PRAISE FOR
DAUGHTER OF THE GODS

"A wonderfully intimate and dramatic evocation of ancient Egypt, where one headstrong young woman dares to become pharaoh. Stephanie Thornton vividly portrays the heat and the danger, the passion and the heartbreak of Hatshepsut's struggle as she defies even the gods to ensure success on the throne of Egypt. A touching love story combines with a thrilling tale of death, courage, and political intrigue to produce a superbly researched and powerfully written novel. This is the kind of book that grabs you by the throat and doesn't let go. A remarkable story, remarkably told."
—Kate Furnival, author of *The Russian Concubine*
and *Shadows on the Nile*

"An epic saga that brings ancient Egypt to life with vivid imagery and lovely prose. Stephanie Thornton is a rising star!"
—Stephanie Dray, author of *Lily of the Nile* and *Daughters of the Nile*

"From her moving love affair with a commoner to her fierce and unwavering commitment to Egypt as a female pharaoh, Hatshepsut crackles with fascinating complexity. Her *ka* must be grinning with pleasure at this richly textured account of her life, one that is worthy of the great queen herself."
—Vicky Alvear Shecter, author of *Cleopatra's Moon*
and *Curses and Smoke: A Novel of Pompeii*

PRAISE FOR
THE SECRET HISTORY

"What a heroine! Stephanie Thornton's Theodora is tough and intelligent, spitting defiance against the cruel world of the Byzantine Empire. Her rise from street urchin to emperor's consort made me want to stand up and cheer. Her later years as empress are great fun to read, but it was her early struggle as actress and courtesan that really had me roaring: either with rage at the misfortunes heaped on this poor girl, or with delight as she once more picked herself up with a steely glint in her eye and kept on going."
—Kate Quinn, author of *Empress of the Seven Hills*

DAUGHTER OF THE GODS

A NOVEL OF ANCIENT EGYPT

STEPHANIE THORNTON

 NEW AMERICAN LIBRARY

New American Library
Published by the Penguin Group
Penguin Group (USA) LLC, 375 Hudson Street,
New York, New York 10014

USA | Canada | UK | Ireland | Australia | New Zealand | India | South Africa | China
penguin.com
A Penguin Random House Company

First published by New American Library,
a division of Penguin Group (USA) LLC

First Printing, May 2014

LIBRARY OF CONGRESS CATALOGING-IN-PUBLICATION DATA:

Thornton, Stephanie, 1980–
Daughter of the gods: a novel of ancient Egypt/Stephanie Thornton.
p. cm.
ISBN 978-0-451-41779-4 (pbk.)
1. Hatshepsut, Queen of Egypt—Fiction. 2. Queens—Egypt—Fiction.
3. Pharaohs—Egypt—Fiction. 4. Egypt—History—Eighteenth dynasty,
ca. 1570–1320 B.C.—Fiction.   I. Title.
PS3620.H7847D38 2014
813'.6—dc23   2013045116

Printed in the United States of America
1 3 5 7 9 10 8 6 4 2

Set in Simoncini Garamond   •   Designed by Elke Sigal

In memory of my mother,
Kristin Louise Crowley

PART I

pharaoh's daughter

1493–1491 BC

Revel in pleasure while your life endures
And deck your head with myrrh.
Be richly clad in white and perfumed linen . . .
In weary quest of what your heart desires
Do as it prompts you.

—"Song of the Harper,"
FROM THE TOMB OF KING INTEF

CHAPTER 1

YEAR THIRTEEN OF PHARAOH TUTMOSE I

The gods erred that day. Or perhaps they were simply cruel.

It was the season of Akhet, and the Nile swelled with Isis' tears and the rich dark silt that would feed the barley and emmer during the cool months of Peret. Hatshepsut and her sister sat rigid as statues at the bow of the royal skiff, shaded from Re's heat by a thin awning of spotted goat hide. The slaves' ostrich-wing fans kept the lazy flies at bay, but rearranged rather than lessened the heat. A trickle of sweat snuck down Hatshepsut's back, and her scalp itched under her wig. Sandalwood oars tipped with gold spread like glittering dragonfly wings behind them as slaves rowed to the steady beat of the drums.

"You fidget like a sparrow." Neferubity laid a hand on Hatshepsut's leg, her nails graceful half-moons and her hands painted with intricate swirls of henna. The paint on Hatshepsut's hands was already smudged and her nails ragged from constant biting.

"A sparrow would be able to fly from this boat." Hatshepsut rubbed the ears of the black dog curled at her feet and scanned the river. This hippo hunt had seemed a good idea until she realized she wasn't to wield a spear, or even a bow to hunt the brown cranes soaring overhead. Not that it mattered—the courtiers from the pharaoh's court in the boats ahead were making so much noise, most of the animals had probably fled to the desert of the Red Land by now.

Rekhyt lined the banks of the river, mostly farmers looking like they'd just been dug from the Nile's black mud, and fishermen struggling not to upset their boats as they bowed to the Great Royal Wife and the rest of Egypt's court. Bare-breasted women looked up from pounding linens upon the rocks and fell to their knees in the murky water, drenching the linen sheaths they'd tucked between their legs. A naked girl ran along the bank, her braided youth lock flapping as she laughed like a hyena. Hatshepsut wished she could do the same instead of being trapped in this boat, wearing a wig that scratched like Ammit's claws. She leaned over the edge of the boat and waved at the girl. *"Ankh, udja, seneb!"*

Life, prosperity, and health.

Neferubity chuckled next to her. "You won't have any life left if Mother hears you yelling like a *rekhyt*." The bells at the ends of her braided wig tinkled as she smiled and shook her head.

"What Mother doesn't know can't hurt her," Hatshepsut said. "Or me."

"I see you're wearing your new necklace. It suits you."

Hatshepsut touched the gold and jasper pennant of Sekhmet, the goddess of war and hunting, a gift from Neferubity for her last naming day. "I thought I might speak to Father when he returns. Perhaps I might serve Sekhmet in her temple."

Neferubity laughed. "Even the lion goddess might not be able to keep you from trouble, little sister."

The boats continued their languid procession until Hatshepsut thought she might jump overboard to escape the boredom. Fortunately, the furious rattle of sistrums and men yelling upriver interrupted her plans.

"They found a hippo." Growing a shade paler, Neferubity pursed her lips, but Hatshepsut jumped atop their bench, sending the little skiff bobbing. The sleek black dog at her feet whimpered, straining on his leash.

"Hush, Iwiw." Hatshepsut knew how he felt.

Their boat crept closer, confirming Neferubity's guess. A hippo calf with rolls of fat ringing its neck shaded itself in a papyrus grove at the edge of an island, its gray skin shiny in the sun. Several boats ahead, Imhotep—the ancient vizier in charge of the government during the pharaoh's long campaign in Canaan—stood and notched an arrow onto his bow. Next to him, glimmering with gold, sat Ahmose, Hatshepsut's mother and Egypt's Great Royal Wife. The courtiers and nobles fell silent as Imhotep let the arrow fly. He aimed too high. The wooden shaft arced into the reeds, sending a black-and-white ibis screeching into the blue sky. The little river cow honked his outrage at the disturbance, then splashed clumsily into the Nile and disappeared into the murky waters with a wiggle of his gray rump.

Neferubity joined the polite clapping, but Hatshepsut glared into the reeds and scratched her scalp. Would her mother notice if she dropped her wig into the Nile? "I'd have hit that hippo from fifty paces," she declared.

It wasn't bragging, because it was true. Neferubity kissed Hatshepsut's temple, smiling fondly as she smoothed her sister's wig. "I'm sure the hippo is glad you weren't behind the bow."

They glided forward, passing the crushed grasses that bore the indent of the river cow's body. Ahead, slaves pulled the first boats of the expedition onshore. There the nobility would enjoy a meal under baobab trees and linen awnings before returning to the capital.

"Perhaps we'll sight a hippo on the return," Imhotep speculated, loud enough for the meager breeze to carry his words. Hatshepsut snorted. The old man would need the blessings of the nine great gods to shoot a sleeping elephant at twenty paces.

She twisted on her bench. "Pull to the side here."

Neferubity glanced at the bank of the island, one that would connect to the shore when Isis' tears receded, and shook her head. The golden disks at her ears flashed with Re's light. "I'm not dumb, little sister."

"You have two choices, Neferubity." Hatshepsut crossed her arms and gave a honeyed smile. "We can either pull to the bank so I can relieve myself in seclusion, or I can do so in front of the entire court of Egypt."

Neferubity studied her for a moment, then heaved a sigh. "We should probably keep your bad manners hidden from the Nubian ambassador for as long as possible."

Hatshepsut shot her a grin. "I'll be right back." In one movement she swiped a throwing stick from the bench of the head rower. The elm shaft, unpolished and lacking balance, was a poor substitute for her own spears, but it would do.

"Hatshepsut!" Neferubity shrieked, as Hatshepsut splashed into the Nile, sending the little boat swaying. Iwiw barked and leapt after her, his rope leash trailing in the mud. They tore through the papyrus grove, the bushy fronds atop the reeds quivering with the breath of the gods. The river was alive, the drone of flies and the waves lapping at the shore marred only by the occasional shriek of laughter from the courtiers upriver. Great Royal Wife Ahmose surely would have noticed their absence by now. And she undoubtedly wasn't happy about it.

Mud squelched between Hatshepsut's toes, coating her gilded sandals. She kicked them off onto a low table of rock. Her mother was going to have her head for ruining them, but she'd worry about that later. She'd have preferred to strip everything off and dive into the river glinting through the reeds, but she settled for tucking the hem of her skirt into its beaded belt. With any luck, the slaves would be packing up by the time they arrived upriver.

Hatshepsut stilled, forcing her breath to slow until her chest scarcely moved. A white egret pecked at the mud under a slender baobab tree on the opposite shore. It was a difficult shot from such a distance, but worth it. She crept closer, out of the reeds, wondering briefly where

Iwiw had gone. Muttering a prayer to Sekhmet, the lion goddess and Egypt's greatest hunter, Hatshepsut lifted the stick, every muscle tensed to send it flying.

"Hatshepsut! Where are you?"

The egret flapped its glorious wings, then launched into the air, soaring away from Hatshepsut.

"Sekhmet's breath!" Hatshepsut stomped, spattering freckles of mud up her white sheath.

Neferubity grabbed her arm and pulled her to an open swath cut through the sedge grass, higher up the bank than the swamp Hatshepsut had trudged through. A sheen of sweat pearled on her sister's upper lip and a pile of dried hippo dung swarmed with flies near her feet, but otherwise Neferubity might have been on her way to a royal banquet. She grabbed the hunting stick and hesitated, glaring as if ready to hit Hatshepsut over the head with it. Instead, she tossed it into the reeds. "You would try Thoth's patience."

"I almost had that egret."

Her sister ignored her. "I don't care if you almost took down a whole pride of lions. Mother is going to kill us."

"Not us." Hatshepsut looked down at her dirty sheath and the mud up to her knees. "Just me."

Neferubity chuckled and released Hatshepsut's arm. "I'll wear my best sheath to your funeral. Let's go before anyone else falls victim to our mother's wrath."

"I need to get my sandals."

"Nice try, little sister."

"Mother will never believe I fell out of the boat if I don't have my sandals," Hatshepsut called over her shoulder, tromping through the swamp before Neferubity could argue.

The sandals lay on the rock where she'd left them, coated with a thick crust of dried brown mud. Iwiw jumped out of the reeds, the hair on his neck on end and his teeth bared. Hatshepsut stepped forward, and he snapped at her.

"Iwiw! Heel."

But his lip only quivered and he continued to growl a low sound of warning. Beyond the dog a menacing gray hulk rose out of the river and trudged through the reeds. Hatshepsut's heart stopped.

A river bull.

His thick hide was cracked with scars, some healed and others freshly pink, from prior fights with other bulls. The hairs on his snout bristled in the air and he flicked his ears, his black eyes like shiny beetles. More dangerous than any lion, the hippo could easily gore her with his tusks, leaving her body mangled and her *ka* unable to pass to the Field of Reeds.

Hatshepsut held her breath and tried to back up, but the gods were against her. The beast glared straight at her, then bellowed, his giant yellow tusks ripping through the air. The breeze had carried her scent to him.

This world seemed to slow, the gods cursing Hatshepsut, and her body turning to granite. The river bull galloped up the bank, reeds snapping and mud flying. Anubis stalked Hatshepsut, a foul smell filling her nostrils and her body going cold as the jackal-headed god reached into her heart to steal her *ka*.

Someone screamed.

Something hard slammed into her shoulder and the world went black. She opened her eyes to a scene worse than Ammit devouring the emaciated bodies of the damned on the Lake of Fire. Neferubity lay facedown, splayed in the mud where Hatshepsut had stood just moments before. The hippo reared up with a roar, and then his colossal jaws scooped into the mud and snapped shut, crushing her sister's thigh in its pink maw. Neferubity screamed, the sound searing itself into Hatshepsut's mind, and the river bull jerked its head to and fro. Neferubity lurched in the air like a drunken dancer.

The hippo bellowed and Neferubity went flying, crashing into a clump of papyrus and mud. The monster stopped still, leveling a yellow stare at Hatshepsut. Then he snorted and lumbered off, disappearing into the river with scarcely a sound.

Panicked screams far in the distance broke the gods' curse. Time hurtled forward and the world snapped back into focus.

"Help! For the love of Amun, someone help!" Hatshepsut raced to Neferubity, tripping into the mud at her side. Her sister was curled up like a newborn babe, her right leg bent at a painful angle and the jagged white edge of bone poking out of the maimed flesh. Neferubity gave a tortured cry when Hatshepsut touched her ribs.

"Everything's going to be all right." Hatshepsut wiped the mud from her sister's eyes and took her hand, alarmed by the slackness of her grip. Neferubity's wig was askew and coated with brown slime, her eyes screwed tight against the pain. She opened her mouth as if to speak but only gurgled, a froth of red blood streaming down the mud on her cheeks to feed the earth below.

"Help is coming," Hatshepsut said, clutching Neferubity's hand as if to keep her sister's *ka* from flying away. Blood poured from her leg, pools of red like broken wings in the mud. The crushed papyrus reeds trembled, and the foul stench of death returned. Anubis circled her sister now—Hatshepsut could almost make out his yellow eyes amongst the reeds. "You have to hold on."

Neferubity's chest heaved and her lungs rattled, the blood seeming to seep out of her body from all directions even as she gasped for breath. Her nails dug into Hatshepsut's palm for a fleeting moment, as if she might cling to this life. But Anubis was too strong; he had her sister tight in his jaws and refused to release such a prize as the pharaoh's eldest daughter.

Neferubity blinked but her eyes were unfocused, her voice less than a whisper. "I'll watch you from the Field of Reeds, Hatshepsut." More blood trickled from her lips. "Make me proud."

Hatshepsut shook her head, the braids of her wig slapping her cheeks. "Don't say that. You'll be here, watching me ruin everything I touch."

"Neferubity?" Their mother's voice trembled, barely penetrating Hatshepsut's mind.

The nobility had arrived, their wide eyes ringed with kohl and mouths slack with shock. Ahmose rushed past the courtiers and stumbled into the mud next to Hatshepsut. "Neferubity!"

But it was too late. Neferubity looked beyond Hatshepsut, her blank eyes already staring at Ma'at's scales in the afterworld. Their mother gave a mangled sob, drawing the body of her eldest daughter to her chest and silently rocking back and forth as tears streamed down her face. The courtiers on the shore wailed, the women clawing at their hair and breasts in the traditional display of mourning.

Hatshepsut stood and stumbled away, watching the whisper of her sister's *ka* depart her body. She stared at Neferubity's footsteps in the mud, evidence that she had been alive only moments ago, and at the imprint of her own body, where Neferubity had shoved her from the hippo's path.

Anubis had claimed the wrong sister.

CHAPTER 2

Her sister was dead.

It had been almost three months since Neferubity's death, long enough for the lotus blossoms left in her tomb to dry and their petals to fragment and blow away, long enough for the offerings of ox leg and milk to sour and draw flies before disappearing entirely. Still, the pain was raw, as if the hippo hunt had been only yesterday.

Hatshepsut reached out to touch a clump of papyrus reeds as the skiff bobbed its way across the Nile from the tombs on the West Bank. The morning was still cool enough; Re's scorching heat had not yet wrung the sweat from her pores. The rowers gave a hippo wide berth, but the lazy river cow only yawned, water filling its giant mouth. Overcome with rage, Hatshepsut grabbed the rower's hunting stick and hurled it at the beast. Fresh pain tore across the cuts on her wrists, dropping pearls of blood into the muddy river. The wooden shaft disappeared into the waters with scarcely a ripple, and the hippo submerged itself below the silty waters, leaving only a foam of bubbles on the surface.

There was a hesitant touch at her elbow, and the head rower stood next to her, his eyes on the planks of the boat. *"Satnesut?"*

Hatshepsut's eyes flicked to where the rest of the rowers stared at her as if she'd lost her mind. Standing on the prow with chest heaving and scarlet ribbons of blood unfurling down her arms, she wondered if perhaps they were right.

Her eyes burned from the tears she'd shed at Neferubity's tomb, even as donkeys brayed and children laughed, while the boat neared the East Bank. The musky scent of incense clung to her skin; the precious smoke had traveled into the sky to guide her sister's *ka* up an invisible ladder formed by the gods' outstretched arms.

But she didn't want Neferubity with the gods. She wanted her here.

Hatshepsut touched the necklace of Sekhmet at her throat, her last gift from her sister. Life continued here in Egypt's capital, despite Neferubity's absence from this world. The rowers—young men clad only in loincloths—grunted as they tied up the royal barque. One tripped in his haste to help her to the dock.

"Hatshepsut!"

She hadn't heard that gruff voice in almost two years, but she would have known it anywhere.

Her brother.

The child of a lesser wife named Mutnofret, Thutmosis was their father's only living son and, therefore, Egypt's "hawk in the nest." There had been three other sons born to Pharaoh Tutmose—although none from the womb of the Great Royal Wife—before either Hatshepsut or Thutmosis had been born, but one by one Anubis had claimed them all, leaving the pharaoh with only a single son and two daughters born from his seed.

Yet Anubis' greed now left Egypt with only the hawk in the nest and one royal daughter.

Thutmosis was younger than Hatshepsut by almost a year but had become a man during the military campaign in Canaan, his shoulders filled out and his lips and cheeks rubbed with red ochre. Hatshepsut took after their father in looks with her dark hair and short stature, but Thut possessed his mother's pale skin and ready smile. Fortunately, he hadn't inherited her affinity for honeyed rolls. Kipa, his wretched pet monkey, munched a fig while sitting atop his shoulder and picking at the braids of his wig. Hatshepsut was shocked as her brother hobbled toward her, leaning on an ivory walking cane and pursing his lips every time his weight shifted to his right foot.

Thut's cinnamon-colored eyes were warm under the thick lines of kohl as he opened his arms to her. "By the great nine gods, Hatshepsut. Now I know I'm finally home." He stood back to look at her, his gaze trailing down Hatshepsut's bare breasts and coarse white skirt. Sand from the desert still clung to her papyrus sandals. "Let me guess. Gallivanting through the Red Land on your chariot this morning?"

Hatshepsut thought to lie, but Thut had always known when she didn't tell the truth. She rubbed her eyes, not caring if she smudged the streaks of kohl that Sitre had painted from her lids to her temples. "Visiting Neferubity's tomb."

"I'm sorry. I wish I'd been here." He pushed the braids of Hatshepsut's wig behind her shoulders. "One day we'll meet our sister in the Field of Reeds."

Hatshepsut hugged him hard, burying her face in his chest and breathing in his scents of linen and sweat so he wouldn't see the tears well in her eyes. These days it seemed she was capable only of crying or flying into a rage. His fingers stroked her sharp shoulder blades so that she didn't want to let go. "It's my fault," she said.

His hand stopped moving. "What's your fault?"

"Neferubity's death. She saved me and I froze." Hot tears streamed down Hatshepsut's cheeks, and her nose started running. "I should have been the one to die."

She feared the loathing in his eyes if she looked at him. She shouldn't have said anything.

"Hatshepsut, it's not your fault Neferubity died."

She wiped the tears and snot with the back of her arm. "Of course it is."

Thut gave her a sad smile and pulled her into his arms again. "The gods do as they please, Hatshepsut. They meant you to live that day, and so you did."

"But—"

"It's not your fault."

He might believe that, but she didn't. And neither did her mother.

Never close to the daughter whose birth had almost killed her and who should have been born a son, Ahmose could now scarcely stand to be in the same room as Hatshepsut. Her golden eldest daughter was dead, and Hatshepsut's *ka* was stained with Neferubity's blood, a crime it seemed unlikely Ahmose would ever forgive.

Thutmosis lifted Hatshepsut's hand to kiss her palm, but his eyes narrowed at the crimson slashes across the pale flesh of her wrists. "I sacrificed a bull to the gods for Neferubity at Iunu. I see you've been making your own sacrifices."

Hatshepsut thrust her chin in the air. "And if I have?"

"Neferubity wouldn't have wanted this." His tone was curt, and she stepped away, wounded. "Find some other way to honor her."

Hatshepsut had already sacrificed her willow longbow and feathered arrows, her favorite golden hunting stick engraved with golden hares, and her hunting dog, Iwiw, all buried with Neferubity in her tomb. She brought cornflowers to her sister every day so Neferubity could enjoy their color and fragrance in the Field of Reeds. None of that changed the fact that it was Hatshepsut's fault her sister was dead.

She glanced at Thutmosis' carved ivory cane, its top painted with red and blue lotus blossoms. Her shining half brother had once been carved in the image of Horus himself. Not so now. "You never wrote of this," she said. "What happened?"

Thut's smile didn't reach his eyes. "An elephant hunt gone awry. The break never healed right." He tapped the walking stick on the ground. "But I managed a nice cane from one of its tusks."

If only Neferubity had been so lucky.

This was the brother who had helped Hatshepsut steal their father's chariot one night to race through the market of Waset. He had taught her how to climb trees and take down an ostrich from thirty paces. Now Thutmosis was broken, and so was she. Only her wound wasn't so easy to see. "We didn't expect you back until after the harvest," she said.

He threaded her arm through his and they walked into the dark interior of the palace, Kipa clinging to his wig. Two girl-slaves fell into step behind them, one offering a tray of watered wine. Thut waved them away, his voice so low that only Hatshepsut could hear it. "Father's health has been deteriorating. He suffers from terrible fevers and chills. After the news of Neferubity, we thought it best to return to the capital."

Thut peered at the position of the sun through one of the clerestory windows. "I have to go—Father waits for me in the gardens. You'll be at my mother's naming-day dinner tonight?"

Hatshepsut stood on tiptoes and kissed his cheek. "Of course."

He opened his mouth as if to say more, but pressed his lips to her forehead instead. "Then I'll see you soon."

Hatshepsut waited for her brother to disappear around the corner and the echo of his cane to fade away; then she cut through the palace kitchens. Two slaves strained a giant vat of beer, while another knelt over a wooden slab on the ground to knead bread dough in a courtyard open to Nut's vast blue belly. Hatshepsut picked her way around a cluster of domed clay ovens, her stomach growling at the scent of the baking flat loaves. She was almost past the palace granary when a hand closed around her wrist and yanked her into a dark storeroom.

Another hand clamped hard over her mouth, muffling her yelp of terror. Ropes of garlic and bundles of dried parsley hung from the low ceiling, and the air was tinged with the scent of earth and dust. She started to bite down on the hand over her mouth, but stopped at the familiar spice of a man's musk perfume. A strong arm snaked around her waist and lips trailed to her bare breasts, fingers running down her spine in a way that made her moan with pleasure.

"Not now, Mensah." She danced out of his arms, smoothing her hair. She had more important things to attend to right now.

"But I want you. Here. And now." Even in the dim light she could make out the glint of his earrings, bright as the flash of his lazy smile. As Imhotep's son, Mensah was accustomed to getting what he wanted, when he wanted it.

Not this time.

"I can't." Her body was responding to his closeness, aching in anticipation of his touch. There had been kisses with other men—boys, really—including twin courtiers who'd caught her in a dark hallway outside a banquet a few weeks ago, but only Mensah made the blood race through her veins like hot wine. Breathless, she kissed him. "Meet me in the stables tonight."

His fingers caressed the nape of her neck, his breath warm on her ear. "I can't wait that long."

"Before dinner, then."

"You're torturing me, woman."

"Think of this as an excellent opportunity to cultivate patience." She flashed him a grin and paused at the door.

"Patience is a worthless virtue." He closed the distance between them with three strides, his mouth on hers in a way that made her want to forget what she'd been planning.

She pushed away, chest heaving. "My brother is home."

"With the pharaoh. My father informed me." He rubbed his jaw, the muscles of his arm bulging under its gold armbands. He smiled, that same grin that reduced the girl-slaves in the palace to tittering birds. "Go to your brother, then. I can't compete with the hawk in the nest."

"I'll see you tonight." In the darkness she gazed at his outline, the shoulders of a bull narrowing to a trim waist. Mensah was the spoiled youngest son of one of Egypt's oldest families, his lineage recorded in the temples back to the pharaohs of old, and she was the youngest daughter of the pharaoh, forbidden to marry and destined only to adorn court banquets. It was natural that their relationship had taken this recent, and rather physical, turn. With him she could forget about Neferubity, at least for a while.

Hatshepsut hurried through the maze of columned hallways to her chambers. The rooms were empty—her servants wouldn't expect her for a while longer.

She yanked off her wig, freeing the snarls in her dark hair, and grimaced at her reflection in the copper mirror before slipping barefoot into the gardens. Palms hung heavy with ripe dates, filling the air with their sweet scent. A tame gazelle glanced up from its breakfast, flicked its ears, and went back to munching a jujube branch. Everything smelled fresh in the cool morning air, and the birds chattered overhead. However, it wasn't the sound of sparrows and finches that greeted her ears, but the low timbre of human voices. A cluster of willows shaded the far corner; one listed dangerously to the center, akin to some of the nobility after imbibing too much spiced wine at her father's feasts. Beyond the trees, as she had hoped, her father and Thut were on the other side in the main palace gardens. Threading her way around several sleeping cats, Hatshepsut crouched behind a hedge of stunted palm trees and juniper bushes.

A little eavesdropping couldn't hurt.

"The Akkadians will have to wait to present their prospective princess to you, Thutmosis," her father said. Hatshepsut could just make out the white of the pharaoh's long kilt through the dense leaves. "I will not allow you to wed some foreign princess before you've married Hatshepsut."

She choked, doubled over as if someone had punched her in the stomach.

As the pharaoh's eldest daughter, Neferubity should have married Thut and been his Great Royal Wife, borne his children and the next heir. To keep the line of succession straight and avoid imposter claims to the Isis Throne, the hawk in the nest always chose a wife from within the family, and the pharaoh's younger daughters were forbidden to marry. Dalliances like hers with Mensah were ignored as long as no children came of such relationships. Hatshepsut took no chances, faithfully using the crocodile dung–and–honey pessary procured at great cost from the Royal Physician. A future without responsibility, a future of doing as she pleased when she pleased: such was the life Hatshepsut had envisioned for herself. Yet that life had been buried along with Neferubity in her tomb.

As Pharaoh Tutmose's youngest daughter, Hatshepsut had never been important. Now she was precious for two things: her royal blood and her womb. The idea of trading her freedom to marry Thut and bear Egypt's future heir made Hatshepsut wish she could trade places with her sister.

She jumped as something touched her foot. A striped cat threaded its way between her legs and into the juniper bush.

"Who's there?" her father's voice rumbled.

Hatshepsut backed away in full retreat, but her bare foot stepped on something thin and furry atop the granite tile. The screech of a cat rudely awakened from its nap rent the morning stillness. Hatshepsut jumped back to avoid the unsheathed claws of the angry feline she had just mauled, but her balance faltered. She slipped and plunged back into a fountain's shallow waters with a violent splash.

Shimmering orange fish darted like underwater flames to avoid their intruder. Drenched and mortified that she might be seen, Hatshepsut struggled to sit up amongst the floating lotus blossoms.

Too late.

The men crashed through the trees, but stopped short when they saw her.

"Hatshepsut?"

The gods were enjoying a good laugh at her expense right now.

Thut bent to pluck a waterlogged pink lotus from Hatshepsut's skirt, scarcely managing to keep a straight face. Kipa scampered from one of his shoulders to the other and bared her little yellow teeth as Thut offered his hand to help Hatshepsut from the fountain. "I'm sure one of your attendants could have arranged a bath if you'd only asked," he said. "Amun knows you needed one."

She flicked some water at him. He only grinned wider.

"What in the name of Amun were you doing?"

The pharaoh's exasperated tone made Hatshepsut wince. The strokes of kohl at his temples turned his glare more menacing under the white leather and red copper of the double crown. The crown was also known as Two Great of Magic, and as a child Hatshepsut had thought it was the crown's magic that made everyone do her father's bidding. Now she realized it was the mantle of authority he wore so easily that made Pharaoh Tutmose such an effective leader.

Hatshepsut's head touched the colored tiles as she swept into a full *henu* before her father. A kaleidoscope filled her open eyes, swirls of green, red, and blue.

"It was nothing, Father," she mumbled into the ground, cheeks on fire. "I was only listening."

"I gathered as much," the pharaoh said. His face was more lined than Hatshepsut remembered. For the first time in her life, her father looked his fifty years.

Still, his eyes smiled at her.

As the pharaoh's youngest child, Hatshepsut had always been indulged, and rarely punished for all the times she'd hidden from her attendants or reprimanded for the countless scrapes she'd received while racing chariots and wrestling her brother. She was her father's favorite, and she knew it.

With a sigh, he touched her shoulder to make her rise. Hatshepsut grimaced at her drenched sheath and the growing lake at her feet. She glanced toward her brother, but met the scrutiny of a third man—one she hadn't noticed until now—standing in the shadow of the hedge.

Each part of his face was not especially noteworthy, but a single scar marred the flesh of his forehead—a thin white slash through copper. This stranger was no typical courtier with the soft belly and pale skin attesting to a life of ease safe from Re's glare. His skin was too dark for the nobility's taste, and his leather armband branded him a soldier in Thoth's division. The man looked positively *common*.

She was staring. Scrambling to mask her flurry of emotions with the servant's laughing eyes on her, Hatshepsut mustered her most imperious tone. "And who is this, Father?"

Her brother motioned the man out of the shadows and into the full light of the garden. "Senenmut of Iuny. I've made him one of my personal advisers."

"Adviser?" Hatshepsut could hardly imagine such a *rekhyt* coming out of the fields to serve the royal house. "How could you be qualified for such a position?"

Thut groaned, shaking his head, but Senenmut's eyes flashed and his lips curled up in a tinge of a smile. Hatshepsut was sure he was laughing at her again. "I am the eldest son of Ramose and Hatnofer of Iuny. I was apprenticed as a scribe to the temple of Thoth at the age of seven," he said. "When my youth lock was shorn, I was sent to work in the military, writing missives for Admiral Pennekheb, son of Ebana. I stayed in the army for a number of years to assist with negotiations and oversee various building projects. Admiral Pennekheb recently recommended me for service to the royal house." Senenmut paused for a moment and crossed his arms before his chest. "So here I am."

Impudent *and* common. The man would make excellent crocodile bait.

Thut motioned toward his leg. "Senenmut took down the elephant that did this before the beast broke more than my leg. The man is fierce with a battle-ax." He looked at Hatshepsut and chuckled. "Although perhaps not as fierce as you, sister."

"I'd recognize a daughter of the lion goddess anywhere." Senenmut gave her a slow smile. "Or perhaps her more diminutive cousin, Bast."

Hatshepsut fumed. The man dared compare her to a house cat? She didn't care if he'd saved Thut or not; there had to be a place for him in Aswan's granite quarries. Years of hard labor would wipe that smirk off his face.

She eyed Thoth's baboon emblem on his armband. "I find it surprising that any god—especially the god of knowledge—would claim you."

Thut squeezed her arm in warning. "Perhaps the two of you should ignore each other. You both possess the terrifying tendency to say precisely what you think."

"Or I could have his tongue cut out."

Senenmut's grin deepened. The man really was a baboon, just like the god he claimed. "I'm sorry you find my qualifications so lacking, *satnesut*," he said.

At least he knew to address her properly.

"Not at all." Hatshepsut crossed her arms in front of her. "I'm sure you're highly qualified to entertain my brother, much like Kipa here." The monkey jumped to the top of Thut's head, raising such a racket, Hatshepsut was sure that she was being cursed in monkey.

Her father cleared his throat and rubbed his temples. "That's enough, Hatshepsut. Your brother and I have much to discuss before we visit Hathor's temple today."

Hatshepsut straightened and met her father's gaze. "I'd prefer to remain here. I deserve to know what you have planned for Thutmosis and me."

So she could plot a way to get out of it.

Father and son exchanged a look. The pharaoh sighed and squeezed her shoulder. "We'll wait for your return before resuming that topic. You may join us on our trip into Waset."

"Thank you, Father." She bowed to him and her brother, but didn't bother to acknowledge Senenmut before racing as fast as she could back to her chambers.

"*Satnesut!*" Mouse dropped the palette of kohl she was grinding as Hatshepsut burst through the door. A Nubian dwarf, Mouse might have had a different name before she'd been brought to the capital, but with her wide ears and overlarge teeth, the nickname had stuck. Her glare at Hatshepsut was as dark as her skin as she picked up the pieces of the broken palette. "I see you've ruined another sheath. What happened this time?"

Hatshepsut ignored the question. "I have to get dressed." She threw open a cedar chest and tore through a stack of folded linen sheaths as Sitre walked into the room.

Her old *menat* grabbed her hands with ones spotted and gnarled with age. "You may run wild outside the palace, but Mouse and I have enough to do today without having to clean up another mess."

Sitre had delivered Hatshepsut into this world, and threatened to take her out of it more times than she could count. Hatshepsut knew she wouldn't win the argument. "I need to accompany Father and Thut to Hathor's temple." She took a deep breath and sat down on an ebony stool. "They're talking about my *marriage*."

"They?" Mouse picked up the sheaths Hatshepsut had flung to the floor. Neither she nor Sitre seemed ruffled at the mention of Hatshepsut's marriage.

"Father and one of Thut's new advisers, Senenmut of Iuny." Hatshepsut twisted in her chair. "I'm thinking of using him for target practice."

"Just don't let his blood splatter your sheath." Sitre raked an ivory comb through Hatshepsut's tangled black hair. Hatshepsut had let it grow since Neferubity's death, preferring her own hair to the infernal wigs her mother forced her to wear. Ahmose either hadn't noticed or no longer cared what her daughter did. Hatshepsut guessed the latter. "I suppose it's only fitting your marriage be negotiated in the presence of the goddess of love, despite your scorn for Hathor," Sitre said. "But you'll have to sit still if you want to look presentable for the cow goddess."

Isis' magic blessed their hands, and soon Hatshepsut's gilded sandals slapped back over the garden tiles. Sitre had dressed her in a soft linen sheath with an overgown of delicate gold and turquoise beads, so she no longer looked like a drowned Nile rat. Her favorite diadem of rosettes and stylized papyrus stalks sat atop her oiled hair, and she chewed the little ball of incense Mouse had given her to freshen her breath. She wouldn't allow Senenmut to fluster her again. She was the flesh and blood of the pharaoh, while he still had the dirt of Iuny under his fingernails. He was beneath her notice.

The men looked up as she approached the stables, the pharaoh's *medjay* guards standing at attention. Everyone's eyes lingered on her.

"Shall we?" Hatshepsut felt a thrill as her brother motioned to the chariots—one plain cedar and the other of electrum hammered with the pharaoh's cartouche—but then she saw the ebony sedan chair and four waiting Nubian carriers, men chosen for the breadth of their shoulders and not the prettiness of their faces. Hatshepsut wished for a chariot, but knew better than to argue, lest she be denied the privilege of going into the city at all.

"Where's Father?" she asked.

Thut's driver took his cane and helped him into the electrum basket, a blinding mixture of gold and silver reserved for the royal family. Fortunately, Kipa was nowhere to be seen. Senenmut stepped into his empty chariot and wrapped the reins around his fists.

"Father had a sudden spell," Thut said. "He'll be fine by tonight."

"In that case—" Hatshepsut stepped into the chariot with her brother and motioned to the driver. "Your services are no longer necessary."

"Hatshepsut—" Thut groaned.

She braced herself, planting her feet firmly in the basket. "Don't worry, brother. I won't kill us."

The horse bolted at the flick of her whip, leaving the guards and Senenmut to scramble in the dust behind them. With any luck, she'd be able to lose them entirely.

They passed along the Walls of the Prince and under the palace's Great Double Gate, the guards a blur of white as Thut laughingly hollered at her to slow down. The gentle scents of lotus blossoms and fig trees were quickly replaced with the pungent smell of animal dung and baking bread, dust, and spices. They careened around a corner and passed a pile of mud-brick houses stacked precariously upon one another. The corner of their chariot almost clipped a wizened old man balancing a basket of silver-scaled fish on his head.

"May you copulate with a donkey!" The *rekhyt* shook his fist at her before realizing he'd just cursed the pharaoh's daughter. Laughing, she turned in time to see the basket crash to the ground as he collapsed in a bow, the fish slithering to the dirt in a flash the same color as the moon.

Thut groaned into his hands, but Hatshepsut only laughed harder.

A brown nanny goat poked its head out of a door and bleated just before they entered the market with its morass of carts and stalls. Hatshepsut slowed the chariot and glanced over her shoulder, stifling a curse to see Senenmut round the last corner. He scarcely seemed winded, but the *medjay* strung behind him panted and heaved, their chests slick with sweat as they clutched their spears for support. She'd have to drive faster next time.

Vendors with booming voices hawked wares of all kinds—hills of elephant garlic and onions, half-starved donkeys, and jewelry so cheap its gilding was already peeling. One cart was piled with dirty linen bundles, likely mummies of ibis, falcons, and dogs available to accompany the recently deceased to the Field of Reeds. The market swarmed with every variety of people, but each *rekhyt* fell to the ground as the royal entourage passed and the *medjay* barked her brother's titles. One man almost dropped his armload of green melons in his haste to press his head to the dirt.

They emerged from the market outside Hathor's temple, and the world fell silent.

The chariots stopped before a freshly swept path; the earth leading to the house of the goddess must be clean of footprints and never touched by the hooves of goats or pigs. Gaudily painted images of the cow goddess smiled benevolently at Hatshepsut from every wall and pillar of the flowery forecourt of Hathor's outer temple. Hatshepsut rolled her eyes. She'd visited this temple only once—when forced by her mother during one of Hathor's holy days—and didn't care to return anytime soon. Love was for fools and old women.

"Such a lovely drive through the city." Senenmut brushed imaginary dust from his arm. "Although it seems you could have run over a few more *rekhyt* if you'd tried harder."

"We'll talk in the shade over there," Thut said, not giving Hatshepsut a chance to respond to Senenmut. "And then I'll see to Hathor's offering while I speak to the High Priestess." He motioned them to a bench near the crocodile pool. Unfortunately, the beasts looked to be mostly asleep. Hatshepsut was sure Ma'at, the goddess of truth and justice, would forgive her if she managed to push Senenmut into the waters.

A *wa'eb* priestess with downcast eyes materialized with a tray of bread and faience glasses of watered wine. A group of musicians and Hathor's dancers practiced in the far corner, their naked bodies slick with oil as they swayed to the sensuous notes of the harps. Hatshepsut felt a twinge of envy at their freedom as her own slipped further away with each passing moment.

She took a slice of honeyed bread dotted with raisins and glowered at the dancers. "When are we to marry?" she asked.

Her brother choked on his wine. "So much for the subtleties of conversation. At least I know I'll never be bored with you as my Great Royal Wife." He wiped his mouth with a linen napkin offered by Hathor's priestess. "It appears we must be married sooner rather than later."

"What happened with the Akkadians to spur this decision?" The bread was suddenly dry in her mouth. Hatshepsut set the piece back on her plate.

"They've offered one of their royal women as a wife for your brother." Senenmut bit into a slice of brown bread slathered with honey. They may as well have been discussing which manure to use in the palace fields, for all his interest in the conversation.

"I already heard that part." Hatshepsut glared at him. "Would you care to elaborate?"

Her brother sighed. "The Akkadians have a ripe young princess they want me to marry as a peace offering."

Hatshepsut stared at him. "That can't happen." It was ludicrous to imagine a foreigner sitting aside the Isis Throne, especially after everything their dynasty had done to rid Egypt of foreign rulers, beginning with expelling the dreaded Hyksos from the Black Land only a few generations ago.

"Of course not," her brother said.

"There *are* benefits to the match." Senenmut said. "Your brother will likely produce several heirs, regardless of whom he marries first. Peace with the Akkadians while he and your father live would be a definite boon for Egypt." He took a long draught of his wine. "Your status in life wouldn't change one fathom."

This time her glare could have frozen the Nile. "Except that it would dilute the bloodline. There could be civil war after Thutmosis dies. Not to mention that it would be an affront to Ma'at." Hatshepsut would have to talk to her brother about his recent choice in advisers; this man had to go.

Thut laid his hand on her thigh. "Obviously, if Princess Enheduanna married me before you, she would become Great Royal Wife and relegate you to secondary status once you and I were married. Senenmut and I have discussed the possibility that if I marry an Akkadian princess first, then any son born to us could inherit the throne before your sons. That is why the marriage is not acceptable until after you've married me."

"So what do the Akkadians want from Egypt instead? Increased trade agreements? Gold from Nubia?"

Thut nodded. "The sand dwellers drive a hard bargain." He studied her before speaking. "None of us sees a way to push back our marriage by more than a few months. Only long enough to prepare."

"A few months?" Hatshepsut's necklace was suddenly too tight.

"Nothing can be allowed to stand in the way of a smooth succession," Senenmut said. "You're both old enough to be married, and the pharaoh's health isn't what it used to be."

"I understand." Her voice was so quiet, she wasn't sure if either of them heard her, but she didn't care.

Thut fiddled with a gold bangle at his wrist, not meeting her eyes.

"Father plans to make the announcement at my mother's naming-day celebration this evening."

"Of course." She didn't realize she was picking at the wounds on her wrists until the scab started to bleed.

Thut and Senenmut continued to speak, something about increasing their demand for copper from the Akkadians, but Hatshepsut didn't hear any of it. She wanted to scream.

She rose, ignoring them both as they stood in response. "I need to return to the palace."

"Of course." Thut touched her elbow, already reaching for his cane. "Are you all right?"

"I'm fine. Just bored with all your blather about copper." She flashed him the brightest smile she could manage. "I'll see you this evening."

Hatshepsut felt their eyes on her back as she clambered into the chariot. She heard none of Waset's sounds on the return trip, smelled none of the scents of the City of Truth. Once inside the palace walls, she started to walk, no destination in mind, needing time to think. Head down, she turned a corner and barreled straight into Mutnofret's myrrh-drenched chest.

Set's blood! Somehow she'd stumbled into the Hall of Women, the last place she wanted to be.

The women's rooms and gardens were a gilded prison used to trap the graceful creatures within. Her father had only two wives, but, like all pharaohs, he had once possessed some of Egypt's most delicate flowers, plucked from their families for the honor of gracing the pharaoh's bed in the hopes of producing the future hawk in the nest. Yet Pharaoh Tutmose had often been gone campaigning and neglected his other women after Thutmosis was born, more concerned with ruling his empire than siring more children, since he already had four strong sons. Then his three eldest sons passed to the West, and aging Ahmose made sure no new women were brought in to threaten her position as Great

Royal Wife; there was already enough rivalry between the pharaoh's two wives to fill the entire Hall of Women with animosity. Now Tutmose's old flowers were withered, breasts sagging past their ribs and faces so lined that no amount of kohl and henna could make them young again. And here they would remain. A woman left the Hall of Women only once: on her way to be mummified by the priests of Anubis.

This was to be Hatshepsut's life.

"My, my, child!" Double chin wagging, Mutnofret giggled as she backed away from her husband's daughter. In her youth, Mutnofret's curvaceous silhouette and exotic features had caught the pharaoh's eye, but now her honeyed cakes were her constant companions. Her pendulous breasts hung down to the waist of her skirt, the nipples painted with red ochre and set with carnelian stones. "Good thing I'm not your mother—she'd have your ear for not paying more attention."

"I'm sorry, Mutnofret. My mind was elsewhere." Hatshepsut didn't wish to get drawn into a conversation about the roast ostrich served at last night's banquet or the latest fashion of headdress. She sidestepped Mutnofret's substantial girth. "If you'll excuse me."

"Of course, my dear." The older woman's kohled eyelids crinkled as she smiled. Her eyebrows were missing, shaved off to mourn the recent death of her favorite cat. The pampered feline had been sent to the Field of Reeds with enough mummified mice and pots of milk to keep it fed for eternity. "I'm sure you have plenty to do this afternoon. You always do—such a responsible girl." She leaned back and examined Hatshepsut. "One day you'll make a fine wife for my son—so dedicated."

Hatshepsut grimaced but managed to slip away from Mutnofret without being cajoled into further conversation. She'd have to make an extra sacrifice to Amun for that little miracle later.

But there was something else she had to do first.

CHAPTER 3

Hatshepsut lay in Mensah's arms, wanting to run, to yell, to throw something. Their lovemaking on the stable floor had been fierce, which her scratched back could attest to, but that only added to the sensation that her world was spiraling out of control. And there was nothing she could do about it.

The horse in the next stall whinnied softly, then fell silent. Hatshepsut raised her hands in the shadows, scarcely able to make out the dark lines of dried blood on her wrists.

Neferubity wouldn't have wanted this. Find some other way to honor her.

She grimaced in remembrance of Thut's words. She knew what had to be done, but that didn't make her decision any easier.

Mensah kissed the top of her head. "You're quiet tonight."

"Just thinking."

"That's dangerous, especially if it's you doing the thinking." He dodged her mock punch. "What are you scheming this time?"

There was no point hiding the truth. Rumors would fly across the Two Lands faster than a heron could fly up the Nile. "Thut wants me to marry him."

Mensah rolled to his side and propped himself up on his elbow. He picked a piece of straw from her hair and twirled it between his fingers. "I anticipated that." His eyes flicked to her as he lay back in the straw. "I also anticipated your resistance."

"Would it do any good?"

"It might. If you wanted it to."

She closed her eyes. His look was too tender—she needed Mensah to be his typical shallow self. "I don't like the idea of fighting a losing battle. I'd prefer to put my energies elsewhere."

"I know precisely where you can put all that extra energy." His finger traced the line of her rib cage, then made a lazy circle around her nipple. His lips curled into a wicked smile. "Your marriage doesn't mean this has to stop."

She swatted his hand away and tugged her rumpled sheath on over her head. "Somehow I doubt Thut would be willing to share his Great Royal Wife."

Mensah gave a bark of laughter. "I wasn't proposing we tell him."

But Hatshepsut could never do that to her brother. Whatever her decision, she'd make it with her entire being, exactly as Neferubity would have done. And as much as Hatshepsut preferred to believe she had some choice in this matter, the simple truth was she had none. She didn't relish the idea of being dragged kicking and screaming before the priests.

She kissed Mensah, letting her lips linger on his.

His fingers threaded through hers. "That felt like good-bye."

She stood, inhaling the scents of hay and horse dung, the final scents of freedom. "You'll find some pretty noble's daughter to take my place soon enough." She poked his foot with her toe and smiled. "Or, more likely, one of the girl-slaves from the kitchens."

He winced as he stood, possibly from the insult, or more likely from the scratches Hatshepsut's nails had left on his back. He towered over her. "It's not a slave or some empty-headed courtier's daughter I want, and you know it."

She touched his chest, reached up to trace his jaw. "I'm sorry, Mensah. I truly am."

"I won't let you go so easily."

She smiled at him, hearing the challenge in his voice. "I wouldn't expect otherwise."

And then she turned and walked away, into the orange haze of dusk and away from the warmth of his arms. It didn't matter how much Mensah fought for her; she'd made up her mind.

She'd honor Neferubity, if it was the last thing she did.

Hatshepsut gritted her teeth as the *medjay* pounded their spears on the ground and opened the giant gilded gate to allow her entrance into the darkened Hall of Women, the entire northern wing of the palace reserved for the royal wives and concubines of Pharaoh Tutmose. One woman with a thick waist and too much henna on her cheeks braided a crown of delicate white lotus flowers as another strummed a harp, filling the night air with fragile notes. The oil lamps flickered as the guards pounded their spears again and a herald announced the pharaoh.

"The Good God, Lord of the Two Lands, Aakheperkare, the Son of Re, Tutmose the Justified!"

The concubines' faces lit up at his presence, but dimmed quickly once they realized the pharaoh had not come for them. Tutmose gifted the women with a smile or caress, but stopped when he saw his daughter waiting in the shadows. He dropped a kiss on a woman's expectant forehead and crossed the courtyard to Hatshepsut. Thut claimed their father was ill, but Pharaoh Tutmose still seemed a lion to her, exuding power and confidence with every step he took.

Hatshepsut performed a neat little *henu*. "How are you feeling?"

"Much better," he said. "The tincture that Gua forced me to take earlier must have helped. Thank the gods—I wouldn't want to ruin tonight's celebration."

"And my brother informs me you have big news for us?" Hatshepsut asked, her voice as sweet as honey.

"I do. I plan to announce both your marriage and Thutmosis' co-regency tonight."

Hatshepsut started. She hadn't realized Thut would ascend the Isis Throne so soon—she'd assumed his crown would wait until their father had passed to the West. Once they married and Thut wore the double crown, Hatshepsut would assume the title of Great Royal Wife. A gift and a curse from the gods.

"I'd like to speak with you about my marriage, Father."

"In a moment, Hatshepsut." The pharaoh motioned her to a small shrine tucked in the corner. A wooden statue of the goddess Isis stood lit by the flickering flame of a tiny clay lamp. In one hand the Goddess of the Throne clutched an ankh, the symbol of everlasting life, and she wore a black crown shaped like a throne. Her dress was painted a bright red, the color of blood and sacrifice, and upon her head was a gold vulture headdress. If Hatshepsut became Great Royal Wife, she would be crowned with the same headdress, and her ties to the mother goddess would be further strengthened if she bore Thut's son. The goddess stared at her, as if trying to discern her heart's desires. Hatshepsut looked away.

She still preferred Sekhmet, but Isis had given birth to Horus and was the mother of pharaohs. If Hatshepsut were to give up her freedom, it seemed only fair that she receive something in return. And she knew what she wanted.

An offering of blue and white lotus flowers had been left at Isis' wooden feet, along with a merry spray of red nightshade berries. Pharaoh Tutmose knelt and retrieved a tiny faience vial from his kilt and doused the wooden statue of the queen of gods. The scent of myrrh rose to mingle with the perfume of the courtyard.

Her father closed his eyes and began to pray. "Hail Isis, blessed mother. I dedicate my daughter to you. May you bless her womb and make her an obedient wife, one who bends to Egypt's will."

Wife. Mother. Hatshepsut swallowed her scream.

"I know this isn't what you'd planned for your life." The pharaoh grasped the shrine to pull himself to his feet. "But I think in time you'll grow accustomed to life as Thutmosis' wife."

"That's what I wished to talk to you about, Father."

He took off his wig, ran his hands over his scalp. "What troubles you, daughter?"

She pulled a deep breath into her lungs and forced out the words.

"I need you to teach me how to rule. Train me as you have Thut, as if I were your son."

The pharaoh's eyes widened. She'd never seen him so shocked. "Absolutely not. You are a woman. A woman cannot rule."

"I won't be relegated to the Hall of Women, content to serve Thut and await a death in childbed."

Instead, she would sacrifice her freedom in exchange for power and a chance to redeem herself.

"I need to do this." She knelt and clutched his hands. "For Nefer-ubity."

Clouds passed before the pharaoh's eyes at the mention of his eldest daughter, the fourth child who had traveled before him to the Field of Reeds.

His lips tightened. "Giving Egypt its next heir will be your most important duty as Great Royal Wife. Your only duty."

"I am well aware of that." Hatshepsut wouldn't think of that now. "But I would be a far better Great Royal Wife for Thut if I could help him from behind the throne."

He gave a stiff shake of his head. "Absolutely not. The pharaoh requires advice from those with a steady heart, yet you possess Sekhmet's temper."

"A temper you've always indulged."

"No longer."

"Father—"

"No." His voice was angry. He straightened under the double crown, towering over her. "You belong in the Hall of Women, at least until you can learn to control yourself."

She tasted the copper tang of blood in her mouth as she watched her father walk away. He had never refused her anything before, but now, when it most mattered, he denied her.

The doors to Mutnofret's apartments closed behind the pharaoh, scarcely muffling the excited squeal of his second wife.

Hatshepsut glanced at Isis' statue. The goddess' lips were curled in a gentle smile, but then the lamp sputtered and her face settled into its wooden stare once more.

"You've heard my prayer," Hatshepsut whispered to her. "Please help my father see the truth."

Hatshepsut would find some other way out of the Hall of Women and into Thut's throne room. She just didn't know how.

Mutnofret's door opened again and the light from within spilled into the moonlit courtyard. Hatshepsut stiffened, expecting another reprimand, but Thut emerged instead.

He walked slowly to sit beside her, setting his cane on the ground and folding his legs beneath him, the right one at an awkward angle. His sandalwood perfume mingled with the scents of lotus and jasmine. Each of his fingers was bedecked with gold rings to match the pectoral on his chest, a giant lapis lazuli falcon representing Horus. He resembled their father in the shape of his chin and the hook of his nose, yet there was something different about him, something smaller. He rubbed his face with both hands. "Father is going to announce that I'm to be co-regent."

"Congratulations." Hatshepsut's voice fell flat.

"Don't sound so excited."

She couldn't answer, numb with desperation and hopelessness at the future that yawned before her.

"I'm not sure I want this." Her brother stared into the night. The concubines had left the harp by the fountain, but their low giggles floated up from somewhere in the darkness. Thut winced and stretched his crippled leg in front of him. "I'm not sure I'll ever be ready to sit on the Isis Throne."

Hatshepsut laughed, the sound too loud for the quiet courtyard. Thutmosis shot her an angry look. "I'm not sure why that's funny."

She kissed his cheek and leaned her head on his shoulder. "It's not, Thut. The whole situation is ridiculous."

Her brother didn't wish to rule, and she wanted nothing else. The gods really did taunt those they loved most.

"Now that we're finally alone, I have to ask: Do you want to marry me, Hatshepsut?"

He was the first, the only person, to ask her opinion. Yet she couldn't bring herself to tell him the truth. For Mensah, she felt a wild hunger, a desperate excitement to have him in her bed that she couldn't imagine sharing with the brother she'd grown up with. She loved Thut, but even when they'd sat side by side as children, reciting the King's List for their tutors and memorizing the course of the Nile, she'd sensed a dullness to his mind and had bristled at his easy compliance with the rules that she constantly tested. At first she had thought perhaps the lessons came easier to her because she was slightly older, but as time had passed she had realized her brother simply didn't thirst for knowledge as she did, that he was content to do as he was told and no more. Thut was an indulgent brother, but that didn't mean he would make a good husband, at least not for her. "I'm not sure what I want," she said. "Do you want to marry me?"

"I'd be a lucky man to have you as a wife, wild heathen that you are." He deflected a mock punch with a laugh, but sobered and tilted her chin to look at him. "I know marrying me wasn't what you'd planned."

Hatshepsut tried hard to make her smile genuine. "Plans change."

He cupped her cheek in his palm. "I love you. I promise to do my best to make you happy."

Thut kissed her nose and looked up into Nut's black belly, as if he might find the answers there. "Father needs me. I'm of age, and he's not as young as he used to be."

"And so you'll do what you have to."

He nodded. "Of course."

Just as she would. Yet she still wanted something in exchange.

Hatshepsut opened her mouth to broach the same question she'd asked her father, but Mutnofret's doors flew open to reveal the concubine in all her glittering splendor. Tonight Thut's mother had managed to outdo even herself. Hatshepsut was sure every jewel she owned was plastered to her body, plus a few more she'd likely pilfered from the pharaoh's concubines for the occasion.

"Hatshepsut!" Mutnofret lumbered into the courtyard and gathered her son into a fleshy embrace. Her grin revealed several missing teeth. "I just sent Thutmosis to find you. Come in, come in. We're all waiting for you!"

Dread spiraled down from Hatshepsut's heart to settle in the pit of her stomach. Thut's arm was around her waist as they entered Mutnofret's cozy dining room, open on one wall to a garden but crammed with more shrines and statues of the gods than even the temples housed. Cats lazed about several of them, including two perched on Sekhmet's lion head. Hatshepsut's patron goddess seemed to sneer with disgust as she walked past. The pharaoh and his Great Royal Wife reclined on their ebony chairs and nibbled appetizers from communal bowls of garlic chickpeas and honeyed figs. Ahmose pursed her lips as if she'd bitten a rancid pickle, but Pharaoh Tutmose beamed with satisfaction. Tonight the succession would be made secure and any possibility of civil war averted once his son and daughter married. He would have fulfilled his last required duty as pharaoh.

"You've been riding your chariot," Ahmose said as Hatshepsut tipped a cat from her chair. "And you're late."

Riding her chariot, amongst other things. No one needed to know about her meeting with Mensah in the stables, especially not Thutmosis or Ahmose. Hatshepsut's mother had managed to find more fault with her than usual since Neferubity's death, a feat Hatshepsut wouldn't have imagined possible. If she had her choice between enduring the rest of this dinner or swimming through a pool of poisonous asps, Hatshepsut knew which she'd pick. Snakes wouldn't be so terrible.

"Yes, Mother, I am late." She knew her mother would expect more elaboration, but she refused to give it.

Tutmose cleared his throat and gave her a warning look. She would try to behave.

As if on cue, matched pairs of slaves arrived with golden platters piled high with all the second wife's favorite treats. They marched out coriander gravy, baked perch from the morning catch, roast gazelle, chilled cucumber soup, melon salad, breads of all shapes with every stuffing imaginable, and fluffy cinnamon and honey pastries to top it off. A massive bowl full of honeyed dates, one of Mutnofret's favorite dishes, was placed right in front of Tutmose's second wife so she wouldn't have to trouble herself by reaching for the delicacies.

Hatshepsut couldn't manage a bite—her stomach was full of hostile butterflies doing battle against one another. She reached for a bit of melon, but her hand brushed against Thut's at the same moment. The butterflies attacked each other as she struggled to sit still.

It took an eternity for everyone to finish eating—Mutnofret alone ate at least three helpings of every dish. The pharaoh cleared his throat as silent slaves removed the last platters. "I believe there are gifts in store for you, Mutnofret," he said.

Mutnofret feigned surprise. "I didn't expect gifts!" She sat up straighter, a difficult task she barely accomplished. "Who wants to go first?" She wiped her mouth, whether to remove the last remnants of the meal or because she was salivating at the impending shower of gifts, Hatshepsut couldn't tell.

"Here you are, Mother." Thut pushed a linen-wrapped parcel toward Mutnofret. She pounced on the offering like a famished lioness upon her prey.

"Oh, what could it be?" Mutnofret threw off the linen to reveal a new pectoral, one shaped with lotus buds and dripping with carnelian and turquoise. "It's gorgeous!" She pulled Thut's ear toward her to kiss his cheek, leaving an imprint of wet ochre. "Thank you, dear!"

Mutnofret looked next to Hatshepsut, eyeing the small package she revealed. Hatshepsut smiled. Any gift would please Mutnofret. "This is from my mother and me," she said, handing over the gift. A quick look at her mother revealed that Ahmose had not lost her sour look from earlier in the evening. If anything, her distaste was now even more apparent.

Mutnofret made short work of the linen wrapping and held up a delicate copper mirror with dancing butterflies engraved on the back. "It's lovely," she gushed. "Hatshepsut, you must have picked this out."

The barb was aimed at her mother. "It's from both of us," Hatshepsut repeated.

Her father interrupted before the usual wifely squabbles could begin. "And now, my wife, I have one final gift." Tutmose stood empty-handed. The staid butterflies on Mutnofret's mirror taunted the angry ones in Hatshepsut's stomach.

The pharaoh stood between his two children but addressed Mutnofret. "You shall soon add pharaoh's mother to your list of titles, as Thutmosis takes his place beside me as co-regent." Mutnofret grinned like a cat with a helpless wren pinned in its claws. Hatshepsut snuck a glance at her brother. His face was a mask, but she caught the way his jaw clenched at their father's words. "And I know you have long dreamed of seeing your only son married," the pharaoh continued. "You shall soon hold your grandchildren in your arms and know that our family's dynasty is secure."

Hatshepsut held her breath and wished for a few moments of forever to postpone the inevitable.

"In two month's time, you will see your dreams turn to reality. Thutmosis and Hatshepsut shall be married!"

Mutnofret squealed like a scalded pig and jumped from the table to sweep the hawk in the nest and his future bride into her meaty arms. Hatshepsut glanced at their father, but he avoided both her and her mother's eyes. One woman's dreams were realized tonight, but another's failure to produce a male heir was flung in her face. Ahmose's expression reflected her pain, her features pulled into a grimace worthy of a mortal wound.

"You two will make such a regal couple!" Mutnofret planted a wet kiss on Thut's cheek and another on Hatshepsut's forehead. "I've never been so happy!" She paused and shook her head, a sly smile on her face as she looked askance at Ahmose. "I'm sure Hatshepsut will outshine her mother's capabilities in bearing sons, don't you think, Thutmosis?"

Thut cleared his throat. "I'm sure my sister will give me many sons."

Hatshepsut's stomach rebelled. She gasped and pushed Mutnofret's meaty arms from her shoulders. "I need air."

She made it to Mutnofret's sitting room, but didn't realize Thut had followed her until he touched her arm. "Hatshepsut!"

She pushed him away. "Let me go."

"Tell me what's wrong."

"Just leave me alone!"

Thut looked about to argue but dropped his hand and released her. It was a good thing; if he'd held her much longer, she would have vomited all over Mutnofret's tiles. As it was, she made it only into the courtyard before heaving the contents of her stomach into an alabaster urn carved with images of the sacred triad of Isis, Osiris, and Horus.

Normally she would have gone to sit under her drunken willows to calm down, but that would have been the obvious place to find her. She didn't want to be found.

Her feet took her through the open arboretum outside the palace offices. Sycamore and willow trees surrounded a deep pool bedecked with lotus-blossom tiles. A waist-high statue of Amun guarded one corner, the god's granite face impassive under the double plumes of his crown.

This would all end if she waded in and allowed the black waters to usher her to Amenti. Egypt had prospered for millennia without her; surely it would continue to do so. Thut could find another wife, a woman content to warm his bed and bear his gaggle of children. She could join Neferubity in the Field of Reeds and wait for the rest of their family to join them one day.

The water covered her ankles, then her calves. She took a deep breath and closed her eyes before stepping in the rest of the way.

"Hatshepsut? What are you doing?"

Senenmut.

A statue frozen midstep, Hatshepsut desperately wished she could disappear into the shadows. She waited a moment's breath and hoped he would allow her to slink away.

It was a futile hope.

"Hatshepsut?" Senenmut repeated himself, this time a fraction louder. "Come here. I have something to show you." He turned and walked back toward the offices.

Hatshepsut felt a flicker of annoyance at his command, but the only other options were to drown herself or to return to her family. Senenmut was the lesser evil.

The walls of scrolls and scent of dusty papyrus comforted her. Hatshepsut had spent countless hours with Neferubity in the royal offices over the past two years, poring over Egypt's tribute requirements of her vassal states, composing missives to foreign dignitaries, and filing court judgments for future reference—all to help prepare her sister to become Great Royal Wife. The idea of drowning herself suddenly seemed ridiculous. All that knowledge had been hard-earned and would be put to good use. She just wasn't sure how. At least not yet.

Senenmut handed her a scroll. The delicate reed paper was marred with black slashes of choppy hieratic script. "Who wrote this?" Hatshepsut squinted, but that didn't help. "It's barely legible."

"I did." Senenmut chuckled. "My hieroglyphs are even worse. My poor handwriting is one of my few faults."

Hatshepsut could think of more faults to add to his list, but reminded herself that not everyone had the benefit of her royal education. She considered pointing out her superiority in learning, for surely this *rekhyt* couldn't speak four languages, recite Egypt's military history from memory, or debate foreign policy and trade agreements as she could. Instead she continued to read, deciphering the scrawled letters as best she could. "You're recommending the enlargement of our temples in Nubia?"

Senenmut nodded. A triumphant gleam lit his eyes. "And the appointment of an Egyptian loyal to the Isis Throne to oversee all of Nubia as viceroy."

His plan was brilliant, not that she'd ever tell him that. Considering his performance earlier this morning, she was surprised at his willingness to share such ambitious plans with her. Either he was looking to boast or perhaps sniffing out a possible ally for this risky venture, knowing of Thut's inherently cautious nature. The Nubians were one of the tribes of the Nine Bows, nine groups of foreigners stretching from the Asiatic sand dwellers in the north to the Nubian kingdoms in the southern deserts. All lived outside the Nile valley—and, thus, in the land of chaos—and each had fought against Egypt at some point in history. "Nubia has been peaceful since my father took the throne," Hatshepsut said, "but they rebel every few years, especially when Egypt has a new pharaoh."

"With an Egyptian viceroy and a massive temple to Egypt's gods staring them in the face, they might think twice about rebelling next time, don't you think?" A boyish grin lit his features.

"Quite likely," Hatshepsut murmured. She'd seriously doubted Senenmut's abilities as an adviser to her brother, but it had never occurred to her that perhaps the man possessed natural talents to make up for his poor birth and lack of manners.

She pushed the papyrus back to him. "Have you shown this to my father?"

He shook his head. "Not yet, but I will. The reconstruction of the temple will require the transport of laborers, so it will have to wait until after the harvest."

"I'll be interested to hear what he says." Their eyes locked for the briefest moment, and she cleared her throat. "If you'll excuse me."

"Ah yes." Senenmut rolled up the paper. "Back to the snake pit?"

"The snake pit?"

"Your mother and Mutnofret, in the same room?" Senenmut chuckled again. "If that's not a pit of serpents, I don't know what is."

A wry smile tugged at Hatshepsut's lips. "I'm hoping to slip back to my chambers without them noticing."

"You think they'll let Egypt's future Great Royal Wife disappear so easily?" Senenmut's eyebrow arched. "I'd ask how you managed to escape in the first place, but I'm sure it was quite a scene."

"It would have been worse if I'd stayed." *Much worse.*

Senenmut blew out one of the lamps. "So, your father made the announcements?"

Apparently he knew about both of the announcements. Hatshepsut had the feeling Senenmut didn't miss much.

"He did." Some of Hatshepsut's earlier dejection returned to cloud her mood. "Thut will be co-regent, and in two months' time I will be his Great Royal Wife."

"A sacrifice of your freedom, but one worthy of your kingdom." Senenmut didn't meet her eyes.

"It's a sacrifice I've known I would have to make," Hatshepsut said, her tone measured as she thought of the pool. The bottom of her sheath was still wet.

"Of course." Senenmut motioned her to the door as he blew out the final lamp. With one puff of air he extinguished the tiny flame. Moonlight streamed through the window. "But I'd imagine it still tastes bitter going down." He looked at her, but his expression was hidden in the darkness. "Shall I walk you back, then?"

For some reason the idea of Senenmut walking her through the moonlit gardens seemed far too *intimate* for her taste.

"I can manage," she said. "If I don't return soon, Father will probably send out the guards."

"As you wish." Senenmut bowed his head and waited for Hatshepsut to exit the office before he closed the door behind them.

"There you are." Thut's relieved voice echoed off the walls of the corridor. Kipa sat on his shoulder, her tail wrapped around his neck as she peeled a pistachio. "We were beginning to worry." His eyes widened as they fell on Senenmut. "The two of you alone and you both survived? I'm shocked."

"Just barely," Hatshepsut said. A girl-slave passed them, and stopped to bow. The royal family was never alone, one reason she loved to escape into the Red Land. "I'm exhausted. I'd like to go back to my chambers."

Thut kissed her forehead. "Of course," he said. "Father just announced that you're to move into the Hall of Women tomorrow. Shall we pick out your apartments and furnishings in the morning?"

She'd as soon pick out her tomb.

"Actually, I was hoping the two of you could assist me in planning the temples in Nubia," Senenmut said, looking up as if the mud brick ceiling was especially fascinating. "It's a large undertaking and I'd appreciate the help."

Puzzled, Hatshepsut looked at Senenmut. She'd seen the plans—they were essentially finished. But she welcomed the opportunity to avoid the Hall of Women for even an extra moment.

"I'm sure we can manage both," Thut said. "In peace, Senenmut."

Senenmut bowed. "In peace."

Perhaps she wouldn't feed him to the crocodiles. At least not yet.

CHAPTER 4

"Hatshepsut, wake up."

She groaned and rubbed her eyes. She'd been living in the Hall of Women for a week now, but still found it disconcerting to wake in chambers that reeked of unfamiliar perfumes accumulated over years. It didn't help that her father had been ill for the last few days. She had tried to persuade Thut to put off their wedding preparations and let her assume some of the pharaoh's responsibilities, but he had refused, wanting to prove to their father—or more likely to himself—that he could rule alone.

Hatshepsut blinked her way back to reality, her mind still immersed in the foggy world of dreams. She was startled to see Senenmut standing in her doorway, illuminated by the yellow glow of a sputtering oil lamp.

"What are you doing here?" Hatshepsut pulled the sheet to her chin, ready to scream, but Senenmut remained by the door.

Only bad news was delivered in the middle of the night.

"It's your father," Senenmut said. "Come quickly. I've already sent a messenger to bring Thutmosis."

Hatshepsut's ivory headrest clattered to the floor as she jumped out of bed. Her linen dress billowed behind her, the angry gray of storm clouds in the darkness.

She barreled into her father's chambers, but stopped short at the fetid smell of death and decay.

"By the gods." She swayed on her feet.

Someone touched the small of her back to guide her forward. A fire roared in the brazier, so the room blazed like a baker's oven at midday. Shadows lurking at the edges of the room chanted mournful hymns to Anubis, meant to ease the passage of the dying to the West.

"Leave now!" Hatshepsut gestured violently at the priests. Senenmut herded them back into the hallway as she sank to the floor at her father's bedside. The pharaoh's breath was ragged—sometimes fast and shallow and other times so slow she feared another inhale would never come. The lion of Egypt was a shrunken husk as he reclined on the bed, eyes closed. The engraving of the hippo goddess Taweret brandished knives of protection upon the pharaoh's ebony headrest, yet Hatshepsut feared the goddess was no match for Anubis. Without his stern expression and booming voice, her father was suddenly small. Mortal.

"Father?" Hatshepsut laid her hand over the pharaoh's. His skin was hot but damp, as if he'd just been dredged from the Nile, his arms mottled with stains the color of pomegranate.

"I don't think he can hear you." Senenmut stood beside her. "The Royal Physician thinks he slipped into this deep sleep hours ago. Yesterday the pharaoh felt worse than usual but didn't wish to bother anyone. He complained of chills, so a fire was lit, but it didn't help. The fever was still high when Gua last checked him." Senenmut retrieved a golden Eye of Horus amulet from the pharaoh's chest and handed it to Hatshepsut. "He believed the illness might be caused by rotting food trapped in your father's body, so he ordered a tonic of garlic and onion juice, then recommended the pharaoh get some rest. And when the servant tried to wake the pharaoh for his next dose of herbs—"

Hatshepsut nodded mutely. Anubis slunk about the shadows,

impatient to catch the pharaoh's *ka* in his jackal teeth and drag him to the realm of the dead.

The door creaked open. Thut seemed younger without his wig and kohl, his face blanched to match the white of his kilt. He knelt at Hatshepsut's side and took her hand without a word.

"You'll be pharaoh before daybreak," she whispered.

Her brother was about to receive the crown to the most powerful country in the world. Hatshepsut expected some reaction from him, but Thutmosis only stared blankly at their father.

Ahmose joined them moments later, rumpled from sleep but still the Great Royal Wife in her pristine robe and the braided Nubian wig she always kept ready at her bedside. Her dark eyes filled with tears as she stared at her husband, but she blinked them away as she knelt at the foot of the bed. She reached out and clasped Tutmose's ankle, her jaw clenched so tightly that Hatshepsut feared her teeth would break.

They settled into silence, but soon Ahmose scrambled to her feet. "I can't do this," she said. She bent to press her lips to Tutmose's forehead, lingering for a long moment as if trying to gather the strength to leave him. "I'll look for you in Amenti," she whispered, one of her tears splashing his cheek. "Wait for me with Neferubity."

The door slammed behind her, leaving only stillness and the promise of death.

They didn't have to wait long to witness the pharaoh's passage to the next world. His breathing grew more labored, each inhale and exhale a struggle against his imminent fate. Tutmose's final breath rattled in his lungs as Re broke through the black line of the horizon, ushering the pharaoh to Ma'at's scales in a haze of golden light. Hatshepsut waited an eternity for the next inhale, but it never came.

He was gone.

"May the soles of his feet be firm. May he rest forever in Amenti." Thut recited the common death prayer, his wide eyes shining.

An ear-splitting keening shattered the peace, an animal wail from the hallway that made the hair on Hatshepsut's arms stand on end. A harried *medjay* burst into the room, the guard's stately demeanor re-placed with something akin to panic.

"It's Mutnofret," the guard choked out. "She heard of the pharaoh's illness." The *medjay* saw the death mask on Tutmose's face and bowed his head before speaking again. He recited a death prayer and then added hopefully, "Perhaps someone else could tell her the news?"

Thut spared a glance at Hatshepsut, but she waved him away. He would benefit from having something to do right now, and she needed time to think. "I'll see to Mother," he said, the relief plain on his face.

Hatshepsut laid her forehead upon her father's feather mattress as soon as Thut closed the door. She had still hoped to persuade the pharaoh to train her, but now that dream would be entombed with her father's mummy. Her fingers clutched the bed linens. "What am I going to do?"

A hand on her shoulder made her flinch. She had forgotten Senenmut. She brushed his hand away.

"You'll do what you've always done," he said. "Fight for what you want, one day at a time."

Hatshepsut stared at him. She hadn't realized her desires were so transparent. Senenmut had risen from the mud of Iuny—no mean feat—but she didn't want his insight. The man's ambition was too obvious. She stood, her elbows cradled in her hands. "There are plans to be made, his body—" She choked on the word; one of her white-knuckled fists pushed against her lips as she squeezed her eyes shut. She wouldn't cry, not in front of him.

Senenmut took a step toward her, but she held her hands up like a shield. "I need to make arrangements for the funeral. There are ambas-sadors and governors to inform—"

"Go to your mother," Senenmut said. "I'll see to the priests, and when you're ready you can take over the arrangements. The ambassadors and governors can wait." He hesitated, then sighed. "What about Nubia?"

"What do you mean?" Her mind seemed lost in a fog, too dense to think.

"They'll see this change of leadership as a chance to rebel."

Of course they would. She knew the pattern from the histories she'd studied with Neferubity, lessons learned in what seemed an eternity ago. As if she didn't have enough to think about right now.

But Senenmut shook his head. "Never mind. I'll discuss the matter with Thutmosis later."

"Thut and I will be married immediately after the funeral." Hatshepsut rubbed her temples. The room felt empty, as if the gods had abandoned them now that Anubis had claimed his prize.

"An extra boon for your brother," Senenmut said.

Hatshepsut looked back at her father's still face, silently cursing him for leaving her too soon. "There's so much I—*we*—needed to learn from him."

"You know more than you think." Senenmut's gaze was hooded. She wasn't sure if he meant her alone or Thut as well. "You will help guide Thutmosis. You were born for it."

But she hadn't been born for it. Neferubity had.

Egypt mourned for seventy days. The country was silent, the Great Double Gate locked. Within the Walls of the Prince, no banquets or festivals that might distract the nobles from their dutiful grieving were allowed. The royal wedding had also been postponed until the end of Akhet in order to avoid the unlucky taint of death, and moved to a day decreed by the High Priest of Amun.

Hatshepsut had been trapped in the Hall of Women, her father's mourning wives her only company, although she'd received several gifts from Mensah. The latest was a basket of almonds and fresh lettuce leaves, both well-known aphrodisiacs. A papyrus note lay nestled inside.

> *I thought you might sneak out tonight so we could nibble on these together. I miss you.*

She burned the note and fed the lettuce and almonds to one of the concubine's dogs.

Hatshepsut had been allowed out of the Hall of Women only once since her father's death, so she could attend the small ceremony that officially transferred the double crown to her brother. A larger coronation waited for the wedding day. Today she received a taste of the freedom she had once taken for granted, as the old pharaoh was laid to rest, allowing her brother to claim his place fully upon the Isis Throne.

"I'll be glad when this is over," Thut said to Hatshepsut as they followed the funeral procession up the sandy path to their father's tomb. She noted the ever-present circles under his eyes and bit back a stinging retort about how she'd been entombed in the Hall of Women. Thut had been especially sweet and gentle over the past two months, bringing her new jewels and enameled boxes of sweetmeats when he'd come to visit; so considerate that she'd wanted to scream every time he'd denied her only request: to allow her to leave the Hall of Women. She would convince her brother of her use in his throne room or go slowly insane while locked away. She just had to wait for the right opportunity.

"I wish funerals didn't have to be at this ungodly time of day." Thut walked slower than usual today, leaning heavily on his cane. Slaves weren't allowed in the royal entourage, so Hatshepsut fanned herself and Thut with a swan's-wing fan, but the meager breeze she created did no good. "Morning would have been better—it's too damn hot to be gallivanting through the desert."

"It's the custom," Hatshepsut said. The court officials attended the public funeral at dawn, but only the royal family and priests accompanied Osiris Tutmose to his final resting place in the Western Valley. The threat from thieves dictated that few knew the location of the royal tomb.

The sledge bearing their father's mummy scraped over the sand. The oxen snorted, two beasts as black as Nut's belly at night. Each wore a wreath of lotus blossoms around its horns, a symbol of rebirth.

"Well, custom or not, it's infernally hot," Thut said. "Only snakes and scorpions go out in the midday sun. And I think most of the snakes are smart enough to have taken cover today."

"Perhaps you should change the law, then." Hatshepsut spared a glance behind them to their father's widows. Ahmose regally picked her way over the path, while Mutnofret huffed her way up the slope like a beast of burden. The front of her sheath was drenched with sweat. "Your mother is having a difficult time," she said to Thut. "You should help her."

He looked behind them. "You don't mind?"

"Not at all," Hatshepsut replied, grateful to Mutnofret for the distraction. "I'll be fine."

They continued in subdued silence to the pharaoh's tomb. The time had come for the symbolic weighing of Osiris Tutmose's heart against Ma'at's feather. If his heart was lighter than the goddess's feather, the dead pharaoh would be found true of voice and Osiris would welcome him into the glory of the afterlife. If not, the beast Ammit would gorge itself on the pharaoh's heart for dinner tonight. Hatshepsut shuddered at the thought of the slavering monster, a fearful combination of crocodile, lion, and hippopotamus.

Priests carried Osiris Tutmose's treasures for the afterlife into his tomb, furniture and art to keep the pharaoh comfortable in Amenti, *senet* boards to occupy his endless days, and crates of 365 blue faience *shabti* statues to come to life and serve the pharaoh in the Field of Reeds, one for every day of the year. The *iniut* banner—a headless cheetah skin stuffed with linen—was tied to a pole in a gilded pot as an offering to Anubis. An ebony chest in the shape of the jackal god carried the four precious canopic jars that housed the pharaoh's internal organs. It was then time for the mummy to take its place in this perfectly choreographed dance of death.

Silently, three priests came from the back of the assembled mourners to begin the Opening of the Mouth ceremony. One wore the snarling mask of their patron god, the black jackal Anubis. The priests reeked of death; as the Controllers of Mysteries, their hearts and minds were filled with the secrets of mummification that no other mortals were permitted to learn. Their long kilts were dyed black to symbolize the rotting flesh of the dead and the fertile soil of Egypt, the cycle of rebirth. The masked priest took his place behind the mummy, and the other two tilted the sledge until the body was vertical once again. Hatshepsut could scarcely believe the remains of her father were wrapped under those linens and hidden behind the solid gold funeral mask. The back of the mask was carved with spells, each meant to protect a specific part of Osiris Tutmose's face as he passed through the challenges of the next world before being reborn.

The High Priest's deep chant started low and gained in volume until it swelled and echoed through the valley. He swung a censer back and forth, cloaking the breath of the gods with the heavy scent of precious incense. Several other priests joined the mournful melody, and the professional mourners keened in accompaniment as they rent their clothes and tore their hair, all three timbres wrapped together in a melancholy song.

A shrill cry rang out to Hatshepsut's right. Mutnofret clung to Thut, eyes puffy and chubby cheeks streaked with rivers of kohl and tears as she alternated between hiccups and inhuman shrieks of grief. Hatshepsut glanced sideways at her own mother. Ahmose blinked and wiped away the single tear that threatened to ruin her flawless makeup. Hatshepsut grasped her mother's hand and gave it a tight squeeze. Ahmose stared straight ahead, but gave a squeeze in response.

The sounds of mourning stopped, leaving a roaring silence punctuated only by Mutnofret's sniffles. The High Priest, a leopard skin draped over his shoulders, came to stand in front of the body. Raising a golden adze, he touched the mummy's eyes to symbolize the pharaoh's successful awakening in the Field of Reeds. The priest picked up a chisel and tapped the mouth as well. He rubbed the entire death mask with cow's milk, symbolically reinvigorating the rest of the pharaoh's face. Now Osiris Tutmose would be able to see and speak in the afterlife. The leopard and jackal priests embraced the mummy to allow the soul of Tutmose to find its earthly form.

Wordlessly, the mummy was lowered back onto the sledge, and the High Priest motioned to the royal family. One by one, each of Osiris Tutmose's wives and children placed a papyrus page from the Book of Coming Forth by Day at his head and feet. The spells would assist the pharaoh along his journey to the afterlife.

"Rest well, Father." Hatshepsut touched the bulge at Osiris Tutmose's heart, the site of the sacred green jasper scarab that was also inscribed with spells for the afterlife. She stepped back to allow the priests to push the sledge into the gloom of the subterranean grave. The final priest carried a green wooden box shaped like Osiris, filled with damp Nile silt and grain. The seedlings would sprout inside the dark tomb, symbolic of the rebirth of the deceased in the afterlife, but then they, too, would wither and die, as did all life. The sound of wood scraping rock slipped into the dark and finally disappeared.

A train of Anubis' priests filed up the sandy path, laden with trays of food and all the other accoutrements necessary for the funeral feast. The priests erected awnings for the royal family so they could enjoy their meal in honor of Osiris Tutmose in relative comfort while the pharaoh awaited his final judgment.

Hatshepsut sat on a linen blanket and attempted a bite of roast gazelle—her father's favorite food—from the bowl she and Thut shared. It tasted like sawdust.

"Admiral Pennekheb has returned to court. He tells me the provincials in Nubia are getting restless," Thut said, as if commenting on the weather. Yet he twisted the gold bangle at his wrist so hard that Hatshepsut feared it might leave a mark.

"Restless? Is it an insurrection?" Hatshepsut asked. This was precisely what Senenmut had predicted and had sought to avoid with his plan for Egyptian monuments and a new viceroy for Nubia, plans waylaid by her father's death. She hadn't seen Senenmut since that night, or had the opportunity to speak with Thutmosis about the possibility of a revolt; Senenmut must have neglected to mention the concern to her brother. Annoyance at the *rekhyt*'s incompetence flared, but she quashed it. She'd deal with him later.

"Do we need to send a division south?" she asked.

Thut stared at her for a moment, then tore a piece of gazelle off its bone and chewed, his mouth open slightly. "It's just a small group causing problems."

"Is it serious?"

"I don't know." Her brother's tone was sharper than usual. "Sending a division or two should take care of it."

"I certainly hope so." Hatshepsut eyed him carefully. If the problem in Nubia was serious, Egypt would need to act swiftly, or the gold shipments would be disturbed, not to mention the havoc that instability would wreak on the southern border.

Lost in thought, Hatshepsut didn't notice that Thut had fallen asleep—still sitting up—until his head dropped to her shoulder. The poor man was exhausted. She shifted on the blanket so he wouldn't fall forward and call attention to himself. Mutnofret caught her eye and winked.

Then Hatshepsut realized there was a way for her to escape the Hall of Women. She chewed her thumbnail, her mind spinning the plan as Thut dozed. It might work, as long as she played her part right.

The remnants of the feast were packed up and taken into Osiris Tutmose's tomb so the former Pharaoh could enjoy his favorite foods as he settled into the afterlife. Hatshepsut watched with a heavy heart as the priests slid shut the massive stone door to the tomb and sealed it for all eternity as the black line of the horizon swallowed Re.

It was done. Now it was time to rejoin the land of the living.

They didn't have to seek out Admiral Pennekheb. As soon as the royal barque neared the dock Hatshepsut saw Egypt's most senior military expert waiting with Senenmut, his cedar walking stick in one hand and a torch in the other.

That could mean only one thing: the situation in Nubia was dire. It took an eternity for the ship to make it to shore and then for the rowers to tie it to the dock. Ordinarily Hatshepsut wouldn't have wasted such precious time, preferring to jump ashore before the crew finished with the rigging, but the citizens of the City of Truth lined the shores, their eager faces lit by torchlight, all yearning for a rare glimpse of the royal family. Protocol must be observed. Hatshepsut couldn't go bolting off the ship, no matter how much she wished to.

Finally, the boat was secure. The instant her feet hit the ground, the two advisers fell into step behind Hatshepsut and Thut.

"*Per A'a.*" Pennekheb didn't miss a beat as he spoke to the fledgling pharaoh. "We must proceed with sending the army to settle things in Nubia. They've murdered Governor Turi. The Egyptian colonists in the area have taken refuge in a fortress built by your father. The Division of Horus awaits your orders."

Thut waved his hand. He seemed pale, even in the torchlight. "Fine. Send the men."

Hatshepsut linked her arm through her brother's. This was her chance. "Thut, if you'd prefer, I can see to this and give you a report in the morning."

He stopped, his face awash with relief. "You'd do that?"

"For you? Of course."

His hand cupped her face and he brushed an errant braid back under her diadem before looking to Pennekheb and Senenmut. "My sister has my full permission to do whatever is necessary."

"Will you join the troops?" Hatshepsut asked before her brother slipped away. His smile disappeared, replaced by a sickly pallor.

"It's entirely unnecessary for you to supervise the troops," Senenmut said. "In fact, your presence might make the situation more volatile. You would give our enemy a highly visible and extremely prized target."

"Nubia rebels every time the Isis Throne changes hands. Each time they've been easily conquered," Thut said.

"We'll see to the details," Senenmut reassured him. "A swift response will ensure our victory."

Hatshepsut noted the slowness of Thut's step as he made his way up the dock alone. The double crown had already aged her brother, while the very idea of ruling invigorated her.

If only she were a man. Hatshepsut would have loved the opportunity to leave the capital, to secure her people's love and the military's loyalty. Instead, she was cursed with a man's *ka* in a woman's body.

She turned on Senenmut and Pennekheb once her brother was out of earshot. "What was that all about?"

Senenmut's eyes followed Thut's departing form. His voice was low when he spoke. "Your brother detests fighting."

"But he fought in Canaan with my father," Hatshepsut said.

Senenmut shook his head. There was a long silence. "Your brother never fought," he finally said, so softly Hatshepsut thought she had misheard him. "He stayed in his tent whenever there was a battle, complaining of one ailment or another."

Thut was a coward? Hatshepsut was so stunned she couldn't speak.

Admiral Pennekheb shifted his weight, leaning on his cane. The lines at his eyes had spread to the rest of his face—a wrinkle for each battle he had fought in the name of Egypt. Pennekheb had served his country for many years, but Egypt still needed him, especially now. "I informed the pharaoh of the insurrection early this morning," he said. "I had hoped that he would be moved to take action, but—"

Hatshepsut whirled on Senenmut, unable to contain her anger any longer. And she was more than angry; she was furious at him, at her brother, and even at her father for abandoning her when she needed him most. "None of this would have happened if you'd voiced your concerns to Thutmosis after my father died."

Senenmut blinked. "I did speak to your brother," he said, measuring his words carefully. "The pharaoh decided not to devote Egypt's resources to averting what he believed was a remote chance of a foreign revolt."

Her fury vanished, leaving her strangely empty. She'd always understood that Thut was cautious, but seeing this new side of him was like meeting a foreigner for the first time, a weak-willed stranger she didn't care to acknowledge. It occurred to her how little she knew the brother she'd grown up with, the man she was soon to marry.

"From now on I need to be informed regarding all military matters," Hatshepsut said, her voice hollow. "In addition to my brother, of course."

"Of course."

"As you wish, *Hemet*," the aging general agreed as the trio walked into the palace. "We should sort out the details regarding Nubia. The Division of Horus is standing by to move out as soon as they receive orders to do so."

"A punitive strike—a fast one—would be the best course of action," Senenmut said. "Take out those responsible for the insurrection and make an example of them. Replace the governor with one loyal to Egypt and keep an occupation force in Nubia until the dust settles."

Pennekheb nodded slowly, rubbing his chin. "I see you paid attention to at least some of my lectures."

"We should have another division standing by to deploy," Hatshepsut said. "I doubt we'll need the extra men, but perhaps if the Division of Thoth were ready?"

"I'll see to it." Admiral Pennekheb looked at her with an expression that might have passed for awe. "If I were a much younger man, you'd not be safe from my suit, *Hemet*. I've rarely met a man with such a quick grasp of military maneuvers, much less a woman." Hatshepsut smiled at his flattery; this man might prove a useful ally. "If you'll excuse me, I'll go speak to the commanders," Pennekheb said. "The men of Horus will be able to move by morning."

"There are some maps of Nubia from the campaigns Osiris Tutmose led into the region a few years back," Senenmut added as an after-thought as they watched Pennekheb shuffle away. "I'll find the scrolls and deliver them to the commanders as well."

"Of course." Hatshepsut nodded her approval as Senenmut turned to go. "Thank you for telling me about Thut," she said quietly.

Senenmut turned back to face her. The smile fell from his face. "I have the utmost respect for your brother, despite his shortcomings."

Hatshepsut shook her head. "Such behavior is inexcusable."

Senenmut sighed. "My father died while we were in Canaan. My mother and siblings would have been destitute if not for your brother's generosity in providing for them."

That sounded like the Thut she knew, not the one who had cowered in his tent while Egypt's blood was shed. "I'm sorry—I didn't know." Hatshepsut's voice was low.

"Your brother is a good man," Senenmut assured her. "But we men all have our weaknesses." His gaze caught hers, but she only chuckled.

"And you possess more than your fair share of weaknesses," Hatshepsut said.

"Perhaps, *Hemet*." Senenmut gave a hollow laugh, but the sound was cut short.

"Hatshepsut."

Mensah stepped into the corridor, a smug smile on his face. "It's been a long time." His gaze traveled over her, lingering on her breasts and hips. "Too long."

She'd always loved the attention Mensah lavished upon her, but right now all she wanted to do was wipe the smirk from his face.

"Senenmut," she said, "this is Imhotep's son, Mensah."

"I'm aware," Senenmut said. "Your name means 'third-born,' correct?"

Mensah crossed his arms over his bare chest. "I suppose my father ran out of names by the time I arrived."

"Indeed." Senenmut raised an eyebrow at her. Hatshepsut knew from Thut that Senenmut was the eldest of six children, none of them named for their birth order. "I'll leave you two to your discussion, then."

She held up a hand. "Wait a moment, Senenmut." Beckoning to Mensah, she walked to the other end of the corridor, wishing they were farther from Senenmut. Mensah stood too close to her for propriety's sake, but she refused to back into the whitewashed wall. "What are you doing?"

"I've commissioned a statue in your honor," Mensah said. "A work of art, for a work of art."

She would have laughed had his expression not been so sincere. "Stop it, Mensah. I don't want a statue."

What she wanted was for him to leave. Now.

"I haven't seen you in months, Hatshepsut." Mensah clasped her hand, but she shook him off. Over his shoulder, Senenmut perused a wall fresco of musicians and naked dancing girls, but every so often his gaze flicked in their direction. Mensah glanced his way, his lips tightening to a hard line. "What's he doing here?"

"Senenmut advises Thut."

"I don't like the way he looks at you. Like he wants to devour you." His lips softened. "That's my job."

She sighed. "Not anymore. I'm not yours any longer, Mensah."

His eyes narrowed. "So you're ending it?"

He seemed to forget she had ended it the night she had left him in the stables. Mensah had a pretty face and they'd had their share of fun, but that was where his talents ended.

"I don't have a choice."

He jerked his head toward Senenmut. "Is it because of him? A filthy *rekhyt* advising the royal family? My family has served the pharaohs since they first sat upon the Isis Throne—"

"Senenmut has nothing to do with us." How could she make him understand? "Mensah, I'm to marry Thut. This is the way things have to be."

He tipped her chin up with his thumb. "But I don't want that. And I don't think you do either."

"I don't, but—"

He kissed her then, pinning her between the wall and his bare chest. She'd never admit it, but his lips still had the power to make her blood race.

She shoved him away. "If you ever touch me like that again, I'll have you castrated and your manhood thrown to the crocodiles."

Chest heaving, she ducked out of his arms without waiting for a response and walked back to Senenmut. Behind her, Mensah cursed, and then his footsteps stomped down the corridor in the opposite direction.

Senenmut had his back to her now, hands clasped loosely behind him. She didn't know how much he'd seen or heard, but, regardless, she'd just given this man more information than he needed. "The frescoes here are quite well done," he said without looking at her. "Are they painted by the same artists as the tombs on the West Bank? I've heard those are spectacular."

Hatshepsut rubbed the pale scars on her wrists but forced herself to stop. "I don't honestly know."

Senenmut gave her a sidelong glance, then cleared his throat.

"I'm off to dig through piles of dusty old maps," he said. "When I lived in Iuny, I thought life in the palace meant luxury and intrigue, but I'm positive some of the farmers out there have more fun pulling turnips and shoveling manure."

Hatshepsut would have laughed out loud had she not been so upset by everything else. Senenmut's griping was a ray of sunshine in the clouds of her day. "Poor, poor Senenmut. I'm sure we can find you a nice plot of land back in Iuny if you'd prefer. One with plenty of manure."

"Watch out," he said. "I might take you up on that offer one of these days. Then who would do your dirty work?" His throaty chuckle reverberated down the corridor as he strolled off to retrieve the maps.

Hatshepsut couldn't stop the smile that broke out on her face. Senenmut was common, ambitious, and more aggravating than a scorpion sting. Yet, entirely against her will, she found she enjoyed his company. She watched him for a moment before shaking her head and heading to her own rooms to begin work on her brother's war.

The thought of Thut pulled Hatshepsut back to hard reality.

A war to wage and a wedding to plan. She would never get any sleep.

CHAPTER 5

"I have something for you." Unannounced, Senenmut strode into the Court of Reeds—so named for its forest of giant reed pillars—his gleaming white kilt brushing his ankles. The thin sheen of sweat covering his chest confirmed that he had run to the throne room to deliver the mysterious something he promised.

The royal audience would begin in a few minutes, and Hatshepsut was ready for the opportunity to hear and pass judgment on *rekhyt* cases. Thut had allowed her more say in state matters over the past weeks, and while she reveled in her newfound power, her eyelids were heavy from another sleepless night spent reading dusty records of ancient court cases by the light of flickering oil lamps. She craved the softness of her bed instead of the hard throne she now occupied, its seat carved with ebony inlays to represent a leopard skin and its stiff back gilded with intertwined lotus and papyrus stalks. She had offered to assist Thut with the royal audience today, and although the crowd rumbled on the other side of the doors, the pharaoh had yet to grace the Isis Throne with his regal presence.

"Oh?" Hatshepsut barely looked up from a petition from the Temple of Amun. The god's temple requested that the Royal Treasury pay for its new irrigation ditches, crying poverty after having sent food for the troops in Nubia. She tore the papyrus in half. Amun's storehouses had more gold than the pharaoh's treasury; the priests would have to dig their own ditches. "It had better be good news, or I'll have you flogged for starting my day with ill tidings."

"It worked."

"What worked?"

Senenmut rolled his eyes. "The invasion of Nubia. It's over."

She leaned forward on her chair. "And?"

"And we won, of course."

Hatshepsut jumped from her throne with a shout of joy. She had never doubted Egypt would win, but Senenmut's words were sweeter than she could have imagined. "When did you hear?"

"This morning. The insurrection was easily subdued, and Admiral Pennekheb installed a new Egyptian viceroy to replace Turi. The rebel ringleaders' heads are now rotting on pikes in the desert sun."

Hatshepsut wanted shouted her triumph to the skies, but she managed to contain herself. "Anything else?"

"Greedy, aren't you?" Senenmut asked with a grin. "No, no other news. Although . . ." His voice trailed off.

"Yes?"

"It might be wise to leave a more lasting reminder in Nubia for those tempted to rebel in the future. Heads in the desert last only so long."

"Something along the lines of the temples in Nubia you planned before my father passed to the West?"

Senenmut nodded slowly. "And another temple, a new one, to be constructed at Semna."

Hatshepsut smoothed her sheath as she sat back down. Senenmut was nothing if not ambitious. The treasury could easily afford the expense if the temples weren't massive. Hatshepsut knew she should wait for Thut's approval, but she rather liked the idea of authorizing the building projects herself.

"See to it that the new monuments are nothing too outrageous."

"Of course." Senenmut kept his expression calm, but his eyes lit up. "I'll have the plans to you by week's end."

"You mean you don't have them ready?" She gave him a wicked grin.

"Not quite yet," he said, "but I have something else for you." He reached into the pocket of his kilt and retrieved a delicate dagger with an ivory handle carved with intertwined sun disks and their rays, a unique motif. The sheath was made of hammered bronze, inscribed with images of a lioness attacking cows and ibexes. Down the middle were flawless hieroglyphs.

The One Who is Powerful, Sekhmet, Lady of Slaughter and Wearer of the Solar Disk

Sekhmet, the lion goddess of war and daughter of the sun. Her patron goddess.

"The ivory is from the elephant I took down in Canaan," Senenmut said. "I'd like you to have it."

Hatshepsut stared at the blade as if it were a viper. "Why should I have it?"

Senenmut smiled, a slow grin she was sure made most women as weak-kneed as a newborn colt. She refused to let its magic affect her. He shrugged. "You seem to be a woman who isn't easily impressed by gold."

"So you're trying to impress me?"

"Perhaps." He didn't take his eyes from her. "Is it working?"

"You'll have to try harder than that, Senenmut of Iuny." She gave him a stony glare. He was a fool for this blatant flattery. She still hadn't taken the knife—didn't plan to—when the side entrance to the throne room swung open. Thut strode into the room with Kipa on his shoulder, the pharaoh's false beard strapped to his chin and the double crown askew on his head. She still wasn't used to the sight; it didn't seem right for her brother to be wearing her father's crown.

"What's this, sister?" he asked. Kipa scampered up the arm of a slave who was carrying a tray of watered wine and green grapes. The monkey grabbed a handful of the fruit and stuffed them in her mouth. "A private audience with the *rekhyt* before the real petitioners are received?" He kissed her on the cheek and smiled to Senenmut as he took his place on the massive Isis Throne, flanked by the golden goddess of the throne; her husband, Osiris; and son, Horus.

Thut's face was still handsome, but his body had softened in the months since he'd returned from Canaan before their father's death. The rounded arc of his pale belly sat atop his starched white kilt, his hairless skin gleaming dully in the square of light streaming from the windows.

He eyed the ivory knife and chuckled. "Ah, the infamous dagger," he said. "Senenmut worked on that pretty bauble almost every night on our way back from Canaan. The rest of the men would be drunk around the campfire or chasing the camp women—" Thut caught himself, shifting on his throne and poking at his golden collar as he looked askance at Hatshepsut.

"I'm well aware that our soldiers don't live like priests while in the field." Her brother's concern for her sensibilities was touching but misplaced.

Thut shot her a relieved smile, but a crimson flush crept up his neck. She wondered if perhaps her brother had availed himself of those same women while he was in Canaan, or if Senenmut had. She continued to ignore Senenmut and pushed the thoughts from her mind—it was none of her business what either of them had done then, just as neither of them needed to know about her dalliance with Mensah.

"Well," Thut continued, "Senenmut was always at work on that little trinket. Took a fair amount of ribbing from the men for it, too." He looked at his friend's outstretched hand and back to Hatshepsut. "Is there a problem, sister?"

Hatshepsut gave Senenmut a hard look. "Not at all." She moved to take the dagger, but Senenmut shook his head. "May I?" he asked Thut.

"Of course." Her brother gestured for him to step onto the royal dais. Hatshepsut gritted her teeth.

Senenmut's fingers brushed hers as he placed the blade in her hand. She shivered, but refused to acknowledge the heat that crept to her face from his touch. But Senenmut noticed. The infernal man saw everything.

"Your brother never stopped speaking of you," Senenmut said quietly. "I figured a woman like you would appreciate a gift from a beast who refused to go down without a fight."

"A woman as wild as you," Thut said to her, laughing. Her brother kissed the back of her hand. "I've always harbored the suspicion that Senenmut planned to court you himself when we returned to Waset."

Senenmut managed a tight smile. Hatshepsut set the dagger on the gilded table at her elbow. It might as well be a snake, for all she wanted to do with it.

"Senenmut has come with news from Pennekheb," she spoke hurriedly. "Your foray into Nubia has been a total success, brother."

"Of course it has." Thut flicked his wrist, and silent attendants emerged from the shadows to hand him the golden crook and flail. "Did you doubt otherwise?"

"It seems the gods have graced you with the gift of foresight." Hatshepsut shook her head, a little annoyed. Thut had been blithely unaware of the maneuverings of his troops since they'd deployed. She had kept him apprised of events as she received news from the admiral, but Thutmosis cared more for the placement of his pieces on a *senet* board than for the movement of his soldiers.

"How long until the betrothal stele is ready?" Thut asked Senenmut. Hatshepsut started; she'd heard no mention of such a monument. Thut noticed her reaction and covered her hand with his. "I had Senenmut design a stele announcing our upcoming marriage to the *rekhyt*. He's the only one I could trust with so important a job."

She wondered if the project had truly been her brother's or if

Senenmut had managed to plant the idea in Thut's mind. She suspected the latter.

"It will be finished by the week's end," Senenmut said. "The stone
is red granite, truly a work of art."

"As it should be if it mentions my name," Hatshepsut said. She remembered too late Mensah's words in the corridor.

A work of art, for a work of art.

Senenmut didn't bother to hide his grin. "So I've heard."

Thut laughed, but Senenmut's gaze held hers. Hatshepsut refused
to look away. Finally, Senenmut bowed, the slightest hint of a smile on
his lips.

"That's precisely what I said when I commissioned the piece," Thut
said, still chuckling. "Humble you are not, sister."

Senenmut backed from the throne, his eyes hidden by his wig as he
took up a position at the bottom of the dais. "I thank the gods every day
for Senenmut," Thut said, quiet enough so only she could hear him. "I
doubt I'll ever find a more able-bodied adviser and loyal friend."

Somehow Hatshepsut doubted Senenmut's motives were quite as
altruistic as Thut believed. Her brother tended to think well of everyone, not necessarily the best trait in Egypt's pharaoh. She intended
to keep Senenmut on a tight leash.

A scribe took his place, sitting cross-legged at the bottom of the
dais, and two servants with giant ostrich-feather fans hovered behind
them as the usual courtiers filed in before the petitioners were admitted. Unlike the *rekhyt*, who arrived wide-eyed and slack-jawed, the
nobility came to the Court of Reeds to see and be seen. At the front of
the line came the vizier Imhotep, followed by his son. Mensah's musk
perfume was so strong that Hatshepsut almost choked as he took his
place beneath them, subtly pushing Senenmut to the periphery as Thut
bent down to discuss something with Imhotep. As Imhotep's only surviving son, Mensah was widely expected one day to take his father's
place advising Thutmosis as vizier, an honor that would make him
strut like a peacock more than he already did.

Imhotep and the other courtiers settled into their gossip, but Mensah's gaze burned into Hatshepsut.

"Filthy *rekhyt*," she heard him sneer at Senenmut under his breath, but Senenmut pretended not to notice and instead struck up a conversation with an elderly noble whose wisps of hennaed hair poked out from under his wig.

Thut leaned toward her and scratched his chin under his false beard. "Are we ready to begin?"

She nodded, and he motioned to a herald. "Bring forth the first petitioner."

The giant ebony doors swung open and the crowd of commoners surged forward into the throne room. The herald scanned his papyrus scroll for the first name on his list. "Siptah, merchant of Waset, come forth!"

The merchant Siptah, potbelly hanging over his stained kilt, jostled his way to the dais. His kohl, crooked and uneven, looked like a drunken monkey had applied it. He attempted a clumsy *henu* and sank in an untidy heap at her brother's feet.

"As Amun endures and as the Pharaoh endures," Siptah said, "so I speak in truth."

"Rise," Thut said. "What is your case, Siptah of Waset?"

Siptah rose and stared intently at the tiles. "Great *Per A'a*, I humbly ask retribution from Merenaset, a lowborn thief of a woman who has stolen from me!"

Siptah's words rose above the din of the hall, and the nobles up front quieted to hear the rest of the tale.

"And what, Siptah, has Merenaset stolen from you?" Thut asked.

Hatshepsut dared to interrupt. "Is the woman here to defend herself against these accusations?"

A barefoot woman in the middle of the crowd stepped forward, so wiry and thin that Hatshepsut could count the ribs that strained against the threadbare linen of her sheath. Although worn, the fabric was spotless and not a hair on the woman's wig was out of place. She swept to the floor in a stiff bow and then was on her feet again, her brown eyes as calm as the Nile on a windless day. "I am Merenaset, *Per A'a.* And it is true—I did steal from this man."

"You see, she admits to the crime!" Spittle spewed from Siptah's lips as he turned to face Merenaset. "You are a thief! A criminal!"

He reminded Hatshepsut of a washerwoman bickering over the price of fish in the market. She was thankful when her brother held up a hand to stop him. "Siptah, you still have not answered us. What has Merenaset stolen from you?"

The merchant turned to face the pharaoh, his visage flushed. "I caught her stealing bracelets from my faience stall. She knows it's true!"

A mixture of groans and excited murmurs arose from the crowd. A case of theft was certainly more interesting than the typical irrigation squabble, but the petty crime hardly seemed to warrant so much drama.

Hatshepsut studied the two petitioners as the herald called for order from the crowd. Beads of sweat marred Siptah's brow, whether from nerves or something else she couldn't tell. Merenaset seemed composed, but every now and then she chewed her thumbnail. Yet her expression toward Siptah was the same one would give a dung beetle before stepping on it.

As soon as the room quieted, Merenaset spoke again, her voice so low it was difficult to make out her words. "I have already admitted I stole from you."

"So you deserve to be punished!" Siptah stomped his foot like a child with a youth lock in the midst of a tantrum.

Hatshepsut cleared her throat, and Thut clapped the golden crook and flail to stop the grubby merchant from going any further. He motioned for Hatshepsut to speak.

"Why did you steal the bracelets, Merenaset?" Hatshepsut asked.

The woman blushed and looked at the floor. The glimmer of tears sparkled in her lashes when she raised her eyes. "I have a daughter,

Hemet. Her father abandoned us before she was born and left me with nothing. I stole the bracelets to trade for something to eat. If I hadn't, there would have been only one way for us to eat that night—"

"It doesn't matter what the reason is! She must be punished!" Siptah's hands balled into fists, and Thut's *medjay* guards stepped forward. The *rekhyt*'s palms fell open at his sides.

Thut leaned in to murmur to Hatshepsut. "The law requires that her ears be cut off. This is a simple case."

"Redress is short, harm is long, and a good reputation is seldom forgotten," she said.

Thut arched an eyebrow at the ancient proverb.

"The law states only that the thief *should* have her ears removed," Hatshepsut added.

Merenaset's plight was not unique—many women were forced onto Waset's streets to earn their bread—but perhaps there was a way to use Merenaset's case to everyone's benefit. Something more useful than a set of bloody ears.

"I don't think a normal punishment fits your case, Merenaset." Hatshepsut's gaze slid back to the woman. "Something needs to be done so this doesn't happen again."

"*What?*" Hatshepsut winced as Siptah's screech hit her ears. "This woman is a confessed thief! Cut off her ears so everyone will know she's a criminal. Ma'at demands it!"

Thut released the crook and flail to his lap. "You will listen to our sister and not interrupt again."

Hatshepsut leveled a glare at Siptah that would have scattered lions. "Ma'at demands that this woman get a fair trial."

Cowed, Siptah took a step back. Hatshepsut spoke again to Merenaset. "Would you be willing to work off your debt?" she asked.

The woman looked at the merchant, blatant distaste apparent in every line of her face. Hatshepsut couldn't fault the woman—Siptah's own mother probably looked upon him with the same expression. "Yes. If that is what is necessary to appease Ma'at."

"Would such an arrangement be acceptable to you, Siptah?" Hatshepsut asked. The sullen merchant was practically salivating at the thought of free labor. He nodded. "Good. Then that solves the issue of retribution. Merenaset will be at your stall tomorrow before Re reaches his zenith. The two of you may work out the details."

Hatshepsut signaled to one of the *medjay* to escort Siptah from the throne room, and turned to Merenaset. "Siptah is satisfied, but that doesn't solve the root of your problem. Once you've worked off your time to him there still won't be bread on your table."

The heavy weight of dejection slumped Merenaset's bony shoulders. "I'll manage."

"Do you have any skills? Or perhaps something you could make and sell?"

"Aside from my poor attempts at picking pockets, I'm afraid my skills are few and far between." Merenaset managed a wan smile. "I can clean and like to believe I have some talent for singing. Unfortunately, neither has helped me so far in this life."

Hatshepsut pondered what tasks Merenaset could perform without a real trade. A solution uncoiled in her mind, simple and perfect.

"Brother, could you arrange for a new chantress at Hathor's temple?"

Thut nodded slowly. "Of course. A chantress would be a perfect position—to sing hymns for the goddess and assist the priests in keeping the temple."

"And occasionally the palace might require sensitive information from someone who lives in the house of the goddess," Hatshepsut whispered. The relationship between the priesthood and palace was never smooth. Many of the gods were unimaginably wealthy due to their land holdings and the offerings made to them, and their High Priests often craved the power that typically accompanied such wealth. The palace had spies in many of the temples, but most were men posing as mere *wa'eb* priests. A female spy could prove a useful asset in a temple of men.

"And your daughter would be able to live at the temple with you,"

Hatshepsut said to Merenaset. That would certainly guarantee the woman's cooperation, not that she really had a choice.

The woman's face blossomed into a grin. "Thank you, *Hemet*." She sank to the floor and pressed her forehead to Hatshepsut's feet. "Thank you so much!"

Hatshepsut spared a glance at Thut. He beamed at her and gave her hand a warm squeeze.

Hatshepsut slid off her stool and crouched next to Merenaset. She pressed Senenmut's dagger into Merenaset's hand, curling the woman's fingers around its ivory suns.

"I want you to have this—protection for you and your daughter."

She heard Thut's sharp inhale behind her, and she didn't have to look to see the fire in Senenmut's eyes. This would teach him not to presume too much about their relationship.

"It's beautiful." Merenaset wiped her eyes. "My daughter and I will thank the gods for your wisdom and goodness every night."

"Our overseer at the Temple of Hathor will speak to the High Priest tomorrow and arrange for your installment as chantress," Thut said. "Our sister has solved your case quite tidily."

"Thank you," Merenaset murmured with a bow before the herald directed her from the throne room.

"Our audience today is at an end. May Amun bless the Two Lands!" Hatshepsut was surprised at the abrupt dismissal, but Thut clapped the golden crook and flail together, and she floated back to her seat. The throng of grumbling petitioners filed from the throne room. Many would return the following month, when the pharaoh held his next audience. Hatshepsut watched as Senenmut joined the crowd and backed from their royal presence. She expected a glare, but instead a wicked smile spread across his face. He was laughing at her. Again.

"Nicely played, sister." Thut looked to the empty table where the ivory knife had lain. "Although I'm sure you bruised Senenmut's heart a bit."

Hatshepsut shrugged. "He'll recover. The dagger will remind Merenaset where her loyalties lie." And it might protect her should any of the priests prove interested in taking advantage of a poor woman and her daughter.

"Criminals should be punished according to the law. Cutting off her ears would have been satisfactory."

"I think Merenaset will likely wish she could trade her ears after she's worked for Siptah for a day."

Thut chuckled. "You're probably right. You usually are." He checked the position of the sun through one of the windows as he handed off the trappings of state—the crook and flail, false beard, and double crown. Re's light warmed his face, the ochre staining his lips. His jawline was soft, but otherwise her brother was pleasant on the eyes. "I'm going to finish writing to the king of Mitanni before it gets too hot to think," he said. "Why don't you go relax in the Hall of Women? I don't want you worn out before our wedding."

"I think I'll go to the offices instead. I'd like to review the tribute amounts sent from Nubia last year. I think they could bear increasing."

Just then there was a burst of laughter below them. Imhotep had already left his seat at the bottom of the dais and was shuffling slowly toward the door. His son had remained behind, surrounded by a gaggle of Egypt's finest sons, all oiled and smelling like the inside of a perfume bottle. One said something to Mensah and motioned toward Hatshepsut, but Mensah only shook his head, his lips pursed tight. Another murmur of laughter rose from the others, but Hatshepsut's icy stare silenced them. Their attention quickly turned against Senenmut, still standing at the back of the retreating crowd.

"Upstart commoner," one said, loud enough to be heard. "Doesn't know his place."

"Don't worry," Mensah answered. "He'll be back in the fields, where he belongs, before you know it. A *rekhyt* like him can't help but make a mess of things sooner or later."

Thut stiffened next to her. "Do you have something you'd care to discuss with me, Mensah?"

Mensah straightened, then bent in a *henu* as polished as his gold pectoral. "Not at all, *Per A'a*."

"Good." Thut offered Mensah the insult of his back, turning to Hatshepsut. Mensah recognized the dismissal and stormed from the throne room, trailed by his flock of followers. Senenmut *was* an upstart commoner, but for once Hatshepsut was glad he could count on her brother's support. Thut had many faults, but he prized loyalty above all else and offered it wholeheartedly to those he cared about.

Thut offered her his arm as they walked down the dais. "Look over the tribute from Nubia if it pleases you, sister. In a few weeks you won't have time to play pharaoh. You'll have more important duties to attend to as Great Royal Wife."

He kissed her forehead, and then Hatshepsut watched her brother make his way toward the side door to the pharaoh's apartments, the sound of his cane and mismatched footsteps echoing off the pillars.

Pharaoh and Great Royal Wife. With a little luck, she could play at both.

CHAPTER 6

Re had risen hours ago, but his golden ascent went unnoticed in the palace as everyone scrambled to prepare for the royal wedding. The ceremony would start after the sun god reached his zenith, an auspicious time for new beginnings, at least according to the priests consulted about the timing. Had anyone thought to ask the bride's opinion, they would have promptly been informed that there would never be a good time for her to marry Thut.

Of course, no one asked her.

Sequestered in her chambers, Hatshepsut endured Mouse and Sitre's ministrations, supervised by a scowling Ahmose. They spoke not a word as they plucked every hair from Hatshepsut's body, scrubbed her skin with sea salt, and painted her nails with henna. A young woman's room on her wedding day should have been full of laughter as women prepared the bride, yet Hatshepsut's chambers were as quiet as a tomb. This marriage meant a new beginning, but felt more like a door locking behind her. These were her last moments of freedom, today the last day she truly owned herself. From now on she would remain in the Hall of Women, and one day bear the future hawk in the nest. Today she sacrificed her freedom for the possibility of helping her brother guide their kingdom.

She had no choice.

"You look like you're going to a funeral," Ahmose said from her place in the corner. Hatshepsut's mother was still beautiful, but her perpetual frown had carved whispers of lines around her lips and eyes, like tiny cracks in otherwise flawless granite.

"So do you." Hatshepsut cringed the moment the words left her mouth.

Her mother sighed. "I suppose I do." Sitre and Mouse stepped back as Ahmose stood and lifted the lid from an alabaster pot to sniff the jasmine perfume inside. "I'd always planned to be mother of the next pharaoh," she said. "Something to give me a purpose in this life once your father was gone."

"I'm sorry I wasn't a son." It wasn't the first time Hatshepsut had spoken the words to her mother, but they still tasted bitter.

"It's not your fault, Hatshepsut." Ahmose set down the perfume and clasped her daughter's hands, her skin cold. For a moment Hatshepsut saw the world through her mother's eyes: her eldest daughter and husband dead, stripped of her title, and required to live the rest of her days locked in the Hall of Women. Such a future might one day await her as well.

Hatshepsut shuddered, then on impulse pulled her mother into her arms.

Ahmose stiffened. It was the first embrace they'd shared since Neferubity's death, and for a moment Hatshepsut feared her mother might push her away. But then Ahmose gave Hatshepsut's back an awkward pat.

"I wish I could make you happy," Hatshepsut whispered, tears stinging her eyes.

"Oh, Hatshepsut." Ahmose stepped back and tipped up her daughter's chin. The kohl that followed the line of her lids to her temples was flawless, but her eyes filled with tears. "You and I are so different, Hatshepsut. I know I haven't provided what you needed since—" She couldn't finish the sentence, staring up at the ceiling with its painted lotus blossoms.

Since Neferubity's death.

Hatshepsut squeezed her mother's hand. "I wish it was Neferubity standing here today."

"No." Ahmose shook her head. "Never say that, Hatshepsut." She led her to the window seat, Re's morning light bathing them in the god's warmth. "It took me many wasted days and even more sleepless nights, but I finally realized why your sister left this world for Amenti."

"I'm glad someone figured it out." Hatshepsut's words were sharp, her voice reminding her of her mother's.

"This life is hard," Ahmose said. "You are so strong, Hatshepsut. I envy your strength and courage. Neferubity . . ." She placed her hands over her heart, as if trying to protect that most precious organ, the center of her being. "Neferubity was fragile. This life bruises us, batters us like a toy ship in a storm. But you—" She gave a wan smile. "You thrive on its challenges."

Hatshepsut shrugged, uncomfortable with the rare praise, and not at all sure of the truth of her mother's words.

"You're all that I have left, *sherit*, but I can finally admit that I haven't been a very good mother to you. All I want in this life is for you to be happy." Ahmose placed her hands on Hatshepsut's shoulders. "Will this marriage make you happy? Can you love Thutmosis as I did your father?"

It was difficult to imagine sharing such feelings with Thut. The last time Hatshepsut had seen her brother naked they both wore youth locks and went swimming in the Nile, trying to drown one another. Hatshepsut would trade Hathor's trinkets of love and passion for Amun's weightier gifts: a crown and the power that came with it. Yet there was no guarantee Thut would be willing to share his power with her.

She pushed the thought away, offering her mother a weak smile. "I don't know. I've never given love much thought."

From the corner Mouse cleared her throat, kohl brushes clenched tight in her fists as she looked pointedly out the window at the position of the sun.

Hatshepsut gave a wry chuckle. "I suppose I won't get a chance to find out if I don't get dressed."

Ahmose still lingered, pressing her forehead to Hatshepsut's. "You're going to be a wonderful Great Royal Wife, Hatshepsut. You'll make us all proud."

Her mother released her to Sitre and Mouse, the two women working to ready her as if Ammit's teeth nipped at their heels. Hatshepsut closed her eyes to let Sitre paint them with malachite and kohl. It was easier to ignore the inevitable. Tonight would come soon enough.

Sitre and Mouse toiled to prepare their mistress until even Hathor would envy her beauty. It was only fitting that the pharaoh's daughter be drenched in gold—the skin of the gods—on her wedding day. Golden earrings in the shape of ankhs, the symbol of eternal life, hung heavy from her ears, and gilded bracelets snaked their way up her arms. Hatshepsut's sheath was shot through with so much gold thread it cascaded like a waterfall of molten metal down her body. Even her skin shimmered with precious gold dust imported from Nubia. The images of bound Hyksos and Hittites imprinted on her sandals would match Thut's, so they might tread on Egypt's foes together as they began their reign. Atop Hatshepsut's wig, Ahmose reverently placed Nekhbet's massive vulture headdress bearing the hooded *uraeus* with fangs bared, ready to strike her enemies, the same headdress that all the royal women of their family had worn at their weddings. Lapis lazuli studded the crown, the blue-and-gold-flecked stone reserved only for royalty and the gods. And hidden under her sheath and the weight of gold, Neferubity's jasper pennant of Sekhmet was tied around her waist with a thread of gold knotted seven times for luck.

Sixteen years old, and she was about to become Egypt's Great Royal Wife. She could certainly do worse in this life.

Sitre and Mouse packed up the cosmetic jars and palettes, leaving behind a faience jug of wine and a platter of sliced melon and figs. Sitre frowned and set down the jars to envelop Hatshepsut in a tight embrace until she felt like a child again, pulled onto a perfumed pillow. Her old nurse held her for a moment. "I'm so proud of you," Sitre said with a sniff, accidentally smearing black kohl onto her cheekbones.

Hatshepsut blinked back the thorns in her eyes. "You're going to make my kohl run."

Sitre, Mouse, and Ahmose all dabbed their eyes, then backed from the room, closing the heavy door behind them. Wistfully, Hatshepsut traced the edge of one of Nekhbet's golden wings with a hennaed finger. She knelt on the cold floor in the shaft of Re's golden light, praying to Egypt's bevy of gods for guidance, but Nekhbet was not inclined to assist her. Neither were any of the other gods or goddesses, for that matter. Her chambers felt as empty as her father's after he'd flown to the sky. A delicate trill of laughter sounded, filling the rooms from somewhere and nowhere all at once. From the corner of her eye, Hatshepsut thought she saw Hathor's tiny statue near the window shift, her cow ears shaking with mirth. Not for the first time, Hatshepsut silently cursed the laughing goddess of love, then turned the statue to face the wall.

Re hung from his pinnacle in the sky. There remained only a few moments of freedom for her to cherish.

Hatshepsut took a long sip of palm wine, savoring the sweet taste as it slipped down her throat. A heavy knock at the chamber's entrance made her start. She touched the corners of her eyes, careful not to smudge the gold dust, and cleared her throat. "Enter."

The massive doors swung open and a lone man was revealed. Hatshepsut's heart stalled to see Senenmut dressed in his best court finery, here to escort her to the wedding. It was suddenly hard to swallow.

Senenmut stepped into the silent chambers, the door open behind him. He bowed in a full *henu*, but paused longer than necessary.

"I suppose you've been sent as my escort?" Hatshepsut tried to infuse her voice with a lightness she didn't feel.

"I have." He managed the faintest of smiles, the kind reserved for the extremely unfortunate, such as a man whose entire harvest has been destroyed by locusts. Or a woman about to be married off to a man that she could never fully love.

"Are you ready?" he asked, clearing his throat. His eyes today were the exact green of freshly split papyrus reeds. Hatshepsut took some pleasure in noting the way those eyes lingered on her.

"Of course. I was born for this." She tilted her chin in the air. "Not that I'd expect you to understand."

"My *rekhyt* mind can scarcely conceive of such a responsibility." Senenmut crossed his arms before him. "As a matter of fact, I think I'll leave you to escort yourself to your own wedding."

"You wouldn't dare." She checked her distorted reflection in the copper mirror one last time, her fingers lingering on its engraved tadpoles meant to confer one hundred thousand days of life upon their owner. She took a final sip of the palm wine.

He said, "I can think of a number of beer houses that would be much more enjoyable than a stuffy royal wedding. A mug served by a comely wench, certainly one with a gentler tongue than yours—"

She didn't realize what she was doing until the palm wine splashed Senenmut in the face. She stood there holding the empty gold cup while the shimmering liquid dripped down his jaw and onto his bare chest.

She was horror-struck, but then Senenmut started to laugh. The sound filled her chambers and she scrambled for a towel. "I don't know why you're laughing."

"I didn't know you cared," he said. "You never cease to amaze me."

She held out a square of white linen, but he only tilted his chin so she had to wipe the wine from his face and chest. Their fingers brushed when he took the towel from her, sending a jolt of heat up her arm, straight to her heart. Even the tips of her ears felt warm. She didn't know what was wrong with her.

He finished wiping his face, then tossed the rumpled linen onto the table. "To the priests, then?"

To the priests. And to Thut.

Hatshepsut wished to ignore the inevitable, to imagine what it would be like to marry someone other than her brother. For the briefest moment, she wondered what it might be like to spend her life with a man more like Senenmut.

While she often loathed the man and still hadn't discounted feeding him to the crocodiles one day, even she had to admit that under Senenmut's raw ambition was a rare mind coupled with fierce dedication that she never would have expected to emerge from Egypt's muddy fields. Whereas Thut was loyal, cautious, and as predictable as the Nile, Senenmut was capricious like a spring windstorm and entirely self-absorbed. It occurred to Hatshepsut that that might explain why she sometimes detested Senenmut so: He and she were too much alike, almost as if Khnum, the ram-headed creator god, had cast them from the same clay on his potter's wheel. Perhaps they should be the ones fated to spend the rest of their lives together, lest they ruin anyone else's chance at happiness.

Laughter bubbled in her throat at the thought, and a nervous giggle escaped her lips before she could stop it.

Senenmut raised his brows. "I think brides are supposed to be contemplative before they meet their grooms. Or did you perhaps have too much of that wine before you threw the last of it at me?"

She glared at him. "I'd have had more if I knew Thut was going to send you to bring me to the priests."

He laughed, then turned and walked toward the door, not waiting for her.

She wouldn't wish marriage to Senenmut on her worst enemy.

"Senenmut," she said, waiting for him to turn around. "The Great Royal Wife does not walk behind a *rekhyt*."

"Yes," he said slowly. "But you're not the Great Royal Wife just yet, now, are you?"

"We wouldn't be talking now if I was."

Once Hatshepsut married her brother, she would leave the Hall of Women only when Thut allowed her. It might be a long time before she saw Senenmut again.

He stepped out of her way to let her pass, but her arm brushed his, leaving a smudge of gold dust. Senenmut touched her hand and their eyes locked. Her fingers lingered for a moment in his—one pale and weighted with sparkling jewels and the other strong, bronzed by Re's touch. Her breath lodged in her throat.

Then she remembered who she was.

Hatshepsut jerked back her hand as if scalded, tripping over a chest behind her in her haste to put space between them. Senenmut caught her in time, his hand around her waist to pull her upright. His fingers trailed down her spine until his hand rested at the small of her back.

She was about to become Thut's property; for Senenmut to touch her like this was treason.

"Let me go." Hatshepsut's heart hammered in her throat.

Senenmut's eyes bore into hers. "The gods shaped us from the same clay, Hatshepsut. Don't try to deny it."

How had he come to hear her thoughts, to use them against her?

She managed to disentangle herself, lifted her chin in the air. "If you touch me like that again, I'll have you thrown into Aswan's quarries so fast it will make your head spin."

"If you say so." Senenmut held her with his eyes. "But I doubt that very much."

Hatshepsut refused to dignify that comment with a response. Instead, she turned and stormed out the door.

The clay pot shattered into a myriad of rainbow pieces. Shards of striped azure and carnelian rained upon the royal dais, the delicate dust settling on Hatshepsut's painted hands.

"Love your wife." The priest intoned the common maxim to Thutmosis. "Fill her belly, clothe her back. Make her happy while you are alive and you will profit from her womb. Neither judge her nor raise her to a position of power."

The horde of assembled courtiers erupted into a deafening chorus of cheers, but to Hatshepsut it seemed as if she were far off in the Western Valley. Only the faintest murmur of the screaming masses penetrated her senses. Someone grabbed her cold hand and lifted her arm in a gesture of jubilation. The murmuring of the crowd grew louder until the monstrous reality broke upon Hatshepsut all at once.

Neither judge her nor raise her to a position of power.

She looked at the man who held her arm so triumphantly aloft, as if he were carrying the severed hand of some barbarian recently conquered. But this golden man at her side was no warrior.

He was her brother.

And now he was her husband.

Hatshepsut glanced down at her gown. The fine film of dust that had settled upon her bathed her tangibly in her own marriage. Her eyes strayed for the briefest moment to the opaque smudge on her arm; its missing gold dust likely still clung to Senenmut's arm. Damnable man—she wished a scorpion might sting him in his sleep or a hippo would overturn his boat one day and crush him in its jaws. He deserved a long, drawn-out death.

At her feet lay the jagged edges of what remained of the clay pot. Made of the finest silt dredged from the depths of the Nile and painted with vibrant blues and reds, it was inscribed with formal prayers in stiff hieroglyphs. Before the brief ceremony Hatshepsut had spared a glance at some of them—typical wedding prayers to be sent on the winds to the gods as soon as the pottery shattered.

May your wife give you a son while you are youthful.
May your home be blessed with peace and prosperity.
May your husband treat you as a treasure—clothe you, feed you, and keep you in your old age.

The petitions were trite, hollow supplications made since time immemorial at the cold granite feet of the gods. Instead, she prayed for

Amun's guidance to keep her place beside the Isis Throne and pleaded with Hathor to grant her patience as she became Thut's wife.

"You could smile." Thut muttered the words through his teeth as he shook her arm, encouraging louder roars from the ocean of nobility that stretched before them.

She formed her lips into a smile so wide she feared her face would crack. After an eternity the crowd quieted for the speech from the pharaoh and his Great Royal Wife.

"Gathered friends," Thut began. "It is a great honor to have you witness the union of Amun's beloved children. We promise to serve you dutifully and guide Egypt into its golden age!"

Then he paused and looked to Hatshepsut.

She stepped forward. "May the gods eternally bless Egypt as they have seen fit to bless the children of Osiris Tutmose today. Join us in the banquet hall to celebrate this great gift from the gods. Wine, food, and dancing for all!"

The crowd erupted into cheers and waved palm fronds as Hatshepsut led Thut from the dais. He had forgone his cane today, so she had to slow her pace to match his, letting him lean on her while maintaining the illusion that he was walking on his own. They waited while the spectators filed into the formal dining hall.

"You did well," said Ahmose at Hatshepsut's side, her cinnamon-colored eyes warm with pride. "As I knew you would."

"Thank you." Hatshepsut blinked once to ease the stinging in her eyes. She was saved from having to find her voice as Mutnofret pulled Hatshepsut into a smothering hug.

"My daughter! You've made me so happy today." Mutnofret's voice lowered to a conspiratorial whisper. "But not as happy as I'll be when you deliver my first grandson. This has been a day blessed by the gods."

It hardly seemed possible, but Mutnofret had gained even more weight since Osiris Tutmose's death; her honeyed rolls had added a third chin to her repertoire. She was beginning to resemble one of her favorite desserts—a huge brown date with no discernable waist or neck.

"The honor is all mine," Hatshepsut said. She tried to step back even as she was enveloped in another myrrh-drenched hug.

"Thutmosis!" Mutnofret released Hatshepsut and yanked her son into her arms. "When are you going to make me a grandmother?"

"As soon as we can." Thut offered a warm smile as Mutnofret cackled. Hatshepsut prayed with renewed fervor for Amun to grant her strength.

A herald shuffled before them and bent into a deep *henu*. His ancient bones creaked as he rose. "The guests await their pharaoh and Great Royal Wife."

"We're ready." Thut took Hatshepsut's hand and kissed it, leaving a film of saliva on her skin. She resisted wiping it off.

The herald opened the door to the banquet hall and banged his heavy staff on the floor to quiet the courtiers. He announced the wives of Osiris Tutmose with little fanfare, but then it was time for the first presentation of the pharaoh and his new wife.

The herald's voice bludgeoned the silence with the titles of the new pharaoh and his Great Royal Wife. "Aakheperenre Thutmosis, great is the manifestation of Re, the strong bull, the great one, divine of kingship, powerful of forms, Thutmosis, Thoth is born!" He continued on. "Eldest great daughter, lady of the Two Lands, King's Great Wife, Hatshepsut!"

Thut pulled Hatshepsut into the banquet room. Re's light spilled from skylights to illuminate the painted images of gods carved amongst the pillars. The nine ancient gods and much of Egypt's younger pantheon bore witness to this royal celebration from their granite columns: falcon-headed Horus; Re, wearing his sun-disk crown; green-faced Osiris; Hathor with her cow ears; and Isis, the goddess of many names. The guests erupted into cheers at the sight of their two new leaders. Hatshepsut played along until she caught sight of the one man in the room who was not celebrating.

Senenmut.

His penetrating gaze shifted to her. He gave a stiff bow and then melted back into the crowd of nobility.

The rest of the evening passed in a blur—platters piled high with roast ox and river fowl dressed in their own feathers, acrobats contorting their bodies into impossible poses, and harps and sistrums played to sustain the jubilation. The oiled bodies of naked dancers gyrated, and the pharaoh's best wine flowed freely. Mensah was there, dressed in his finest linens and wearing almost as much gold as the royal family. The last son of Egypt's eldest family stood surrounded by all the up-and-coming young men of court, as if he were a pharaoh in his own right. His ancient father had been sickly of late and had received permission from Thutmosis to retire to their family estates prior to the wedding. Rumors already flew as to whether Mensah would replace his father, but it seemed strange that he hadn't yet pressed the issue with Thutmosis, at least not that Hatshepsut had heard of. But then she hadn't seen Mensah since the day she'd attended the Court of Reeds. In fact, it seemed Mensah was doing his best to ignore her even now, keeping his eyes on the pretty acrobats while reigning over his followers. Perhaps she was finally rid of him.

The room filled with the overpowering scents of roasted meats, sweat-slicked bodies, and the melting perfume cones worn on the heads of men and women alike. No one appeared to notice if Hatshepsut's smiles ever rang true.

After sunset, Sitre escorted Hatshepsut away from the banquet and returned her to her chambers. The old *menat* exchanged the golden wedding finery for a loose white sheath—one so delicately woven as to be transparent—and took away the wig and jewels that denoted her new position. Even Sekhmet's jasper amulet came off, leaving her naked and vulnerable.

Sitre folded the gold wedding sheath, worry written plan in the lines knit above her brows. "Hatshepsut, do you know what Thutmosis will expect of you tonight?"

A nervous laugh bubbled in Hatshepsut's throat. She nodded.

Sitre clasped Hatshepsut's hand. "It will hurt for a moment, but the pain will pass. I'm sure the pharaoh will be gentle."

Hatshepsut could only stare. She'd given Mensah her maidenhead; it had never occurred to her that Thut would wonder why she came to him already a woman.

Sitre stroked Hatshepsut's short curls. "I've never seen you so terrified."

"I'm not terrified," Hatshepsut snapped. "I want this to be over."

"Soon, *sherit*." Sitre frowned and shot her a look akin to pity. Then she bowed and left.

Hatshepsut perched on the edge of her bed and clutched the plush mattress like one of the caged doves in the palace aviary. Time was not kind. Each moment dragged into eternity—it was all she could do to sit still while she waited for Thut. She jumped at every noise, and her stomach mimicked the acrobats at the feast, contorting into impossible positions.

The ebony door creaked open and Hatshepsut jerked to her feet, her heart pounding like a drum before battle. A head poked around the heavy panel, and Hatshepsut sank back into the mattress. "Mouse! What in the name of Amun are you doing here?"

"He's on his way, *Hemet*. The pharaoh just left his chambers." Mouse bit her lip. "I know I shouldn't say anything, but Sitre told me you were nervous. You don't have to worry, at least not if the girl-slaves in the kitchens are to be believed. They say the pharaoh is a lamb in bed." She winked. "A quick lamb."

Hatshepsut exhaled slowly, not knowing whether to laugh or cry. "Thank you, Mouse."

The attendant scurried out after making a tiny *henu*. Hatshepsut stood and turned around, but the sight that greeted her only made things worse. Stretched out before her was what would shortly become her bed of torture. Soon those linens would be twisted around naked limbs as Thut became her husband in body as well as name. She almost wished she came to Thut a virgin tonight and that she hadn't known such heights of pleasure with Mensah, for surely she'd never know such passion again. She was so engrossed in her thoughts that she didn't hear the door open.

"You looked beautiful today." Thut's low murmur in her ear sent a jolt of shock through her body. Hatshepsut jumped, but before she could pull away, her brother's arms bound her to his chest.

"Gods, but you scared me!" Hatshepsut stepped away from him, burned by his touch.

"Hardly the reaction I intended, sister." Thut's eyes traced the lines of Hatshepsut's body through her sheath and he gave a satisfied sigh. "The sight of you makes me feel as if I'm drunk without wine."

And yet, she could smell the wine on his breath. She sent another silent prayer to Hathor as Thut laid down his cane and stepped closer. "Are you nervous?" he asked.

"No." She swallowed hard. "Are you?"

Even in the moonlight, she could make out the flush that spread across his cheeks. "A little. I don't want to hurt you."

"I'll be fine." Hatshepsut tried to relax, shoving unwelcome thoughts from her head. She had written her future in her mind without even giving Thut an opportunity to prove himself; there was still a chance that he might surprise her, that she might find happiness with him. She forced a smile. "I'm a lucky woman."

Thut untied the gilded rope that held his kilt, the silhouette of his manhood hard and erect. His hands felt clammy as he undid the strings at her shoulders and let her sheath fall in a heap at her feet. She fought the urge to cover herself. "And I'm a lucky man," he said, running his fingers over her nipples.

She shivered, but he touched his lips to hers, picked her up, and managed to carry her to bed despite his limp. He laid her out on the feather mattress as if making a precious offering to the gods, spread her legs, and entered her with one swift stroke.

And even as he filled her body, Hatshepsut cried out at the emptiness that overwhelmed her *ka*.

Part II

GREAT ROYAL WIFE

1492 BC – 1488 BC

The kisses of my beloved are on the other bank of the river,
A branch of the stream floweth between us,
A crocodile lurketh on the sandbank.
But I step down into the water and plunge into the flood.

—EIGHTEENTH DYNASTY LOVE SONG

CHAPTER 7

YEAR ONE OF PHARAOH THUTMOSIS II

Hatshepsut awoke to darkened chambers and the soft snores of her husband beside her.

Husband.

It was a foreign word, a weight that couldn't possibly belong to her. And yet it did.

She had lain awake long after Thut had sated his desire, and now her abused body protested even the slightest movement. A flicker of consternation had marred his features when he had first entered her, and then he had lost himself, finally stiffening with a grunt and falling upon her. Several times during the night, Hatshepsut had woken to the sensation of his fingers at the cleft of her legs, and she had done everything in her power to bring him to a speedy climax. She hoped she would soon find herself with child and could beg off this portion of her marital duties.

She pulled the rumpled sheath over her head and slipped from bed. Her brother's chest rose and fell with each muted snore, his jaw prickly with a day's worth of stubble. He might sleep through the priests' hymns as Re rose, but she wouldn't waste the day in bed.

Turning away, Hatshepsut ran her hands over her scalp, still burning from the monstrosity of a wig she'd endured all yesterday. She planned to sneak out undetected, but the door's hinges gave a shuddering groan.

"Leaving so soon?" Thut's voice was thick with sleep.

"I have things to attend to," she said. The first item on the list was to have the door oiled. "Shall I send your slaves to see to you?"

She'd sacrifice a vial of myrrh to Hathor if she managed to escape without Thut demanding an encore of last night's performance.

He interlaced his fingers behind his head and reclined against the wall. "Send Mensah to meet me in my apartments instead."

"Mensah?"

"I've elevated Imhotep's son to the position of Cupbearer of the King. Their family is the highest in the Two Lands, at least after ours. It seemed only fair, after his father's retirement."

Hatshepsut choked but turned it into a cough. She'd have preferred that Thut make Mensah governor of one of Egypt's provinces, preferably one at the ends of the kingdom. Now he'd be constantly underfoot.

Thut yawned. "Tell him to bring breakfast so we can discuss the trade agreements with the Akkadians. I'm starving."

"Of course," Hatshepsut said. The priests of Re had begun their hymns on the other side of the gate to the Hall of Women, their faint chants welcoming the sun god and praising his success in defeating Apep, the god of darkness and chaos, throughout the night. She was almost out the door when Thut stopped her.

"Oh, and sister—"

"Yes?" She wanted to get out of there and take a bath. A very long bath. And when she returned to her chambers she wanted Thut gone. And the sheets changed.

"No more work. You have only one job now."

Naked, he crossed the room to wrap her in a tight embrace, then stepped back and stroked her flat stomach to the bones of her hips.

"You might already carry Egypt's heir. I don't want you overtaxing yourself and jeopardizing your health."

"Of course, brother," she assured him. Perhaps a few weeks of running their kingdom alone would convince him of how much he needed her help.

"Good." He grinned. "And I wouldn't want you worn out this evening, would I?"

Hatshepsut managed a smile. This was to be her life now, at least until Thut could get a son on her. If that was the solution to reclaiming her bed, then she would do everything in her power to ensure that she became pregnant as soon as possible.

Sitre waited for her across the courtyard in the empty bathing pavilion, buckets of hot water already prepared and fresh linens laid out. Thut had retired all their father's women to their various estates, allowing only Ahmose and his own mother to remain, out of respect for their stations as wives of the former pharaoh. The sunny courtyard that had hummed with the idle gossip of Egypt's faded flowers echoed instead with the angry slap of Hatshepsut's sandals.

"You're a godsend." Hatshepsut didn't wait for help undressing, but pulled her sheath over her head while Sitre poured the pails of steaming water into the waiting granite tub, a gift from the Cretan ambassador. She sank into the warm water, unable to stop the groan of pleasure that escaped her lips. "I'm not getting out of here all day."

"Then I'll tell Senenmut he'll have to brief you out here on all of his building plans," Sitre teased as she added a mixture of juniper oil and milk to the bath.

Hatshepsut was glad the water was hot, a good excuse for the sudden heat in her cheeks. "And the Akkadian ambassador," she said. "Perhaps the thought of negotiating trade agreements over a bath would throw him off enough for me to secure all the cedar I want."

Her stress melted away as the juniper relaxed her tense muscles. Morning sunlight danced on the water's surface, and Sitre buzzed about the pavilion like a giant dragonfly on a mission, stopping here and there to straighten a pot or fold a towel while she hummed a little tune to herself. It was a song Hatshepsut remembered from her childhood, an old lullaby Sitre would sing to her before she drifted off.

The sweet one, sweet in love in the presence of the king,
The king's daughter who is sweet in love,
The fairest among women, a maid whose like none has seen.

Hatshepsut grimaced. That was enough of that.

"Sitre?"

"Hmm?" Her old *menat* didn't look up, but continued to arrange the clay pots of various unguents and bath oils, some of which smelled like a flower garden in full bloom and others a pungent animal musk.

"If I needed something, some sort of potion to help me conceive faster, do you think you could find one?"

She felt ridiculous asking, but knowing from experience that there were ways to avoid unwanted pregnancies, she figured there had to be ways to speed the process.

"You're that eager to get Thutmosis out of your bed?"

Not only that—a son of Thut's would guarantee she'd never be shoved into obscurity. A son meant power for any wife of the pharaoh.

Hatshepsut picked at a flaw in the granite tub with her nail. "I don't know how many nights of it I can take."

"I've heard some women travel to the temple of Hathor and expose themselves publicly to the statue of the goddess."

"Does that work?"

"I'm not sure." Sitre shrugged and replaced the lid on a silver pot shaped like a pomegranate. "You're young. It won't take long for you to find yourself heavy with child, but there's an old crone in the city who may be able to help. She was once a chantress in the temple of Isis."

"So she dabbles in magic?"

"I've heard more than one woman swear Djeseret helped her conceive."

Hatshepsut stood and accepted the linen towel Sitre held out for her. The bathwater pearled on her skin as she stepped from the tub. "If you could arrange a meeting with this Djeseret—"

"I'll seek her out today." Sitre helped her dry off. "You'll soon be heavy with child. Then you'll barely fit on your bed alone, much less with the pharaoh."

That evening Hatshepsut sat alone in her rooms, curled up before the brazier as the merry fire warded off the night's chill. It was the season of Peret, when fresh mud bricks were laid out to dry and pale green seedlings stretched their faces to touch Re's warmth. A time of new beginnings.

The crickets chirped their nightly song in the garden while the fire popped and crackled inside. Mouse had snuck Hatshepsut the tribute ledgers from the northern governors earlier in the day, and the seasonal tribute from the Sinai had just been received. Hatshepsut had spent much of the evening happily reconciling the current ledgers for the Royal Treasury to determine how much could be spared for Senenmut's building projects in the south. There would be plenty for the temples as well as enough to start building tombs for her and Thut on the West Bank. Hatshepsut planned to be buried near their father, but she had yet to discuss the idea with her brother. He'd likely tell her to focus more on creating life and less on dying.

She knew she should stop for the evening, but the thought of Thut waiting for her kept her in her chair. Mensah had already breached the inner sanctuary of her office once this evening to coolly remind Hatshepsut of her appointment with her brother, but she'd sent him away with an earful of sharp words. She was even less impressed with her former lover now that Thut had promoted Mensah and he was able to order her about. Still she lingered.

Gentle footsteps alerted her to someone's approach. Mensah had likely come with orders to fetch her this time. An excuse ready to fly from her lips, Hatshepsut was surprised to see Sitre enter the dimly lit office. Her dark face blended into the shadows so that it was impossible to read her expression.

"I've brought Djeseret as you requested, *Hemet*," Sitre murmured. "I'll see that you are not disturbed."

"Thank you."

A hunchbacked figure swathed in a white linen cloak shuffled into the room. An ancient hand spotted with age and tipped with ragged fingernails reached from the hidden folds of the rough fabric to push back the hood. The crone's face was as white as the room was black. Skin, hair—everything except her eyes. One eyelid drooped to obscure its rheumy pupil and the other sparkled bright with the color of freshly spilled blood. The hag's decrepit face was littered with deep canyons; wrinkles crisscrossed jowls hanging from old bones.

She was albino.

No wonder the woman was credited with great powers. Those like her received special gifts from Isis, the goddess of mothers and magic.

Unbidden, the gnarled woman sank into a chair with a great exhalation. Hatshepsut could smell the reek of garlic and onion along with something else, an herb she couldn't put a name to.

"Thank you for coming to see me," Hatshepsut began, but the witch held up a hand to stop her.

"Your *menat* tells me you need to quicken your womb." Djeseret's voice belied her age, as smooth as honey and filled with the cadence of youth.

At least the woman wasn't going to waste her time.

"If that's possible."

"Oh, it's possible." The crone cackled at some joke known only to her. "Anything is possible with Isis' help."

"Of course," Hatshepsut said. "I'm just glad the great goddess has seen fit to send you to me. With Isis' good graces, how long do you think it will take before I conceive?"

"Isis works on her own timetable, *Hemet*. I only stoke the embers, not predict when they'll flame." Djeseret stood and retrieved two burnished snake wands from her robe and slowly traced Hatshepsut's body. Their silver tongues seemed to flicker in the firelight. She stopped, then a clawed hand retrieved a small green bag emblazoned with the golden scarab, the symbol of rebirth. "Brew these herbs into a tea and drink it each morning as you break your fast. It will soften your womb and allow your husband's seed to take root."

Hatshepsut took the bag and sniffed carefully. The notes of nettle, anise, and fennel filled her nose. "Will this work?"

The wattle of flesh under Djeseret's jaw swayed as she chortled. She reached into her cloak once more and pulled out a tiny ivory statue of Hathor and an amulet depicting the fertility god Min. The god's giant phallus was unmistakable as it stood at attention. She eyed the jasper insignia of the Sekhmet at Hatshepsut's neck. "The lion goddess of death does not welcome new life, *Hemet*."

Hatshepsut reluctantly unclasped the necklace, tucking its warmth into her palm.

"Wear this at all times," Djeseret instructed, handing Hatshepsut the amulet. "If you pray faithfully to Min, Hathor, and Isis they will grant your wish."

Hatshepsut took the cold stone in her other hand. "Thank you." She expected the audience to end, but Djeseret remained. The crimson eye scrutinized Hatshepsut, making her feel as if beetles were crawling up her flesh. "Is there something more?"

When Djeseret finally spoke her voice was hauntingly low, with an otherworldly vibration. "You have a unique path before you, my child, one not tread by most mortals. Most of us walk the earth and are swept into obscurity soon after our life is spent. But not you." Djeseret's unblinking red eye remained focused on her. "Not you."

Hatshepsut's heart pounded. "I don't know what you mean. I am only the wife of—"

"*Your* name will live forever." The unwavering voice cut her off. "You shall do great things while you walk this land. When you pass to the West your eternal name shall be repeated for generations."

Hatshepsut could find no words to answer the woman. It was Thut's name that was to be lauded through the ages while hers became a whisper in time, a woman's curse. And yet what Djeseret prophesied was entirely different, intoxicating, even.

"And my brother?" she asked, but Djeseret silenced her with a wave of her hand.

"There is more, a price Isis shall extract from you in exchange for this great gift." Djeseret's voice was detached, disembodied from her eerie white body. "The gods will pour down a storm upon you from which you cannot emerge. While your name shall be repeated for all eternity, your praises sung, and your everlasting *ka* safe throughout the ages, your mortal life shall take a twisted path."

Hatshepsut sat back as if stung. "A twisted path? What does that mean?"

"You shall be the downfall of those you love." Djeseret's voice was a strangled whisper. "Egypt will prosper, but those closest to you shall find only anguish and ruin."

Hatshepsut sputtered in protest. "You don't know what you're talking about."

Djeseret blinked once, then heaved her ancient bones to stand. "The gods don't ask permission before they cast your fate, *Hemet*. You have no control over your destiny."

"I will not cause those I love to suffer, no matter what you believe." The heat of Sekhmet's angry breath filled her mind as she glared at the woman. "Find your own way out. Sitre will pay you for the herbs."

The old crone bowed slightly before covering her dingy hair and limping silently from the room. Hatshepsut stood alone in her cold office; the fire in the brazier had burned out sometime during the audience. Djeseret's words pummeled her like a multitude of fists.

Your name will live forever.

You shall be the downfall of those you love.

Egypt will prosper, but those closest to you shall find only anguish and ruin.

"Son of Set!" She punched the wall, wincing and muttering several more curses at her scraped knuckles, but noting with some satisfaction the delicate crack that now ran up a fresco of a hunting scene.

The albino taunted paying customers with ideas of glory, only to yank both back with prophesies of doom. She should be whipped for fraud.

Stomping over to her desk, Hatshepsut flung open a box of ebony and threw Hathor's statue, the amulet, and the packet of herbs inside before slamming it shut. The oil lamps flickered with the impact. "The crazy old witch likely would have poisoned me with this."

"Hatshepsut?"

Mensah was the last person she wanted to see right now, yet here he was. She swallowed another curse, knowing precisely why her brother's steward dared intrude upon her for the second time that evening. "I believe you're supposed to address me as *Hemet* now that I'm Great Royal Wife."

He glanced about, one eyebrow arching to his wig. "Might I ask who were you talking to?" He paused for effect. "*Hemet.*"

She sighed. "Only myself."

Mensah would relish telling Thut that his wife was losing her mind, but she couldn't find it in herself to care.

"I see." He cleared his throat. "The pharaoh awaits your presence in his chambers. He instructed me not to return without you this time." He stepped closer and glanced about her empty offices, his stern facade melting into a tantalizing smile. "But perhaps he wouldn't notice if his Great Royal Wife took her time. The pharaoh may be Horus here on earth, but I'd imagine he has a difficult time satisfying Sekhmet in his bed. I, on the other hand—"

She didn't think. She slapped him. Hard.

"Speak to me like that again," she whispered, "and I'll ensure that same pharaoh has you so thoroughly dismembered that the murder of Osiris shall pale in comparison."

The color drained from his face, and he held his face with one hand. "You don't mean that."

"Perhaps not." She ignored the sting of her palm. "But do you really want to chance it?" Turning her back, she dropped Sekhmet's red jasper amulet into a worn reed basket, letting her fingers linger on Neferu-bity's gift. She blinked hard and barely glanced at the box of herbs before brushing past Mensah. "And I'm not Sekhmet anymore. I haven't been for a long time."

The oil lamps flickered as she walked down the corridors toward Thut's chambers and her last responsibility of the night.

One final duty, and then she hoped to forget this day had ever happened.

CHAPTER 8

The moon had waxed and waned twice now, but Hatshepsut still refused to touch Djeseret's stash of herbs. Instead, Sitre had found her a terracotta amulet of a naked mother suckling an infant and tied it round her waist with seven knots. Yet each month she continued to purify herself with natron and oil at the appearance of her moon bloods. Exposing herself before Hathor's statue was beginning to sound more appealing with each of Thut's nightly advances. She hoped it wouldn't come to that.

Tonight her brother intended to celebrate the Opening of the Year with the Festival of Intoxication for Hathor. Years ago, Re had raged against humans for violating Ma'at, so he had sent Hathor to destroy mankind. She transformed into the lion goddess Sekhmet and Egypt's fields ran red with the blood of her rampage. Seeing this, Re realized his mistake and ordered Sekhmet to stop, but she was too gone with bloodlust to listen. Knowing he had to halt her some other way, Re stained seven thousand jugs of beer with pomegranate juice and poured the red liquid into her path. Believing the beer to be blood, Sekhmet gorged herself and passed out in a drunken stupor. When she awoke, her bloodlust had passed and she returned to being Hathor. Thus the goddesses of love and violence shared a common history.

Now, to commemorate the salvation of mankind, a perfect year could only begin in a celebration of complete and utter drunkenness.

Tonight Thut had spared no expense; in addition to countless jugs of red beer, four thousand loaves of bread would be distributed to the people of Waset while dancers, singers, and acrobats would entertain at the palace. None of the nobility would see their beds until well after the Dog Star rose just before dawn. Hatshepsut was thrilled at the rare opportunity to leave the Hall of Women, and hoped that as an extra boon her brother would be too exhausted to visit her chamber later that evening.

She hummed to herself as she reached the gilded doors to the banquet hall, allowing a girl-slave clad only in a collar of lotus flowers to attach a perfume cone to her wig and offer her a bouquet of mandrake fruit. Hatshepsut inhaled the scent of the little green apples before taking a bite and sucking the magical juice with the promise of Hathor's pleasures and then spitting out the fruit's poisonous flesh. The scent of jasmine washed over her, and the low buzz of hundreds of voices swelled as she was admitted into the beehive. Lithe acrobats contorted their bodies like sedge grass in the wind, and elegant dancers flew through the air; one narrowly missed a tray of roast swan complete with feather garnish. Beer flowed freely, and raucous laughter mingled with the lyres and pipes from the musician's stand. Thut lorded over it all from his dais—a kingdom in miniature the perfect size for him, complete with rivers of wine and mountains of food.

The crowd parted for Hatshepsut to make her way to the royal dais, but the revelry continued unabated with a flick of her wrist.

"What do you think?" Thut hollered over the din as she arranged the pleats of her skirt. He lifted a blue faience cup of beer so fast that the red liquid sloshed over his hand. "I think I could drink to drunkenness tonight—my insides are as dry as straw."

She chuckled. "It looks as if you're well on your way."

"It's the perfect opening to Hathor's sacred month—don't you agree?" Thut was obviously proud of himself, preening like an ostrich in mating season.

"I'm sure the goddess approves."

"All this, and that's the best you can do?" He gave a mock frown. "Where is that golden tongue that makes all the foreign ambassadors fight to kiss your feet?"

Hatshepsut pointed her hennaed toes before her. She rather enjoyed the idea of the Akkadians and Phoenicians kissing her feet. "I'm sure Hathor will be impressed," she added.

"I hope so." His eyes grew warm and his fingers brushed her stomach. "Perhaps, then, the goddess will grant me my greatest wish."

She forced a smile, thankful for the haze of mandrake clouding her mind and the boy-slave that appeared with a plate of duck slathered in onion sauce. Her foot tapped in time to the beat of the drums. She didn't want to be a silent observer of the festivities, but yearned for one night during which she could enjoy herself.

Tonight would be that night.

The hum of conversation filled the hall as the music slowed and came to a halt. A servant balanced a massive plate of stewed pigeon on the head of a trained monkey, but Hatshepsut waved them away. She took a long draught of beer, thick and red with a hint of pomegranate. Her stomach protested at the duck. She needed something other than food right now.

The music began again, this time faster and syncopated with a deep Nubian drumbeat.

"I'm going to dance." Hatshepsut drained the glass of beer and pushed away her plate.

"What?" Thut spoke too loud over a bite of roasted swan, a victim of his hunting excursion earlier that morning.

Hatshepsut twirled her fingers in the air. "Dance. I'm going to dance!"

She bounded down the steps and waded through the sea of nobility to Hathor's temple dancers. The girls' oiled bodies pulsed to the drum's common beat, mingling with the noblewomen in their transparent white linen. As protocol demanded, the men stood to the side, but their eyes followed Hatshepsut as she took her place. She could almost hear their thoughts as they stared at her hennaed breasts and flowing linen skirt.

Men were simple creatures sometimes.

She closed her eyes and her hips found the beat. The music from the rams' horns and sistrums swept over her and infused her *ka* with the heady rhythm. Everything else faded away. Her feet moved fast, a grin leaping to her lips as some of the crowd clapped in time. Hathor's naked dancers cheered her on; a pretty one with brown eyes as big as a gazelle's took her hand and they twirled about the floor together. Faces became a blur. Dizzy laughter bubbled in the back of Hatshepsut's throat, but then the music slowed, changing to a sensuous crawl.

A glance at the dais revealed that Thut wasn't watching her, but appeared engrossed in the other dancers, ignoring a boy-slave at his elbow with his platters of honeyed dates and slices of chilled melon.

The drums quieted to a low rumble and the lyres took the lead. Lust and longing infused each note, begging for a partner to hold, a strong chest to melt into. Now alone on the floor, Hatshepsut swayed hypnotically to the music; the timeless notes soothed her troubled *ka*. Gone were the heavy worries of irrigation canals, bowing to foreign ambassadors, and plotting to avoid her brother's amorous advances. She was just a girl at a feast and there was nothing except this moment, this one flawless dance.

She might have stayed there for eternity.

Time melted away—she may have danced for moments or hours. The last strain of the lyre reverberated through the hall long after the musician plucked the string, an intangible echo of all she yearned for. Hatshepsut blinked a few times to get her bearings as the nimble dancers moved around her and the music reverted to a faster tempo.

She looked to the Isis Throne, but it was vacant and the dais empty.

A survey of the floor didn't reveal her brother there either. Thut had disappeared and left her to preside over the feast he had organized.

She might have expected as much. Perhaps her breach of etiquette had angered him, but she didn't care.

The room swayed from the mixture of mandrake and her annoyance at Thut's disappearance. She pushed through the waves of naked dancers and drunken court ladies to the quiet of the gardens.

The night air chilled the sheen of sweat on her skin and gooseflesh rippled over her body. Hatshepsut wrapped her arms tightly around herself and collapsed on one of the benches tucked into the corner of the main garden, shivering as its cold seeped through her linen sheath. This oasis in the middle of the palace was drenched with night's shadows and cloaked in silence, the trees and flowers painted a stark black. The scent of her jasmine perfume mingled with the damp lotus blossoms, beauty and everlasting life intertwined. The Dog Star had risen to its pinnacle in Nut's black belly, ushering in the Opening of the Year and heralding the Nile's Inundation. She closed her eyes and focused on the meditative chirp of crickets, cradling her head in her hands, elbows perched on her knees.

A branch snapped and blighted the cricket's unchanging song. Her head jerked from her hands so she could see who dared to intrude upon her peace.

"I didn't know you could dance," Senenmut said, his voice quiet under the stars. The darkness shrouded him and deepened the bronze of his bare chest while shading his long kilt a murky gray.

"Only on rare occasions." Hatshepsut straightened. Despite the dark and chill of the night, she felt a little warmer upon seeing him. "It's unseemly to dance with commoners."

"That was hardly the way we *rekhyt* dance." Senenmut pulled a date from its branch and tossed it to her. "Far too many clothes on." He avoided her eyes as he took another fruit and popped it into his mouth. "Although I'm surprised Thutmosis didn't fetch you."

She chewed the date and shrugged. "My brother lets me do as

I please." The mandrake made her head light, and she slid over on the long bench so Senenmut could sit. He looked as if the seat were a crocodile waiting to pin him with its jaws. She chuckled. "I promise I won't bite."

"Unless you lose your temper." He gave her a lazy smile that made her forget her next thought. The man was trouble.

"Ha." Her face screwed up in a mock pout. She plucked a pink lotus blossom from the pool to keep her hands busy. The flowers had not yet sunk below the surface, but claimed a bit more time this evening before their rebirth the next morning. In the light of day the petals would have been a vibrant shade of fuchsia, but now they, too, were washed with gray. She shook droplets of water from the blossom and inhaled its perfume of the gods, noticing another intoxicating scent: cinnamon and honey. Senenmut's scent. Her heart beat faster, perhaps another effect of the mandrake.

She should excuse herself and return to the banquet, but right now that was the last thing she wanted to do. Absentmindedly, she plucked the petals from the lotus and let them float like feathers to her feet. "What are you doing here, Senenmut?" she asked, watching them fall.

"It was hot in the hall. I thought the gardens would be a refreshing change."

"Not that." She gave an exasperated sigh, but then caught his grin. He was baiting her, as usual. "Why are you at court, serving my brother and jostling for power against all the other petty courtiers? I'm sure Thut could elevate you to governor of your *nome* if you asked. Before the next inundation, you could be back in Iuny with a pretty little wife and a hut full of urchins just like you."

"The world can't handle more than one of me."

"At least we agree on one thing." She chuckled at his pained expression. "Is this truly all you want in this life?"

"No." He didn't hesitate. "I want more. And I think you do, too."

"Me?" Her hand fluttered as if to dismiss him. "I'm Egypt's Great

Royal Wife. I share my brother's throne, and, one day, I'll bear the next pharaoh. The gods have given me the blessings of a hundred women."

The words sounded like a recitation, even to her ears.

"Perhaps. But that's still not enough for you, is it?"

She laughed, but the sound was shrill. "Don't presume you know anything about me, Senenmut of Iuny. You don't know me at all."

"Whatever Thutmosis gives you will never be enough." He moved as if to take her hand, but stopped. "I've already received more than my share of blessings in this life. What more could the son of a simple scribe want? Yet it's still not enough."

Hatshepsut's throat constricted at his words—it was as if he had seen into her *ka*.

"You have indeed risen fast." She stood and allowed the remainder of the lotus blossom to fall to the ground. She picked another from the pool, wishing for the scent to linger a while longer. "The gods favor you."

"I'll settle to be favored by the pharaoh and his Great Royal Wife."

Hatshepsut rolled her eyes, making sure he saw it. "Thut certainly favors you. I merely tolerate your existence in this life."

A grin split Senenmut's face, and the white of his teeth gleamed in the darkness. "That's high praise coming from you. Are you sure you haven't had too much mandrake?"

"I am nothing if not benevolent." She gave him a cheeky grin, then sobered. "Still, you're not like the other courtiers, with all their polished manners and artful lies." She took a deep breath, the mandrake loosening her tongue. "In fact, I think I've grown accustomed to having you underfoot."

"Like a pebble stuck in your sandal or an uncomfortable boil, I'd imagine."

"Exactly." She chuckled, touching her toe to his, feeling the warmth radiating from him. "Usually I'd be happy to see you feeding the carp at the bottom of the Nile. But sometimes—"

Before she could say more, the voices of other partygoers intruded into the garden. A woman laughed, a tinkling sound echoed by the man's deeper timbre. The couple was likely on their way to find a secluded corner for a tryst, a common activity at these banquets. And as this celebration was in honor of Hathor, the goddess of love, the mood was certain to blur the lines of etiquette among some of the revelers.

The same conclusion could be drawn of her and Senenmut, should they be seen in this garden niche. She could only hope the shadows would mask the heat of her cheeks as it spread like wildfire to her ears. But in the back of her mind a faint voice questioned if sharing a dark alcove with Senenmut might be worth the consequences.

Hathor was mocking her. She knew there was a reason she'd always scorned the goddess of love.

"Enough about my untimely demise by those nasty carp." Senenmut gestured to the path. "We should be getting back."

Their feet crunched the pebbles of the path as they walked without speaking, Hatshepsut a few paces in front of Senenmut. The giggles and moans of Hathor's couple became more urgent, the man's rhythmic grunts broken by a woman's ecstatic scream. Hatshepsut felt her face regain its scarlet blush.

Senenmut cleared his throat. "You go in. I'll follow in a while."

Hatshepsut almost thanked him, but thought better of it as she sauntered back into the banquet, stepping around sticky puddles of wine and passing a woman vomiting into a painted urn held by a girl-slave. Taunting Senenmut was her favorite sport, but she couldn't afford another slip like the one just now in the garden. She was determined not to let him see how he had managed to get under her skin.

Senenmut was entertainment, nothing more.

CHAPTER 9

"What do you mean, the pharaoh is indisposed?" Hatshepsut stood outside Thut's chambers, arms akimbo as she glared at Mensah. She'd barely slept after playing hostess for her brother's little party last night, the one he'd mysteriously disappeared from. Now she needed his official seal to demand the Sinai's stingy governor increase the shipments of turquoise to the royal court.

"The pharaoh has given strict orders not to be disturbed until he says otherwise." Mensah repeated his instructions, his upper lip curling into a sneer. The *medjay* on either side of the door gazed forward like statues.

"I am the Great Royal Wife." Hatshepsut pointed out the obvious, trying to keep her tone level. "If I need to see my husband on official business, I'm sure he didn't mean to exclude *me*."

"The pharaoh left explicit instructions, *Hemet*." Mensah's voice didn't waver, but she got the distinct impression he was enjoying his power to refuse her. "Not even you are to be allowed to breach the sanctum of his chambers."

She arched a perfectly kohled eyebrow. Either Mensah was trying to make her life especially difficult, which was entirely likely, or Thut was hiding something.

"Why?" Her eyes narrowed. "Is he ill? Feeling the effects of too much wine?"

"I am not at liberty to say," Mensah said. "Perhaps the two of you can discuss it this evening over dinner."

"So I'm supposed to wait around and then scurry to my brother's table? What crumbs shall he feed me then?" Hatshepsut dropped her hands, still holding the apparently unimportant Sinai papyrus her brother had asked her to attend to. She hadn't gotten to bed this morning until well after Re had risen and had tossed and turned once there, reliving the scene in the garden with Senenmut until she was too exhausted to think any more.

"Fine. If you see my brother before then, please convey the message that I eagerly await his company over dinner." She handed Mensah the rolled papyrus, now rumpled from being squeezed in her fists. "The pharaoh needs to sign this before then. The messenger is waiting to begin the trip to the Sinai to deliver it."

Mensah bowed and took the papyrus in his thick sausage fingers. "I'll give it to him when I see him."

"Thank you." Hatshepsut was curious to discover what her brother was hiding, but at the same time she didn't really want to know. Anything Thut made a point to hide from her never ended well, including the frogs he had snuck into her bed when they were young. Hatshepsut hoped for her brother's sake that this latest subterfuge wouldn't be as juvenile.

By dinnertime she was starving and more than a little on edge, her stomach rumbling at the thought of food as she snapped at Sitre and Mouse while they dressed her. Mensah bowed this time, a little too obsequiously for her taste, and opened the doors to Thut's apartments to allow her entrance.

Reed mats softened the pharaoh's tiled floor, surrounded by a plethora of artifacts sent from foreign countries whose ambassadors were eager to please Egypt and her divine ruler. There was a golden elephant statue from Nubia that Hatshepsut had pretended to ride when she was young, a giant alabaster urn carved with griffins from Akkad, and a two-headed limestone stele from the Phoenicians. Slaves melted into the shadowed murals as they bowed to the Great Royal Wife amid tables strewn with tureens and platters. Hatshepsut touched a rose granite statue of Amun, one of the many likenesses of the hidden god of the air peppered throughout the room. Kipa slept atop the head of another across the room, her tail twitching each time she snored. Thut had decided to keep Amun's statues when he had redecorated, perhaps as an invocation to the supreme god to guide him, as he had their father.

Hatshepsut rounded the corner into the cozy dining room, but stopped short as she saw its lone occupants ensconced on a single couch, their limbs intimately entwined. Her brother seemed to be feeding the woman from a bowl on his lap, her eyes closed and full lips open in anticipation.

The girl with gazelle eyes from the feast.

"And who is this?" Hatshepsut asked without thinking.

Thut's hand stopped, a dripping bite of green melon suspended midair. His companion's eyes snapped open in surprise. She seemed to be of sturdy *rekhyt* stock, with eyes the color of wet earth during the Inundation and thick bones beneath her many curves. The girl scrambled to the floor in a clumsy *henu*, her face hidden under the thick braids of a very cheap Nubian wig.

"This is Aset." Thut gave Hatshepsut a sheepish look and sucked the sticky melon juice from his fingers. His statement explained everything and nothing. The woman kept her eyes averted, too frightened to meet the gaze of the Great Royal Wife, as he helped her to her feet.

"Aset?" Hatshepsut asked, dumbfounded.

"Aset of Waset," the girl said. "Dancer in the temple of Hathor."

A common name for a common girl.

Hatshepsut rubbed her temples. "I remember you from the feast last night."

"Yes, *Hemet*."

"And your parents?"

"I have no family." Aset raised her eyes. "I never knew my father, and my mother passed to Amenti a few months ago."

Hatshepsut recognized the grief in Aset's voice and, despite herself, felt sympathy for this little dancer. Life in a temple was easier than most, but it would still be a lonely existence without any family.

"One day you shall be reunited with your mother in the Field of Reeds, as Thut and I shall be greeted by our father when we pass to the West." Hatshepsut took a seat opposite the one recently occupied by the two of them. This promised to be an interesting meal.

She motioned to a boy-slave to pour her a glass of wine, hoping it hadn't been too watered. Thut cleared his throat and signaled to the waiting slaves as he took his seat. Aset sat with him, but put a decent space between them. At least the girl had manners.

"Aset will be staying in the Hall of Women." Thut took off his gold bracelet, then put it on again. It was obvious he expected a challenge.

"I gathered as much," Hatshepsut said. Filling the Hall of Women was Thut's right and duty as pharaoh, but she'd wait until they were alone to give him an earful for surprising her like this. He'd made her look like a fool, yet this meant Thut would no longer monopolize her bed each night. She turned to Aset. "The gardens in the Hall of Women are lovely this time of year. The purple saffron blossoms are my favorite part of Akhet."

Who knew if her brother's interest in this girl would outlast the Nile's floods.

Thut's shoulders relaxed and he mouthed two words to her.

Thank you.

Hatshepsut didn't wait for the others to serve themselves as she tore a tiny piece of roasted quail from its bone and dipped it in garlic sauce.

She would be civilized toward the woman her brother had chosen. It wasn't as if Aset had a choice.

Then again, neither did she.

The morning light slanted through Hatshepsut's windows to bathe her in Re's golden touch. She yawned lazily, stretching from fingers to toes. She had spent a delicious night utterly and completely alone in her bed. And she had actually slept. Hatshepsut was more than happy to gift the rest of Thut's evenings to Aset as long as he spared her the occasional night. Great Royal Wife or not, she could ensure her future power only by fulfilling her duty of birthing the future hawk in the nest.

Yet there was plenty of time for that.

As Thut and his newest consort would undoubtedly be indisposed again today, this was the perfect time to attend to something he might not approve of, although Hatshepsut had already received his permission for the first part of her plan.

"Mouse." Hatshepsut poked her head into the sitting room and beckoned the dwarf. "Please ask Dagi to have the royal barque ready in an hour. I'd like to go across the river." She bit her lip. "And I have a message for you to deliver to Senenmut as well." Hatshepsut scrawled a note in hieratic, too excited to waste time executing the formal hieroglyphics on the papyrus.

"And do you require an answer from *Neb* Senenmut?" Mouse asked.

It seemed strange to hear Senenmut's name associated with a noble title, a recent gift from Thutmosis to his favored adviser. "No," Hatshepsut said. "Just deliver the message."

Mouse bowed and scurried off on her missions as fast as her squat little legs would carry her. It didn't take long for her to return.

"I took the liberty of having the kitchens stock the boat with a basket of food." Mouse winked. "For two."

"Two?" Hatshepsut was already dressed in a simple white sheath and soft calfskin sandals, but the Nubian wig Sitre had chosen remained on its ebony stand. Hatshepsut checked the copper mirror and tucked a tuft of dark hair behind her ear. "And who will be joining me for lunch?"

Mouse shrugged, a wicked gleam in her eye. "I thought perhaps *Neb* Senenmut."

"We're picking out a spot for my tomb, Mouse, not going on a picnic." Hatshepsut hadn't planned to spill the secret, but she didn't want Mouse thinking this was all a ploy for her to spend time with Senenmut. It wasn't.

At least she didn't think it was.

"Oh." Mouse's lips twisted into a pout. Apparently the idea of her mistress cavorting on the sands of the West Bank was more interesting than determining one's eternal resting place.

"But thank you for the food. We'll probably be gone all day, and I'm already starving."

"Enjoy yourself. And try not to get dirty."

"I'll do what I can," Hatshepsut called over her shoulder. She couldn't wait to be free of the palace, at least for one morning. A giggle slipped under the doorway as she passed Thut's apartments, followed by her brother's muffled voice. She stopped in her tracks.

She'd heard those same sounds before. In the garden that night of the Festival of Intoxication.

She cared less that Thut had been so brazen as to have a tryst with Aset in the gardens than that she had been in the same garden alone with Senenmut. Thut loved Senenmut, but not enough to forgive him the treason of a private interlude in a moonlit garden with his Great Royal Wife. It was only by the grace of the gods that Thut hadn't stumbled upon Hatshepsut and her adviser. Senenmut wouldn't have survived the encounter.

Her adviser.

Hatshepsut stopped walking. Senenmut was loyal, someone with the intelligence to assist her and the backbone to tell her when she was wrong. A rare gifts from the gods, even if it was in the guise of an arrogant and ambitious *rekhyt*.

"May I help you, *Hemet?*" Mensah appeared out of thin air. "I'm sorry to inform you that the pharaoh—"

"I'm not here to see my brother. I'm on my way to the docks."

"Of course." Mensah bowed and stepped out of her way. The soft shuffle of his sandals seemed to follow her, but when she turned to ask if he needed something, he had disappeared.

Good. The last thing she wanted was for Mensah to report to Thut the details of her trip across the Nile.

Sunlight hit Hatshepsut in the face as she emerged from the palace. She wanted to run, but restrained herself to walk at a dignified pace down the path to the river's edge.

Senenmut was waiting for her, standing on the dock next to the sailor Dagi.

Hatshepsut attempted to suppress the grin that threatened to break upon her face, but she had as much luck as squashing a sneeze.

"A lovely day for a boat ride, isn't it?" Senenmut asked as she approached, a lazy smile spreading across his lips and making her suddenly warm. He, too, had dressed casually for today's excursion—bareheaded and wearing only a short kilt. His single adornment was Thoth's leather armband high on his bicep.

"It certainly is," Hatshepsut said.

Dagi bowed and gestured for the two to board a painted cedar ship that loomed high over the other boats. A giant Eye of Horus was emblazoned in gold on the side, and red and white royal pennants snapped in the breeze. A grin crinkled the sailor's ruddy cheeks. "I'm mighty pleased to be summoned today. I feared the crew and I'd be put out to pasture after Osiris Tutmose was taken to his tomb."

"No such luck, my friend." Hatshepsut boarded, and Senenmut followed behind her. "I've plans for the valley, so your services will be needed more often."

"Good." Dagi shoved off thick ropes that tied the boat to the dock and freed the vessel before he stepped aboard. "That's what I like to hear. Wouldn't want the wife to make me take up farming again." His grimace elicited a chuckle from Hatshepsut and Senenmut. "Them dusty old sails can't wait to be unfurled. And your little attendant lugged down two baskets the size of baby rhinos."

She smiled. "As long as they're not so heavy that they sink the ship."

Dagi seemed to contemplate that. "I doubt they will. Close, but not quite."

Hatshepsut and Senenmut ignored the goat-hide awning and took their seats on the prow to enjoy Re's morning light, far enough from the rowers to be out of earshot.

"So, is this a pleasure cruise or does your invitation have a more sinister undertone?" Senenmut closed his eyes and leaned back, hands clasped behind his head.

Her tongue tied itself in knots at the sight of him in the sun, the lines of lean muscle stretching across his chest and shoulders. Why in the name of Amun had she asked Senenmut to accompany her? Sometimes she doubted her own sanity.

The striped sail snapped in the breeze behind them, a rainbow of red, yellow, and blue. Today the Nile sparkled green in Re's warmth. They passed wooden water wheels turning lazily in the muddy channels that fed Egypt's crops of flax, barley, and emmer.

"Hatshepsut?" Senenmut peered at her, his brow furrowed.

She took a deep breath and tucked her feet beneath her; she liked looking at him. "By *sinister*, do you mean 'Is there work involved?' Because there might be."

He shook his head, eyes closed again. "A morning boat ride on the Nile, the sun on my face, and a picnic. I knew it seemed too good to be true."

"You can have all that, but I have a job for you as well."

"A secret one, judging from the apparent lack of entourage today." He peered at her through one eye, his expression hooded. "Does the pharaoh know we're out here?"

"Thut gave me permission to visit the West Bank. He thinks I'm going to visit our father's tomb."

"So, he doesn't know what you're really up to?" Senenmut frowned. "For that matter, neither do I."

She waved her hand. "Thut's too busy with his latest concubine to care."

Senenmut's eyes opened a little wider. "That didn't take long."

"Thut can be very efficient when he wishes to be."

"You disapprove of the girl?"

"Actually, no. She seems malleable, a *rekhyt* dancer in the Temple of Hathor. Anything that keeps Thut from my bed—"

His jaw clenched. The last thing she wanted to discuss with him was her brother in her bed. Hatshepsut smoothed her linen sheath over her legs, needing something to do with her hands. "It looks as though she'll be keeping Thut indisposed for some time."

Silence fell, and then Senenmut asked, "Does Mensah know you're out here?"

"Mensah? Why would he need to know?"

"He seems to hold some claim to your affections."

"That was a long time ago." She wanted to add *when I was young and stupid*, but held her tongue. "And I don't need either Mensah or Thut's permission to pick out my tomb."

"Planning on dying soon?" Senenmut closed his eyes again. Re's light danced on his face.

"No, but I'd hate for my *ka* to disappear into oblivion simply because I hadn't planned ahead."

"Your father began planning his tomb the day he took the Isis Throne."

"Yes," she said. "Some tombs on the West Bank are for royal families going years back, but farther south, the valley is completely empty. Essentially we can make a fresh start."

"We?" Senenmut looked at her.

"You seem to have a knack for architecture, Senenmut of Iuny," she said grudgingly. "First in the military and now with your temples in Nubia. I thought you might like to try your hand at something everlasting."

"And your brother? Am I designing his tomb as well?"

Hatshepsut shook her head. "I hope to outline my tomb and then present him with the sketches. He can follow suit or do something different. There's no decree that says he has to be buried in the valley. Although since our father is there—"

"I'm sure he'll mimic you."

She shrugged. "Possibly."

"I believe I'm up for the challenge of building your tomb, but I'd like Ineni on the job as well." Senenmut dipped his finger into the green waves of the Nile and started to sketch something on the dry planks of the bench. "There's no one in the capital with more architectural experience."

"He designed my father's tomb," she said. "I think the two of you would make a perfect team."

"What are you thinking in terms of design?"

"Something simple. Inaccessible."

"Like a cliff tomb?"

She looked at the picture he'd created from damp wood and water. A cliff rose from a valley, a tiny dark doorway perched under the ledge. From there, a narrow shaft descended into the mountain. She nodded. "Precisely."

The design faded in the heat, but its imprint remained in Hatshepsut's mind. Now they just had to carve it into stone.

The boat lurched as it docked, and Senenmut shaded his eyes as he stood, looking out at the desolate golden sands before him on this, his first visit to the forbidden Western Valley. "The land of the dead."

Hatshepsut stood and brushed the wrinkles from her sheath. "Shall we?"

Dagi was already on shore, the plank outstretched for them to disembark. Hatshepsut was halfway down the incline when her sandal caught a warped section of wood. She stumbled forward and was about to pitch headfirst into the river, but Senenmut's arm snaked around her waist to stop her.

"You all right, *Hemet?*" Dagi asked, his arms out to help her.

Hatshepsut pushed an imaginary strand of hair from her eyes. "Except for my pride, yes."

"We promise not to tell anyone you almost took an unscheduled swim. Right, Dagi?" Senenmut's voice was infused with laughter. She enjoyed the feel of his arm around her, perhaps a little too much.

"My lips are sealed," Dagi said.

Senenmut's arm fell away, replaced with his open palm on the small of her back to guide her down the final steps of the narrow plank.

"We'll be back in a couple hours," Hatshepsut said to Dagi.

"The food'll be ready." He handed a skin of water to Senenmut and bowed as the two started up the thin path cut through the sands.

The sun-baked earth yawned unendingly before them, sparse tufts of grass tucked into pillows of brown sand. An ever-present haze of shimmering heat clouded the far-flung cliffs. Tucked within those sepulchral rock faces were uncounted tombs, the final resting places for pharaohs, queens, and other royalty from dynasties long since past. It was here that Neferubity had been buried what seemed a lifetime ago. A trained eye could discern a shadowed entrance here and there, but most of the tombs had long since disappeared beneath blankets of sand, just as the inhabitants had intended. To those who still walked the earth, the valley was empty, forsaken. But for those buried within its rocks, this was a city teeming with centuries of Egypt's most illustrious *kas* as they departed the underworld each night to reunite with their earthly bodies. Each time the angry winds of a *khamsin* blew, the secret rooms with all their precious treasures were protected anew, providing a deterrent against tomb robbers for centuries. And of course the handful of guards paid by the throne to protect the valley also assisted in ensuring the perpetual sleep of those buried here.

Senenmut and Hatshepsut walked in silence. The lazy hum of the river disappeared until they heard only rocks crunching underfoot. A thin sheen of perspiration clung stubbornly to her skin as Re's heat intensified. They reached the foot of the cliffs and paused for a moment to rest in the meager shade of a boulder off the path.

"Anything strike your fancy?" Senenmut took a long drink from the water skin. He dragged the back of his hand across his mouth and tossed the jug to Hatshepsut.

The water tasted like leather, but she drank her fill. "These cliffs are too easy to access. Farther up they get steeper. Dangerously steep."

"Perfect." Senenmut offered his hand to help her stand. He looked to the west. "What is that?"

Where they stood they could see only the Red Land, with no trees and no view of the Nile, yet still there were wonders to be found. Hatshepsut shaded her eyes, smiling at the sight of the secret community nestled into a rock amphitheater. "The Place of Truth."

"It looks like a village, but that's not possible, not here on the West Bank." Senenmut glanced at her. "Or is it?"

"My father founded the town," she said. "For the workers building his tomb."

"A secret village of stonecutters?"

She nodded. "And plasterers, craftsmen, artisans. Everyone needed to build a royal tomb."

"And they stay out here, hidden in the desert, of their own accord?"

Hatshepsut cocked her head at him. "Of course. At least after we drag them out here in chains and whip them into submission." He blinked, and she laughed. "The servants in the Place of Truth are paid three times their normal wage and are allowed to work on their own tombs on their days off. They're sworn to secrecy about what they do, but those who live here are honored to be chosen for such a position."

Senenmut stared awestruck at the village. "A secret city of Egypt's most talented artisans."

"I don't suppose you'd like to meet them?"

His eyes widened. "Could I?"

"Of course." She grinned. "But only if you can keep up."

Their skin glistened with sweat by the time they reached the border stones of the Place of Truth. Headed toward them, a workman in a loincloth carried a box of paints in one hand and a leather satchel in the other, his head bent against Re's glare. He glanced up at their approach, continued on his way for a moment, then dropped into a full *henu* in a puff of dust.

"Please rise," Hatshepsut said, sneaking a glance at Senenmut. He watched her without speaking, his expression unusually serious. She returned her attention to the workman, recognizing his thin nose and the cleft in his chin. "You are Aka, are you not?"

An easy smile spread across the worker's face. "I am indeed, *Hemet.* You have a fair memory."

"I met you when I accompanied my father to inspect the paintings on his tomb," she said. The trip had been years ago, before her father left for Canaan. "Your work was among the finest I've ever seen."

Aka's ears turned red. "You are too kind, *Hemet.*" He bent to pick up his satchel. "I'm afraid we weren't expecting you today. The women of the Place of Truth will be frantic to sweep their steps and scrub the children's faces."

Hatshepsut laughed. "I don't mind dusty stairs or smudged cheeks. I've asked *Neb* Senenmut to help design my tomb. He was unaware of the existence of the Place of Truth until today."

"As are most people," Aka said. "I'd be honored to accompany you into the city, if you'd like."

They followed Aka into the tiny town, entering through tall white gates that opened onto the single main street, so narrow that the buildings on either side shaded it from the sun, leaning toward one another as if to listen to the gossip from within one another's walls. Children played tag in the alleys, and two boys raced hoops with wooden sticks. They glanced at the newcomers, seemingly unimpressed, at least until Aka hissed and motioned them to their knees. Several women stepped outside to see what the commotion was about, including one breastfeeding a chubby-cheeked infant, and another holding a string of lamp wicks she'd been braiding, but they all fell into deep *henus* at the sight of the Great Royal Wife.

"You must be hot and thirsty after your trek from the river," Aka said. "My house is at the end of the street and my wife just brewed a fresh batch of barley beer."

"That would be lovely," Hatshepsut said, slowing her pace as they approached the market, trailing quite the crowd behind them. She waited for the inevitable as Senenmut inspected the copper goods, wooden furniture, and inlaid baskets.

"They're the finest I've ever seen," he said, straightening after examining an ivory jewel box with stark black hieroglyphs running down the center. "All of it."

"I told you they were the best," Hatshepsut said, sharing a smile with Aka. She shifted on her feet, eager to keep moving to allow the illusion of a breeze, then glimpsed something—or someone—from the corner of her eye. The man ducked into a dark alley so fast she had to stand on tiptoes to see past Aka to ensure she wasn't imagining things.

The artisan glanced behind him. "Is something wrong, *Hemet*?"

"I'm not sure," she said. "I thought I recognized someone."

Senenmut followed her gaze. "Another artisan?"

She shook her head. "Someone from Waset."

Aka removed a perfectly folded square of linen from his pocket and wiped his brow. "The water carriers are here today to refill the well. These hills have no water, so we rely on a handful of water carriers from Waset to supply us every week," he explained to Senenmut before looking to Hatshepsut once again. "Perhaps you recognized one of them."

"Perhaps," Hatshepsut answered slowly, shaking her head as if to clear it. "Or perhaps the heat is making me see things."

Senenmut studied her with concern. "Your face matches the ivory on this box. We should get you out of Re's glare."

"Please," Aka said. "Follow me."

The interior of Aka's house was dark, a result of the tiny windows cut high in the walls, but much cooler than the air outside and immaculate with its expertly woven reed mats and sparse furniture. His tiny sparrow of a wife fluttered about, producing two alabaster cups and a clay jug of beer so thick it almost required chewing. Senenmut set down his cup with a grin. "This reminds me of home," he said to the mistress of the house. "And for that I thank you very much."

Aka's wife flushed at the compliment, bowing to Senenmut over hands stained from grinding her husband's paints. "I hope we'll be seeing more of you," Aka said to Hatshepsut. "Your father visited the West Bank often before he flew to the sky. In fact, you remind me very much of him."

"I do hope to come here often to check the progress of my tomb," Hatshepsut said, smiling at the compliment and setting down her own empty cup. This project would provide a perfect excuse to leave the Hall of Women on a regular basis. Surely Thut couldn't deny her that.

They parted from Aka at the north gate; he was headed to the south of the valley to paint scenes on Mutnofret's tomb, but pointed them west toward some promising cliffs. Hatshepsut inquired whether there was anything the Place of Truth needed and promised to send a new flock of geese to replace the one Aka told her had been eaten by desert dogs the month before.

"We're getting awfully tired of dried fish." Aka laughed, then bowed once more and continued on his way.

Hatshepsut and Senenmut, having refused Aka's offer of donkeys, walked toward the west in silence, and Hatshepsut found her mind wandering back toward the little town with its crooked houses and streets filled with laughter. For a moment she imagined what her life would be like if she lived there, brewing her husband's beer and grinding his paints as Aka's wife did, instead of in the palace. The idea made her feel warm and pleasant, but also bored. She wanted more from life than the comfort of a dark house and the protective walls of the Place of Truth. Not only that, but she didn't even know how to brew beer.

Hatshepsut banished the idea. The gods had chosen a different path for her; it wouldn't do to worry about what might have been.

She and Senenmut walked in a companionable silence broken only by Senenmut's occasional humming, a sound that lightened Hatshepsut's heart as they picked their way around boulders and climbed over hills of broken limestone. Re had scarcely moved when Hatshepsut found what she was looking for: a perfectly terrifying vertical incline. The cliff began at the base of an ancient riverbed, long since dry, and stretched up into the sky.

"This is it." If she craned her neck she could just make out the pinnacle. "Can you build here?"

"You *would* have to pick the most dangerous spot in the valley, wouldn't you?" Senenmut shielded his eyes from Re's glare as he looked up. She could see his architect's mind take measurements as he surveyed the site. "It will definitely require some fancy engineering, but Ineni and I can make it happen. If this is what you want."

"It's what I want," she said. From the entrance she would be able to see not only Re's daily ascent, but also have a bird's-eye view of the tomb that housed her father's *ka*.

It was perfect.

"Then I'll make it happen." Senenmut's eyes caught hers as he spoke. Something about the way he spoke hinted that only for her would he attempt such a monumental task.

She looked away.

Out here in the desolate valley they were alone, surrounded by silent and ancient cliffs. The only witnesses were a pair of buzzards that circled the sky and the gods' whispers in the wind.

The warm breeze whipped the hem of Hatshepsut's sheath, bringing her the faint scent of cinnamon and honey. Senenmut didn't move; he stood as rigid as stone until she reached up to touch the narrow white scar on his forehead, wondering for a moment where it had come from. She wanted that moment to last forever, standing on a precipice from which they could never return.

"Kiss me," she said.

When their lips touched, it was as searing as the winds of a summer *khamsin*, leaving Hatshepsut breathless in its wake. Senenmut's arms slipped around her and she clung to him, never wanting to let go.

And yet she was Egypt's Great Royal Wife. This was treason.

She gasped. "We can't do this."

The blood coursed through her veins and made her light-headed, his hands in her hair as he clutched her to him. His chest heaved as Hatshepsut pressed her forehead to his heart, feeling its furious beats mirror the pounding of her own heart.

Senenmut would find his entrails missing and his body impaled on a pike in the main square of Waset if Thutmosis were to discover them. Hatshepsut would endure a life locked in the Hall of Women, if not worse.

Nothing like this could ever happen again. And yet Hatshepsut both hoped and feared it would.

"I'm sorry." She gave a shaky exhale. "In another life—"

He stepped back and ran his hands over his scalp. "Never apologize. I've waited since the day you fell in the fountain to do that."

She couldn't stop the grin that spread across her face. "Have you really?"

"I probably shouldn't have told you that." He rolled his eyes, then fell serious. "But I'd face your brother and an army of *medjay* to do it again."

"I don't think that's necessary." She stood on tiptoes, brushing her lips to his. It was reckless, but she didn't care. This time the kiss was only a whisper, one that tasted of tears. A final good-bye.

Senenmut groaned. "Amun's blood, woman. You're going to be the death of me."

"We should get back before Dagi suspects something." She broke his gaze, not trusting what would happen next if she continued to look into his eyes. He touched her cheek, then his hands fell open at his sides.

The trek back to the barge was silent, heavy with the burden of many words left unsaid. The gods toyed with them, dangling happiness in front of them before they yanked it out of reach.

The speck of the boat grew larger as they approached the dock, until Hatshepsut could see the contents of Mouse's baskets spread about the boat. A look askance at Senenmut showed his face set in rigid lines, his jaw clenched tight.

"Did you find what you were looking for?" Dagi asked merrily. He offered Hatshepsut his hand as she walked back up the narrow wooden plank, setting each footstep carefully this time.

"I think so." She took her seat close to the prow. She felt a stab of remorse as Senenmut sat on the opposite side of the deck, still close enough that she could smell cinnamon on the air.

She tasted none of the pomegranate salad or melon stuffed with raisins that were offered to her, heard none of Dagi's constant chatter as the little boat skimmed the green waves. When they arrived at the palace's dock, she paused to thank Dagi and his crew.

By the time she finished, Senenmut was gone.

CHAPTER 10

Hatshepsut floated in the dark waters of the pool in the Hall of Women, a white sliver of moon hanging high in Nut's belly. Despite the cool air, the water still held a trace of the day's warmth, yet the remembrance of Senenmut's lips made the blood hot in her veins.

She'd avoided returning to the Hall of Women all afternoon, but eventually had grown tired of wandering restlessly up and down the palace corridors. She had arranged for a new flock of geese for the Place of Truth and then sent for Ineni as a welcome distraction. The old architect had been close with her father, but Hatshepsut had always been struck by how differently the gods could sculpt two men. Where Osiris Tutmose had been wiry and muscular, even in his final years, everything about Ineni was pale and round, like a soft roll pulled fresh from the oven. He often even smelled like just-baked bread.

"Ineni," she had exclaimed as he entered the palace aviary, ignoring his *henu* amidst the cooing of doves and twitter of songbirds. "I'm afraid I must pull you from your retirement. I require your expertise in building my tomb."

The architect's pudgy cheeks had dimpled with his smile. "I'm happy to be of service to the royal family once again."

"Senenmut was adamant he wanted to work with you on the project."

"He's already seen me. I'm glad for his strong back." Ineni chortled. "You've chosen a rather ambitious undertaking, *Hemet*. But, then, you are your father's daughter." He held out a tiny papyrus scroll tied with brown string. "I almost forgot. Senenmut asked me to deliver this to you. He sought me out before I received your summons. He seemed in a bit of a hurry."

"Thank you." Hatshepsut had pocketed the message, where it now lay tucked in her sheath, discarded on the tiles near the pool, taunting her and tempting her.

An invitation or a farewell? Or something else entirely?

She turned in the water to swim a bit more in what was proving a vain attempt to clear her heart. The sheet of warm water rolled over her body when a shout penetrated her waterlogged brain.

She looked up to see Mensah struggling within the clutches of two guards who protected the Hall of Women. They held him by the arms, his face as red as a beet as they attempted to drag him toward the ornate gilded gate. "The pharaoh is ill, you dimwitted jackals," he yelled. "The Great Royal Wife needs to come now, before it's too late!"

"Our apologies, *Hemet*," one guard stuttered. "The cupbearer pushed past us—"

"Let him be." She motioned impatiently, wiping water from her face. "Thut is ill?"

"Very. You must hurry."

She motioned for them to turn around, and pulled herself from the water. Her fingers seemed to be tied in knots, the linen towel gnarled together. "What happened?"

Mensah peered over his shoulder. "He complained of a headache, then started slurring his words as if he'd had too much wine. He was ranting about trade agreements with the Hittites when he fell. He hit his head—there's blood everywhere."

"Blood doesn't scare me."

Mensah's hand was clammy on her wrist, but she ignored the breach of etiquette. "Gua isn't sure if he's going to wake up," he said.

Amun's breath. This was her fault, punishment from the gods for her betrayal today.

She ran through the corridors, wrapped in the damp towel and almost slipping several times on wet feet. Slaves stared at her open-mouthed as she ran through patches of shifting moonlight.

She'd betrayed Thut and now he might die. Anubis had already claimed Neferubity and their father; the jackal god couldn't be allowed to take her brother, too.

"Please, Sekhmet," she whispered. "I'll do anything."

She rounded the last corner before the pharaoh's apartments and skidded to a stop.

Thut had no heir, no one to take his place on the Isis Throne. If he died, she would be the last surviving child of Osiris Tutmose, the only possible successor.

She choked at her blasphemy. The gods should strike her dead and feed her heart to the demon Ammit.

Mensah yanked her arm so hard that he almost pulled her shoulder from its socket. "Hurry, Hatshepsut. We might be too late."

Two *medjay* guarded Thut's apartments, their bronze spears and black-and-white ox-hide shields held at attention. One had a face as blank as the desert sands, but the second man's face and arms were painted with primal black swirls of permanent war paint, a sign of his foreign birth.

The first guard banged the butt of his spear on the door, but the painted man stopped his comrade. "Forgive me, *Hemet*," he said, "but you can't go in there."

"Don't be a fool. The pharaoh is ill and I must attend him."

His eyes bore into hers, his mouth set in a firm line. "I'm sorry, *Hemet*, but the pharaoh gave specific orders that he wasn't to be disturbed."

She stopped, taken aback. "What? But Thut hit his head." She turned on Mensah. "How could he—"

He shoved the guard out of the way. "Stand aside, you worthless dog. The pharaoh requested the presence of his Great Royal Wife."

She opened her mouth to protest, but Mensah kicked open the door and pushed her into the room. The door slammed shut behind her.

Thut was most certainly not unconscious.

He stood at the far end of the chambers, partially obscured by the two-headed stele from the Phoenicians, his chest heaving and smeared with blood. And yet his teeth shone white in the torchlight, the grin of a hyena.

Nothing made sense until her brother raised his cane. There was a flash of ivory and a crack like a whip. A spatter of crimson blood on Thut's face. A moan.

Two thick *medjay* hauled a man to his feet, arms pinned as Thut raised the cane again. "You were my brother!" he screamed, spittle flying. "I trusted you!"

Senenmut.

His nose gushed a river of scarlet and his left eye was swollen shut. His head lolled against his chest, a dark stain blossoming below his ribs.

"Thutmosis." Hatshepsut could barely hear her own voice. A cool hand touched hers and she turned to see Aset beside her, shaking her head, little bells tinkling from far away.

Her brother froze, the cane hanging in midair as if ready to strike the head from one of Egypt's enemies.

"How kind of you to join us, sister." Thut's eyes narrowed. "Now our party is complete. I do wish you'd thought to fully inform me of your jaunt into the Red Land today."

She swallowed hard. "We went to choose a location for my tomb."

Thut clenched and unclenched his fist. "Yes, I'm well aware of your plans. Mensah told me everything, about your trip into the Place of Truth and the liberties you allowed this foul *rekhyt* with your body."

So it was Mensah she had seen in the market, a face so hidden in shadows she had doubted her own eyes.

Thutmosis slammed the flail into Senenmut's nose, producing a dull crack like a melon breaking. This time there was no moan, no sound at all. "How long has this been going on?" he demanded.

"Only today. And it was only a kiss—"

He was before her in an instant, his face so close she could smell the incense on his breath. The storm in his eyes could have obliterated every village in all of Egypt. "Don't play coy with me, sister. I was willing to overlook your whoring before we married—" He sneered. "Yes, you think I'm a fool, but I knew you didn't come to my bed a virgin. It didn't take long to ferret out the truth from the girl-slaves. Why do you think I promoted Mensah?" He gave a strangled laugh. "I wanted to keep an eye on both of you. I thought you might betray me, but not like this. Not with him." He raised the cane again, poised to beat Senenmut once more.

"Stop!" Her voice trembled. She wanted to throw herself between Senenmut and her brother, but that would only ensure Senenmut's death sentence. "Please. You're above this."

Thut's fingers curved around her throat. "Do you know what I could do to you, Hatshepsut, what I *want* to do to you? I could kill you with my own hands. Deliver you to Anubis so you could never betray me again."

She shoved him away. There would be a necklace of bruises ringing her neck tomorrow. "I made a mistake."

"You betrayed me!" Thut roared.

An unexpected blow to the side of her face sent her stumbling back and exploded white fire in her eye. She braced for another blow, but it never came. Instead, Thut's cane clattered to the floor and he gave a strangled sob. Aset was at his side, her pale hand on his arm. "Perhaps your Great Royal Wife tells the truth," she murmured. "Or perhaps her offense is worthy of your forgiveness?"

There was a long silence, Thut's cheeks fading from purple to the shade of parchment.

"I can never forgive her. And I don't want her excuses." Thut studied Hatshepsut, his eyes flat. "You might care to know that I didn't have a chance to summon Senenmut after Mensah told me of your little excursion. He showed up at my door to ask my permission to leave court." He gave a hollow laugh. "Your precious lover planned to abandon you."

He was lying, she was sure of it. Thut was only trying to hurt her.

But then she recalled the letter from Senenmut still hidden in her pocket, and Ineni's mention of him being in a hurry. She glanced at Senenmut, slumped unconscious between the *medjay*, his chest barely rising and falling.

He would have left her.

Thut cleared his throat. "Senenmut will die a traitor's death, impaled on a stake and his body burned. His name and *ka* will disappear from both this world and the afterlife. The court will be told he left the City of Truth to return to his family in Iuny. You shall never speak of this and will never again leave the Hall of Women. Do you understand?"

The law gave Thutmosis every right to execute Senenmut, but it would be her actions that led to his death. Another stain on her *ka*.

"Please, Thut, not his *ka*. It was my fault—"

"I'm well aware whose fault it was." He turned to the *medjay*. "Get that thing out of here." He touched Aset's cheek tenderly, then grimaced and turned his hands over. They were wet with blood. "Leave us."

Aset seemed about to say something, but stopped. She frowned at Hatshepsut, then bowed to Thut and disappeared into the shadows. The guards followed, the door closing with a final thud.

Thut jerked his head toward the ground. "Lie down."

Hatshepsut hesitated, her skin prickling with dread.

"I said, lie down. And take off that towel."

Her life was no longer her own; today's events had taught her that.

She took her time folding the damp linen, willing her hands to stop shaking. Slowly she lay on the cold tiles. Her nipples puckered, the tremors spreading up her whole body now.

"Am I not man enough for you?" Thut undid the rope at his waist.

"It's not enough that I've been cheated of my leg, but now you'd rob me of my manhood, too?"

She let him push her legs apart, and he slammed into her with a grunt. Hatshepsut swallowed her cry, but that only enraged him more, and his fingers dug into her shoulders, his thrusts growing increasingly impatient. Her mind became numb, then her body. Still not finished, he finally rolled away, his member soft and flaccid, and scrambled for his bloodied kilt. "I loved you. I'd have given you everything." His voice cracked, his hard eyes shining in the torchlight. "But I wasn't enough, was I?"

He hobbled off, and she curled into herself, touching hesitant fingers to her swollen eye and looking down at her bruised body. Blood coated her legs, her breasts, her hands.

Senenmut's blood.

The next morning she received a message from Thut, delivered by one of the guards who had dragged Senenmut away. He wouldn't meet her eyes.

The punishment is complete.

She bit her lip and nodded, hands clasped tight in her lap. She refused to cry before this man.

Before snapping to attention and departing, he set two small packages on the table: a small linen bundle and an ebony box tied with worn leather thongs. Her mind still numb, she unwrapped the linen first.

Inside was a leather band, damp along the edges and embossed with the ibis-headed Thoth, god of knowledge and writing. Her fingers came away with a vibrant streak of fresh blood.

She clasped Senenmut's armband to her chest with a moan, hands trembling as silent tears streamed down her cheeks. It took some time to muster the strength to open the box. As she peered inside, her *ka* fled her body, unable to bear the horror. She slid to the floor, choking for breath.

A meaty organ, dark red and the size of her fist, slick with fresh blood and covered by a loose web of blue veins. The top contained several white, wide holes where it had been severed from its owner.

A heart. Senenmut's heart.

The heart controlled the body and housed a man's memory, his personality, his *ka*. Without his heart, Senenmut could not be judged in the afterlife and would simply cease to exist, as if he had never been. She would never see him again, not even in death.

Eyes closed, she slammed the box shut, but couldn't find the strength to leave the floor. Sitre and Mouse helped her to her bed sometime later that day, but still she clung to the box and armband, the last remnants of Senenmut's existence. The room had gone dark when the haze finally lifted from her mind and she realized what she must do.

Fumbling to strike an oil lamp, she blinked against its sudden flame and dug frantically through a reed basket to find what she needed: a slender bone needle, one that Sitre often used to mend the hems of her sheaths.

By the light of the lamp, she began to carve the worn side of Senenmut's armband, the leather shiny where it had rubbed against his skin. Skin that was no more. Her eyes filled with tears and her finger slipped, and the needle stabbed her opposite wrist, a fresh cut atop those she had carved into her flesh when Neferubity had died. She continued on, not caring when her own blood smeared the leather.

When she was finished, she surveyed her handiwork, the figure of a man and a single word in hieroglyphs.

Senenmut.

Thut had sought to obliterate him completely, to kill Senenmut and destroy his body, to cut out his heart so he could never arrive in the Field of Reeds. But as long as Senenmut's name and figure remained somewhere in this world, he could rise again. She had killed him, but she would keep him alive in the afterlife.

She owed him so much more, but this, at least, she could give him.

She tucked away the scrap of leather, hiding it in the bottom of the old reed basket with Sekhmet's red amulet.

Remnants of another life.

Only then did she remember Senenmut's note. Frantic that Sitre might have already taken the sheath to be laundered, she breathed a sigh of relief when she found it flung over a chair. Untying the string and carefully unrolling the delicate paper, she didn't realize the tears had escaped until they dropped to the paper, blurring the single line of Senenmut's almost illegible script.

I'd wait my whole life for you.

CHAPTER 11

Hatshepsut had slept only once in the dark days following Senenmut's death, but fanged demons and the albino witch had stalked her dreams.

Your name will live forever.

You shall be the downfall of those you love.

Egypt will prosper, but those closest to you shall find only anguish and ruin.

Senenmut was dead. Thut despised her. She'd betrayed and been betrayed.

A man was dead at her hands, and not just any man. A man she might have loved, had she been given the chance.

She didn't sleep again, only turned her back toward the door and stared at the swirl of lotus flowers and frolicking red and white calves painted on the wall. It was then that she noticed a line of uneven notches carved into the plaster. She touched their rough edges, counting each one. Seventy-seven.

A lucky number.

A story from her childhood floated to her mind about a farmer's daughter brought to her father's palace as a concubine at the beginning of his reign. Hatshepsut had once come upon her mother talking about the girl with Sitre.

"An unlucky end for so lucky a woman," Ahmose had said, shaking her head over her needlework. "She should have felt honored to be chosen for the pharaoh's bed."

Then her mother had looked up and seen Hatshepsut in the doorway. After that, the discussion had turned to talk of eye paints and perfume.

Hatshepsut rolled over for the first time in days. Sitre sat next to her bed, eyes closed and hands resting on her lap. An onyx grinding stone with half-ground pebbles of kohl lay forgotten at her side.

"Sitre, what happened to the girl who last lived in this room?"

Her *menat*'s eyes fluttered open and she reached out to touch Hatshepsut's cheek. "So, you've decided to join the land of the living again."

For now. That didn't mean she was going to stay.

"The girl in this room? What happened?"

Sitre shook her head. "One shouldn't speak ill of the dead."

"I want to know. She was one of my father's concubines, wasn't she?"

"Yes, she was." Sitre sighed. "And an ungrateful one at that. She asked to go home, but of course that wasn't allowed."

"But she left on her own, didn't she? After seventy-seven days."

"How did you know that?"

Hatshepsut glanced at the carved notches on the wall, envisioning the hennaed hand that had etched them. "Lucky guess. What happened to her?"

"She hanged herself with a linen belt, *Hemet*." Sitre's eyes flicked to the worn cedar beam running across the ceiling. "And don't you go thinking you might want the same end. I'd follow you to the Field of Reeds just to wring your neck if you did."

Hatshepsut rolled onto her back, imagining a body dangling from the beam. It was a tempting thought, but she didn't deserve an easy escape. She'd have to find another way out of the Hall of Women.

Sitre's hand touched hers. "This came for you a while ago."

In her palm lay a pink lotus blossom, a little wilted but still fragrant. Attached was a scrap of papyrus.

Hatshepsut opened it, heart pounding at the thought that this might be a final message from Senenmut. She wasn't sure she wanted to read it if it was.

Her blood went cold at the familiar handwriting.

FORGIVE ME.

Mensah.

She crushed the flower and paper together in her fist, singeing them in the flame of an oil lamp before letting the fire overtake both. She would never forgive him, not as long as she lived.

"Was that from Mensah?" Sitre's voice was soft, as if she feared that speaking too loud might cause Hatshepsut to break.

Hatshepsut nodded, unable to find words.

"Thutmosis has made him vizier." Sitre glanced at Hatshepsut. "I thought you might wish to know."

To know that her former lover had betrayed her and been rewarded with an elevation to the second-highest position in the Two Lands? How many punishments could she bear before the gods managed to destroy her?

"Sitre?"

"Yes?" She had gone back to grinding the kohl.

"I need to bribe a priest of Anubis."

The grinding stopped. "Should I ask why?"

"I need to mummify something."

Sitre's face softened and she patted Hatshepsut's hand. "I'll get you whatever you need, *sherit*. I always will."

It took a few days, but Sitre found a *wa'eb* priest of Anubis, one with the stench of death clinging to him, who was willing to tell her the forbidden secrets of mummification in exchange for a pair of gold bracelets. Muddling through his instructions as best they could, the women washed Senenmut's heart with palm wine; swathed it in sacred linen discarded by the gods' temples; and filled the ebony box with natron, myrrh, and cinnamon. Hatshepsut choked back a sob at the sweet smell of the familiar spice. Then, alone, Hatshepsut buried Senenmut's heart in a quiet corner of the Hall of Women, under the shade of a sycamore tree.

"I will see you again in the Field of Reeds," she whispered, smoothing the earth and sand. "I swear it."

Tears threatened to overwhelm her, but she pushed them away, embracing Sekhmet's fury until she felt like a caged lion, ready to devour the first person who crossed her path. She hoped Mensah might be that person—she'd dreamed up at least a hundred unique ways to torture him in exchange for his treachery—but locked away in the Hall of Women, she'd likely never see him again. She'd have to content herself with imagining his body being pushed from a cliff or torn limb from limb by jackals. For now.

Sitre had finally thrown her out of her own chambers, after she'd hurled a faience urn against the wall and watched with some small satisfaction as it fractured into hundreds of blue fragments, like tiny shards of the sky.

She had to do something, anything. Otherwise she'd soon run out of vases.

There was one task she wasn't looking forward to. She picked up the box inlaid with mother-of-pearl figures of Horus and Hathor that Mouse had prepared at her request and crossed the empty courtyard, catching sight of her mother's chambers from the corner of her eye. Mutnofret had cited poor health and retired to a rich estate in the Nile delta—one renowned for its beekeepers and date farms—so now Ahmose was finally left in peace. Normally Hatshepsut might have slipped past, but a visit with her mother offered a welcome distraction. She rapped on the portal.

"Enter."

The door groaned on ancient hinges. Her mother sat on a leather footstool, embroidering a colorful hem on a new sheath. "The dutiful daughter descends from on high to check in on her mother." Ahmose spoke without malice, setting down her sewing and looking up. She gasped. "What happened to your eye?"

No amount of kohl could cover the evidence of the fight with Thut. The bruise had faded to a sickly shade of yellow around the edges.

Hatshepsut's hand fluttered to her eye. "It's nothing—just a disagreement with Thut. How are you?"

"I may die from boredom soon. The only excitement I've had in months has been the arrival of that new chit, Aset." Her mother's lip twitched and she stabbed the fabric with the slim bone needle. "I was surprised to hear that Senenmut left court to return to his mud hut in Iuny. I thought the *rekhyt* and Thutmosis were close. Didn't you spend some time with him as well?"

Hatshepsut nodded, unable to speak. If only Senenmut really had gone to Iuny. But she wouldn't talk of that with her mother, or with anyone, for that matter. She blinked hard and motioned to the inlaid box of sweets she'd brought as a gift. "I'm on my way to visit Aset now."

"Why in Set's name would you do that?"

"Because I like her." Not to mention she was indebted to her, not that candied dates and honeyed almonds could adequately thank the girl for saving Hatshepsut's face from being beaten to a bloody pulp. "I have no reason not to."

"She's competition for your husband." Ahmose spoke as if she were talking to a dullard. "And for a son."

Hatshepsut's eyes flicked heavenward. "I know my duty, Mother. But Aset is not going to usurp my position. She's a commoner, for the love of Amun."

"A commoner with plenty of colorful gossip following her from Hathor's temple." Ahmose glanced at the door and her voice dropped to a conspiratorial whisper. "They say she managed her place at the

Festival of Intoxication only because she poisoned Hathor's senior dancer. Rumor has it she mixed ground elder flower into her bread."

"Tongues will wag about any girl singled out by the pharaoh."

"There's more," her mother continued. "It seems the High Priest of Hathor also enjoyed Aset's many charms. Apparently he was quite put out at the pharaoh's demand to release her from the temple."

"Next thing you know, she'll have seduced Amun himself."

The gods knew Aset had already seduced Horus, or at least his representative here on earth.

Ahmose pursed her lips and waggled her needle at Hatshepsut. "You mark my words. That girl is trouble."

"I have a spy at the temple of Hathor." She'd contacted Merenaset only once, shortly after her audience at court, and received a report that she was enjoying her official duties as chantress and that the High Priest of Hathor had a collection of the goddess's best offerings hidden in his personal storeroom. Hatshepsut had suspected as much, and she had filed away that information for future use. "Would it make you happy if I asked for a report on Aset?" she asked her mother.

"Yes, as a matter of fact, it would. I saw Thutmosis with her yesterday—it's sickening how he fawns over her. I had hoped your brother would have more sense than to start plucking *rekhyt* from every field in Egypt. He must be looking for someone like his mother."

Hatshepsut didn't wish to listen to a recital of the ills her mother had suffered—imagined or otherwise—at Mutnofret's hands. "If Aset pleases Thut and he makes her happy, then so be it. Perhaps Hathor smiles on them."

The gods knew Hathor certainly didn't smile on Hatshepsut. And she preferred to keep her distance from Thut, at least for now.

Ahmose shrugged and picked up her sewing again. "Keep your friends close and your enemies closer. I wouldn't trust that girl any more than I would an angry scorpion."

Hatshepsut kissed the top of her mother's head and inhaled a trace of lotus perfume. "Then I shall be careful not to step on her."

The former Great Royal Wife snorted before resuming her attack on the embroidered orange fish. "Have Sitre bring you a cut of cold ox flesh. Hold it over that eye to take down the swelling."

Hatshepsut shut the door and leaned her forehead against the cool wood. Beaten and disgraced, she now had to court her replacement and find her way back into Thut's good graces.

Anything to keep from thinking of Senenmut.

Girl-slaves scattered like tittering sparrows when Hatshepsut was announced into Aset's airy chambers, some of the largest in the Hall of Women. The rooms had once belonged to a daughter of the Hittite king, but like the rest of the old generation, the woman had been retired to lands near the Atef-Pehu oasis, left to shrivel and die like the grapes those lands were so famous for.

The apartments were mostly empty, containing only a bed with crisp white sheets and feet carved like cattle legs, several gilded chests and reed baskets, and a scuffed gaming table left behind by the Hittite princess. Aset's slaves had abandoned a game of *senet*, the blue faience and alabaster pawns strewn about the board. The match hadn't been going well; one of the pawns had drowned in the House of Life and several had already been knocked into the afterlife.

"*Hemet.*" Aset sank to the ground and pressed her forehead into the woven reed rug. A rough wooden crate appeared to have exploded next to her, gaudy necklaces and rumpled linens strewn about the floor. A pair of worn reed sandals poked from the box along with a chipped wooden statue of Hathor. A thick ivory trinket of some sort lay at the bottom.

There were no jars of elder flowers or anything else out of the ordinary. Hatshepsut's mother would be disappointed.

Hatshepsut managed a smile but winced at the pain that knifed through her eye as Aset scrambled to her feet. Hammered gold bracelets similar to a pair of Thut's glimmered at the girl's wrists, but she still wore the same cheap Nubian wig from her first encounter with Hatshepsut. Her painted lips and netted dress of blue faience beads belonged on one of Waset's prostitutes. The netting strained against her full breasts, threatening to snap and shower beads over the tiles.

Hatshepsut cleared her throat. "I wondered if you might enjoy some company this afternoon."

"Of course. It would be my honor to entertain Egypt's Great Royal Wife." Aset glanced about the chambers as if trapped. Then again, she was.

Hatshepsut's gaze strayed to a pair of black granite statues on the window ledge. The tall one bore Thut's pointed chin and broad forehead, while the shorter possessed Aset's wide eyes and upturned nose. A closer inspection revealed Thut's cartouche etched into his kilt, an epithet praising his loyal and beautiful concubine on the woman's sheath.

Aset bit her lip. "The pharaoh gave those to me this morning before he went hunting."

Hatshepsut read the rest of the inscription. She pursed her lips. "So your *kas* will always be together in the Field of Reeds, even if your bodies disappear."

Aset didn't answer.

It had been a mistake to come here, she realized, but it was too late to leave now. Another penance from the gods.

"Do you play?" She gestured to the *senet* table.

"Not very well." Aset ran slender fingers over the alabaster pieces. Her nails were ragged, bitten to the quick.

Hatshepsut handed over the box of sweets. The inlaid figures of Hathor and Horus seemed to mock her now. "I thought we might enjoy these. The dried apricots are soaked with honey made from bees fed only cornflower blossoms."

"Thank you." Aset opened the box and popped a date rolled in crushed almonds into her mouth. "I hadn't expected a visit from you so soon," she said, chewing as she spoke. "Not after the other night."

A honeyed apricot stuck in Hatshepsut's throat. So much for small talk. At least she could be thankful that Aset had seen only the beating, that she'd left before Thut had ordered Hatshepsut to the ground. "I'm sorry you had to see that."

"I've seen worse." Aset glanced at her eye. "But the pharaoh does have a temper."

"Thut has always been slow to anger but dangerous once he's crossed."

"Like a hippo on a sunny day."

Hatshepsut tried to smile but failed, the comment reminding her of another death long ago. Neferubity and Senenmut's deaths were a result of her own stupidity. Inviting Senenmut to the West Bank had been dangerous, but she'd chanced it anyway. She had only herself to blame.

She shifted on the hard wooden seat. "Actually, I wanted to thank you for stopping Thut. My relationship with my brother is—"

"Complicated?" Aset moved her first pawn. Hatshepsut stared at her. This girl was more than a simple dancer. She considered the word *complicated*, testing it as one would a fine wine.

Finally, she nodded. "You might say that."

Aset chewed another date and rolled the knucklebones. "Not even the gods get along. It stands to reason their children might not either."

Hatshepsut gave a wry smile. "I don't recall Sekhmet and Horus being the best of friends."

And yet, before her sat the very embodiment of Hathor. Thut probably couldn't help loving Aset.

"Horus and Sekhmet are the god and goddess of war," Aset said. "It must be difficult to be agreeable to others when you're always trying to bend them to your will and wreak vengeance upon their heads when they don't cooperate."

Hatshepsut smiled. "Exhausting, too."

"But Hathor managed well with both." Aset glanced up from the game. "I'd like to as well, if that's possible."

Hatshepsut thought about the gossip circling Aset—the High

Priest as her lover and the elder flowers as her weapon. What would she do if she were in Aset's place? It was one thing to warm the pharaoh's bed and yet another to have the ear of the Great Royal Wife, especially if she planned to be the pharaoh's favorite. It was in Aset's best interests to play both sides, but that didn't mean a friendship with the concubine couldn't benefit Hatshepsut, too. She'd just have to be careful.

Despite herself, she found she liked the girl. Aset lacked the polish of court, but her candor was refreshing. She reminded Hatshepsut of another *rekhyt*, one she'd never see again.

She shoved that thought away as quickly as it had come.

Hatshepsut's last pawn was mired down in the House of Three Truths, but she didn't care that she was losing the game. "It may be some time before Thut and I are on speaking terms again, but I don't see why you and I can't be friends."

Aset moved her pawn onto the House of Rebirth to win the game. "You can join us for dinner, if you'd like. Thutmosis promised he'd harpoon an elephant fish for me on his hunting expedition." She grimaced. "I hate fish."

"You're going to have to acquire a taste for Thut's hunting spoils if you're to stay on his good side."

"Then I hope he can catch more than fish."

"Wait until he takes down an ostrich. You'll never hear the end of it."

Aset groaned.

Dining with Thut was the last thing Hatshepsut wanted to do, but avoiding him wouldn't do her any good either. She'd have to face him sooner or later; it would be better to do so on her own terms.

Yet another punishment.

"Dinner would be lovely, Aset. Thank you for the invitation." She smoothed her sheath and stood to go, but paused for a moment. "I think you and I are going to get along just fine."

Aset grinned, deep dimples clefting her cheeks. "I hope you're right."

Aset's girl-slaves slunk into the shadows as Hatshepsut passed them, her chin held high. The door closed behind her with a thud, followed by a twitter of nervous giggles and Aset's muffled command.

She sighed, remembering her mother's advice.

Keep your friends close and your enemies closer.

Only the gods knew which Aset would be.

The dinner did not go well. Thut managed to ignore Hatshepsut entirely, his lips pursed as if the slaves had served him the bitter gall of ostrich instead of elephant fish seasoned with coriander and cumin. Her fingers brushed his once, but he pulled back as if scalded, then threw down his linen napkin and excused himself. Aset and Hatshepsut finished the meal in awkward silence.

Two months passed. Hatshepsut did contact Hathor's temple, but received a scroll from the head scribe informing her that the chantress Merenaset no longer served the goddess of love and beauty. So the truth of Aset's arrival at the palace might never be known.

Thut allowed Ineni to begin work on both Hatshepsut's cliffside tomb and his own. He might not like Hatshepsut, but he wasn't willing to jeopardize her eternal *ka*, at least not yet.

Contrary to Hatshepsut's predictions, Thut had planned his tomb outside the royal necropolis, fearful that grave robbers might plunder his body if he were buried near any other tomb, no matter how ancient. He had pleased Ineni to no end by picking a site far less treacherous than Hatshepsut's. The excavation for the well shaft on Thut's tomb hummed steadily along, but Hatshepsut's progressed far more slowly, due in part to the difficulty in reaching the spot, but also because of Thut's order that she have no say in the project. She couldn't bring herself to care.

Her hope for the future waned. Without Senenmut and her place next to Thut's throne, she spent her days pacing and eating out of sheer boredom. She read every scroll Mouse could smuggle to her until she had them all memorized. She even attempted to take up embroidery for lack of anything better to do. She was now convinced no woman should ever learn to sew; gouging out her own eyes with her needle would be more enjoyable.

She was rereading the reports on the tombs that Ineni had given Mouse and had already read to the bottom of the papyrus at least five times without absorbing any of the information. Another letter had arrived from Mensah today—one that made her so furious she couldn't get it out of her mind—begging for forgiveness and claiming he'd told Thutmosis what had happened in the desert only to protect her. She was about to give up on the tomb reports when she saw Aset lurking in the doorway.

Over the past weeks, she and Aset had spent countless hours playing *senet* and gossiping, warming to each other without Thut's shadow hovering over them. This closeness with another woman was something Hatshepsut hadn't experienced since Neferubity had died, and she had been scarcely more than a girl then. She and Aset talked about everything—Thut, their affinities for Sekhmet and Hathor, and their shared love of dancing. Everything, save Senenmut. Aset had broached the subject once, but Hatshepsut had quickly steered the conversation to calmer waters. She was no fool. Anything she said to Aset might find its way to Thut.

"I'm sorry to interrupt." Aset hesitated at the door. "I can come back if you're busy."

"Not at all." Hatshepsut gestured to the chair opposite her. She'd attempted to set up a sort of office in her apartments in the Hall of Women, but only after realizing she couldn't bribe the guards at the gilded gate to let her sneak out. She and Thut were barely on speaking terms, but she'd find a way out of here. She just wasn't sure how. Or when.

Aset sat gingerly on the cedar stool and bit her fingernails, looking everywhere except at Hatshepsut.

"Is something wrong?"

"Yes. Perhaps. I don't know." Aset sat on her hands, but her foot still twitched. Hatshepsut waited for her to speak again. "When is that Akkadian princess coming to court?"

Hatshepsut stifled the laugh that bubbled in her throat at Aset's mournful expression. The concubine enjoyed her status as Thut's favorite, but the pharaoh still did his duty and visited his Great Royal Wife's bed, often unsuccessfully. Hatshepsut's terse interludes with Thut had dwindled significantly since Aset's introduction to the Hall of Women. Now Aset feared she would be jostled from her place as the pharaoh's favorite with Thut's newest acquisition, the Akkadian princess whose marriage contract had sped up his union with Hatshepsut. Whether Aset was upset because she actually loved Thut or because she feared losing her place as favorite, Hatshepsut couldn't tell.

"Princess Enheduanna won't arrive for a few months." Hatshepsut wrapped an arm around her friend. "She isn't scheduled to leave Akkad for a few more weeks and then she will have a long journey up the Nile before she reaches the City of Truth."

"Thanks be to Hathor for that." Aset's smile was full of sunshine. She seemed about to say something else, but stopped. Her smile faded and the nail biting resumed. She wouldn't have any fingernails left if she kept it up.

Hatshepsut covered the girl's hands with her own. "Is there something else?"

"There is," Aset answered slowly. "I think it's good news, but you may not."

Hatshepsut knew what she was going to say. What her mother had endured was about to happen to her. And there was nothing she could do about it.

"I didn't need to perform my monthly purification this moon." Aset looked through her lashes at Hatshepsut. "I'm pregnant."

Hatshepsut's lips ceased working. There was a moment's pause until she could mold her expression into a smile. "Congratulations. I'm so happy for you!"

She gathered her friend into her arms, hoping she couldn't feel her *ka* quaking. Taweret, the hippo goddess of fertility and childbirth, had not yet blessed her with the quickening of her womb. Her moon bloods had ceased only days earlier. And yet, in two short months Thut had gotten a child on Aset.

What if Hatshepsut wasn't able to conceive? Or if she failed to produce a boy?

Thus far, she was an utter failure as Great Royal Wife.

The questions tumbled through her mind at an alarming rate. Aset could feasibly conceive multiple children before Thut's seed took root in his Great Royal Wife's belly, mangling the direct line to the Isis Throne. She might be cast aside. Replaced.

Hatshepsut swallowed her panic.

Aset stepped back, a glowing smile beaming from her pretty face, which was even more radiant now that she carried the pharaoh's child.

"I'm so glad you're happy," Aset said. "I worried you might be upset."

"Upset?" Hatshepsut choked out the word, wiping her sweaty palms on her sheath. "You're doing your part to ensure Egypt's security. The more children Thut fathers, the better."

But she'd sacrifice a young lion to Sekhmet if Aset's babe were a girl.

Aset's face darkened at the mention of Thut fathering more children, presumably upon multiple women. Surely she had to realize that the pharaoh would seek out other bedmates as her waist thickened. It was common for pharaohs to call for parades of Egypt's most beautiful females, ones with well-braided hair and firm breasts whom Taweret had not yet opened up to give birth.

Hatshepsut felt a moment's remorse at her tactless words, but Aset brightened. "Of course," she said. "And this baby will be the first of many."

"I'm sure of it." Hatshepsut's lips were about to crack from the smile she'd plastered on her face.

Aset bit her lip and looked at the floor. "I know the gods will choose my child, but I've always wished for a daughter. Someone to teach to dance and tell all my secrets." Her face had a dreamy, far-off expression, as if she could envision such a future.

"Have you told Thut yet?"

Aset shook her head. "I wanted to tell you first."

Hatshepsut's smile wavered. Perhaps history would stray from its origins and allow her and Aset to remain friends, to avoid the pattern that Ahmose and Mutnofret had begun. "Thank you. That means so much to me."

Aset yawned into the back of her hand. "I'm sorry," she said sheepishly. "I can barely keep my eyes open these days. I'd stay in bed all day if I could."

Hatshepsut threaded her arm through Aset's and led her toward the door. "Go rest. After all, you might be carrying Egypt's heir." She swallowed hard to wash down the sour taste of the words. No matter how she liked Aset, it was not the job of a *rekhyt* to birth the future hawk in the nest. That responsibility was hers and hers alone.

Aset's hands framed her flat belly and she gazed down in a moment of wonder before she pulled Hatshepsut into a last hug. "I'm so excited!" she said. "And I know you'll conceive soon—perhaps we'll even be pregnant together!"

Hatshepsut couldn't answer, only watched as Aset's dancer's body swayed to silent music down the hall to her chambers.

She retreated to her apartments, the tomb plans all but forgotten. This new situation threatened to cut the fragile ties between her and Aset. Hatshepsut had only one aspiration left in this life: to regain her control as Great Royal Wife. Without that, she was nothing.

There was plenty of time for her to conceive, but the sooner, the better.

And yet there might be a way to speed the process.

She'd ignored the box of Djeseret's herbs and amulets these past months, but now they beckoned with the promise of a heavy womb. Isis, Hathor, and Taweret had all received countless pleas from Hatshepsut to conceive Egypt's heir, but to no avail. If the goddesses had forsaken her, perhaps the dried herbs and Min's amulet would at least ensure she didn't trail too far behind Aset.

She threw open the lid of the ebony box and removed the worn leather pouch, its gilded Eye of Horus staring into her *ka*. She despised herself for succumbing to the albino witch's promise, even as she clutched the hope the purse held. This was simply a matter of practicality, a measure to secure Egypt's peaceful future. It was her duty. And her salvation.

She slipped the magic amulet into her pocket and made her way back to the airy bedchamber, past the bed she'd shared with Thut. Sitre looked up from organizing a jewelry box as Hatshepsut pressed the precious bag into her *menat*'s hand. "I need you to brew these into a tea for me."

Sitre recognized the bag. "Of course, *sherit*. I heard from Aset's handmaid, she's not had to wash her linens in over a month."

"Word travels fast." By sunset the news would have spread to every farmer and fisherman on the Nile. She hoped that by next month the same *rekhyt* would proclaim her own pregnancy.

CHAPTER 12

The herbs were bitter but potent.

As Aset's belly swelled, Hatshepsut could scarcely rise from her couch each morning. When she did manage to pull herself to a somewhat erect position, it was only to heave the remnants of yesterday's meals into the limestone toilet basin. Sitre and Mouse had to rinse the pot quickly, lest any noxious odors further upset their mistress's fickle stomach.

"The babe is strong." It was the first acknowledgment from Sitre of the inevitable and happy truth: Hatshepsut was with child, her monthly courses having been tardy for several weeks now.

"Strong?" Hatshepsut could barely raise her head from her limestone pillow. She wished she could stay on the decadent coolness of the tiled floor all day.

"He's already attached himself strongly to you." Sitre hovered over Hatshepsut and stroked her forehead.

"Why didn't Aset have to endure this misery?" Hatshepsut asked, feeling the need to retch again.

Sitre chuckled and wrung out a towel from the washbasin to place on the back of Hatshepsut's neck. "It's different each time for every woman. And this will pass soon enough."

"I'll try to remember that."

"Have you told your mother?"

Hatshepsut managed to shake her head. "Not yet. I planned to tell Thut today. I can't wait to have my bed to myself again."

"He'll be thrilled. Two babes in so little time—"

"You mean he'll be extremely proud of himself." Hatshepsut struggled to her feet. "At this rate he'll have a string of heirs to choose from."

Sitre helped her stand. "That's what your father thought."

"True." Her father had sired four legitimate sons and two daughters, but only one of each had survived. Hatshepsut's hand fluttered to her stomach, marveling that Egypt's future heir could be growing within her. A son would clear her path to the throne again, something not even Thut could deny. She'd have her old life back. Almost.

She prayed every day to Isis to forget Senenmut, but the goddess turned a deaf ear to her pleas. And so it should be. His death was a scar her *ka* would bear until the day her heart was weighed against Ma'at's feather.

She sank to her knees before a new shrine to Isis and Taweret. She'd also included Djeseret's tiny statue of Hathor, although the cow goddess of love stood behind the other two goddesses. The musky scent of incense filled her nose as she began her daily chant to the protectors of expectant mothers. She'd never been so dedicated in her prayers, but, then, she'd never needed the goddesses' blessings so much.

She prayed for a boy.

Princess Enheduanna arrived just as Hatshepsut felt the first flutter of life in her womb, like a tiny bird opening its wings to fly for the first time. The nobility had gone to the river to welcome the Akkadian princess to the City of Truth, led by Mensah in his new vizier's robes, and all strutting like gaudy peacocks in their best linens and jewels. Thut had gifted Aset with the privilege of leaving the Hall of Women to greet Enheduanna in a closed cedar litter, so she might see but not be seen. He'd also given her a priceless bolt of gold linen blessed by a priestess of Hathor. Her slaves had transformed the material into a flowing tunic that somehow managed to hide the swell of her belly. There had been no gifts for Hatshepsut.

"I wish I could stay behind," Aset had muttered to Hatshepsut that morning in the courtyard. "I wish the whore's boat would sink."

Hatshepsut's lip twitched. Aset had taken it into her head that Enheduanna resembled the Akkadian goddess of love, Ishtar, courtesan of their foreign gods. Now Aset referred to Enheduanna only as "the whore" or "the prostitute." Of course, that was only when they were alone. The moment she slipped up in front of Thut promised to be terribly entertaining.

"And what if the princess can swim?" Hatshepsut had said. "You'll be far more useful at the docks than shut away here. Perhaps you can manage to trip Enheduanna before she bows to Thut."

"So she falls on an already hideous face." Aset had flashed a wicked grin, then kissed Hatshepsut on the cheek. "I'll see what I can do."

She had climbed into the waiting litter and let the linen curtains flutter shut. The slaves' footsteps had disappeared and the palace had fallen silent, as if holding its breath.

Hatshepsut watched from the audience window above the Walls of the Prince, uncaring if Re beat down upon her. She shielded her eyes, the timid breeze shifting the translucent linen over her swollen belly. The official excuse for her absence from the procession was a difficult pregnancy, and while she was still sick in the mornings, she'd heard the whispers spoken about her, had demanded that Mouse and Sitre spare no details.

"They claim the pharaoh banished you from his bed." Mouse had made that report weeks ago, finding the tiles on the floor terribly interesting as she spoke.

"I'm pregnant. Thut doesn't need me in his bed, nor do I have any desire to be there."

"He still calls for Aset." Mouse glanced up, then stared at her bare feet. "Almost every night. The court thinks she might replace you if her babe is a boy."

Hatshepsut felt her cheeks burn. "I don't care what the court thinks. They would do well to remember that *I* am Great Royal Wife, daughter of one pharaoh and wife to another."

Sitre folded her arms under her heavy breasts. "Then perhaps you should start acting like it."

"I don't know what you're talking about."

Sitre grabbed her by the shoulders and glared at her. "You've been headstrong and wild since the day you fell from your mother's womb, but you aren't stupid. People realize it's no coincidence Senenmut left court the same time you disappeared into the Hall of Women. Your chair is empty next to the Isis Throne, your sun disk setting while Aset's rises."

"My sun disk isn't setting."

"You're locked in the Hall of Women, ignored by the pharaoh, and ready to drive me mad." She threw her hands up in exasperation. "If you don't do something, I'll soon have to knock some sense into you."

Hatshepsut shook her off, sure that things between her and Thut would improve. But they hadn't so far.

And now she stood alone above the Walls of the Prince, watching the garish parade of courtiers snake its way up Waset's streets and under the Great Double Gate, her brother triumphantly leading the entourage of his latest concubine. He rode in a golden chariot drawn by a sleek black stallion, while an open, gilded litter carried Enheduanna behind him. The Akkadian princess was not ugly—far from it. Her bare breasts were like ripe melons swaying with the movement of the litter, and although her ruffled blue skirt and coiled silver crown reeked of her foreign blood, her black hair shone like polished ebony and her cheekbones were as high as Ishtar's. Slaves had strewn the path with white and blue lotus petals, the crowd cheering wildly at the sight of the foreign princess given to their god. Yet another of Egypt's vassals paid homage to the pharaoh's greatness. Everything was as it should be.

Thut and Enheduanna passed under the Great Double Gate, continuing to the main courtyard until they passed from sight. Only then did a carved cedar litter come into view, its white curtains drawn.

Aset.

Hatshepsut climbed down the stairs into the courtyard of the Hall of Women, waiting with hands clasped before the colossal gilded gate. The guards pounded their spears on the ground, and her heart echoed the sound. Then the gate swung open and Thut entered, Enheduanna on his arm.

"This is the Hall of Women, your new home," Thut said. His eyes fell on Hatshepsut and he gave a tight smile. "And this is Hatshepsut, my sister and Great Royal Wife."

Hatshepsut felt like a hippo before the princess's tiny waist and full hips. Even the woman's bow was as graceful as a swan's, the bracelets of silver on her wrists and ankles tinkling. Her musk perfume was so strong even the winds must have been heartsick.

"We are pleased to welcome you to the Two Lands." Hatshepsut forced her lips into a smile. "I hope your journey was pleasant."

Thut helped Enheduanna to her feet, his fingers brushing the firm flesh of her breast. The nipple puckered at his touch.

Hatshepsut swallowed the bitter taste in her mouth, saved from saying any more by the arrival of the cedar litter. Slaves pulled away the curtains and Aset emerged, still graceful but encumbered by her swollen belly.

A smile flickered over Enheduanna's full lips, gone so quickly that Hatshepsut thought she might have imagined it. But, no, the Akkadian's eyes still laughed as Aset scrambled to Hatshepsut's side.

No matter the cloth of gold, Aset still looked and acted like a *rekhyt*. Hatshepsut felt her cheeks burn with anger and embarrassment for her.

"And this is Aset," Thut said. "As you can see, both my women currently carry my seed."

Aset's hand clutched Hatshepsut's behind the folds of their skirts. Her nails bit into Hatshepsut's palm.

Enheduanna smiled and dared to bring Thut's hand to caress her stomach, then lower. "As will I," she said, her musical voice heavily accented. "Very soon."

Thut called for Enheduanna that night.

Ignored by Thut, Hatshepsut and Aset rubbed goose lard and almond oil over their bellies as the last days of Peret slipped into the season of Shomu, when donkeys were piled high with the fruits of the harvest and led to market. Aset had developed a penchant for pickled turnips, the smell of which made Hatshepsut more nauseated than usual. They ignored Enheduanna as she paraded past them each night in a cloud of perfume on her way to the pharaoh's chambers, clad only in her rainbow of foreign skirts and the newest jewels Thut had showered upon her. Often Aset would fall asleep in Hatshepsut's bed, hands clasped under her chin and knees tucked up to her expanding belly, its stretched flesh now marred with a web of angry purple lines. Sometimes they would lie together, hands on the other's bellies, giggling at the tiny kicks they felt within.

And yet, every day Hatshepsut sent silent prayers to the goddesses, begging for a daughter for her friend. And a son for her.

But Hatshepsut also thanked the gods for Aset. Time hadn't dulled the void left by Senenmut's death, but she tried to comfort herself with the idea of him in the Field of Reeds, preferably shoveling dung, as he'd once joked about. She wanted him happy in the afterlife, but not too happy, not since he had planned to abandon her anyway.

Everything was as the gods willed it.

Now if only she could make herself believe that.

She was tying the bow on the linen wrapping hiding a pair of turquoise scarab earrings—a gift for Aset—when a frantic pounding at her door startled her. The package slipped through her fingers and fell to the floor. Alarmed, she squatted to retrieve it as Sitre opened the door.

Aset stood in the courtyard, face flushed in the morning sunlight as she clutched her swollen belly, her waters breaking and raining down upon the tiles. She opened her mouth to speak, but a spasm of pain tightened her distended stomach and her fingers gripped the wood of the doorframe, knuckles as pale as the moon while she mouthed a prayer to Taweret.

"Help me move her," Sitre said.

Hatshepsut grimaced as Aset transferred her viselike grip from the doorframe to the soft flesh of Hatshepsut's arm.

"Help me!" Aset's primal cry rent the air as the three women shuffled inside.

Those two words sent a dagger of fear into Hatshepsut's heart and she recited her own silent prayer to the hippo goddess of childbirth. This was what she would endure a few short months from now. She could rule all of Egypt, but the threat of childbed terrified her.

It wasn't the first time she wished she'd been born a man.

"This way." Sitre led Aset to Hatshepsut's bed and helped her kneel so the bed supported her upper body.

"Is this it?" Aset's voice was small, her face half-buried in the feathered mattress.

Sitre took her station behind Aset and rubbed her back to relax her. "Your waters broke, Aset. Taweret willing, your babe will be born soon." She looked to Hatshepsut. "The child is early, but the birthing pavilion was arranged a few days ago, wasn't it?"

Hatshepsut nodded. "Should we move her?"

Aset whimpered as the next pain began. "What about the midwife?"

"You'll be fine," Hatshepsut said. "Sitre has delivered plenty of babies." Aset didn't need to know that the last one had been seventeen years ago and now stood awaiting instruction from her *menat*.

"Aset, I need to see how far along the baby is." Sitre washed her hands in a basin. "That way we'll know if we can move you." Aset moaned in response, a birth pain full upon her. Sitre patiently waited for it to pass, then felt for the babe's head. Her eyes widened in surprise and a ready grin split her lips to reveal two rows of crooked teeth. "This child is ready to enter the world. It's time for the blocks."

"I can't," Aset moaned. "It's not time."

Hatshepsut had never felt more useless. Sitre returned to her position to knead Aset's back. "We need the blocks."

Aset wailed in agony.

"I'll get them," Hatshepsut said.

She flew to the birthing pavilion, a darkened arbor off the Hall of Women used by scores of women over the years to deliver royal infants. It was customary to give birth outside so the blood of life could return to the earth, and also to allow the desert breezes to confuse the demons from the netherworld that sought to steal the *kas* of the mother and child. One bright morning seventeen years ago, surrounded by Sitre and the goddesses, Ahmose had given birth to Hatshepsut. The pavilion held only the few accoutrements necessary for the impending royal birth: an ivory clapper to ward off evil spirits, a pile of amulets to Hathor and Taweret, a large clay bowl, plenty of fresh linens, and the birthing blocks. The bricks were gaily painted with vibrant scenes of happy new mothers surrounded by the bevy of gods and goddesses called upon for a safe delivery. This was dangerous work Aset embarked upon, one that many women never returned from, claimed instead by Anubis.

Hatshepsut pocketed several amulets and an ivory clapper, then hurried back to her own chambers with the bricks.

Aset was still draped across Hatshepsut's bed, moaning and writhing from side to side as if to shake the babe from her swollen body. Sitre took the blocks from Hatshepsut. "This babe is in a hurry."

"Come to the blocks." Hatshepsut wrapped her arms around Aset's waist to help her stand and positioned her feet squarely on the blocks. "Taweret will keep you safe." She looped one of the amulets around Aset's neck and placed two more at her feet.

Aset squatted, sitting on the blocks and howling with each pain. It didn't take long before the head emerged, a dark swirl of hair followed immediately by the rest of the body.

A boy.

Hatshepsut snapped the ivory clapper together so that the loud crack would scare off any spirits seeking to harm Aset or her son. The flood of disappointment that surged through her was thrust aside at Sitre's next words.

"The cord."

The umbilical cord, pulsing with Aset's blood, was wrapped tight around the child's neck. The baby's face matched the blue of the cord. He still hadn't made a sound.

"What's wrong?" Terror made Aset's pupils huge as Sitre untangled her son and massaged his chest.

Hatshepsut pushed sweaty tendrils of hair from Aset's eyes and blocked her view with her body. "Everything's going to be fine. Give Sitre a moment."

Aset tried to shove her away. "Let me see my son!"

Hatshepsut sent a prayer to Isis to spare the child just as she heard the first cry. The child opened his little pink mouth and howled at having been so rudely expelled from the comfort of his mother's womb. They didn't need a priestess or the seven Hathors to decipher the child's destiny. His first sound had been a gusty *"Ny!"* and not the ill-fated *"Mbi!"*

Aset's son would live.

"Congratulations." Hatshepsut wanted to cry and laugh at the same time as she hugged her friend and helped her off the blocks to the waiting bed. Sitre cut the umbilical cord with a bronze knife, wrapped the infant in white linen, and handed the precious parcel over to Aset's waiting arms. The child nursed greedily, sucking loudly and leaving all three women to marvel at the perfect fingers and toes, the whorl of dark hair on his crown tangled with traces of the womb.

"Thank the nine gods he was early," Sitre muttered under her breath, so quietly that Aset couldn't hear. "If the babe was any bigger, he'd never have made it out. We would have lost them both."

"Thank the gods," Hatshepsut repeated.

The entire court waited to hear news of this birth. Hatshepsut was tired and Re hadn't even reached the pinnacle of Nut's belly. Aset must be exhausted.

"Thut will want to know he's the father of a healthy baby boy." Hatshepsut hoped no one would notice the note of envy that crept into her voice. The eldest son would not be hers. She had failed yet again.

"Thank you. For everything." Aset barely looked up from her baby as she nibbled the traditional honey cake that all new mothers ate to keep demons from the netherworld at bay. The monsters walked upside down, had mouths for anuses, and ate their own feces, but were repulsed by the sweet taste of honey. Aset would have been a tempting target for them, her cheeks flushed and brown hair lit with a halo in Re's afternoon light.

Hatshepsut left them to dream together. To her surprise, she found Thut waiting in the hallway. He leaned against the wall with his eyes closed, but straightened as she closed the door, a soldier on alert. She caught a whiff of natron, a sign that he had purified himself for Taweret.

"How is she?" he asked, arms clamped in front of his chest.

"Aset is well. She's resting now."

"And the child?" He took a step toward the door, but stopped short.

"You have your son."

His face was transformed. He whooped and pulled Hatshepsut into a giant hug, lifting her off her feet and spinning around. She laughed with him, feeling for a moment like the old times, before they were married and everything fell apart. His sentiment would echo through the kingdom as fast as a falcon's flight, an unstoppable wave spreading to every farmer and fisherman along the Nile. Hatshepsut only wished she were the instrument of such joy. But her time would soon approach, and, with any luck, her fully royal son, the true heir, would be welcomed with the same joy.

Thutmosis shoved open the door and strode into the room. "I want to see my son!"

He planted a kiss on Aset's forehead and plucked the sleeping infant from her arms. "You've made me the happiest man alive, Aset. I love you."

Standing forgotten in the doorway, Hatshepsut turned to go, embarrassed to intrude on such an intimate scene. Thut's next words stopped her in her tracks.

"His name will be Tutmose."

Their father's name. The name Hatshepsut planned to call the son of her own body. Instead, her brother had bestowed that precious gift upon the child of a common-born dancer. As much as she loved Aset, she couldn't swallow the slight.

She stepped back into the room. "That was the name I'd chosen for my child, should the gods grace me with a son."

Thut and Aset looked up from their happy cocoon. Her brother shrugged. "Your child will have a different name, one blessed by the priests." He hugged his son to his chest and pressed his lips to the baby's forehead. "But this, my firstborn, is Tutmose."

Hatshepsut's face tightened. Either Thut was being deliberately cruel or incredibly thoughtless. "May we discuss this later?" she asked. This discussion would end in disaster if she continued now.

Thut shook his head, his gaze fastened on Aset and his tiny son. "There's nothing to discuss. It's only right that my firstborn should carry our father's name. We'll find another name for your child." His eyes swept over her rounded belly. "And who knows? You may bear a girl."

He'd already deemed her a failure.

Hatshepsut's hands ached to slap him, claw his eyes, and make him take back those horrible words. Aset's huge brown eyes implored Hatshepsut to let the matter drop.

Gnashing her teeth, she forced herself to concede. She would never win now that Thut had made up his mind. It was small consolation to know that Ma'at would judge him harshly for this one day when he passed to the West. Ammit might devour Thut's heart before he reached the afterlife, but Hatshepsut would make him regret this move in this life.

She blinked back hot tears.

"As you wish," she whispered.

CHAPTER 13

"Is it a boy or a girl?"

The Royal Physician cleared his throat and shifted his weight from one hip to the other. "I took the sample of your urine and sprinkled it on both the barley and emmer seeds. The test is not always accurate, but if the barley sprouted, the child would almost surely be a boy."

"And if the wheat were to sprout—"

"The child would likely be a girl."

"And which was it?"

Gua frowned. He pursed his lips together, holding back the words Hatshepsut so desperately wanted to hear. Finally he heaved his shoulders into a shrug. "Both the barley and wheat have sprouted, *Hemet.* The test is inconclusive."

Hatshepsut closed her eyes against her disappointment. She had known the test would likely be futile, but she was weary of watching Thut parade Aset's son before her.

With Aset's dancer's figure returned, she had been welcomed back into Thut's bed as soon as her period of purification had ended. Then, just a few nights ago, she had crawled into bed next to Hatshepsut, her feet cold and her skin prickled with gooseflesh.

"Enheduanna is pregnant," she whispered. Her hot tears spread in a stain upon Hatshepsut's back. "He sent me away to spend the night with her. What if she has a boy?"

And what if Hatshepsut had a girl? Nothing would ever be the same.

But she had smiled and dried Aset's tears, patted her hand. "Thut will always love you and your son. Only the gods know what will happen."

"I love you, Hatshepsut." Aset had wiped her nose with the back of her hand. "And I've been doing everything I can to convince Thutmosis to forgive you. He'll come around eventually—I know it."

And yet so far he hadn't.

The past month had been torture and now there would be two more months to endure before Hatshepsut would know whether she was mother to a royal princess or the future hawk in the nest.

"Thank you." She motioned to Mouse to show the physician from her chambers, then rubbed her belly. "You're going to keep me in suspense, aren't you?"

There was a resounding kick against her hand. She giggled and patted the spot. It shouldn't matter if she had a boy or girl; she would love this child no matter what.

But it would be better if it was a boy.

When her time came there were no gushing waters or screams. The net of henna tattoos painted on her abdomen had done its duty to keep the child tucked safely within her womb until the babe was ready to emerge. Those painted ochre threads were stretched to their breaking point as Hatshepsut's labor began. Surrounded by Sitre, Mouse, and her own mother, she clamped her lips against the screams that threatened to break as she strained and struggled for two full days to bring new life into the world. It wasn't until the full moon that her child decided to be born, the smell of warm earth and flowers wafting through the night air to mingle with the salty scent of sweat from

Hatshepsut's skin. Finally, in the darkened arbor of the birthing pavilion, supported by the same bricks that had held Aset, she felt a perfectly formed and healthy baby slide from her womb and into Sitre's dark hands.

A girl.

Hatshepsut startled as Sitre snapped the ivory clapper. Her daughter whimpered, but the sound was an icy fist around Hatshepsut's heart.

"Mbi!"

Quiet, but unmistakable. The first cry of a child bound to die.

Hatshepsut hushed her with kisses and a hennaed nipple. Wide-eyed, her daughter suckled greedily, scarcely the demeanor of a babe about to be claimed by Anubis.

Hatshepsut was enraptured with the little creature as tears streamed down her cheeks and she looked into eyes as bright as Nut's belly. The tiny girl yawned and clutched her mother's finger with the strength of one much bigger than she.

She would not die. Anubis would have to claim Hatshepsut before he could tear her daughter into the afterlife.

Sitre looped an ivory amulet of a rising moon around Hatshepsut's neck, and her mother left to seek the pharaoh and inform him of the birth of his daughter. Thut arrived dressed in a sleeping robe and as rumpled as if Ahmose had pulled him from bed herself. She probably had. The kohl around his eyes was smudged; he had either been sleeping or otherwise engaged, likely with Aset or Princess Enheduanna. Perhaps both.

Regardless, Thut hadn't been waiting outside her door as he had for Aset. That stung more than Hatshepsut would ever admit.

She set aside the honey cake she'd been nibbling and the other women shuffled from the garden. Thut frowned and held the baby far from his chest. His daughter stared at him with wide eyes and whimpered once but didn't cry. "She has your nose and lips," he said.

"And your ears."

"Perhaps." He handed the bundle back as if the baby had been possessed by an upside-down demon. At least he had held her long enough to claim her as his own. His gaze slid toward the gate.

"I won't keep you any longer." Hatshepsut hugged her daughter close, breathed in the new scent of her.

"You'll have a boy next time." Thutmosis offered the platitude as he would a trinket. "I'm glad to see you've delivered safely."

"Neferure and I are fine, thank you." The name she had chosen for her daughter rolled from her tongue—"Beauty of Re," one of the sweetest sounds she had ever heard. This baby would be her sunshine, the radiant light in a life that had been gray until now. She refused to ask for Thut's approval of the name, still stinging from his theft of their father's name. She had carried and birthed the child; she would name her daughter, Thutmosis be damned.

"Neferure?" His eyebrow arched. He seemed poised to attack the name, but his gaze darted to the gate once again. "I suppose the name will suffice."

Their daughter chose that moment to cry, the tiny mewl of a kitten that made Hatshepsut's breasts tingle with a rush of milk. She positioned Neferure to nurse, but Thut grabbed her hand. The baby howled, but her father ignored her.

"What are you doing?" Infuriated, Hatshepsut swatted his hand away, but Thut pulled Neferure from her arms. The child's cries brought a regiment of women armed with angry scowls. Ahmose, Sitre, and Mouse all looked ready to attack if Thut didn't release the infant.

"You're not thinking of feeding her yourself, are you?" Thut asked. Neferure's face was now as red as the radishes that grew in the palace garden.

"I most certainly am," Hatshepsut replied. She reached for the child, but Thut held her just out of reach. Had the battered flesh between her legs not protested, she'd have lunged from the bed to throttle him.

He thrust the wailing infant into Sitre's arms and shook his head at Hatshepsut. "You will bind your breasts, and as soon as Gua deems you ready, you'll be back in my bed again. I will get a son on you and, in the meantime, a wet nurse will be found to feed this girl."

Hatshepsut's fingernails bit into her palms. "I will do as I wish with my body. You have no right—"

"I have every right." Thut's voice rose above their daughter's howls. "And you would do well to remember it." He strode to the gate, pausing only to fling his last order to Sitre. "See to it that a wet nurse is found for the child tonight."

The gate slammed. Ahmose was the first to move. She took Neferure from Sitre's arms and brought her to Hatshepsut.

"There's no reason you can't take care of her now." She murmured the rebellious words as if she feared her stepson might overhear. "You have fourteen days of cleansing, far from Thutmosis' eyes."

Hot tears trickled down Hatshepsut's cheeks. Her mother wiped them away with her thumb. "It's hard, Hatshepsut, but bearing the pharaoh's son *is* your duty."

"I hate him." Hatshepsut finally dared to say the words aloud. She had admitted her mistake to Thut, had more than paid the price. Still he tormented her. "I hate him more and more with every day."

"Don't think about the pharaoh right now," Sitre said. "Think about your perfect daughter instead."

She was right. Neferure yawned, her tiny pink hand splayed over Hatshepsut's pale breast like a little lotus blossom. The trace of her daughter's eyelashes fluttered against the softest skin she had ever seen.

She had just met this little person, but already she loved her more than anything else in this life. Neferure would be her lasting achievement, her gift to this world.

Nothing Thut could say or do mattered in the face of such perfect love.

CHAPTER 14

"Enheduanna is going to have a boy."

Aset crossed her arms over her breasts, her scowl as black as a desert panther. Neferure and Tutmose squealed, splashing naked in the shallow fountain in the main courtyard of the Hall of Women, Re's light on the water throwing dancing reflections onto the walls. It was a truly perfect day, no matter the news of the Akkadian princess.

Hatshepsut tucked the edges of her sheath into her belt and kicked off her sandals. "We're not gods. None of us can predict the future."

"The Royal Physician predicted she'd have a boy."

"That's what Gua predicted for her other babies, too," she reminded Aset quietly.

Aset's scowl softened and she almost smiled. "And look how those turned out."

This latest pregnancy was Enheduanna's third, the first two having ended in early stillbirths. Gua had been right about both—each was a boy, formed like flawless granite, and, like the perfect stone, destined never to draw a single breath of air.

Despite the girl's sufferings, Aset refused to have anything to do with the Akkadian princess and managed not to be in the same room with her, but Hatshepsut had attended the burials of both mummified infants, placed amulets on the tiny bodies, and chanted prayers to Anubis for their safe passage to the West.

She might not care for the Akkadian, but not even Enheduanna should have to endure the burden the gods had placed upon her. A haunted woman with empty eyes and pale skin had replaced the haughty princess who had entered the Hall of Women. Enheduanna was no foreign goddess, but a woman like any other.

"We should take her amulets to Taweret." Hatshepsut tossed off her wig and jumped into the fountain. She swept Neferure into her arms, tickling her slippery ribs and giggling as they chased Tutmose in circles. She shouted over the laughter. "And maybe say some prayers for her."

Aset rolled her eyes, raising her voice to be heard. "I'll pray to Hathor that Thutmosis tires of her and sends her on the first boat back to Akkad."

Hatshepsut glanced up to reprimand her. Enheduanna stood in the courtyard, surrounded by her slaves, close enough they all must have heard Aset.

"I heard screaming." Enheduanna's accent was still thick despite her time in Egypt. She tilted her chin in the air, crimson spreading up her chiseled cheekbones. "I thought someone was hurt."

"Just playing." Hatshepsut gestured to her dripping sheath with a weak smile. "You're welcome to join us."

Enheduanna glared at Aset. "Perhaps some other time." Then she turned on her heel and stormed off. Girl-slaves still dressed in the Akkadian style trailed behind her like colorful geese, whispering behind their hands as they glanced back at the fountain.

Hatshepsut set down Neferure and handed her a lotus blossom, waiting until Enheduanna's door had shut behind her before frowning at Aset. "You're cruel to her."

"Nothing she doesn't deserve." Aset shrugged. She grinned, the dimples she so hated denting her cheeks. "You look ridiculous."

Hatshepsut bent, scooped water into her hands, and flung it straight at Aset. Her friend shrieked and sputtered as Hatshepsut swept one laughing child under each arm and ran. Aset gave chase, their golden laughter scattering cats and echoing through the courtyard.

Like Enheduanna's, Hatshepsut's life was different than she'd imagined, and it had its share of hardships. But she had physical comforts, a beautiful daughter, and a friend she loved.

That was much more than some women could claim.

The haunted woman disappeared, replaced with one in perfect health and vibrant motherhood. Enheduanna's skin glowed, her hips spread, and her breasts and stomach swelled. Yet one morning she took to her bed, complaining of a headache. When Hatshepsut stopped by at dusk, the room was as warm and dark as a womb. She'd brought a tonic of honey and chamomile, but the unconscious concubine burned with fever, her skin flushed and breathing ragged.

"Can I do anything to help?" she asked Gua.

"Pray for her." The Royal Physician sighed and packed up his leather satchel, leaving a golden Eye of Horus on Enheduanna's forehead. "You might stay with her so she's not alone."

She sat with Enheduanna, but not by herself. She sent for Aset.

"I came only to see if the rumors are true." Aset stayed by the doorway, her nose wrinkled at the rancid smell of death. Anubis lurked in the dark corner, patiently awaiting his prize. "I'm not staying."

"Not only are you staying," Hatshepsut said, motioning toward a pile of fresh linen, "but you're also going to use those towels to wash her."

"Why in the name of Hathor would I do such a thing?"

"Because it's the decent thing to do. And then you'll be able to tell Thut that you helped nurse poor Enheduanna back to health. He'll sing your praises to eternity."

There was a long silence, then a dramatic sigh. Aset tossed a towel in a golden ewer of water, barely wrung out the linen, and slapped it on Enheduanna's forehead. She gave the concubine's hand a perfunctory pat. "There, there," she said to the unconscious girl. "Everything's going to be all right."

She was wrong. By nightfall Enheduanna's body was cold, she and the unborn babe both claimed by the jackal god of death.

Hatshepsut and Aset folded Enheduanna's arms over her swollen stomach, then chanted prayers as the priests of Anubis slunk away into the night with the body. At least Enheduanna would receive a decent burial here in Egypt, not sewn into the skin of a ram and tossed into a barren pit as would have happened in her homeland.

"Sekhmet's breath," Aset whispered as they watched them go. "I feel terrible. Guilty, actually."

Hatshepsut glanced about the dim chambers, strewn with damp towels and amulets. Anubis' stench overwhelmed Enheduanna's musk perfume. "Guilty? Why?"

"I hated her, wished her dead more than once." Aset choked and clutched Hatshepsut's hand. "But I didn't mean it. You don't think the gods heard me, do you?"

Hatshepsut squeezed her hand. "The gods do as they wish. Nothing we say or do can sway them once they've made up their minds."

She'd learned that the hard way.

"Neferure! Be careful!"

Hatshepsut bolted off her chair. Her daughter stood on tiptoe below a rickety shelf, about to pull a rack of ancient papyrus down upon her head. She scooped the little girl into her arms and righted the shelf, feeling the prickle of her daughter's shaven head against her cheek. The clump of hair on Neferure's scalp was scarcely long enough to gather into a youth lock on the side of her head, the fine strands of mahogany woven into a tiny braid and tied with a jaunty yellow string.

"Mama scared?" The girl's chin wobbled, but Hatshepsut tickled

Neferure's ribs until she giggled. She'd never encountered such a sensitive child as her daughter, so different from herself when she was that age. A single harsh word could send Neferure into a flurry of tears that might last all afternoon.

"Yes, you little monkey, I was very scared." Hatshepsut tried not to look too stern, instead covering her daughter's chubby cheeks with kisses. "Would you like to go see the animals?"

"Yesh!" The imp placed her little hands, still sticky from the honey she'd eaten at lunch, on Hatshepsut's cheeks and planted a sloppy kiss on her lips. Neferure squirmed from her mother's arms and grabbed her hand, yanking her in the direction of the Hall of Women's new royal menagerie. Thut had ordered the pens and cages near the women's quarters built shortly after Enheduanna had first conceived to better entertain what he had anticipated would be his growing brood of children. Instead, only two small children served as the menagerie's meager audience.

The pharaoh and all of Egypt waited for the births of more royal children. Thut took more concubines, filling the Hall of Women with idle chatter and a permanent haze of perfumes. He called Aset to his bed most evenings, but even she failed to become pregnant again. More often than not, Thut couldn't summon his manhood to do his duty when he visited Hatshepsut's bed. It was as though the pharaoh's seed had suddenly withered and died.

And yet, despite all that, Tutmose and Neferure thrived, growing as fast as papyrus reeds.

"Monkeys!" Neferure scampered as fast as her bare feet would carry her, past the fowl yard with the hawks soaring overhead to her favorite animals. The silvery primates chattered in high-pitched voices and jumped from limb to limb when they recognized their favorite visitor. The pharaoh's daughter could always be relied on for tasty treats.

The Keeper of the Menagerie, a long-limbed man named Sebi, lumbered around the corner and offered a frayed basket of green grapes to

Neferure. "I was beginning to wonder if we'd miss you today, *satnesut*," he said, bending down to the girl's height.

Neferure popped a grape into her mouth, but smiled sweetly upon seeing Hatshepsut's pointed look. "Thank you," she chirped. The vervets began talking in earnest now, begging the princess for the precious treats she held. Thut's little monkey, Kipa, now gray around the snout, leapt forward and swiped the grapes from her hands. Neferure squealed with glee. "Monkeys, monkeys, monkeys," she sang, dancing from one foot to the other.

Hatshepsut smiled, enjoying the moment. Her daughter was growing too fast. She wanted to hold on to each instant and draw it out to eternity, cherish each new word and discovery.

"Mama, look!" Neferure pointed up the path. Three figures were coming toward them.

Hatshepsut shielded her eyes from Re's glare to see Thut and Aset swinging Tutmose between them as they walked toward the menagerie. Thut leaned heavily on his cane, but together they managed. "It's your father." Hatshepsut waved and Aset returned the gesture with her free hand. "I'll bet Tutmose wants to see Adjo."

Neferure wrinkled her nose and let out a ferocious roar to imitate the old lion. Adjo was missing almost all his teeth and had only a few patches of hair left, but Tutmose loved him as dearly as Neferure adored her monkeys.

"That was a very good roar, my little monkey," Hatshepsut whispered as the entourage drew near. "Now, remember what I taught you about meeting your father."

Neferure's pretty face grew suddenly somber as she scrambled to perform a *henu*. The bow lacked grace, but was adorable nonetheless.

"You may rise, Neferure," Thut said. He bent to his daughter's height and tugged on her youth lock. "Are you being a good girl for your mother?"

"Yesh." Neferure clambered to her feet as Thut pulled something from the pocket of his kilt.

He held out both fists. "Pick one."

Neferure thought hard, the tip of her tongue between her teeth, and tentatively poked the left with her little finger. Thut grinned and opened his palm, revealing a new green ribbon—Neferure's favorite color. "For my best-loved princess," he said, and tied it over the yellow string at the end of her youth lock.

He might be a terrible husband, but Thut had proven himself a decent father to Neferure, even if she wasn't the son he'd wanted.

He laid his hand on Tutmose's shoulder. "Are you ready to see Adjo?"

"Adjo!" Tutmose yanked his father's hand toward the lion's den.

"I'll take him," Aset said. "You haven't seen Neferure in a few days—I'm sure she'd like to spend some time with her father." Aset intercepted her son and gave Neferure a hug. "Then perhaps you and I can play dress-up later today. I have a new green sash that would look beautiful on a little girl who loves the color green."

Neferure leaned closer to whisper in Aset's ear, loud enough so everyone could hear. "I love green."

"You do?" Aset pretended shock and tweaked Neferure's nose. "Then it will look perfect on you!"

"Would you like your father to help you feed the monkeys?" Hatshepsut asked Neferure as Aset straightened.

"Yesh!" Neferure thrust her hands into the mound of fruit and handed a bunch of plump grapes to her father. Thut watched Aset and his son skip off, then plucked a grape from its stem and threw it to the ground before the chattering vervets. Kipa recognized the pharaoh and jumped onto his shoulder, chattering as if catching up on old times. Neferure giggled.

This was as good a time as any to bring up a subject Hatshepsut had wished to discuss for some time. She took a deep breath and cleared her throat. "I'm going to hire a tutor for Neferure."

She wasn't asking permission, mostly because she could predict Thut's reaction.

"Whatever for?" Thut put Kipa on Neferure's shoulders. "She's a girl. She'll marry Tutmose as soon as she comes of age and bear his sons."

"And she'll be his Great Royal Wife. She should be educated. As I was."

He glanced at her from heavily kohled eyes. "It seems to me you could have done with a little less education."

"And you with a little more," Hatshepsut said under her breath.

"Would you care to repeat that?"

Neferure looked up at her father's tone, but Hatshepsut smiled and kissed her daughter's forehead. "You're doing a wonderful job feeding those monkeys."

Thut's eyes narrowed as Neferure went back to playing with the vervets. "You would do well not to contradict me in front of her."

"If our father saw fit to have his daughters tutored, I see no reason why his granddaughter shouldn't receive the same privilege."

"She's too young," Thut countered, but Hatshepsut was prepared for that excuse as well.

"A child is never too young to learn. Tutmose is already receiving lessons, and Neferure handles a brush and ink well enough to scribble. She's old enough to start learning basic hieroglyphs."

"Hieroglyphs? When will she ever need to write anything? That's what scribes are for."

Sekhmet's breath. Hatshepsut wanted to throttle him.

"Scribes aren't always reliable," she said, struggling to keep her voice even. "Especially if you can't read the characters yourself. Our daughter is royal. She will not be ignorant."

"Fine." Tight-lipped, Thut waved his hand to dismiss both her and the conversation.

Hatshepsut felt a flush of triumph. She'd have gone ahead with the tutor anyway, but it was better to have an understanding with Thut to avoid any future disagreements. After all, these days she made it a point not to deal with her brother if she could avoid it.

"I need to go inside," Thut said. There were beads of sweat at his temples, tiny glistening drops bleeding into his kohl, yet it wasn't that hot outside.

"Is something the matter?"

He shook his head and pushed hard with the heel of his hand above his heart. "I don't feel myself today."

"Perhaps you should get some rest."

Her brother appeared ready to agree, but smiled at something behind her. She turned to see Aset and Tutmose on their way back from the lion, the little boy running down the path. Hatshepsut had already ceased to exist.

"And, brother, at your leisure, I have plans regarding some improvements to Karnak temple. Obelisks and whatnot." This was one of those projects Thut wouldn't let her take part in anymore, but she itched to get her hands on the temple plans. He'd have to acquiesce sooner or later if she badgered him enough. At least that's what she told herself.

"Fine, fine." Thut waved his hand again.

There was much chattering from Tutmose to his father about the lion, little of it discernible, but Thut played along. Aset shot Hatshepsut a sympathetic look over her son's head.

"Have fun with the monkeys, Neferure," Aset said. "I'll see you this afternoon. I have a new dance to show you, too." She planted a kiss on the girl's scalp as the pharaoh and Tutmose walked back up the red dirt path to the palace. Aset hurried to catch up with them, then paused to wave at Hatshepsut and blow Neferure a kiss.

Neferure had the love of not one, but two mothers. And although she hadn't borne him, Hatshepsut had been surprised to discover her love for Tutmose. She thanked the gods again for bringing Aset into her life.

Kipa and one of the other monkeys hung upside down by their tails, causing Neferure to try to stand on her head. Hatshepsut held the basket of grapes with one hand and was brushing the dirt from her daughter's hair with the other when a scream rent the air.

"Thutmosis!" Aset's yell sent the monkeys screeching and scampering for the safety of the treetops.

Hatshepsut turned in time to see Thut stumble off the path and fall headlong into the red dirt. She waited for him to rise, but he didn't move. Aset collapsed to her knees, and Tutmose's forlorn wails joined his mother's as Aset tugged on her husband's arm.

"Thutmosis, get up!" Aset's voice was panicked.

Hatshepsut dropped the grapes. They burst underfoot as she ran to Thut's side as fast as her feet would carry her.

"Help me," she said to Aset, but Thut was too heavy for both of them, his limbs like sacks of grain. Sebi hurried over and used his heft to help roll Thut over.

"I'll get Gua," he said, shooting a worried look at the pharaoh's face, as white as alabaster.

Thut was barely conscious, his breathing erratic and his glassy brown eyes rolling with terror. He gripped Hatshepsut's hand with the strength only those confronting Anubis could possess. She felt for his heart, which was pounding as it raced ahead to Ma'at's scales in the afterlife.

"Thutmosis." Aset's eyes bulged from their sockets. Tutmose sat on her lap, his tears tracing wet paths down the dirt on his face. "You have to get up. Our son—"

Neferure began to cry, a peripheral sound that barely reached Hatshepsut's consciousness until she felt her little hand on her shoulder.

Anubis was quick this time, unwilling to allow the pharaoh's *ka* to linger in this life when the jackal god had already been intoxicated by the scent of death. Thut opened his mouth once, then twice, looking like one of the carp freshly pulled from the Nile. His eyes pleaded with Hatshepsut. His fist a vise on hers, the pharaoh managed to push two words out of his throat.

"Help Tutmose."

And then he was gone. The grip on Hatshepsut's hand slackened, and the heart that had raced so ardently rested from this life and prepared for the next. Thut's glazed eyes stared past her, and Aset sobbed quietly, arms wrapped tightly around her son, as she stared at their husband. Hatshepsut gently pressed Thut's eyelids to forever close them to this world. His face was smudged with red dust, a premature death mask that would soon be replaced with one of gold.

She became aware again of Neferure, the whisper of the girl's tiny hand on her back.

"Father hurt?" Her lower lip trembled.

Hatshepsut nodded and drew Neferure onto her lap, treasuring the sweet smell of life on Neferure's sun-kissed skin. The two women and their children surrounded the pharaoh, a funereal wreath around the dead. Pounding footsteps heralded the approach of Gua and the *medjay,* their spears ready to slay any enemy who threatened their pharaoh. But it was too late—their weapons were useless against Anubis, Guardian of the Dead. Nothing could call Thut back to this world now that his *ka* had flown into the sky.

And that meant one thing: Hatshepsut would be regent, ruling Egypt single-handedly until her two-year-old stepson came of age.

PART III

REGENT

1488 BC – 1481 BC

O my heart—
May naught stand up to oppose me in the presence of the
    lords of the trial,
Let it not be said of me and of that which I have done,
"He hath done deeds against that which is right and true."

—*BOOK OF THE DEAD*, FROM THE PAPYRUS OF NU:
    PRESERVING THE HEART

CHAPTER 15

The double crown dwarfed Tutmose's head, falling over his brow to almost obscure his bright eyes. The combined red crown of Lower Egypt and the white crown of Upper Egypt was an enormous weight upon such a young boy. The *uraeus* ringed the shaven head of a child who had barely seen two harvests, the stealthy cobra poised to strike anyone who dared threaten the new pharaoh.

The High Priest of Amun chanted a hymn and climbed the steep steps through a heavy cloud of incense onto the dais. The scent of myrrh was thick in the air as Tutmose eyed the leopard skin draped across the priest's shoulders, the cat's mouth frozen in a yawn of death. Hatshepsut wondered how her stepson would feel in later years, given such power but unable to recall the day it was bestowed upon him. If he remembered anything at all, it would likely be the sight of the leopard, its empty eye sockets watching him as he sat stock-still upon the throne.

And what would she remember if she were in his place? The heavy weight of the double crown? The expectant looks on the faces of her courtiers? Or a rush of terrible joy?

She pushed the thoughts away. The gods had seen fit to make her regent, a position few women in Egypt had ever managed, and even fewer had handled successfully. Egypt under her hand would grow and prosper, and Tutmose would become pharaoh when he came of age, just as the gods willed it.

The priest finished his hymn to Amun and handed Tutmose the ceremonial crook and flail, the same ones her father and Thutmosis had held when passing judgment in the Court of Reeds. Her stepson squirmed upon the hard seat of the Isis Throne, the sacred triad of gods spreading their arms to wrap the little pharaoh in a golden embrace.

Hatshepsut nodded to Tutmose, their secret cue for him to stand. He grasped the crook and flail and tottered to his feet. The double crown slipped down to his eyebrows, and she had to resist the urge to straighten it upon his head. A small group of nobility gathered below the dais for the ceremonial crowning of a child who wouldn't be ready to rule for at least a decade. Amidst the faces was the new pharaoh's mother. Today anxious pride was evident in Aset's twisting hands and beaming face. And yet underneath her expertly applied kohl, dark circles of grief ringed Aset's eyes.

The High Priest of Amun stepped aside and his voice boomed across the hushed throne room to announce the new pharaoh's titulary for the first time. "Tutmose, the being of Re is established; Horus strong bull arising in Thebes; two ladies enduring of the kingship like Re in heaven; golden Horus powerful of strength, holy of diadems; king of Upper and Lower Egypt; Menkheperre, Son of Re Tutmose, beautiful of forms!"

The courtiers clapped politely at the boy wearing the trappings of the highest office in the Two Lands. Hatshepsut's gaze lingered for a moment on each of their faces. Her hand had selected them all. Each was a man she inherently trusted—aging Admiral Pennekheb; jovial and hardworking Ineni; and two courtiers new to her inner circle, twin brothers Ti and Neshi, now Chief Treasurer and Chancellor. They were all men who would continue to support her while she served Egypt in her new role, and each was eager to impress the new regent. Mensah wasn't there; her brother's vizier had been put under permanent guard in his chambers until Hatshepsut could finalize her plans for him.

She wore no golden headdress or double crown to proclaim her new position, but she was now the acknowledged leader of Egypt, although her role as regent would last only until Tutmose reached adolescence. All her struggles were brought to fruition today. There would be no obstacles placed in Hatshepsut's path as she sought to continue the golden era for Egypt that her father had begun.

This time, she wouldn't fail.

Unbidden, Djeseret's curse surfaced in her mind, words Hatshepsut had forgotten for almost three years.

Your name shall live forever.

You shall be the downfall of those you love.

Egypt will prosper, but those closest to you shall find only anguish and ruin.

As regent, Hatshepsut's name was inextricably linked to that of three pharaohs: her father, her brother, and now her stepson. Chiseled onto monuments, her likeness and name would forever be tied to young Tutmose, and both etched into eternity. Egypt would prosper under her hand, but she scoffed at the last words of the portent of gloom. Those closest to her—Aset, Tutmose, and Neferure—would never suffer because of her, not if she could help it. Neferubity and Senenmut had long ago settled into the Field of Reeds, but Hatshepsut's hand hadn't caused Thut's death. Thinking about her brother, Hatshepsut admitted a certain dose of grief at Thut's passing. One by one, Anubis had recalled her family members, leaving only her mother, Mouse, and Sitre as fragile links to Hatshepsut's childhood.

The witch who had prophesied the curse was a fraud. She had to be.

As soon as the ceremony finished, the nobles dispersed and a *menat* whisked Tutmose off to the nursery. Thut's passing had postponed the search for Neferure's tutor, but Hatshepsut promised she would find someone to teach both children as soon as the seventy days of mourning ended.

Admiral Pennekheb and Ineni stopped her after the ceremony, both of their expressions as serious as if etched onto their tombs.

"We hoped to have a word with you." Pennekheb scanned the crowd, his eyes young in the face of one so old. "Alone."

"Of course," Hatshepsut said. They followed her to her office. The servants had moved many of her belongings over earlier that day, after a fair bit of sweeping and dusting. She sat in her father's old chair and rubbed her hands over the worn wooden armrests, then motioned for the men to take the seats opposite her.

"What is this urgent matter that is making you forgo the festivities?"

The two traded knowing glances. "We're concerned for your safety," Pennekheb said.

"My safety?" That was the last thing on her mind. "Here in the palace? I have the *medjay* nearby, at least most of the time."

"Nearby? Most of the time?" Pennekheb groaned and shook his head.

"You're the regent of the Two Lands now." The topic only somewhat dampened Ineni's perpetual smile. "Do you realize what would happen if someone decided to harm you?"

"Or if they succeeded?" Pennekheb asked.

She hated that they were right. "The Isis Throne would be fair game for anyone, at least until Tutmose comes of age," she admitted. She rubbed her temples, feeling a headache coming on. "I promise to increase my guard. And Tutmose's as well."

"A prescient idea. I would propose keeping a personal bodyguard with you at all times," Pennekheb said. "One can't be too careful."

"I really don't think that's necessary." She didn't care to always have someone lurking in her shadow.

Pennekheb didn't hesitate. "It *is* necessary, at least until the dust settles on the succession. There could be any number of possible domestic coups, not to mention foreign uprisings. Do you have anyone in mind for the position of bodyguard?"

"No," Hatshepsut answered. "But I'm quite sure you do."

The men exchanged a quick look, confirming her suspicions of a conspiracy. "One of your brother's former guards, a man named Nomti, is held in high esteem by the other men. He was elevated to the *medjay* in your father's later years, based on his service in the Division of Thoth. Of all the present guards, he should most please you," Pennekheb assured her. "He will protect you with his own life and isn't afraid to speak his mind."

Ineni's eyes twinkled and his cheeks dimpled with a fresh smile. "It's what got him removed from Osiris Thutmosis' service."

That piqued Hatshepsut's curiosity. "I like him already. What did he do?"

"You can discuss that when you interview him." Pennekheb stood, his joints creaking in protest, and Ineni followed suit. "We just wanted to make sure you were protected. I'm quite sure Nomti can recommend other men who would be suitable for guarding the pharaoh."

"Thank you, gentlemen." Hatshepsut rose to show them out. "Whatever would I do without you?"

Ineni gave a little bow, hand over his heart. "We wouldn't care to find out, *Hemet.*"

She watched them depart, Pennekheb leaning on his cane like a willow in the breeze, while Ineni shuffled beside him like a hippo searching for shade. They were an unlikely pair of councilors, but strong and steady. Hatshepsut beckoned to a waiting attendant. "I require a meeting with Nomti, one of Osiris Thutmosis' former *medjay.* Summon him to the palace immediately."

She pushed back the billowing sleeves of her tunic, grinning at the mountain of papyrus scrolls on her table. In the meantime, she had work to do.

Nomti was announced before the horizon swallowed Re that evening. He had to duck to avoid hitting his head on the top of the door. She immediately recognized the swirling vortex of tattoos on his face and arms, the face that would send most of Egypt's enemies cowering into a corner. A foreigner, probably a Hittite. Gooseflesh crawled up her arms. She didn't care to think about the last time she'd seen the man, outside her brother's chambers.

"Nomti, I've summoned you because my advisers believe I should have a permanent bodyguard with me at all times." She turned her back to him so he wouldn't see how he'd disconcerted her. Could she trust this man with her life? Almost two heads taller than she was, with shoulders like an ox, he could certainly hold his own against anyone who sought to harm her. But he'd been there the night Senenmut had died, and he might have had a hand in carrying out her brother's orders.

"Your advisers are wise men."

"They believe you would be the best man for such a post. Do you agree?"

"I do. If the gods will it."

She finally turned to face him. He stared straight ahead, hands clasped behind his back. "I understand you were released from service by Osiris Thutmosis?"

The black lines around Nomti's eyes hardened. "Yes, I was."

"And?"

"Osiris Thutmosis didn't take kindly to a guard questioning his edicts."

"Did you ever question my father?"

The tattoos around his eyes softened at the mention of the elder Pharaoh Tutmose. "Your father was a good man, *Hemet*. He welcomed the opinions of those who spoke their mind. Your brother did not."

"May I ask what my brother did that made you question him?"

"I asked Osiris Thutmosis if it was fair to beat a defenseless man."

Her body went cold. She shouldn't ask any further questions, but couldn't stop herself. "And what man was that?"

"Senenmut of Iuny. I served with him during the campaign in

Canaan. He was reckless, but a brave man with a good *ka*. He came to see the pharaoh just before you did that night."

"I remember."

His eyes flicked to her face for a moment, but then he looked away. "I didn't hear everything that was said, but Senenmut resembled a pile of meat when he was dragged from the pharaoh's rooms afterward. I asked the pharaoh whether Ma'at would agree with such treatment. He dismissed me on the spot."

"I see."

And then Senenmut was executed, his heart ripped from his body.

"It was brave of you to question my brother." She struggled to keep her mask in place. "If you're prepared to accept the position, I'd be well served to have you as my bodyguard. I've been accused of having a temper, but I always welcome honest opinions."

Nomti's lips turned up, probably the closest gesture to a smile he ever managed. "I would be honored to accept, *Hemet*. It will be a privilege to protect the royal family again."

"I'll expect you tomorrow morning. I hope you're an early riser— I'll be in my offices before Re rises."

Nomti bowed, then paused at the door. "May I offer you some advice, *Hemet*?"

"Of course. Everyone else does these days."

"It might be best to surround yourself with more men who are loyal to you. Like Senenmut."

She flinched, swallowed hard. "Senenmut is dead."

"I hadn't heard of his passage to the West."

"My brother had him executed the night he was beaten."

Nomti cocked his head at her. "I believe you were misinformed, *Hemet*. Senenmut was banished, not executed."

She shook her head, trying to keep her voice level. "My brother only wished for the court to believe he'd returned to Iuny. I have Senenmut's heart buried in my garden to prove otherwise."

Nomti arched an eyebrow at her. "I don't know whose heart is in the dirt of your garden, *Hemet*, but it is not Senenmut's. I watched him being thrown onto the boat bound for Aswan, destined for a life of hard labor, but there are rumors he was released and is back in Iuny, serving the Temple of Thoth."

She stared in shocked silence, unable to draw words into her mouth. She'd spent the past three years locked in the Hall of Women, surrounded by walls tall enough to silence all rumors of the outside world. Rumors and perhaps the truth, too.

Hope flickered deep in her *ka*. He might be alive.

"*Hemet?*"

She blinked. "Are you sure?"

"I know only what I saw. Senenmut might not have survived the journey to Aswan, mangled as he was, but he wasn't executed. At least not that night."

"Thank you, Nomti. I'll see you in the morning."

She waited until the door closed before falling to her knees. Perhaps the gods had played a terrible trick on her. What if Thut hadn't found it in himself to order the murder of his friend?

Hope was a terrible thing.

She needed the rest of the story. And there was only one other person who might possess it.

Hatshepsut ignored the hasty *henus* of courtiers and slaves as she made her way to the Hall of Women. The name was no longer accurate, as she'd dismissed the rest of Thut's women so only Aset remained in the northern wing of the palace. The massive gilded gate was wide-open, no scowling guards standing at attention. Desperate to finally leave the chambers she so despised, Hatshepsut had moved into the pharaoh's rooms as soon as they were emptied, relishing the lack of flowers and perfume, the final feeling of freedom. It was a presumptuous move for a regent and she knew it, but she didn't care.

Aset smiled and waved as Hatshepsut entered the courtyard, then motioned for quiet with a finger over her lips. Tutmose poked a black dung beetle with a stick, and Neferure lay cuddled on Aset's lap, sucking her thumb and idly fingering a linen rag doll that Aset had given her for her second naming day. The doll was from Aset's childhood, its face drawn on anew with Aset's kohls and malachite eye paints. Neferure was the only daughter Aset would ever have now that Thut had gone to the West.

Neferure's face brightened as she spotted her mother. "Mama!" She leapt from Aset's lap and into Hatshepsut's arms, and just as quickly writhed to get down, pulling Hatshepsut's hand as she pointed to the giant black beetle scurrying across the fountain. "Bug! Bug!"

"It's a scarab," Hatshepsut said, kissing the top of her head. "He's a very special bug related to Khepri, the god of rebirth."

"Sca-rhub." Neferure ignored the religion lesson to try out the new word as Tutmose stalked the beetle. As the children became entranced with their six-legged visitor, Hatshepsut signaled for their *menats* to take over.

Aset stifled a yawn behind her hand. She looked worn, but it wasn't as if the duties of the pharaoh's mother—making sure Tutmose ate his vegetables and attended his lessons—were strenuous. More likely it was still grief at Thut's passing that etched the lines around her lips and stole the luster from her skin. A faience jug of wine sat on the table next to her, its clay seal bearing Thut's cartouche and first regnal year discarded on the ground.

"Tutmose did well at the coronation." Aset's breath smelled strongly of wine, not for the first time since Thut's death. She watched the children's antics with the scarab. "He'll be a strong pharaoh one day."

It seemed presumptuous to gauge Tutmose's future talent as a ruler based on his ability to sit still as a child, but Hatshepsut wasn't going to say that to Aset. She shifted in her seat. "I had an interesting conversation with one of Thut's former *medjay*, a guard named Nomti."

Aset rubbed the back of her neck but didn't take her eyes from the children. "The name sounds familiar."

Hatshepsut continued. "He was dismissed from Thut's service the night Senenmut was banished to Aswan."

Aset's eyes jerked to Hatshepsut's. "He told you that?"

"He told me Senenmut wasn't executed, but banished to the quarries," Hatshepsut said. "Is that true?"

The long silence was interrupted only by the children's squeals and the hushed admonitions of their nurses. Aset bit the edge of her thumb, but finally nodded. "Yes."

"And you never told me?"

Hatshepsut's tone was so sharp that Neferure looked up with wide eyes, but a nurse quickly distracted her. Hatshepsut lowered her voice. "Don't you think that's something I'd have wanted to know, that I hadn't caused a man's death?"

"Thutmosis made me swear I wouldn't tell you." Aset clasped her hands in her lap and looked up with sad, wide eyes. "I couldn't disobey him."

"He made you swear because he wanted to punish me."

Aset stared at her a long moment. "That, and because it was by my request that he didn't kill Senenmut."

"What?"

"I asked Thutmosis not to kill Senenmut." She shrugged. "Maybe it was Hathor speaking through me—I don't know—but it didn't seem right to kill a man who'd acted out of love."

"Senenmut wasn't in love with me."

Aset sipped her wine and said nothing.

"And my brother listened to you?"

"A man will do all manner of strange things for the woman he loves."

"And Thut loved you." Hatshepsut had thought at first that he might have been acting to spite her, gifting Aset with lands and spending most of his free time in her chambers, but it had become clear over the years that he truly loved the woman. Hatshepsut might never forgive him for his treatment of her, but some small part of her was glad that both he and Aset had enjoyed love, at least for the short time they were together.

"Senenmut was one of Thut's best advisers," Hatshepsut said, changing the subject. "Someone I'd like to have back at court."

Aset frowned and set down her wine. "You think that's wise?"

"What do you mean?"

"You're regent now, the most powerful person in all Egypt. And you're a woman. Don't you think any man would jump at the chance to share your bed, to use you as his puppet?"

Hatshepsut gaped, at a loss for words.

Aset held up her hands. "Isn't there a chance that you'd be vulnerable if Senenmut returned? After all, he planned to leave you that night anyway."

"We don't know that. He might have planned to return." The words sounded ridiculous the moment they were out of her mouth. "And I would never let a man use me like that." But she remembered Senenmut's ambition, his thirst for power. Would he try to use her to stand in the shadow of the Isis Throne?

She shook away the thought. Such worries were absurd, at least until she knew whether he was even alive. She stood to go, arms crossed before her chest. "Is there anything else I should know about that night?"

Tutmose chose that moment to reappear, carrying the twitching scarab between his fingers. Khepri's minion squirmed, apparently unimpressed at being plucked off the ground by a two-year-old and carted about like a trophy.

"Mama, look!" He shoved the massive beetle in Aset's face.

Aset wrinkled her nose and stepped back. "That's very exciting, Tutmose. Why don't we put the bug back on the ground, where it belongs?"

Tutmose's lower lip trembled and Neferure lifted her arms to Hatshepsut for a hug. Hatshepsut squeezed her tight. "I've got to go, monkey, but we'll play later tonight and have dinner. Does that sound like fun?"

"Yesh." Neferure planted a wet kiss on her mother's cheek and hugged her neck. As soon as Hatshepsut put her down she was off, chubby little legs pumping as fast as they could. Tutmose chased her, the scarab forgotten.

"I'd best go watch them," Aset said.

Hatshepsut touched her arm. "Thank you."

"For what?"

"For saving Senenmut. You're a good woman."

Aset smiled and kissed Hatshepsut's cheek. "It was the right thing to do."

That was true, yet sometimes the right thing was the hardest to do.

Hatshepsut had written to Cretan kings, Nubian vassals, and the High Priests of every god in Egypt. But this brief invitation to court was the hardest she'd ever tried to write.

The rest of the palace had long been silent, so only the moon and a sputtering oil lamp kept her company. Crumpled balls of papyrus littered the floor, and her fingers were stained with so much ink that they'd be black for days. She bit her lip and scanned her latest attempt at the letter.

Greetings, Senenmut:

By the blessings of the gods, may this letter find you well. My daughter, the princess Neferure, is now two years old, and I wish to have her educated by a tutor I trust. Please reply with haste if you are amenable to such a position.

May the soles of your feet be firm,
Hatshepsut, Lady of the Two Lands

She frowned as she reread the letter. She was probably a fool, but she had decided to assume Senenmut was alive, letting hope overcome her *ka*. If he wasn't, the letter would be returned with its messenger. She would deal with that setback when it came, not before.

This was a formal request, and one she wanted accepted. She wished she could offer him a loftier position, but she didn't want to court the gossip that would inevitably ensue. Should he accept her offer, he would surely prove himself capable and clear the way for future promotions.

The letter would have to suffice. She scattered sand over the ink, rolled the papyrus, and bound it with a red string tied in a double knot. Mouse's lusty snores threatened to wake the dead from the other side of her slaves' door, but she tiptoed past it and down the pharaoh's private corridor to the Hall of Women. Aset's room was perfectly silent, her friend's head propped up on a cedar headrest and her lips turned up in a gentle smile. Hatshepsut shook her awake.

Aset groaned like she was birthing a camel. "This better be good. I was having the most wonderful dream about Thutmosis."

"I need this delivered to Senenmut," Hatshepsut said. Nomti would never agree to leave her for so long, and the only other people she might trust with so important a letter were Sitre and Mouse. Her attendants were too old to undertake such a journey.

Aset blinked, then struggled to sit up. "You mean you want me to leave the palace?"

"Please," Hatshepsut pleaded. "I can't trust this to a regular messenger."

"You'd let me travel from the Hall of Women?"

"Thut is dead." Hatshepsut spoke softly.

"But I'm the pharaoh's mother. Is it safe?"

Hatshepsut was taken aback, having thought Aset would jump at the opportunity to take a trip. She hesitated for a moment—perhaps Aset knew better than she did the dangers that lay outside the palace walls—but shook off her doubts. "It should take only a couple days to travel to Iuny and back. Nothing will happen to you or Tutmose while you're gone. Dagi will take you upriver on one of the smaller boats and even accompany you into the city to deliver the letter."

Aset seemed to mull over the idea, then nodded slowly. "If I leave now, then Tutmose and Neferure will hardly notice I've been gone."

Hatshepsut hugged her. "Thank you, Aset. I owe you."

"I'm sure I'll find a way for you to repay me." Aset tapped her chin with her finger. "I just have to figure out what to wear."

Hatshepsut watched her friend rise and start riffling through her many ebony trunks, then padded silently to her own bed. Now she had to wait for a reply.

The next few days were going to be torture.

CHAPTER 16

D ays passed.

Hatshepsut lay naked on the cooling room's granite slab, limbs spread so her skin touched only the cold stone. Wet reed mats hung from windows, chilling the meager breeze to provide some cool air during the day. More mats soaked in shallow silver trays filled with water. Girl-slaves waved falcon-wing fans, wafting the tepid air over her flushed body. This was the only habitable room in the palace now that they were at the height of Shomu. It was too hot to think, much less move.

"Did the priests of Anubis addle your brains, you thickheaded buffoon?" Aset's shrill voice sounded from the other side of the door. "I don't care if the regent gave orders not to be disturbed—I'm the mother of the pharaoh, and I have information she'll want to hear."

Hatshepsut sat up to tell the guards to let her in, but Aset pushed through the door on her own. She was sweat stained, her wig plastered to her head and a thin sheen of perspiration on her upper lip. Hatshepsut dismissed the bath slaves with a wave of her hand. "I see you got past Nomti's guards."

Aset waved everyone from the room. "People scatter like ants if you act like you're in charge. Anyway, those guards have been clubbed over the head a few too many times."

"I'll remember to tell that to Nomti."

Aset mopped the sweat from her brow and handed over a rumpled papyrus. Hatshepsut unrolled it, letting the string drop to the ground. She had to squint to scan the lines. "I don't understand." She frowned. "This is the letter I wrote."

"I found Senenmut's mother, widowed and living on the outskirts of Iuny," she said. "I tried to deliver the letter to her, but she's a *rekhyt*."

"So?"

"She can't read."

Hatshepsut wanted to kick herself. Of course the woman couldn't read.

"So you left?"

"No, I read it to her. I didn't think you'd mind me opening it."

"And—?"

Aset shook her head. "Senenmut won't be coming to court."

"Why not? If it's the position, I plan to promote him as soon as I can, possibly make him Steward of the God's Wife or Steward of Amun—"

Aset laid her hands over Hatshepsut's. "Senenmut's not coming back because he died in the quarries. He's dead."

Hatshepsut shook her head so hard her earrings slammed against her neck. "That's not possible. Nomti said he was still alive."

"Nomti was wrong. I heard it straight from his mother's mouth. He's gone to the West."

"No."

Hatshepsut refused to believe it. But the bright light of hope in her *ka* dimmed, leaving her emptier than before. She had lost him a second time.

"His death was probably a gift from the gods after so long," Aset whispered and squeezed Hatshepsut's hands. "Two years at the quarries would be enough to make anyone pray to Anubis to come for them."

"But I thought he was alive. I thought after all this time—"

She couldn't get the words out. Instead, she hurled a clay pan at the wall, showering the room with water and shards of terracotta. It didn't make her feel any better.

"You thought you could apologize to him," Aset said. "That you could live again."

Hatshepsut sat down, hard. "How did you know?"

"I may be a *rekhyt* myself, but I'm not stupid. Something broke in you when Senenmut left, but you changed the day you heard he might still be alive." She touched Hatshepsut's cheek. "It seemed you might be happy again."

She gave a wan smile. "I suppose now we'll never know."

"That's up to you." Aset straightened. "You can choose to be miserable for the rest of your life, blaming yourself for what happened, or you can thank the gods for the short time you had together."

"I'm not sure I feel like thanking the gods for anything right now." She stood, picking up her damp sheath and slipping it over her head. "I need to get dressed."

"Perhaps you should stay here for a while longer, clear your mind—"

"The day is ruined." Hatshepsut straightened her shoulders as if preparing for battle. "There's other unpleasant business I might as well attend to."

Two guards stood at attention outside Mensah's cell in the palace. His new room was adjacent to a set of storerooms, stocked full of onions and garlic, from the smell of them. Clay jugs of wine stood in lines on wooden racks in the hall, fermenting for a second time. The former vizier would be lucky to be harvesting onions or straining grapes when Hatshepsut finished with him. She had a mind to banish him to Aswan so he could share the experience of what he'd done to Senenmut. Ma'at's justice demanded that someone pay for everything she'd been through, for everything Senenmut had suffered. It might as well be Mensah.

The guards opened the door for her, but her eyes took a moment to adjust. Mensah's chamber was windowless, filled with the sour smell of stale urine and fear. Nomti had done well when she'd told him to find the most uncomfortable room in the palace to hold the traitor.

A guard struck the wick of an oil lamp and it flared to life, illuminating Mensah sitting cross-legged in the corner. He blinked against the sudden light and tried to shield his eyes from the lamp. Black stubble covered his scalp, grown during the time he'd been locked away, and his cheekbones had taken on leaner lines, yet his face and body were still chiseled like the statue of some pompous god. He wouldn't be so pretty when she was finished with him.

She took the lamp from the guard and motioned toward the hall. "I'll call for you when I'm done."

Mensah bowed in a sort of *henu*, arms bound behind his back in copper shackles. She left him with his forehead pressed to the dirt, and circled him like a lioness about to devour her prey. She intended to play with her food before she destroyed him.

"I'd offer you a chair, but, as you can see, I haven't any at the moment." He dared glance up at her, but she pushed his face back into the ground with her foot. "I wondered when you'd come."

"More like you wondered when you'd have to pay for what you have done," she said. "I come seeking Ma'at's justice."

"As you should." He kept his face to the dirt. "But perhaps you might like to hear the whole story before you order me thrown into a sack and drowned in the Nile."

"I have more creative ways to watch you die. And I don't need to hear the story. I lived it. You followed Senenmut and me into the desert, embellished the tale to my brother, then lied to me so I would come watch the drama unfold. You destroyed a man and ruined three years of my life."

"Is that how it seems to you?"

"Of course that's how it seems." She tipped his chin with her foot so he had to look her in the eyes when next he lied. "Because that's how it happened."

"That's only part of the story. Didn't you get my message?"

"The drivel about trying to protect me?" She threw her hands up. "I won't stand here and listen to your lies."

"It's not a lie. I was only trying to save you."

"Thut beat me that night, locked me in the Hall of Women for three years, and ordered Senenmut's death. How is that saving me?"

"Senenmut was dangerous for you. Don't you see?" Mensah sat back on his feet, his shoulders slumped. "Let's say I ignored all I saw in the Western Valley. Do you honestly believe you and Senenmut wouldn't have found yourself in a similar situation later, that you wouldn't have done something more reckless than just kissing him?"

She didn't answer.

Something in his face seemed to break. "I loved you, Hatshepsut. I'd have done anything for you. Thut would have discovered you two sooner or later, and he would have had you both killed. I had to save you, even if it meant hurting you."

She swallowed, clenching and unclenching her fists. "I wasn't yours to save. And you didn't have to follow me in the first place."

"Thutmosis ordered me to."

"Because he thought I'd be unfaithful with you." She laughed, the sound hollow. "And you were bound to obey, following your orders with relish. My brother seemed to believe that Senenmut and I shared more than a kiss. Who else might have planted such an idea in his mind?"

Mensah shrugged. "The pharaoh jumped to his own conclusions. I told him only what I saw."

"So, you thought to control my fate?"

"Not control. Only save you from yourself."

"But then you lured me to Thut's chambers with the lie of his illness. I had to watch my brother beat Senenmut and then face his wrath."

"I have no excuse for that." He hung his head. "I was overcome when I saw you with Senenmut in the valley. You cast me aside and took up with a *rekhyt*. Any man would have been beside himself with jealousy."

"But you're not any man, Mensah. You were vizier to Osiris Thutmosis, and the son of one of Egypt's most noble lineages."

"And you're the daughter of Sekhmet. You don't know the power you hold over men, Hatshepsut. I'm only a man. I loved you."

"But you betrayed me."

"And I'd betray you again to save your life." He tilted his chin in defiance. "I'd die for you if I had to."

"That won't be necessary." She stared at him, still angry, but much of her fury and lust for revenge suddenly deflated.

"We could be good together, Hatshepsut. You rule the Two Lands now, but I could help you. My family has helped Egypt rule for centuries. You wouldn't have to be alone."

The man had gall.

"You shall be stripped of your land and titles. You shall take up residence at the Temple of Amun and do the god's bidding as a *wa'eb* priest."

Reduced to rags and forced to do the work of a *rekhyt*. It was more than he deserved.

"You are the regent of Egypt. The land sails in accordance with your command." He bowed his head. "I will do as you wish."

His voice stopped her at the door. "I still love you, Hatshepsut. Think of what I said."

"Speak of it again and I'll have your tongue cut out."

She slammed the door behind her and stormed past the wine jugs and around the corner, cursing under her breath. It would have been easier to kill Mensah and be done with him forever, yet she didn't want that stain on her heart, hadn't been able to bring herself to order his execution.

Was that mercy or weakness?

She stared out a window at the Nile and drew a shuddering breath. She'd let him live.

She hoped only that she wouldn't one day regret the decision.

Hatshepsut sat stiffly upon her throne in the Court of Reeds, a simple ebony chair dwarfed by the empty Isis Throne next to her. One day little Tutmose would join her for audiences, but for now she sat alone upon the royal dais. This, the deliverance of Ma'at's justice to her people, was her most important job, and also the most exhausting, especially since she'd expanded the sessions to last all day. She'd settled cases this afternoon concerning the accidental death of a farmer's prized ox at the hand of his neighbor, a widow's plea to rescind the banishment of her eldest son for shirking his annual season of labor at the Temple of Amun, and so many more cases that she'd lost count. Hatshepsut didn't have the heart to turn anyone away; to lose a day's work was a huge sacrifice for a farmer or fisherman. If they could stand outside all day waiting to be heard, she could manage to sit upon a throne once a month to hear their cases.

"I believe that was the last one, *Hemet*." Kahotep, an ancient herald who'd once snuck her almonds from his pocket, peered at his scroll. "I'll make sure there's no one else."

She rubbed her temples and twisted from one side to the other to find some relief for her aching back. Neferure had been ill these past days, feverish and lethargic, so Hatshepsut had stayed up with her, despite the assurances from Gua and several priests that she would be fine. She straightened as Kahotep reentered the throne room, stopping between two colossal sphinx statues.

"There's only one more, *Hemet*," he said, studying his scroll before rolling it up. "Senenmut of Iuny."

Her legs would have given way beneath her had she not already been sitting down.

A dark figure strode into the room, his gait measured in perfectly equal strides as he crossed tiles painted with images of Egypt's enemies. He was dressed in a long kilt and formal wig, his face leaner and his nose possessing a decided list to the right, likely a final gift from her brother. Otherwise he looked as if not a day had passed since that terrible night.

It was really him.

She struggled to swallow, feeling as if a viper had wound itself around her throat.

His gaze was inscrutable, but his eyes met hers for a fleeting moment before he bowed in a full *henu*, forehead to the floor and arms stretched before him.

Mottled scars crisscrossed his bare back, layers of stiff white ridges mangling his copper flesh.

Her hands flew to her mouth, too late to stifle a gasp of horror. Those were not the markings of a normal whip, but the infamous strips of sun-dried hippo hide used by the overseers at Aswan's quarries. Twenty lashings with such a weapon were enough to render a man unconscious, and a hundred meant certain death. Senenmut seemed to have received some number in between. She swayed in her seat. "By the gods."

He stood stiffly. "As Amun endures and as the pharaoh endures—"

She raised one hand to cut off the court recitation and just stared at him, unable to form any words.

He didn't move. "The gods have been generous to you, *Hemet.*"

Hemet. She cringed at the formality.

"They have. I'm glad to see your mother decided to deliver my summons—"

"Summons?" Senenmut straightened. "My own curiosity has brought me here today, not your summons."

"But I don't understand." She frowned. "I sent a message to Iuny requesting your presence at court."

"My mother delivered no such message."

"She claimed you were dead."

"As you can see, I am not." His tone was perfectly measured, betraying no hint of emotion.

"Your mother lied." It wasn't an attack, merely a statement of fact as her mind struggled to make sense of his presence.

"Please forgive her impertinence. My noble mother was likely under the impression that returning to court would not be in my best interests."

"I hope your impression differs from your mother's."

"That remains to be seen."

"And yet you are here."

"As I said, I wished to see the truth of our regent with my own eyes."

Perhaps. Or perhaps now that Thut was dead, the final barrier against Senenmut's return to Waset had been removed, making possible the resumption of his old life at court as well. His arrival had not gone precisely as she'd planned, but either way she was grateful to the gods for his presence.

"You escaped Aswan?"

His eyes narrowed, a flicker of some emotion gone so quickly that she might have imagined it. "After two years of hard labor and bribing the overseer, yes."

If anyone could find a way out of Aswan, it was Senenmut.

"In my message I offered you the position of tutor to the Royal Princess Neferure. And Steward of the God's Wife," she added hastily. She might have offered him the double crown if it would make him stay. "Of course, I'm prepared to compensate you handsomely if you do return to court." She sat, hands folded in her lap, glad he couldn't see her damp palms or the perspiration she felt gathering at her temples. She cursed herself for dismissing her fan bearers.

"The God's Wife?"

"God's Wife of Amun. One of my titles."

He gave a deep exhale and rubbed the bridge of his nose. "You wish me to be your steward?"

"And my daughter's tutor."

She waited for him to respond, to reject her outright or possibly accept. Instead he watched her; then his chest rose and fell in a silent sigh.

"I am not the same man I was three years ago, *Hemet*." His voice was quiet. "You should know that."

He was right. Gone was the self-assured councilor with the easy sarcasm and ready smile. He was obviously scarred, but surely his *ka* couldn't have changed that much.

"And I am no longer the same woman."

"No, I suppose not." His gaze flicked over her, making her more than aware of the bull's tail at her waist, the crook and flail in her hands, and the golden vulture crown over her wig. A heavy pectoral of carnelian, turquoise, and gold covered her breasts. She was scarcely a woman now, dressed in all the trappings of the pharaoh. The heavy *uraeus* bared its fangs at her brow, ready to strike her enemies.

Senenmut would never be her enemy. Still, a voice in the back of her mind asked what might have prompted his return. She was under no illusion that he had come for her, and if she had been, his coolness now would have disabused her of the notion. Yet she knew him, knew he'd crave a position at court and the power he'd once had serving the pharaoh.

She hoped she could still trust him.

She sat straighter on her throne. "Are there any impediments to your accepting such positions?"

Myriad possibilities raced through her mind. For all she knew, he might be married to a *rekhyt* with breasts like watermelons, father to a brood of sons bearing his crooked smile.

"None, *Hemet*." He cleared his throat. "'May I greet the mistress of the land, and may I attend to the errands of her children.'"

She recognized the line from the ancient pages of the *Story of Sinuhe*. "So you accept?"

"I do."

She kept her face a mask, despite the unmistakable wave of happiness that surged through her.

Senenmut straightened. "On one condition."

"What might that be?"

"That I have full control of what your daughter is taught, and over your household."

She leaned forward on her throne. "And what do you have in mind?"

"To focus on the current state of your treasury, especially to ensure the Gods' Houses aren't taking advantage of their royal patronage. It would also be wise to inspect the tax revenues received from your nobles. Your father knew that his courtiers excelled at finding ways to avoid paying the full amount they owed to the royal house and he always watched them carefully, a practice I believe might have grown lax under the previous pharaoh."

Hatshepsut couldn't miss his avoidance of her brother's name. She wondered how long it had taken before Senenmut could hear her name without cringing. Perhaps he still did.

"That sounds like a good place to begin," she said, her voice soft. "And my daughter?"

"Neferure should receive a royal education beginning with a study of Egypt's great nine gods and ancient religious texts, and then moving on to learning the languages of our neighboring kingdoms, specifically those of Canaan and Crete. Like the pharaoh, she should also be immersed in the politics and military history of the Two Lands from a young age. I'll find someone else to instruct her on writing hieroglyphs, of course." His face lit with a flicker of a smile that disappeared so fast that Hatshepsut might have imagined it.

She recalled his terrible handwriting and almost chuckled. Instead she gave a solemn nod. "Of course." He could dress her slaves in cloth of gold and teach Neferure to walk on her hands for all she cared at this point. "Neferure will make an excellent pupil."

"She is her mother's daughter."

Again Hatshepsut strained to discern Senenmut's true meaning. Was that an insult or court flattery?

She stood, unwilling to draw this out much longer. "One of the slaves will take you to your new apartments. I'm pleased to have you back with us."

This was not the reunion she'd rehearsed in her head so many times. Far from it.

He bowed his head and backed from the dais, disappearing between the black granite sphinxes and out the giant ebony doors. She waited a few moments before leaving through the side door, scarcely noticing when Nomti fell into step behind her. She'd grown accustomed to his presence over the past week; he was her stealthy shadow day and night.

"Senenmut has returned to court," he said. It was the first time her new bodyguard had offered his thoughts to her without being asked for them.

"I've offered him the position of Neferure's tutor." She purposely omitted the part about his being her new steward. Word of that would spread soon enough.

"I'm pleased. He's a man worthy of your trust." Nomti took his position at the entrance to her chambers. "Watch closely, *Hemet.* Others may not be so happy at Senenmut's return."

She wasn't even sure Senenmut himself was pleased. "What do you mean?"

"There were grumblings before your father flew to the sky, some who believed Senenmut had risen too high for someone with such humble ancestry. There were those who were happy when he disappeared, most especially Mensah and his followers."

"I've taken care of Mensah."

At least she hoped she had.

"His is an ancient family," Nomti continued. "He did not take well to your brother's promotion of a *rekhyt*."

"My eyes and ears will remain open."

"As will mine, *Hemet.*"

She closed the door behind her, glad for the sanctuary of her chambers. Mouse had left a platter of dried fruit and a loaf of brown bread with a jug of red wine from Amun's vineyards. She poured a glass and drank it in one gulp.

No word for almost three years, but here he was. Aloof in the throne room, Senenmut had seemed sedate and perfectly composed. The more she thought on it, the more she was sure he sought only a position at court, no matter how humble.

She pulled her sheath over her head and slid between her bed's cool linen sheets, arranged her headrest, and stared at the blank white ceiling.

It didn't matter. He had come back.

CHAPTER 17

"Where are we going, Mama?"

Neferure climbed the spokes of the massive chariot wheel as if it were a ladder; she hung on to the top and looked back at Hatshepsut with an upside-down grin. Her daughter had recovered from her fever but still wore a healing amulet around her neck, the bones of a young mouse tied in seven lucky knots to keep any lingering demons at bay.

"We're going somewhere you've never been before, monkey, to Karnak. It's the biggest temple in our whole kingdom." Boy-slaves secured a black mare to a second chariot. Nomti stood to the side, waiting to accompany the group into the city.

"Will there be animals?"

"If we're lucky. And you're going to meet your new tutor today. Won't that be fun?" Hatshepsut tickled her daughter, smiling at her giggles as she quashed her own flurry of nerves. Since Senenmut would be in charge of teaching Neferure about Egypt's pantheon and her responsibilities to those gods, Hatshepsut had thought it fitting for them to become acquainted in a temple steeped in Egypt's history. Or perhaps she wanted to torture herself.

Bored with her makeshift ladder, Neferure skipped to the other wheel and climbed to its pinnacle. She seemed about to jump into the chariot's electrum basket when a dark shadow fell from the doorway. Neferure glanced up, then scurried to the ground, attaching herself to her mother's leg and popping her thumb in her mouth.

Senenmut stood at the entrance of the royal stable, dressed this morning in a pristine white kilt, the golden armband of the palace secured high on his right arm. The sight of his broad shoulders made Hatshepsut's legs feel as weak as a newborn colt's.

Neferure's brown eyes stared up at her. "Neferure, this is Senenmut," Hatshepsut said. She leaned down to stroke her daughter's smooth head. "Your new tutor."

Neferure studied him for a moment, her kohled eyebrows knit together. She had spent every day of her life within the Walls of the Prince and rarely saw a face that was unknown to her.

Senenmut stepped forward with a smile so deep it sparked in his eyes. "I'm honored to meet you, Neferure." He reached into the pocket of his kilt, pulled out a small bag, and handed it to the princess. "I thought you might like some marbles. They're most fun when used in a slingshot."

He might have been joking, but it was difficult to tell for sure.

Neferure held the gift close and presented Senenmut with a sunny smile. "Are you coming with us?"

Hatshepsut picked up her daughter, balancing her on her hip. "Yes, he is, monkey. Are you ready?"

"Yesh." Neferure squirmed out of her mother's arms. She clambered into the larger of the two chariots and beckoned for Hatshepsut. Senenmut stood ready to help her into the basket. She hesitated, then touched her hand to his. The brief contact made her heart trip.

She could not be seen swooning like a kitchen slave with a stable boy. Especially not in response to Senenmut.

Hatshepsut secured Neferure and took the reins as Senenmut

joined Nomti in the smaller chariot. "Senenmut, I believe you may remember Nomti from the Division of Thoth. He also served as one of my father's *medjay*."

"Of course," Senenmut said. "And in the service of Osiris Thutmosis, if I recall?"

"Only temporarily," Nomti said.

Senenmut studied Nomti for a moment, shook his head, and looked to Hatshepsut. "Shall we?" he asked.

She flicked the chariot's reins and the horses trotted out of the royal stable and into the bright morning light. They might have taken one of the royal skiffs to Karnak, but she had wanted to go through Waset itself. Thutmosis had rarely left the palace to visit the city's shrines and temples, but now, as regent, she would resurrect her father's custom of riding a chariot through the city.

The City of Truth was a cacophony of yelling voices and braying donkeys. She wanted to urge the horse to run, but the farther they got from the palace, the tighter Neferure clung to her mother's legs. Waves of naked children and dusty *rekhyt* dropped to their knees as the royal chariots paraded down the street. A resounding cheer arose from behind once they'd passed.

"*Ankh, udja, seneb!*"

"They're cheering for us, Neferure." Hatshepsut made her voice heard over the crowd. "Life, health, and prosperity. Can you wave to them?"

The sight of Neferure's hesitant hand waving back encouraged the people to cheer even louder. Hatshepsut's heart threatened to burst with pride.

Her cheeks ached from grinning by the time they reached the entrance to Karnak's vast complex to the gods. The dun-colored walls stretched into Nut's blue belly, carved with hieroglyphs and massive images of the gods. This was the largest of Egypt's temples, a sun-drenched maze of pylons, chapels, and open-air courtyards dedicated to the multitude of Egypt's gods. Solemn *wa'eb* priests dressed in white linen and with shaven heads emerged, scurrying to take the horses and help the party from their chariots.

An apprentice priest motioned to the massive door cut into the boundary wall of the temple. "This way, please." His voice was as soothing as water trickling from a fountain. The outer courtyard contained two shallow pools used by the priests to purify themselves each day before they entered the sacred compound. A young girl—another *wa'eb*—emerged from the sanctuary of the temple with a bundle in her arms and bowed to them. Hatshepsut and Neferure followed her to the closest of the pools, and Senenmut fell into step behind the first priest, the men disappearing from sight as they made their way down to the other lake. Nomti remained behind to guard the entrance.

Surrounded by palm trees at the boundary of a shimmering lake, a polished red granite slab reflected some of Re's light back to the sun god. Upon this the priestess laid out two linen sheaths, startling white in the morning sunlight, and two pairs of new leather sandals, one large and one small. "I'll return to lead you to the temple once you've bathed and changed."

Hatshepsut helped Neferure undress before she took off her own clothes, and shivered in the cool morning air. Then mother and daughter held hands and walked into the lake.

"Mama, it's cold," Neferure whimpered.

"I know, monkey. But you can't insult the gods by praying to them with dirty feet."

Hatshepsut cupped her hands and poured some of the sparkling blue water over Neferure's shoulders, then bundled her shivering little body in linen as quickly as she could before purifying herself with Amun's blessed water. The coarse linen scratched her skin, so different from the translucent material she was used to, as soft as down. She almost forgot something she'd brought along, retrieved the treasure from her sheath, and tucked it into her pocket. The small bulge against her thigh reassured her.

When both were clothed in the rough dress of the priesthood, the young priestess led them back to Senenmut. He was similarly garbed in a priest's crisp white kilt, with plain leather sandals on his feet.

"You're ready now." The original *wa'eb* gestured to them to follow him through the courtyard. This time Senenmut walked at Hatshepsut's side.

"You could pass for a *rekhyt*," he said.

"I rather like it," she said. "I may decide to dress like this from now on."

"And give up all your gold and jewels?" He slowed his pace to fall into step behind her. "I doubt that very much."

So he thought her greedy? Vain? Selfish?

She squared her shoulders, chin tilted as if marching into battle. She didn't care what he thought.

The courtyard stretched before them, the carefully cultivated grass and trees an oasis of green in the midst of the city. The open-air complex was so vast that few of the city's thousand sounds floated above the looming walls. Hidden in every corner and alcove were myriad shrines and temples dedicated to almost all of Egypt's gods and goddesses. Meandering through the buildings and open courtyards were various animals sacred to the gods themselves—cats treasured by Bast, the precious ibis and baboons of Thoth, and the rams of Amun. Occasionally an animal's snort disturbed the tranquility, but otherwise the compound was a silent refuge tucked within the city.

As they walked past one of the small temples, Neferure tugged on Hatshepsut's hand. "Mama, that one's broken," she said, pointing to a structure that had fallen in on itself.

"The temple of Mut," the priest informed them. "The infidels ravaged the sacred building and it has yet to be rebuilt."

"Infidels?" Neferure struggled with the mouthful of strange syllables, as if Senenmut's marbles filled her mouth.

"Not that long ago, Egypt was ruled by bad people named the Hyksos. They didn't take care of the land." Hatshepsut looked at the pile of rubble that had been Mut's sacred monument within Karnak.

The mother goddess likely still seethed from such disrespect and neglect.

Dropping Neferure's hand, she walked to the dilapidated ruins, drawn to them as to someone injured or bleeding. The stones of the crumbling wall were warm under her hands as she traced the faded outline of Mut carved into one of the blocks.

Senenmut approached, his footsteps muffled by the earth and grass.

"You could rebuild this." His quiet words were a caress that perfectly mirrored her thoughts.

"I know." She didn't look at him. The next words jumped from her tongue unbidden. "Will you design it for me?"

There was a silence broken only by Neferure's happy exclamations in the distance. Hatshepsut focused intently on the image of Mut's vulture headdress and willed the maternal goddess to sway Senenmut's answer, if only to beautify the goddess's own domicile.

"Of course."

Hatshepsut closed her eyes and sent a silent prayer to Mut in gratitude. The sound of Neferure calling her name was a welcome distraction.

"The red granite from Aswan would certainly do Mut justice," Senenmut said. "I can write to Amenhetep and have him measure the blocks as soon as you're ready."

"Amenhetep?" She'd never heard the name before.

"The overseer of Aswan's quarries."

The man he'd bribed to set him free. Those three years would always sit between them, a wall never to be breached.

"Mama! Come see the towers!" Neferure barreled past Senenmut to grab her mother's hand. Hatshepsut allowed herself to be dragged to the manicured path, feeling Senenmut's gaze upon her back. She looked to where Neferure pointed, the shafts of two perfect obelisks piercing the sky. Their golden caps glinted so brightly it was impossible to look at them, the embodiment of the sun god's rays here on earth, for long.

"Those are obelisks." Senenmut crouched next to Neferure. "Do you know who built them?"

The braid of Neferure's youth lock wiggled back and forth like a garden snake as she shook her head.

"Your grandfather," Senenmut said. "You never got to meet him, but he was an impressive man, a pharaoh to be remembered through the ages. Do you know Ineni?"

Neferure nodded. "He gives me cakes."

Hatshepsut chuckled, knowing Ineni would happily plead guilty to the charge. Senenmut's grin matched her own, the first one they'd shared since his arrival.

"Ineni is a very nice man and an old friend of mine," he said. "He helped your grandfather build those obelisks. Would you like to see something else they built together?"

"Yesh." Neferure held out her chubby little hand for Senenmut's. He took it and the two walked together to a nearby building, Hatshepsut and the priest trailing behind them. The sight of the thick white scars crisscrossing Senenmut's flesh stabbed her *ka*.

They walked to the hypostyle hall, a project Osiris Tutmose had commissioned soon after he had assumed the Isis Throne. Its tall cedar columns had each been painstakingly carved by a master craftsman to represent a single stalk of papyrus. Together the painted columns created a bright marsh of the precious reeds, an ancient symbol of creation since the days of the first pharaohs. Re's light streamed through the roof to bathe the room with a golden glow, and dust motes swayed lazily in the air. Hatshepsut lagged behind to listen to the exchange between her daughter and Senenmut.

"Do you know what these pillars look like?" Senenmut pointed with his free hand to the top of one of the columns.

Neferure looked hard at where Senenmut pointed, her lips pursed together. She glanced to her mother for help, but Hatshepsut only shrugged. "What do they look like, monkey?"

"Plants," Neferure answered. "Big plants."

"That's right," Senenmut said, gifting her with another smile.

Neferure beamed, but it was Hatshepsut who glowed at Senenmut's words. She had done well in asking him back to court, even if he did make her feel jumpier than a desert fox.

The High Priest joined them then with a *henu* so deep that the paws of his leopard skin brushed the ground. He was marked by the gods, a wine-colored stain the size of a thumbprint under his right eye, and several matching stains on the pale underside of his arms. "*Hemet*, the sacrifice is ready."

Hatshepsut took Neferure's hand as they followed him outside through hundreds of black granite statues of the gods, past Mut's crescent lake, to the middle sanctuary of Amun's temple, the ceiling open to Nut's blue belly. A clutch of priests had gathered under the ancient statue of the plumed god, their monotonous voices intoning a prayer, while a precious white bull lay on a raised altar, legs bound together and long horns bedecked with cornflower garlands. The beast, so close they could smell its sweat, snorted at Egypt's regent and her daughter. Hatshepsut had arranged for this sacrifice as soon as Thut had died, a gift to the supreme god for his blessing upon her reign as regent, but it hadn't seemed appropriate to have the ceremony until after the period of mourning had passed.

"Be very still," she said to Neferure.

She took her place near the High Priest as he brandished a knife and slashed the bull's neck with an expert stroke. Blood poured into a bowl of gold decorated with scenes from the god's life. Some splattered on her white sheath, and a coppery tang mixed with the heavy blanket of incense in the air. The bull knocked over the bowl in a final struggle against his ropes and blood sloshed onto the granite step, staining it with a sluice of red. Neferure gave a shrill cry and buried her face in Hatshepsut's leg, her little fingers digging into her mother's thigh. The animal's eyes rolled back and its body stilled.

Hatshepsut had made offerings to the gods before, but this was her first sacrifice as Egypt's regent. Where they might have ignored her before, now the gods would have to hear her.

Lord of ma'at, god of the gods,
Creator of men, maker of all life,
You are Amun, the lord of the hidden.

She chanted with the priests and stared at the polished tiles through the braids of her wig, sending an additional prayer to the invisible god for plentiful harvests and the wisdom to guide her people.

There was something she wished for, an impossible dream she had refused to speak aloud since Tutmose's crowning. Just the thought of it might offend the gods, but she no longer cared.

"Please take Neferure back to Mut's temple," she said to Senenmut. Her daughter's face was as white as clouds, her eyes round little moons as they stared at the dead bull. "There's something else I must attend to."

She slipped off her sandals so as not to defile Amun's home with dust and followed the path to the invisible god's inner sanctuary, so sacred that few men ever set eyes on its façade. The red and black flecks of the granite entrance gleamed dully in Re's fleeing light. The offerings of the day—loaves of flatbread, jugs of pomegranate wine, and bouquets of lotus blossoms—remained piled in the outer sanctuary. A single priestess and a musician were the only people within, the priestess tidying the gifts to the god while the man strummed his lyre. His eyes were clouded with a milky haze, his vision taken but replaced with the rare gift of attending the invisible god.

"No one may enter the god's inner sanctum," the priestess said, then gasped. "I'm sorry, *Hemet.* I didn't realize—"

Hatshepsut held up a hand and smiled. "There's no need to apologize."

The priestess gaped and retreated with the musician, leaving Hatshepsut alone with the god.

Painted scenes of Amun's cult statue being transported in a veiled shrine covered the outer walls of his innermost sanctuary. The door to the tiny inner temple was sealed with dull yellow wax, the holy center admissible only to the pharaoh and the High Priest. However, as regent, Hatshepsut was also now allowed within the sacred confines.

She retrieved the small faience bottle of precious myrrh oil from her pocket and left it on the offering table with the rest of Amun's gifts, then carefully peeled back the wax seal with her fingernail. A blue shroud covered the massive granite shrine, cloaking the invisible god's golden statue. The faint glow of gold shone through the sheer material as the hidden god reflected the light of the torches. The hieroglyphs covering the walls with permanent hymns to Egypt's supreme god moved in the flickering light, and the scent of fragrant oils clung to the air. Unable to see the Great Cackler, but feeling his presence, Hatshepsut's knees buckled and she fell into a full *henu*, arms outstretched with her forehead pressed to the damp flagstones. Something cold pressed upon her chest, as if her heart was already being weighed against Ma'at's feather.

"King of the gods, I have come here as your humble servant and daughter in gratitude for the blessings you have rained upon my country and myself." She spoke into the ground. "I hope and pray for your daily guidance, that you will aid me as you did my father when he wore the double crown. Everything I do, everything I've ever done, is for Egypt. I only hope to prove myself worthy of the Isis Throne."

Of course, not even the regent could sit upon the Isis Throne. That belonged only to the pharaoh.

She remained prostrate on the floor in the hope of receiving even the slightest reassurance from Amun. The air cooled and her shoulders ached. Pins burrowed into her legs, but there was no sound, no divine light, no rustle of movement from the shrine.

Nothing. The god of gods refused to acknowledge her.

Hatshepsut ignored the painful tingling in her legs and, head bowed, backed from the god's dark presence into a rare afternoon rain.

She retraced her steps, covering her head and swearing under her breath the entire way. Amun's silence was almost as terrible as hearing the god hurl curses upon her head.

Perhaps his silence *was* a curse.

Then she tripped, forcefully, as if someone had shoved her, falling to her knees on the altar of Amun's middle courtyard. She scrambled to her feet on the damp tiles and looked up to see the ancient statue of the Great Cackler watching her with glaring granite eyes, rain pouring down his face. There was a crack like a whip snapping in the air, and a fissure at the god's neck opened as if an invisible sculptor had hit his chisel too hard. A shower of granite dust exploded into the air and was quickly eaten by the rain.

Amun, the god of gods, bowed his head to her.

Then a second crack rent the air, a boom of thunder, and the ancient head crashed to the ground, shattering the white tiles with the impact. The force cleaved the head cleanly in two, from the chin to the left ear. The god's glazed eyes stared blankly at her from the ground.

She blinked and shook her head, then opened her eyes to see the statue still staring at her. She reached out to touch Amun's face, the granite under her hands broken and all too real.

The High Priest came running, leopard paws bouncing off his chest and sandals slapping the wet tiles. "*Hemet*, are you all right?"

She wiped her arms, shivered. "I don't know what happened."

He stared openmouthed at the statue, wrung his hands as if strangling a pheasant. His fingers were long and thin and fluttered like bird wings, the wine stains like blood trickling down his arms. "This is a bad omen. A terrible omen."

She'd be condemned if word got out that Amun's statue had collapsed in her presence, that she had caused the damage. That the great god had condemned her.

"Don't tell anyone I was here. Please."

"I cannot keep such a secret in good conscience, *Hemet*. This is a message for you, something the other High Priests must be informed about."

"Please. I'll fund Amun's building projects, the new chapel you requested here at Karnak."

His gaze lingered on the statue for a long moment before he gave a tight nod. "I'll keep everyone out for as long as I can. You must go now."

The High Priest shuffled out from the same direction he'd come. Soon the courtyard would be crowded with priests and priestesses, all horrified at the desecration of the god's sacred altar.

The statue was stiff and cool, now empty of the god's presence. Perhaps the granite had simply failed, a weak vein in the aged stone damaged by the rain causing the head to fall.

A shriek of laughter overwhelmed Hatshepsut's mind, the hot roar of the desert wind mixed with the loud cackle of a goose.

Your name will live forever.

You shall be the downfall of those you love.

Egypt will prosper, but those closest to you shall find only anguish and ruin.

Amun's voice, echoing Djeseret's prophesy of doom. Hatshepsut stumbled from the courtyard, chest heaving, and pressed her back into Karnak's walls to keep her knees from buckling again.

She'd have done anything not to hear those words again.

CHAPTER 18

Shomu drew to a close and the *rekhyt* finished bringing in the harvest of oats, wheat, and barley that would feed Egypt for another year. The Nile's benevolence meant plenty of grain to add to the storehouses and stockpiles of food for leaner years. Hatshepsut could ignore Amun's curse when the land was so blessed; she could believe she had imagined the hidden god's voice in her head. The High Priest had kept his word, and she hadn't spoken of the incident to anyone.

She would take the secret with her to her tomb.

In order to give the gods their due, Hatshepsut had already sat idle during the first two unlucky days at the end of the year, and recited spells from the *Book of the Last Day of the Year* over a piece of newly woven linen, which she tied around her neck to avoid the wrath of the gods. Now the people held their breath, hoping the five Days of the Demons at the end of the year would pass with a whimper instead of a roar. Osiris' and Horus' days had already gone by, but today was Set's day, the most terrible of all.

She couldn't stomach another day of mindless boredom, and sent Mouse to inquire whether Senenmut might be willing to join her in breaking the rules.

"Senenmut will do whatever you want." Mouse sniffed. "That man would walk across a bed of scorpions if you asked him to."

"You must be growing senile if that's what you think," she said. "Senenmut can scarcely stand to be in the same room with me."

"And you must be blind." Mouse rolled her eyes to the ceiling, blowing a puff of onion-scented breath in Hatshepsut's direction. "That man swallows you with his eyes. I'm surprised there's anything left of you after the past few weeks."

Hatshepsut's cheeks flushed. She had noticed his gaze on her when he thought she wasn't watching, but the look on his face had never been a happy one. More as if he were in terrible pain.

She herded Mouse out the door, then double-checked her reflection in the copper mirror. Hathor's cow face smiled benignly from the handle, mocking her. "Leave me alone," she whispered to the goddess. She slammed the mirror onto the table. Facedown.

Still, her heart did a traitorous little jump when she entered her offices.

Senenmut was already seated at the table, shaking his head in disbelief as he ticked off lines in the ledgers with his stylus. "You must be the gods' most beloved subject this side of the Nile." He gave a dry chuckle at her pointed look. "Pardon me, *Hemet*. On both sides of the Nile."

She had recently promoted him to the Steward of Amun, a sort of reward for the completion of Mut's temple at Karnak, and he wore the gold pectoral of his new office across an otherwise bare chest. She had granted him the position he sought at court and the power he craved. Everything she thought he wanted.

But it wasn't enough.

Still he was aloof. She knew he craved more titles, wanted to help her rule Egypt. She just didn't know how much more he desired.

Her leg barely touched his under the table. She refused to move and kept her eyes to her papyrus, bit the end of her brush until the wood was as mangled as if a rat had gnawed it. Senenmut cleared his throat as if he were about to say something, but was interrupted by a rap at the door.

The brush still touched her lips as Hatshepsut raised her eyes to his. She looked away, fearful Senenmut would be able to read the lust written plain across her face. Maybe it was more than lust. She didn't know, would never get the chance to find out.

"Enter," she said.

The door creaked open to reveal Nomti and Kahotep, the old palace herald. Her bodyguard held a large woven basket in his arms.

"What is that?" She eyed the basket warily. After a bountiful harvest, it was likely some sort of extravagant bribe, a gift with a lofty request from some mayor or courtier seeking a favor. Why couldn't people ask for what they wanted, plain and simple?

"This just arrived with a Nubian messenger," Kahotep said. "The boy looked like he'd been running for days, so I sent him to the kitchens before he collapsed."

"Nubia?" Hatshepsut's eyebrow arched in question. She wasn't expecting anything from Nubia; the troubled region had been strangely quiet lately.

"I asked the messenger to repeat his message to me so you could receive it straightaway." The herald shifted from one foot to the other. "He only said that General Pebatjma wished to send this gift to you. He was explicit that it is for your eyes only, *Hemet*."

Senenmut moved out of the way as Nomti set the basket on the table. "I don't know that name—it sounds Nubian," he said. "Is he one of the Egyptian officials you appointed to the region?"

She shook her head. "I've never heard of him. I just appointed Khui as the new viceroy of Nubia. His report last month said things were going well."

"I should open this for you." Senenmut's tone brooked no argument. "You don't know what it could be—scorpions or snakes, maybe worse."

"That seems a little dramatic."

"*Neb* Senenmut is right," Nomti said. "It could be dangerous."

She rolled her eyes at their stern looks, but threw her hands up in the air. "Then I suppose you may have the honor."

Inside the basket was another basket, followed by another. Nestled inside was a large stone box, one carved with crude Nubian symbols. A rancid smell leapt into the air as Senenmut drew off the stone lid. He slammed the box shut, but it was too late. She had already glimpsed the putrid contents.

Viceroy Khui's head, or at least what was left of it.

Rotting black flesh and empty eye sockets writhing with white maggots sent her retching in the corner. On her knees at the edge of the room, Hatshepsut roared, "Bring me that messenger!"

"*Hemet*, I'm so sorry." Kahotep looked about to weep as Nomti raced from the room. "I should have checked inside the baskets first before sending the boy to eat."

She wiped her mouth with the back of her hand and struggled to her feet. "Find Admiral Pennekheb," she said. "We'll need his expertise before we move against the Nubians."

She paced while slaves scrubbed the flagstones of the remnants of her lunch.

"We should have expected something like this," Senenmut said. He looked far too relaxed, leaning against her desk, while she felt like a panther, ready to spring. Instead, she paced.

So much for Set's day passing with a whimper.

"The Nubians will pay for this," she said. "I don't care how long it takes. I won't be humiliated."

Pennekheb arrived and Nomti returned, dragging the Nubian messenger behind him. He shoved the boy into the middle of the room, and Senenmut barred the door.

"What's your name?" Hatshepsut prowled before him, prepared to do battle.

"Awa." The youth held his head high and dared her with his eyes, his gaze piercing her like an arrow.

"You will bow before your regent!" Nomti slammed Awa to the

ground and stepped on his back to force him into a *henu*. He shoved the basket under the Nubian's nose. "Who did this?"

"The greatest ruler Nubia has ever seen," Awa shouted. "General Pebatjma!"

Hatshepsut stopped before Awa. "So your miserable leader dares start an insurrection against the mightiest country on earth?"

"Together with a thousand men, we've taken back our kingdom!" Awa looked up, only to have Nomti slam his face into the floor again. There was a crunching sound from the boy's nose, like a walnut cracking open.

"At what expense?" Admiral Pennekheb asked, as if inquiring about the weather. Of everyone in the room, only he appeared to have his emotions in check.

"We've overrun the fort and slaughtered all the Egyptian men. We separated their heads from their bodies and burned them so they can never rise in the afterlife." A maniacal grin cleft Awa's black face as he lifted his head. Blood ran from his nose to his mouth and covered his front teeth with a slick of red. "Nubia will never fall to Egypt again!"

His words fanned Hatshepsut's anger into rage as she thought of all those men, their hopes of the afterlife obliterated by the swords and torches of madmen.

"Fall to Egypt?" she yelled, hot with fury. "Your kingdom was an unruly state of warlords without a law to protect its people until Egypt came along and offered her guidance. And this is how we are repaid? By constant revolt and rebellion? Our yoke has been soft upon your backs, but nothing says it has to stay that way."

Awa spat at her feet. "Better dead than ruled by a woman."

Senenmut looked about to smash his foot into the boy's mouth, but Hatshepsut beat him to it. This time when Awa spit, two of his teeth clattered to the floor.

She motioned to Nomti. "Lock up this traitor. And see to it that Khui's remains are taken to the priests of Anubis."

Senenmut yanked Awa to his feet and passed him into Nomti's custody. The atmosphere of the room had changed, charged like the afternoon sky before a thunderstorm.

"We must invade."

Hatshepsut's words were a clap of thunder.

"Immediately," Pennekheb agreed. "I'm surprised they waited so long to rebel after the succession."

"They probably weren't expecting a new pharaoh," Senenmut noted wryly. "It would have taken them a while to muster the men and supplies needed for a coup."

"Regardless of how or why this happened, the rebels must be rooted out and utterly destroyed," Hatshepsut said. "I won't allow Egypt's borders to shrink while I guard the throne, nor can we afford to let the gold shipments from Nubia be disrupted."

"We have four divisions available to us here in Waset: Horus, Thoth, Set, and Re," Pennekheb said. "The men can be ready to march in a few days. The other *nomarchs* can call on their reserve troops to supply us with several more divisions." The admiral looked confident. "Don't worry, *Hemet*. We'll bring the Nubians to heel for you. This generation won't rebel again."

Her father had once regaled her with stories of his conquest in Nubia; the pharaoh had sailed home to Waset with the naked body of the Nubian chief hanging from the prow of his boat. Osiris Tutmose's presence on the front lines had guaranteed the army's loyalty to the royal house and ensured that Nubia saw the strength of the pharaoh himself, ending the chance of further rebellions while Tutmose lived. Unfortunately, her brother had shirked the opportunity to prove his worth in battle when he'd been given the chance. Now the Nubians had risen again—a safe gamble if they thought the ruling house was weak or inept. With a child on the throne and a woman as regent, Egypt surely seemed vulnerable to open insurrection. But if Nubians saw firsthand the full might of Egypt and the declaration of power behind the throne, they might think twice before revolting again. Plus, this was an opportunity to secure the loyalty of Hatshepsut's military, something that might prove useful in the future.

"I'm coming with you," she said.

The room fell silent.

"Absolutely not," Pennekheb countered. His tone was even, but both of his frail hands clutched the top of his cane. "The battlefield is no place for a woman, no matter how capable you've proven yourself elsewhere. Not only that, but this will be a much bloodier affair than our foray into Nubia when your brother took the throne." He glanced at Senenmut, squared his shoulders. "I'm sure your steward agrees with me."

Senenmut looked at her, his expression inscrutable. There was a pause so long that she wished she could hear his thoughts. "She should go," Senenmut finally said.

"You can't be serious." Pennekheb threw his hands up.

"As long as you're not planning on joining the men on the front lines. I don't doubt you might do something foolish in Egypt's name."

He knew her well, but she was no fool.

She glared at him. "I'm not a soldier. But my presence is necessary."

Pennekheb's mouth fell open in disgust. He shook his head. "No, I absolutely won't accept this. It's too dangerous to risk the regent's life on a border skirmish. No one else can be trusted to take up the regency if something happens to you."

"I'll be perfectly safe," Hatshepsut said. "The Nubians won't stop fighting until they realize I won't allow them to carve away pieces of my kingdom. Let them see firsthand whom they're dealing with. There will be no mercy for those who survive."

Pennekheb stood in stony silence, glowering. "I won't have the death of the regent on my hands."

Hatshepsut snorted. "Let's hope it doesn't come to that, shall we?" She grinned wickedly. "Then it's settled. We go to war!"

CHAPTER 19

The bedraggled ostrich feathers from her stallion's bridle fluttered in the desert air. Weeks ago, the jaunty plumes had pranced in time to the horse's trot as they traveled the edge of the Nile's moist black bank, but now, covered with the thick film of red dust that coated everyone and everything, the feathers sagged, exhausted in the heat.

Hatshepsut, Admiral Pennekheb, Senenmut, and the Royal Treasurer Ti rode in chariots at the front. The commanders and a company of archers marched behind them, the biting head of a snake that slithered closer to Nubia and the impending war. The plodding footsteps of thousands of soldiers coughed up dust and sand behind them.

Leaving Waset and the palace behind with the promise of a war not yet fought had been exhilarating for Hatshepsut, but they'd been at this slog along the desert border for what seemed like an eternity, Re scorching their backs as they traced the Nile's curves. Their ranks swelled with each city they passed and the *nomarchs* delivered the reserve troops Admiral Pennekheb had guaranteed. Egypt's sands stretched behind them as they passed the rapids of the First Cataract and then the Second and crossed Nubia's borders. Isis hadn't wept yet to flood the river, but the waterfalls roared and lifted everyone's spirits as they trekked past. But both times the river had calmed and left the landscape precisely as it had looked since they'd left Waset, a never-ending expanse of undulating brown.

Only Re's movement overhead marked the passage of time, the buzzing of flies breaking the monotonous sounds of thousands of marching feet. The Third Cataract beckoned and past it, the city of Dongola. It was there that Admiral Pennekheb was sure the battle to retake Nubia would commence. This would be their last night camped together. Many of the men behind Hatshepsut carried cumin seeds in the pockets of their loincloths, symbolizing faithfulness to the wives and lovers waiting for them back home. Some of these men wouldn't live to see another sunset, but would instead be buried here in Nubia with their memories and those seeds.

Hatshepsut shaded her eyes and squinted toward a disturbance on the horizon. Nomti reined his stallion to a trot. "It looks like a runner."

Her elbow bumped him as she tried to get a better look. She'd ordered her own chariot, but Nomti and Senenmut had joined ranks with Pennekheb, all vehement that she needed a guard with her. What they meant was painfully obvious: Nomti wasn't there to protect her from the Nubians, but rather from herself.

"They might be our scouts," she said. The dust cloud loomed larger until she could make out two men like growing ants on the horizon. Their short kilts and light skin branded them as Egyptians.

"I'll find out what they've seen." Senenmut spurred on his horse and Pennekheb called a halt for the rest of the procession. The two disturbances in the sand inched closer to each other and eventually collided. It took only a few moments for Senenmut to reverse course.

If Hatshepsut had been on her own, she would have raced ahead to meet him. But she wasn't alone, and hadn't been since the moment they'd left Waset.

Sand sprayed from his horse's hooves as the animal reared to a halt. "The Nubians are camped over the next rise just outside Dongola," he said. "They think we're still several days off, compliments of the reports our spies have planted."

"Send more scouts," Hatshepsut said to Pennekheb. "I want a full account on the layout of the terrain."

"I'll ready the troops," the admiral said, the years melting from his face. "Tomorrow we shall have our victory!"

The red of blood and fire spread across the sky as the black line of the horizon swallowed Re's body, an omen of death and destruction to come. The troops feasted on double rations of bread and beer to give them strength for the coming challenge, but Hatshepsut spent the night in her tent, prostrate before a makeshift altar to Set and Sekhmet. Her prayers to the warrior gods tumbled together and her joints grew stiff, but still she muttered the words. At some point, the gods blessed her with the precious gift of sleep.

It was Senenmut who woke Hatshepsut as he entered her tent well before dawn, his copper scimitar already strapped to his hip. He shook her gently. "It's time. The admiral has a plan to give us an advantage, but we need to move within the hour to keep the element of surprise."

His words chased away the last dregs of sleep. Her joints protested as Senenmut helped her from the reed mat tossed over packed sand. "This is what we've been waiting for," he said. His hand lifted as if to brush a stray hair from her cheek, but dropped quickly to his side. "A day generations will remember."

He clasped her hand to his chest, closed her fingers around something small and hard. "I asked Mouse to find this for you. It's been a long time since I've seen you wear it, but I thought you might want it today."

She looked down to see Sekhmet's red jasper amulet on a white string, the necklace Neferubity had given her so long ago. The stone was warm in her hand, as if alive, and for a moment it seemed that the lion goddess bared her teeth to growl before settling back to her complacent smile.

"I'd forgotten all about this," she said, slipping the amulet over her head. "I hope the goddess will forgive the oversight."

He smiled, that slow, lazy smile she hadn't seen since the day in the Western Valley. "I think Sekhmet would forgive her favorite daughter almost anything."

It was suddenly hard to breathe. Senenmut would be in the midst of the fighting today, traveling with the division of his beloved Thoth in an officer's capacity, while Nomti kept her a safe distance away. She wanted to tell him to be careful, but the words stuck in her throat.

He bowed, turned on his heel, and let the tent flap fall behind him.

She listened until his muffled footsteps faded into silence. "Protect him, Sekhmet. Keep him safe, and I swear I'll do anything you ask of me."

Her eyes felt gritty as she splashed her face with water from a copper urn and allowed slaves to replace the loose sheath she'd worn last night with the short kilt of her soldiers. Upon this were layered broad bands of thick brown leather until they covered her entire torso. For the first time, she placed the pharaoh's blue battle crown—the *khepresh*—upon her bare head.

Today she was not just regent, but also the supreme commander of the armed forces of Egypt. She would dress the part.

She strode from her tent but stopped at the sight before her. The Egyptian army stood ready, a sea of brown faces illuminated only by a few smoking torches. Archers stood at attention and scores of infantry brandished spears and cowhide shields. The air crackled with anticipation.

"Take me to the front of the line," Hatshepsut said to Nomti as she climbed into her chariot.

"Don't get any ideas." He eyed her as if he expected her to leap from the basket at any moment.

"I'm not going to fight," she said. "But I won't hide in my tent either."

The gilded chariot circled to the front of the Division of Horus, the image of the falcon god emblazoned on each man's leather armband and the linen standards hanging limply in the warm air. This group of elite soldiers would lead the way and be the first to engage the Nubians outside Dongola. There would be heavy casualties.

Hatshepsut tried to commit each man's face to memory. These were Egypt's sons, husbands, fathers. The next time she saw many of them, they would be corpses on the battlefield.

She focused on her men as the chariot halted and projected her voice in the hope that the mouths of men would carry her words.

"Men of Egypt, sons of Sekhmet and Set! Before you waits an enemy determined to bring Egypt to her knees, flaunting the might of our great kingdom and inciting chaos and violence within our borders. Today we will bring these criminals to heel, and you shall be guaranteed your place of honor in the Field of Reeds. Let Ammit feast on the hearts of these rebels!"

She shook her spear in the air, prompting a roar so loud it could likely be heard all the way to Dongola. The noise crested to a deafening crescendo as the men pounded their shields with their spears. A nod to Admiral Pennekheb prompted the signal to move out. Thousands of men marched past her chariot with a salute, ready to discover what the gods had in store for them.

She spied Senenmut's chariot as the division of Thoth drove past. His gaze lingered on her and then he raised his spear to her in salute.

His form disappeared over the rise. She prayed to Sekhmet that she would see him again.

Alive.

"The first reports are here." Nomti held aside the opening for the messenger. Hatshepsut's tent was a nest of activity as advisers buzzed to and fro and the wind kicked up outside. She wanted to see the action rather than hear secondhand reports about the battle that was unfolding in her name.

The messenger was covered with dust, beads of dirty sweat

dripping from his temples. She held the golden ceremonial mace her father had taken to war against the Nubians and used it to impatiently motion the runner to a map of Dongola's surrounding area. Miniature toy soldiers sat upon the frayed papyrus—those of Egypt in polished white alabaster amongst the ebony of Nubia's troops.

"What's happening?" she asked.

"The Division of Horus has broken into the Nubian front line. Our surprise attack caught them off guard, but they regrouped quickly." The runner's chest heaved as he pushed out the words. "Our soldiers met with heavy casualties, especially the archers at the front of the regiment's line, but they've managed to break the Nubians."

That was good news. If the Nubians scattered, it would mean chaos among their ranks.

"And the other divisions?"

"The Division of Thoth has also moved in to provide reinforcements to Horus, to ensure that their line remains strong."

Senenmut's division. Hatshepsut kept her face a mask. She had to trust the gods to protect him.

"Are the other divisions preparing to move in as planned?"

The messenger nodded, wiping his brow with the back of his hand. She sent him away with a flick of her wrist and set down the mace, impatient for more news. She had to get out of the tent.

She was halfway out the door when Nomti stepped in front of her.

"Where do you think you're going?"

"To the top of the rise."

"Absolutely not."

"I refuse to stay while all those men fight for my kingdom. I need to see what's happening."

Nomti shook his head. "And if our forces have to retreat?"

"That will never happen."

"We can't know for sure."

"Well, if they did retreat—which they won't—I'd have to leave here anyway. I promised to keep away from the front, but I never said I'd stay hidden away in a field tent."

Nomti sighed. He had served her long enough to know that she would do whatever she wished. "Fine. To the rise, but no more."

"Agreed."

His whip cracked overhead and the horse bolted. The wind roared, as hot as Sekhmet's breath, spewing angry dust devils into the air and washing the imprint of her soldiers' footsteps from the sand. If this continued much longer, the desert would soon claim all evidence of this battle, tucking the fallen soldiers into a blanket of sand for all eternity.

The view from the dune's crest was something she'd remember until the day her *ka* flew to the sky. The back lines of the Egyptian infantry swarmed like locusts, a protective wall to fill any chinks in the divisions. The center teemed with thousands of men, mounted and on foot, light and dark, each side trying to devour the other. The gods circled the battle, cackling amidst the sandstorm and throwing back their heads to roar with bloodlust.

An ant of a man broke free from the melee and ran in their direction, slowly taking on legs, arms, and a head. Hatshepsut moved to grab the reins, but Nomti flicked them out of reach. "Don't you dare," he said.

The runner arrived minutes later, his bare chest spattered with someone else's blood. His legs gave way and he barely managed to gasp out his message. "The Division of Thoth is fully engaged. There are heavy casualties, but the Division of Horus has penetrated the Nubian lines. The Division of Set has also been engaged."

Hatshepsut's throat constricted at the mention of deaths within the ranks of Thoth, but she gave a tight nod.

The next hours crawled by, Sekhmet seeming to slow time so she could guide each bronze arrow to its mark. Several more runners came to report the ebb and flow of the battle. At one point the Nubians resurged and delivered countless Egyptians to Anubis' waiting jaws. The wind died down to make the torment of Re's brutal heat unbearable, but calmed the storm of sand as the rebels were pushed back to Dongola.

The haze of evening approached and a final runner tore up the rise. This one was different—panting and out of breath, but with a gleaming smile shining like a beacon as he neared the royal chariot.

Thirsty for news, Hatshepsut didn't even allow him the moment to bow. "We've won, haven't we?"

"The rebels have been pushed back within the city, and the Divisions of Horus and Thoth have pursued." The messenger's smile never faltered. "Admiral Pennekheb wishes to know your orders regarding the destruction of the city and the taking of its inhabitants."

"Assemble the rebel chiefs and their families—I'll deal with them personally. Women and children will stay behind with the occupying force of Egyptians to work the gold mines. The Division of Re will remain in Dongola to ensure the Nubians don't rise again."

The runner repeated the message to commit it to memory, then retraced his steps back down the dune.

Nomti checked the position of Re's sinking body. "It may be some time before the admiral and the others finish. Shall we return to the tent?"

"I'm not going back. I'm going down there to deal with the chiefs."

"Absolutely not. They'll bring the traitors to you."

"The fighting is over." Hatshepsut stepped out of the chariot, crossing her arms before her. "I'll walk if I have to."

Nomti glared at her, a black look borrowed from Ammit before the demon devoured the hearts of the dead. Hatshepsut turned and started to walk in the direction of Dongola.

"Fine," Nomti growled, and she smiled into the dusk. She would have looked rather foolish walking onto the battlefield, but she'd have done it if she had to.

He offered his hand and pulled her back into the chariot. "But you're not going within a stone's throw of the city."

"Or within an arrow's shot." Hatshepsut swallowed her laughter as Nomti glared again. She wouldn't push her luck.

It didn't take long before they came across the first body, that of a grizzled Nubian warrior past his prime. A bearded vulture perched on the man's ribs, digging into exposed intestines. The bird looked at them, and the shiny innards clutched in its beak glistened in the setting sun. More buzzards circled overhead, drawn by the scent of blood.

Hatshepsut shuddered as they passed three massive burial mounds among the sands, the resting places of Nubia's chiefs from the time before Egypt had conquered these uncivilized lands. In her youth, her tutor had often regaled her with tales of the hundreds of sacrificial victims forced to accompany their chief to the afterlife, their throats slit or, worse, heads removed. These people were savages.

The chariot continued to weave through the maze of slaughtered men and dead horses until they approached the rear of the Egyptian troops. The men were pitching tents and lighting celebratory bonfires as twilight fell, but wild cheers broke out as the soldiers spotted Hatshepsut.

She held up a hand to stop them. This was their victory, not hers. "Thanks to you, Egypt is secure once more!" she shouted into the roar of men's voices. "Ammit gorges tonight on the hearts of Nubia's vile betrayers!"

The soldiers laughed and gave a hearty cheer. Then the crowd parted as three Nubian chiefs bound at the neck were shoved forward, tripping as the men jeered at them.

The leaders of the resistance.

All wore giant gold hoops through their ears and spotted calfskin loincloths. Fans of ostrich feathers topped their crowns, but one also wore a black panther hide draped across his shoulders, scarcely darker than his skin. The Prince of Miam. Another of the princes tripped on his copper shackles and fell face-first into the sands, yanking the others to their knees. A group of women with bare breasts and rainbow-colored skirts followed, a gaggle of naked children trailing behind them. A girl about Neferure's age had salty white streaks of dried tears down her cheeks, but she held tight to her little brother's hand.

"Take the children away," Hatshepsut said. The youngest amongst them would be judged worthy to be raised by Egypt's nobles, and possibly sent back in future years as proper Egyptians to rule their native lands. For now they would be gifted to Amun's temples as slaves.

One of the women howled and clawed at a soldier as he stole the infant from her back, but she quieted at the chief's barked reprimand. Soldiers rounded up the children and herded them away, spears pointed.

"You are traitors and as such shall die traitors' deaths," Hatshepsut said, her voice strong. "Perhaps Nubia will learn its lesson this time." At her signal, soldiers armed with axes stepped behind the rebels. They grasped the feathers of the men's crowns and the women's braided hair. The Nubians didn't have time to protest before the copper axes hit their targets. The Prince of Miam clutched his neck in a vain attempt to staunch the flow of blood and slid to the ground, gurgling and gasping as the other men fell next to him. One of the women moaned as she sank to the ground, and the sand filled with pools of blood.

Hatshepsut swallowed the bile that rose in her throat and gritted her teeth before turning to address her men. She had done what she had come to do: subdue Nubia and ensure the love of her soldiers.

"Tonight is yours," she told them, hoping no one would notice the hoarseness of her voice. Someone handed her a skin of fetid water and she took a swig, relishing its sour taste on her parched throat. The taste of life. "Tomorrow we attend to the dead, but tonight is for the living. Double rations and wine for all!"

Two of the soldiers—archers she remembered from this morning—came forward. Both brandished spotted black-and-white leather shields, but one wore the bronze armor that denoted his position as a company commander.

"Where are the rest of the officers?" Hatshepsut asked.

"Inside Dongola, securing the city," the bronze officer said. "They wanted to lock down the storehouses."

These men wore faces as somber as if they had lost the day instead of winning it.

"Please come with us, *Hemet*," the commander said. "There's been an injury. I've been sent to fetch you."

The festive mood in the air was sucked away in that moment, leaving Hatshepsut alone in the night's dark void.

Senenmut.

"An injury?" she echoed the words back, unable to force her tongue to form any other sentence.

He didn't answer, only nodded.

The flames of the bonfires were suddenly too bright, the shouts from the men too loud, but she followed the officer toward one of the makeshift tents erected on the battlefield as a temporary infirmary. She tried desperately to see which god's emblem the man wore on his leather armband, but it was too caked with dried blood and dust to tell.

Vivid images of the grizzled old Nubian she and Nomti had first come upon assailed her, forcing her to imagine the same death wounds on Senenmut. She stumbled and nearly fell.

"Are you all right, *Hemet*?" Nomti's hand reached out to steady her, and the officer glanced over his shoulder.

"I'm fine," she said.

She couldn't bear the thought of losing Senenmut, and would never forgive herself if it was too late to tell him of her feelings for him. He carried the other half of her *ka*; she knew that now. She had forgotten the fickleness of the gods, how they loved to toy with mortals. She had barely survived the first time she thought Senenmut was dead; she wasn't sure she could endure that again.

Her feet were boulders as they approached the infirmary tent, her tongue thick and heavy in her mouth. She clung to the safety of uncertainty, dreaded to see Senenmut stretched out as his lifeblood leaked from some fatal battle wound.

"Wait outside," she said to Nomti.

He opened his mouth to argue, but she swept past him. This was her duty to see through, not his. She didn't need witnesses if it truly was Senenmut inside. The officer lifted the tent flap, and the lamplight from within seeped into the dusk. Hatshepsut steeled herself and stepped inside.

Rows and rows of good Egyptian men were laid out before her, most on cots but some on the ground, all wrapped in bloody bandages. The tent was close and stuffy, thick with the metallic tang of so much blood. Some men nursed broken limbs braced by fresh wooden splints, but others were ashen, mumbling prayers to Anubis and preparing themselves for the journey to Ma'at's scales. She stopped at the foot of each cot to give a gentle word to those who were not long for this world and offer congratulations for the few hardier souls. All the while, she managed to box up the panic that threatened to overwhelm her.

"Over here, *Hemet*." The officer pulled back a sheet erected around one of the cots. Hatshepsut took a step forward, desperately hoping she wouldn't see Senenmut lying there.

CHAPTER 20

It was Pennekheb.

Her heart cried out in relief even as guilt stabbed that same miserable organ. The admiral had given Egypt the best years of his life and now lay on a plain military cot, his trunk wrapped in white linen that matched the sparse hair scattered upon his chest. The bandages and cot were wet with blood.

Hatshepsut sank next to him and clasped his age-spotted hand. His eyes fluttered and he gave a weak smile. "We've routed the rebels once again, haven't we?"

"With your guidance," she said. "Egypt couldn't have done this without you, my friend."

"I may have earned my retirement this time." Pennekheb coughed, the sound wet. "One of their spears took a liking to my ribs."

Hatshepsut looked to the physician for confirmation. He nodded and placed a golden Eye of Horus near the wound. She didn't ask for the prognosis—the stain of blood had already overcome most of the bandages. A red drop pearled at the loose corner of the linen wrappings and finally fell, swallowed by the earth and followed by a steady trickle.

Pennekheb coughed again and spat out blood. A line of pink saliva oozed from the corner of his mouth. Hatshepsut wiped his chin with a clean bandage.

"You need to rest." She tucked the scratchy blanket around his legs and swiped her eyes with the back of her arm while her back was turned.

"Your father would be proud of you." Pennekheb managed a wan smile. He closed his eyes. "*I* am proud of you."

Anubis prowled outside the tent, not yet sated by Egypt's *kas*. It didn't take long for the jackal god of death to come for the admiral. Pennekheb didn't fight, only slipped peacefully into the dark sky, his body drained of its lifeblood.

Tears slid unchecked from Hatshepsut's eyes. Pennekheb had given his life to Egypt, and now the Nubians had killed him before his time. Enraged, she slipped out of the tent to discover the victory celebration in full swing.

"Follow me," she said to Nomti.

The horses had been unharnessed and stood nearby, chewing stray clumps of trampled grass and awaiting their grooms, but at a signal from Hatshepsut they were quickly bridled once again.

The chariot rolled back toward the desert, night falling fast.

The closest Nubian corpse, a young man with a pale dusting of sand on his dark skin, his arms and legs bent at impossible angles, lay just outside camp. A scorpion skittered into the open maw of a dead horse nearby. The rebel had been cut down by a battle-ax left in his abdomen. The entrails lay outside his tunic like giant worms, crusted with a thick film of black blood.

Hatshepsut steeled herself against the urge to retch and forced her eyes away. Nomti clicked the reins and the chariot started from the scene, but her hand on his arm stopped him.

"I need only a moment."

As if in a dream, she stepped down from the chariot and walked to the dead man. The lavender intestines quivered as she pulled the ax from his stomach with a sickening squelch. She stared at his right hand.

"Don't, *Hemet*. Someone else will do that."

"Egypt's men died today. Pennekheb died today." She clenched the handle of the ax. "This is the only thing I can do for them."

Stepping on the man's outstretched forearm, Hatshepsut hacked into the dead man's wrist.

She managed two strokes before the sound of bones crunching became too much to bear; then she collapsed into the desert's unforgiving sands, gasping for breath.

"Hemet—" Nomti was at her side, trying to pull her back to the chariot.

"Let me do this!" Since she was unable to fight and barely allowed to witness a battle waged in her name, the least she could do was collect the hands of the enemy for the official tally of Nubian casualties. Trapped in a woman's body, today of all days she craved equal footing with the men who had risked their lives for her. This was a weak sort of vengeance for the men who had died, but it was all she could offer them.

Hatshepsut struggled to stand and made her way back to the half-butchered hand. Forcing herself to stare at the grains of sand above the mutilated wrist, she finally freed the hand from the rest of the arm and threw the offensive appendage into the basket. Her palms were sticky with blood and she wiped them on her kilt before clambering back into the chariot. They continued in silence, stopping every so often so she could free a Nubian rebel of his right hand.

Now the Nubians would pay for all eternity for their crimes in this life. If Ammit didn't gobble up their hearts the instant their sacred organs were laid upon Ma'at's scales, at least they would be forced to roam the afterlife without a hand. All the *kas* of the afterlife would know their shame. The hands would be smoked to preserve them and counted later, providing a tally of the enemy dead.

They returned to the Egyptian camp to find the evening revelry to

Sekhmet far progressed. The Egyptians had taken several cows from Dongola as the spoils of war and the choicest cuts roasted over the bonfires' flames. Wine flowed and the men belted out off-key verses, the ecstatic songs of men who have stepped to the boundary between this world and the next and been allowed to return.

Be faithful, resolute, alive,
You and the Two Lands that has no enemies;
This life is no more than a dream,
so seize the day before it passes!

The world snapped into focus. The fires cracked and popped with magnificent clarity and sharpened the smells of roasting ox and the empty desert air. Hatshepsut waded through the crowd, but stopped every few moments as a soldier with a belly of beer congratulated her or offered his exaggerated account of the battle. She asked if any of the officers had returned from Dongola, but no one knew.

Finally, Hatshepsut spied the glint of bronze armor working its way into the crowd. Her *ka* cried out in relief and she pushed through the mass of soldiers, heading in the direction of the bronze glare. But she realized her mistake as she got closer. It wasn't Senenmut coming toward her, but Ti. Her treasurer smiled and waved as he jostled over to her. The thick armor plates seemed out of place on such a thin man.

"The rebels are dead, the gold shipments secure, and Dongola is safely delivered into your hands, *Hemet*." He shouted over the din of the party, his grin contagious. "What a glorious day!"

"One for history." Hatshepsut smiled, and looked past Ti to scan the crowd.

"And my tomb—I'm going to have this day plastered on the walls of my burial chamber," Ti said. "The Nubians defeated, a woman regent out severing hands from the dead rebels—"

"You saw that?" She stared down at her hands, the skin taut with dried Nubian blood.

"The men are in love with you after that little display. You could ask them to jump from a cliff and they'd all race to be first."

At least something good had come of Pennekheb's death. Hatshepsut flushed at Ti's compliment as he bowed to excuse himself. "Is there anything else I can get for you, *Hemet*? Some wine or ox flesh?"

"No, thank you. Although I haven't seen the other officers return." Hatshepsut hoped she sounded nonchalant. "Have you seen Senenmut?"

"He was finishing up an inventory of one of Dongola's storehouses, trying to determine what we can take on our return trip to Waset," Ti said. "He fought well today, not that he'd ever mention it. I'm sure he'll be here soon."

Senenmut wouldn't be in the thick of the festivities if he could avoid it. She and Ti parted ways, each in pursuit of the evening's distractions. But it wasn't to the bonfires or her tent that she walked.

A newly beaten trail wound away from the camp and met up with the main path from Dongola—the soldiers had been down to gather drinking water. The bonfires cast an ethereal glow into the sky and lit Nut's dark belly with a translucent orange haze. The farther Hatshepsut traveled from camp, the more the cricket chirps and the murmur of the Nile's lazy waters overtook the men's laughter and song. Her feet tread less on sand and more on the moist vegetation clinging to the earth near the water. It was a fine line between the scant Black Land and the immense Red Land here.

The riverbank was empty and silent, save for the lonely call of an occasional frog. Hatshepsut had hoped to find Senenmut, but instead she found her first moment of solitude since leaving the City of Truth. The clean scent of the Nile and Nubia's damp earth filled her nose, overpowering the smells of campfires and death that clung to her skin. Desert grit covered her body and filled her mouth, ears, and eyes. She splashed water over her face and scrubbed her forearms with river grass until they were raw and every trace of rebel blood had been washed downriver.

Finally clean, she felt exhaustion overwhelming her, seeping into her bones. Each step felt as if invisible hands clung to her feet. For a moment she imagined the *kas* of the dead dragging her down, but she willed the image from her mind.

Her newly erected tent sat on the outskirts of camp, dingy white and set apart from its companions, and identified by the red and white pennants it flew. Inside, her eyes were greeted with the warm glow of a single oil lamp and the interior's profusion of colors. Vibrant hues of green, yellow, and red danced in a riot of geometric designs, a happy escape from the tedium of Nubia's tawny sands.

Half-asleep, she kicked off her sandals and sat on her cot. Then something stirred in the shadows.

Someone else was in the tent with her, sitting on a low stool at the edge of the lantern's circle.

Senenmut stood in one fluid motion, but she had already closed the gap between them. The blood in her veins sang with her need for him, the restraint of the past months shattered in an instant. He kissed her then, a kiss that radiated life, a kiss she'd waited three years to receive.

"I thought you were dead," she said, gasping at how right it felt to have his arms around her, to know that he was finally hers.

"I may as well have been," he said, one hand cradling the back of her head while his eyes burned for her. "I need you, Hatshepsut. I always have."

His mouth was on hers then, ravenous, his hands in her hair and then everywhere. He picked her up and she clung to him, tasted the cinnamon of his lips and the sweat on his skin. The kiss chased away all the longing and worry that had haunted her these past months. It all dissolved as they fell together under the canopy of the rainbow-hued tent.

A loud crash and a muffled curse outside the tent woke Hatshepsut. Two men—one with a voice still slurred from Sekhmet's feast and the other mostly sober—bickered over a broken beer jug until the latter realized they were outside the regent's tent. There were several more curses, the shuffle of feet, and then silence fell again.

The hazy fingers of morning weaseled their way through cracks in the canvas. Senenmut lay stretched out on his back next to Hatshepsut, his bare chest gently rising and falling.

She sat up, fingering Sekhmet's amulet still at her neck, and grinned at the scattered heaps of their clothes on the floor. The coarse wool blanket scratched her skin, her mouth was dry, and her muscles ached as if she'd been run over by a chariot. For the first time in years, she was happy. Truly and deliriously happy.

She watched Senenmut sleep, then reached out and traced his temple. He smiled, eyes still closed. "Good morning," he said, making her wonder how long he'd been awake.

"Good morning."

He rolled to his side and propped himself up on his elbow so he could explore the curves and valleys of her body. He smiled that lazy smile, the one she'd missed so much. "You know," he said, his thumb brushing the indent of her hip, "I'd have started war with the Nubians long ago if I'd known this was the reward."

"I wish you would have." A heavy warmth seeped into her limbs and made it impossible to move. "We were utter fools to wait so long."

Senenmut rolled nearer, one hand planted on either side of her as his head dipped lower. His lips made their way down her thigh, his light breath on her flesh making her shudder with pleasure. "I'd have had you on the floor of your throne room on the day I returned if I thought I could get away with it."

"That would have given the slaves something to talk about."

"I intend to give them plenty to talk about."

She didn't want to answer questions about her relationship with Senenmut—not yet. This was their secret and theirs alone, at least for now. She never wanted to leave the cot, this tent. If only they could stay like this forever.

But the camp was stirring. More sounds came from outside the tent, groans from soldiers paying for their dedication to Sekhmet last night, and laughter from those more fortunate. Men's shadows marched across the rainbow panels of her tent.

She traced the scar on Senenmut's forehead with a ragged nail. "I've always wondered how you got this."

"I got caught stealing a set of pens from the offering table at the Temple of Thoth." Senenmut smiled. "My father found them, introduced me to the back of his hand for the first time, and apprenticed me to the temple the next day."

"And set you on your path to the army and to the palace," Hatshepsut said. "To me."

"I suppose so," Senenmut said. "I'll have to remember to thank my father for the beating when I meet him in the Field of Reeds." His face hovered over hers, the intensity of his expression making her blush even as she wrapped her legs around him, teasing him. She must look like Ammit after all this time with the army, living like a man, but she'd give up all her perfumes and paints, gold and jewels, if it meant waking up next to this man every morning.

Yet she was regent. And as much as she might wish to, she couldn't spend the morning abed with the man she loved.

Loved.

She knew without a doubt the word was true. She'd never sought Hathor's blessing, but the cow goddess had granted it just the same. And for that she was grateful.

"You should go now," she whispered to Senenmut, her back arching as his lips brushed the curve of her neck. "Before the whole camp wakes up."

He drew back as if slapped. "Of course."

He stood, turning his back so she was confronted with his scars again.

"What's wrong?" she asked.

"Nothing."

"You're a terrible liar, Senenmut."

"I forgot," he said, his voice so cold that she shivered. "I'm just a *rekhyt,* someone you can use and then send on his way."

"What are you talking about? I don't want to explain myself to every man outside, at least not yet."

He tied the kilt around his waist, then turned to face her. "You don't know what you want. You never have."

She stood, scrambling to cover herself. "How dare you speak to me like that—"

"I'll speak to you however I want, *Hemet*. I've earned at least that much."

Hemet. His mouth twisted with the title and his eyes flickered with pain. Old pain, the kind that lingered and festered, the type that could destroy a man. Then it was gone, replaced with the dull flame of anger.

"Thut is gone and I'm regent." She stood and took a tentative step toward him, the wool blanket around her waist. "I can do what I want."

He gave a bark of laughter, turned from her, and lifted the tent flap. Re's bright glare cut into the tent. "You mean like you did last time?"

"What are you talking about? We both wanted that kiss in the valley."

Soldiers passed, their curious eyes glancing inside, but she no longer cared.

Senenmut stopped and shook his head as if he couldn't believe what he had heard. "You asked Thutmosis to dismiss me after that kiss. He took great joy in informing me just before he broke my nose."

She stared at him, openmouthed. She could almost hear her brother crowing from the Field of Reeds. "My brother's final revenge."

"What?"

She laughed but the sound was hollow. "My brother told me you'd asked his permission to leave court, that you planned to leave me."

"What?" The tent flap fell, guttering the daylight. "When did he say that?"

"Right before he beat me." She wouldn't speak of the rest, of Thut taking her on the ground. Some things were better left unsaid. "Then he sent me your heart the next day."

"My heart?"

"What I thought was your heart. It must have been a pig's, maybe a goat's." She glanced up at him. "I had it mummified, buried it in my garden."

"You mummified my heart?"

"So Anubis could still judge you. It wasn't that difficult."

Now she understood his coldness since his return to court. As if he didn't have enough reason to hate her—

He gave a long, slow exhale and ran his hands over his scalp. "All this time—"

"We both thought the worst of each other." She waved her hand, couldn't look him in the eyes for fear of what she might see. "But it doesn't matter anymore. You can leave if you wish."

He closed the space between them, stopping a handsbreadth before her. They didn't touch, but she could feel the heat of him, was drawn to it like a lotus to the sun. He held her hands and turned them over, traced the pale scars on her wrists with his thumbs. "If I knew what was good for me, I'd have left you long before that day in the valley." She opened her mouth to berate him, but he smiled. "Unfortunately, I've always been a fool where you've been concerned."

The wool blanket fell to her feet. His cheeks under her hands were rough, covered with a day's dark stubble. She kissed him, tasted the saltiness of his lips, breathed in the exotic scent of cinnamon. This time when he took her it was even more urgent than before, as if he were trying to capture the time they'd lost.

Afterward, lying face-to-face with her chest pressed to his, she touched the scars on his back, hesitant at first and then feeling their rigid edges under her fingers. He kissed her palm, wove his fingers through hers.

"I'll make it up to you, all those lost years," she said. "I swear it."

"You already have," he said, kissing each of her fingers. "Although there's still one thing I can't believe."

Her heart fell. "And what is that?"

"You really mummified my heart?"

She laughed, almost wanting to cry as she remembered the desolation of those early days without him. "I did indeed."

He pulled her on top of him, their damp flesh pressed together, almost as close as they'd been only moments earlier when he'd moved inside her. His thumb followed the outline of her bruised lip. "Then some pig is rolling in the mud in the Field of Reeds right now, wondering how he got so lucky."

She wrinkled her nose with a huff and slid down to nestle in the crook of his arm, wanting to be close to him. He moved—too far away for her liking—but then she felt his lips trail kisses down her spine. "You have Sah's belt on your back." He kissed the spot again. "Three perfect freckles, all in a line. And one is fainter than the others, like the constellation."

"Do I?" She shivered as his fingers traced a line up the back of her thigh. If she could carry only one memory with her to the Field of Reeds, this would be it. Entwined with the man she loved, flush with a perfect victory, her future bright.

Her skin tingled as his fingers circled the delicate brown spots. "You're my beautiful star—my *nefersha*." He covered her body with his, hugged her to him. "A star, even if you are as haughty, infuriating, and temperamental as Sekhmet herself."

"Some of my best qualities."

He laughed. "Gods, but I love you, Hatshepsut."

Those words would never get old.

CHAPTER 21

The days tumbled by and Akhet had almost passed by with its season of easy sailing before the army returned to Waset, triumphant with the heavy spoils of war. This was a superstitious season, when wine should be drunk all day instead of beer, and it was said a man destined to die on the sixth day of the second month would likely meet Anubis as a result of intoxication. It was said that some lucky children born during this season were gifted by the seven Hathors with a future death by copulation, while those born on an unfortunate day during the last month were doomed to die of old age with an offering of beer poured in their face. But Hatshepsut didn't care about superstitions now. She knew the gods favored her.

The long trip home had been a gift from them, one that Hatshepsut had done her best to prolong, using the excuse of wishing to visit with Egypt's *nomarchs* along the way. Each day her ears were filled with praise for the glorious campaign in Nubia, but as soon as Re fell, Senenmut would sneak into her tent and they'd spend the dark hours, while the sun god battled Apep, in each other's arms, making love and dreaming of the future. She'd remember each of those nights until the gods called her to the sky.

With mixed emotions she watched Waset come into view, eager to return to Neferure and share the spoils of the Nubian victory with the City of Truth, but reluctant to hear the gate at the Walls of the Prince clang behind her. She'd relished her absolute freedom in the deserts of Nubia, surrounded by her people and spending time with Senenmut. Now she returned to the heavy responsibilities of ruling Egypt. Things couldn't remain the same.

Upon their arrival at the palace, she spent the morning with Neferure and Tutmose, their lessons canceled for the day. It had been only a few months since she'd been gone, but both of them had grown. Three years old now, Tutmose was as sturdy as a date-palm trunk, with scratched knees and elbows, while Neferure was like a delicate piece of sedge grass. Hatshepsut would have liked to play with the children all day, but the governors of each province stretching all the way to the Great Sea had sent their annual reports regarding exports and what tribute they would send to the palace in the way of grain, copper, turquoise, gold, and other precious metals. In addition to all of that came the tribute pouring in from Nubia: ivory, ebony, and ostrich feathers, along with sacks of gold dust and herds of cattle. It would be a monumental yet mundane task to reconcile the ledgers, and one Hatshepsut felt a responsibility to oversee.

"I'm glad you're back, even if you're as dark as a girl-slave." Aset hugged Hatshepsut, then stepped back with her hands still on Hatshepsut's shoulders. "And skinny, too. Didn't they feed you on the campaign?"

"Mostly sandy bread and stale beer. But it was wonderful."

Aset felt her forehead. "You've bitten too many mandrake berries. Sleeping on a cot, surrounded by foulmouthed soldiers, and bumping about a chariot hardly sounds wonderful."

"It was nice to see something of Egypt outside Waset." Hatshepsut steered the topic to calmer waters. "Did you know I'd barely been outside the City of Truth until now?"

Aset shrugged. "There's nothing I could possibly want outside these palace walls."

"But Egypt has so much to offer. Some of the cities I saw might have been in Phoenicia or Canaan for how different they were."

"Then I'll live vicariously through you." Aset smiled, glancing over her shoulder at Tutmose play-spearing one of the palace cats. It was a good thing for the cats that his aim still belonged to a three-year-old. "We can talk about your trip over dinner."

Hatshepsut had planned to eat with Senenmut; she craved his company even though they'd spent the last night in her tent making love until dawn. She yawned into her hand. "I'm exhausted. I think I'll have a tray sent to my chambers. Perhaps tomorrow?"

"Of course." Aset cocked her head to the side, then gave her another quick hug. "Well, it's good to have you home."

She returned the hug. "And it's good to be home."

And it was true, except that the whitewashed walls pressed in upon her and the air in the corridors tasted stale and brittle. She yearned for an open stretch of sand, the freedom of Nut's vast belly blanketing her at night.

But such things were not to be. Not anymore.

She arrived at her office to find her Chancellor and Chief Treasurer already there with Senenmut, bent over piles of papyrus and the remains of a meal spread out over the long table. Neshi and Ti were aristocrats, twins raised within the Walls of the Prince, both thin and effeminate. In fact, they were the same twins who had once cornered her outside a banquet before Neferubity had died, and both had plied her with ineffectual kisses. Hatshepsut had discovered their more potent bureaucratic abilities soon after Thutmosis had passed to the West. Ti especially had proven his worth when the final spoils of war from Nubia had been tallied and added to the Royal Treasury.

"The tribute will be good this year." Senenmut looked up from his tabulations. "Very good."

Hatshepsut bent over to inspect his scroll, glancing at Ti and Neshi to make sure they were absorbed in their work before caressing the back of Senenmut's neck. She'd been delighted to discover the other night that her merest touch there could drive him mad. Their relationship would remain a secret until he was better established at court, but that didn't mean she couldn't tease him a little. He shifted in his seat, picked up his brush, and scrawled almost illegible hieroglyphs down the margin of his papyrus.

> *Keep doing that if you want me to do something that would embarrass Ti and Neshi.*

She chuckled, straightening in a hurry as Neshi glanced up. "Impressive figures," she said.

"The harvest was more than ample this year." Ti tapped the end of his brush on the paper as he added some figures. "Tutmose is lucky to receive the throne during a year of plenty."

Neshi cleared his throat and the twins exchanged a glance. Senenmut didn't seem to notice, blotting out his hidden message and rolling up the scroll. She straightened. "What is it? Out with it."

Ti wrinkled his nose. "We don't wish to bring bad tidings."

"But we'll tell you if you promise not to kill us."

She gave them a look of mock severity and drummed her fingers over the thick gold bands on her forearms. "This must be important for you both to risk your necks."

Neshi stroked his smooth chin but avoided her eyes. "We decided it would be best if you heard from us."

"And not the gossips," Ti said.

"By the great nine gods," she said. "I'm going to lose my patience, and then I can guarantee you'll both be a head shorter by morning."

Senenmut chuckled, reached for a glass of lukewarm beer. "This sounds highly entertaining either way."

Neshi wrinkled his nose at Senenmut. "There's a priest of Amun who has been making overtures for the throne. I believe you know him. He used to be a cupbearer and then vizier to Osiris Thutmosis?"

Senenmut's face turned dark. "Mensah? You let him live?"

Hatshepsut raised a hand to stop him—that was a long story she didn't care to tell in front of Ti and Neshi. Perhaps she'd made the wrong decision in sparing his miserable life.

"Has he committed treason?" If so, she'd have him thrown onto a spike in front of the palace and his body burned. Mensah was out of second chances.

Ti shook his head but his eyes laughed. "Hardly. He thinks to marry you."

Senenmut choked on his beer, but Hatshepsut sat dumbstruck, then burst out laughing. "Where on earth did you hear such nonsense?"

"From my spies at Amun's temple." Neshi shrugged. "It pays to be informed."

"Does he think me an idiot?"

Ti looked to his brother. "We're not sure what he thinks."

"If he thinks at all," Senenmut muttered.

She rubbed under her eyes, careful not to smudge her kohl. "The jackal hasn't even had the courage to broach the subject with me yet."

"Do you want him to?" Senenmut asked. Hatshepsut thought she detected a note of jealousy. It was evil of her, but she rather liked the sound.

"Perhaps he thinks to woo you first." Ti gave a wild grin.

"Trade my throne for a *wa'eb* priest and imperil the whole country?" Hatshepsut tsked as she picked up her stack of papyrus again. "He must be mad."

"That jackal's not a *wa'eb* anymore," Neshi said. "He's risen to Second Lector Priest in the temple of Amun now. Many of his supporters at court think it would be a good match, especially considering his lineage and former position as vizier."

Hatshepsut cursed Thutmosis all the way in the Field of Reeds for elevating Mensah to vizier. She might have confiscated Mensah's wealth and property, but his family was ancient. He'd always have friends in high places.

Ti whistled. "Perhaps he's deluded himself into believing his pedigree and your crown might be a better combination to continue the dynasty than little Tutmose."

"Facing a stake in Waset's square might change his mind." Senenmut crossed his arms and leaned back in his chair, testing her.

"No. Send him to the fortress at Buhen," she said. "He can govern it for all I care, but get him out of Waset before he does anything he'll regret. That should teach him a lesson."

"A geography lesson, certainly." Ti laughed. "Buhen's the edge of the civilized world."

"Precisely." She gave a wicked grin. "And there's nothing to say he'll actually make it that far."

There were all sorts of dangers on the road to Buhen—lions, snakes, and bandits, to name only a few. Maybe his horse would step in a scorpion hole and throw him along the way. In any case, she wouldn't waste more time or energy on the fool.

She scanned the figures Ti had added at the bottom of his papyrus. Her eyes widened at the amount of copper the governor of Sinai promised to send. "The treasury will overflow this year."

Ti chuckled. "We might have to build a bigger treasure house just for the copper."

Neshi peered over her shoulder and let out a low whistle. "Lucky us."

"This calls for a celebration." Hatshepsut motioned to one of the boy-slaves waiting outside. Moments later, a wonderful vintage of date-palm wine appeared with four blue faience glasses.

"To Hapi, the fat old Man of the Fishes!" They pounded their glasses on the table. The wine tasted of earth and air, dates, and a hint of honey. "May the god of the Nile bless us with another bountiful Inundation and harvest next year!"

The four of them sipped their wine as they chipped away at the mountain of papyrus scrolls. Hatshepsut traveled her way up the Nile through the ledgers as the hours slipped by, moving farther away from the City of Truth with each *nome*'s accounts. Finally, as slaves came in to light the lamps, she gave voice to an idea that had blossomed slowly in her mind.

"Tutmose and I should take a journey down the Nile. A royal procession to celebrate our victory in Nubia."

And to boost her own popularity with her people.

The men's brushes stopped moving and they all looked up at her.

"That's a good idea," Senenmut said after a moment. "An extremely good idea."

"It's not often that the *rekhyt* get to see the living god or regent," Ti said. "And Osiris Thutmosis never went on procession."

"My father never had a chance either," Hatshepsut added. "He took me to visit some of the religious centers near Waset when I was young, but that's as close as he got to a true procession."

"He had his military campaigns," Neshi said. "That gave the people a chance to see their pharaoh and his might. But that was a decade ago. A procession is long overdue."

"How big would your entourage be? And how long would you be gone?" Ti was already sketching a long column of figures.

"I'm not sure how long." She thought for a moment. "Several weeks? The Nile is sluggish at this time of year. The group should be small—myself, Aset, some servants and guards."

"The children?" Senenmut asked.

Hatshepsut nodded. "Of course."

"And your favorite Chancellor and Treasurer," Neshi said.

Hatshepsut grinned. "That goes without saying. I don't know what I'd do without you."

"That's certainly workable," Ti said.

Their easy acceptances pleased Hatshepsut. "Appropriate the funds, and we'll be on our way as soon as Isis ceases her tears and the Nile recedes." Her stomach rumbled; she realized she hadn't eaten since the morning meal with the children. "Shall we continue this tomorrow?"

"We'll be here before Re wakes," Ti said.

She stood, eager to tell Aset and the children about the procession. The children's tutors would have to join them for so long a trip, or Tutmose and Neferure would fall behind in their lessons. A tutor schooled in military traditions had been acquired for Tutmose shortly after Senenmut's arrival, but Senenmut was still officially Neferure's tutor, despite his absence while in Nubia.

Hatshepsut stopped with a start. If both the children's tutors came, Senenmut would travel on the same ship with her, the two of them confined in very close quarters for weeks on end.

There was no way they'd be able to keep their secret for much longer.

The day of embarkation dawned crisp and clear. Three cedar boats with Horus' giant gold eyes emblazoned on their hulls sat at the dock, red and white royal pennants listless as they waited for the breeze. Hatshepsut, Aset, the children, and their servants would sail on the first boat, with the courtiers on the second. The final barge would carry a stable of goats and oxen ready to be slaughtered for the expedition's dinners, and a floating kitchen to prepare the majority of their meals. All that remained now was for the passengers to board.

Hatshepsut's loose traveling sheath brushed her legs as she made her way to the royal nursery to collect the children. Aset was helping her son pack the last of his carved wooden soldiers for their journey.

"One is missing," she said to Hatshepsut, looking slightly frayed as she smoothed the braids of her wig. "It's been a crisis."

Tutmose crawled about the ground, scrambling under chairs and behind chests. Then he stood, brandishing an ebony figure in his fist. "Found it, Mama!"

"Crisis averted." Hatshepsut grinned as Neferure came running toward her. "Are you ready for our trip, monkey?"

Her daughter nodded. "I said good-bye to Nana."

"Good girl." Hatshepsut planted a kiss on Neferure's smooth head. It was probably a good thing Ahmose would remain behind; the former Great Royal Wife was growing frail and had no desire to leave the comforts of the palace to be crammed on a boat for several weeks. Her body may be tired, but her tongue was as sharp as ever. In such close quarters Ahmose would have sniffed out her daughter's relationship with her steward, and Hatshepsut didn't want to find out whose blood would have been spilled as a result.

"I think we're ready." Aset held the linen bag of soldiers in one hand and her son's hand with the other. "All soldiers present and accounted for."

They made their way through the maze of whitewashed corridors into the bright morning sunshine. A low hum began at the causeway and grew into a lion's roar.

"What's that?" Tutmose asked.

Across the river, the brown banks of the Nile seemed to shift, like sand in a storm. Only it wasn't sand, but a swarm of *rekhyt* along the river's edge. "Our people," Hatshepsut said. "They're very happy to see us."

And it wasn't just her stepson's titles that were carried on the breeze, but the exuberant cries of her own name shouted by Waset's citizens. She held Tutmose's hand and waved back. It took only a moment and soon he was waving in unison with her, even as Neferure hid behind Aset's legs. The crowd threatened to scream itself hoarse, the sound refusing to ebb until they were all aboard.

The cedar barque swayed lazily along the sparkling surface of the Nile, a line of overdressed nobles waiting to board the second boat. Red and white pennants snapped to attention on the first boat, the gilded oars all raised in stiff salute.

"Impressive, isn't it?" Senenmut emerged from belowdecks, dressed in a short kilt and without his wig. "They've been chanting your name for ages. And Tutmose's, of course."

"Of course." Hatshepsut glanced at Aset, but she had her back turned and Neferure on her hip, pointing out an egret swooping overhead.

"Remind me to speak to whomever arranged our cabins," Senenmut murmured.

"Why? Is there a problem?"

His voice dropped. "My room seems to be next to yours."

"Precisely as I'd arranged." Although with only four cabins, there weren't many options. Hatshepsut and Aset had their own chambers, but the children shared the third with their *menats*, and Senenmut, Nomti, and Tutmose's tutor would have the last. Their slaves would sleep on reed mats outside the doors. The next few weeks would be cozy.

Senenmut sighed, but it did little to hide his grin. "I'll never get any sleep so close to you."

She glanced at Aset and the children, her voice a whisper. "We're going to have to be discreet."

"That's not what I meant."

"No? Then what is it?"

Now it was his turn to whisper, offering her a teasing smile. "Sometimes you snore."

She'd have smacked him, but he sauntered away to Neferure, asking loudly whether she had seen any crocodiles yet. He glanced back once, still grinning, but Hatshepsut was called to answer one of Tutmose's questions, something about how often they could expect a hippo to overturn the boats.

The barges eased from their moorings and slipped fully into the Nile's muddy embrace. A handful of fishing skiffs made of lashed papyrus darted back and forth like pale dragonflies, crisscrossing the waves while showering the glassy brown waters with a bright confetti of purple and red anemone petals. The other vessels followed at a comfortable distance, a parade of nobility housed within the royal barges. It wasn't until the dark smudge of the city on the horizon became a mere haze that Hatshepsut tore her eyes away from their home.

The sails unfurled to take advantage of the scant breeze, pregnant with the wind's first kiss. The boats continued merrily along their way that first day, carried easily down the lethargic Nile, the banks laden with precious silt now that the floods had receded. They passed a frenzy of life: bare-breasted women on the edges of naked fields, pulling in reed baskets of water from rickety wooden swapes; men driving plows and throwing barley seeds to be trampled underfoot; and small cities of brown and white goats grazing beneath palm trees. Neferure and Tutmose shrieked with glee at every soaring ibis and sleeping crocodile as Hatshepsut watched the multitude of mud brick huts that poked their heads above the green.

This was her Egypt.

Late that afternoon, the boats floated by the island where Neferubity had flown to the sky, now a peaceful green knoll rippling with a carpet of sedge grass and papyrus fronds along the riverbank. Hatshepsut spared a moment to murmur a prayer for the *kas* of the dead; she liked to think her sister and father watched her from the Field of Reeds, and were pleased with all she'd done for Egypt and their dynasty. Everyone else was belowdecks, so the air was empty save for her whispered words and the grunts of the rowers, but then Aset came up, complaining about her oven of a cabin. Hatshepsut smiled, glad for the company.

"I feel like I've rolled in the pens of the menagerie." Aset sniffed herself and grimaced. "I smell like it, too."

"Wonderful, isn't it?" Hatshepsut hugged her and laughed.

Aset blew a tired puff of air and tucked a damp strand of black hair back into her wig. "You're touched, aren't you? All this sun and wind, and you've finally lost your mind."

"You'll get used to it," Hatshepsut said.

"The heat? Or you being mad?"

"The heat. It grew on me in Nubia."

"I just want a bath. I don't suppose you lugged along that Cretan tub, did you?"

"No, but there's a perfectly good river at our disposal. We'll go for a swim before we dock at Gebtu for the night."

"We can do that?"

"You're traveling with the pharaoh and the regent of Egypt." Hatshepsut grinned. "We can do anything we want."

The royal barge anchored alone in the middle of the river, and they watched the rest of the entourage trek ashore for dinner as special guests of the town of Gebtu.

"Try not to get into too much trouble out here," Senenmut said under his breath; he was the last from their boat in line for the skiff that would ferry them into town. "Although I'm not convinced that's possible with you around."

Hatshepsut grinned at his formal kilt, gold pectoral, and stiff wig. He would have to sit through an interminable parade of dinner courses and stiff conversation while she had the privilege of swimming naked in the Nile. "I have no idea what you mean."

"Of course not." He straightened, rubbed his chin, and gave a thoughtful nod. "Yes, I think Neferure would enjoy hearing *The Tale of the Eloquent Peasant*. It's a truly admirable piece of literature."

She raised an eyebrow, but his gaze flicked to the other side of the ship, where Aset waited with the children. Neferure and Tutmose played hide-and-find amongst the rowers' benches, but Aset stared in their direction. Hatshepsut cleared her throat. "I've never cared for that tale. I've always failed to see the allure of the story of a *rekhyt* advising his pharaoh."

Aset turned away and clapped for Tutmose to come out from under a bench. Senenmut dropped his voice and grinned. "You'll pay for that one day. Watch out for crocodiles."

"Thanks for the advice."

A smattering of domed pigeon coops crowded the shoreline, their clay surfaces pockmarked with roosts. Hatshepsut's stomach rumbled at the thought of roast pigeon, but she was glad to avoid a stuffy meal of laughing at bland jokes and discussing the harvest tallies with the town officials. Nomti and the other guards scouted the area for hippos and crocodiles and, finding none, gave the group permission to toss aside their dirty clothes and jump into the river. The children splashed and giggled, little river otters at play.

"Stay close to the boat, you little monkeys!" Hatshepsut leaned back to wet her hair, letting the river fill her ears. She hadn't shaved her head since leaving for Nubia, so her hair curled round her ears when she didn't wear a wig. She had it in her mind to leave the infernal thing in her trunk during the entire procession.

"Are they at all like you and Thutmosis when you were young?" Aset glanced at the children and scrubbed her arms hard with natron soap, as if she'd never be clean again.

"Sometimes. Neferure reminds me more of my sister. Thut and I were terrible trouble when we were younger." She frowned. "I don't want our history to repeat itself with Tutmose and Neferure."

"I think the two of them will be happy together one day." A dreamy smile warmed Aset's face. "More like Thutmosis and me." She winced. "I'm sorry. I didn't mean it that way." She swam over to Hatshepsut and wrapped her in a wet embrace. "I still miss him."

"He worshipped you." Hatshepsut knew Aset still kept the black granite statues Thut had made for her, the two of them kept side by side on an altar in her apartments. "He's waiting for you in the Field of Reeds."

Thut had worshipped Aset and Tutmose. Sometimes the memory still hurt.

"Do you think you'll ever love again?" Hatshepsut's question came in a rush, as if she feared she wouldn't get the sentence out unless it was blurted in a single breath.

Aset shook her head. "No one could ever love me like Thutmosis. His love was the greatest gift the gods could have given me, and, despite my empty bed, I'll be thankful for it until the day Anubis comes for me."

Hatshepsut grinned. "No one says your bed has to stay empty."

"You're incorrigible." Aset splashed her, then gave her an odd look. "What about your empty bed?"

Hatshepsut glanced at the shore. Their secret would be out soon; Aset might as well hear the truth from her own mouth. "It's not empty anymore."

"I'd suspected as much."

"You did? How?"

"You're far too happy these days. You don't brood nearly enough." She smiled. "So, tell me: Who is it?"

Hatshepsut hesitated, clinging to the last precious moment of her secret before finally answering. "Senenmut."

Aset's smile fell. "But he's a *rekhyt*."

"That's a bit hypocritical, isn't it?"

"It's different for a woman, and you know it. Thutmosis was expected to take plenty of wives, sire multiple heirs. You're the regent and it's your duty to keep the throne safe for my son. Taking up with that *rekhyt* does exactly the opposite." She swam over so Hatshepsut had to look at her. "What will happen to the succession if you become pregnant?"

"I've taken care of that." As soon as they'd returned to Waset, she'd started using the pessary the Royal Physician had once recommended. She counted back, and her heart stuttered. She hadn't needed to purify herself since before the battle at Dongola.

Her courses were late. Dear gods, how could she have been so careless?

"I'm sure Senenmut is a good romp," Aset was saying, "but couldn't you at least choose someone a little less ambitious?"

Hatshepsut swam back from Aset, her thoughts crowding her mind like a flock of pigeons. This baby could cost her position as regent. A son would mean competition for Tutmose's throne, or perhaps put her in a different position altogether, one she'd only dreamed of.

To have Senenmut's child. The thought made her both quake with joy and tremble with terror. A son with his crooked smile. The threat of childbirth.

Aset's lips pursed as if she'd been sucking lemons. "How do you know he doesn't want the throne?"

"Because I know Senenmut. He's not like that."

And yet she felt the tiniest flicker of doubt. She shoved it aside.

"Are you sure?"

"As sure as I can be about anything in this life." Her eyes narrowed. "You don't like him, do you?"

Now it was Aset's turn to look offended. "I once saved his life, Hatshepsut. I just don't want to see you or Tutmose hurt."

The children were hollering to get back on the boat, Tutmose trying to climb up the thick rope to the deck while Neferure waited patiently for assistance. Hatshepsut swam to Aset and clasped her arms with wet hands. "Senenmut would never hurt any of us. I trust him."

"That's what I'm afraid of."

"I love him, Aset, and he loves me. Please be happy for me."

"I'll try." Aset sighed. "Just don't do anything you'll regret."

CHAPTER 22

T he boats made good time the next day, passing naked boys swimming in the muddy waters of the Nile and finally spotting the glow from Nubt's lamps as the horizon swallowed Re. The white walls of the city's famed temple to Set towered over the sprawl of squat mud-brick buildings. While Amun reigned supreme in the capital, it was the powerful and ambivalent Set who controlled the rest of Upper Egypt. Osiris Tutmose had commissioned this temple shortly before he had gone to the West, and Hatshepsut yearned to see her father's work.

This city, the sacred center of Set's worship since before the pha-raohs, did not sleep tonight. The entire town crammed at the edge of the river to greet the visiting nobility. The crowd fell to the ground in one simultaneous *henu* as the ship bumped the dock. A thin and im-peccably dressed man clambered to his feet, cleared his throat several times, and shifted from one foot to the other as if he had pebbles in his sandals.

"Welcome to Nubt!" The harsh twang to the mayor's vowels re-minded Hatshepsut they were no longer near the capital. His smile revealed a set of worn teeth and pulpy gums, the result of too many years of eating bread milled with Egypt's ever-present sand. "Set, our

patron god, is pleased to open his city to the pharaoh and his entourage. We are happy that you could join our humble city as we feast
and make merry in your name!"

"We are honored by your attention," Hatshepsut called as the skiff
reached the shore. "May the gods bless your city!"

The mayor presented her with a papyrus collar woven with fragrant
cornflower and blue lotus blossoms, looping it over her neck before
both her feet touched shore. In his haste he almost knocked the wig
from her head, not that she'd have minded the excuse to drop the thing
into the Nile. Tutmose grimaced when the mayor offered him a smaller
necklace, but he ducked his head when Aset frowned at him.

Chariots and sedan chairs formed a line at the end of the dock, a
multitude of shapes and sizes likely apprehended from every possible
source within the city. Hatshepsut chose one of the chariots, as litters
hoisted Aset and the children aloft. The procession wove its way
through the riotous crowd and down streets so narrow she could have
touched both walls had she spread her arms. They passed whitewashed
mud-brick homes, most with tables or beds on their roofs. Nubt's citizens peered down to catch sight of the pharaoh and regent, a story to
pass on to their children and grandchildren for years to come, and
showered them with a rain of cornflower petals. The narrow alleys
opened up as they entered the town center. Dusty market stalls had
been hastily shoved into doorways and the ground swept clean of most
of the animal dung, although a bag of dried lentils had been spilled
and forgotten. Garlands of fuchsia lotus blossoms draped every tree
and building to imbue the air with a heavenly perfume. Thousands of
tiny lamps with dancing flames lined the square, and tables covered
with linen cloths had been set for dinner. Jugglers, acrobats, and musicians huddled to the side, waiting with an entire program of entertainment.

Hatshepsut allowed the mayor to lead her to the largest of the
tables. She had lost sight of Senenmut in the crowd, and Aset and the
children were seated at the very end of her table, far out of earshot as

the volume of voices reached a steady hum. Seated in the middle, with the mayor and Ineni on either side of her, Hatshepsut found that the giant plates of marinated olives, steaming mashed turnips, freshly baked bread, and roast quail stuffed with cloves of garlic made her stomach groan in anticipation. She'd spent the day sorting through allocation requests from the gods' temples and had forgotten to eat. The mayor tore off a quail's leg and offered it to her; she happily accepted.

"Did you have fair weather?" he asked, his hands aflutter. "This time of year is usually pleasant sailing, but one never can tell. And I've heard dreadful stories of those nasty hippos upsetting more than one boat. Of course, I've never left Nubt—born and bred—but word does travel. Do you have turnips this flavorful in the City of Truth? I don't imagine you do—Nubt is known all down the Nile for having the best turnips in all Egypt. Now that the gold has run out it's our claim to fame, that and the temple, of course. And with the garlic? I doubt the gods could create a better-tasting dish! But listen to me! It isn't my desire to flow on like the Inundation."

The man never once paused for breath. He didn't eat more than two bites from the time they sat down, and those must have been swallowed whole. Fortunately, nodding hadn't precluded Hatshepsut from helping herself, and now she was full, despite having picked around the turnips. She hated turnips.

"Is the Temple of Set open this evening?" Hatshepsut took advantage of a rare pause to interrupt the mayor.

His head bounced up and down like one of Neferure's toy balls. "For you, the temple can be opened at any time."

"I hear it's an architectural marvel." She dangled the bait before him. "Ineni here is my chief architect and would love to hear all about it." She grinned at her portly adviser's pained expression and stood. Silence fell over the gathering. "If you'll excuse me, I think I'll take some air on my own."

The chatter continued as Nomti fell into step behind Hatshepsut. This was an opportunity she wasn't going to miss, to view the temple alone and in the shrouded darkness of night instead of in the glare of day.

The temple's white walls loomed high over the square, even in the gloom. Two glowing yellow eyes glared down at her from the top of the gate, a scrawny temple cat with two gold hoops in its ears who likely wished it could trade Egypt's regent for a plump mouse. The stars twinkled brightly, easier to see now against the crisp darkness of the sky without the dull glow of the city's lamps. The temple was deserted, so Nomti remained at the entrance of the outer gate so Hatshepsut could wander alone. Even the offices of the High Priest matched the darkness of Nut's belly. Beyond the sprawling plaza stood the main temple itself, its massive hypostyle hall filled with papyrus-topped columns the height of ten full-grown men. Most Egyptian monuments were crammed from floor to ceiling with adulations of the gods or lively scenes reenacted for the benefit of the dead, but here the temple walls were bare, unfinished. Puzzled, Hatshepsut ran her hands over the smooth granite, still warm from Re's heat.

"The walls are as bare as the desert, the barren domain of Set." Senenmut stepped into one of the rectangular shafts of moonlight that filtered through the open roof and leaned against a granite column, arms crossed in front of him. "Shouldn't you be back at the square, learning more about turnips?"

She groaned. "I am now an expert on everything to do with the wretched things."

He shot her the crooked smile she loved so much. "So I heard."

They were finally alone. She let herself be pulled into his arms, savored the taste of wine on his lips.

"I see someone missed me." Senenmut chuckled.

"Shut up and kiss me."

He did.

They undressed each other and made love slowly, her back pressed into the flagstones as he hovered over her, bringing her to the edge of ecstasy several times before they finally fell over the precipice together, their sweat-slicked bodies clinging to each other as they gasped at their shared pleasure. Afterward, they sat twined together on the ground at the base of a pillar, her back against his bare chest and their legs stretched toward Set's outer courtyard.

"I told Aset about us."

Senenmut didn't answer at first, but his fingers stopped stroking her hair. "And?"

"She wasn't happy."

"I can imagine."

"She'll come around. Hathor is her patron goddess, after all." She leaned her head back and looked up into Nut's black belly, the stars glowing like dull marbles through wisps of clouds. Now was probably as good a time as any to tell him. "There's something else."

He made a questioning noise in the back of his throat, the sound vibrating into her spine.

"I think I'm pregnant."

He stiffened behind her and perfect silence settled over the courtyard, as if the gods waited to hear his reaction. She held her breath, her lungs close to bursting.

"Are you sure?"

She nodded, unable to trust her voice.

"I don't think I've ever been so happy." He pulled her tight, the joy rippling from his body in waves. His grip loosened. "What about you? Are you happy?"

She hesitated, then nodded, surprised at the truth. The terror was still there, but somehow it was smaller in the face of his joy. "Yes. Although this does complicate things."

"Children always complicate things." He chuckled. "Just ask my mother."

She smiled, leaned back into his chest. "She did have six. That's more than enough complications for anyone."

Laughter rumbled in his chest. "I'd give you at least a dozen if I could."

"Gods, I hope not." Not that many, but one or maybe two. Perhaps Egypt could handle that. "Your mother wasn't regent, you know."

"I know. Everything is as the gods will it, Hatshepsut." He twined his fingers with hers. "There is always order amongst the chaos, even when it's not possible to see. Set somehow always manages to push his way into life; there are things you can't predict or control."

"Perhaps for you mere mortals."

"Don't tell me you've decided you're a goddess now." Senenmut laughed. "Egypt was almost destroyed by the first Sekhmet; she would certainly crumble before two lion goddesses."

Hatshepsut touched the amulet of the lion goddess at her neck. "Not a goddess, but no longer a plaything of the gods either. *I* control my own life now." It was a bold statement, but she'd spent too many years cowering before Hathor, Taweret, and Isis. She glanced toward the towering statues of Set at the entrance: curved snouts, pricked ears, and forked tails. He wasn't a god she wished to offend. "I still honor the gods, of course."

"I forgot that none of the rules of this life apply to you." Senenmut stroked the back of her neck, making her shiver and her skin prickle with gooseflesh. "Remind me to make sacrifices to Set on your behalf. Just in case."

"There's more to pleasing the gods than slaughtering bulls and lighting incense." Like this temple they sat in. "If I could, I would cover Egypt with monuments to the gods."

"With your name on them, too, I suppose."

"Naturally." She glanced around, happy to be able to see something her father had made, built of solid granite that would last to eternity. "Do you know what my favorite part is?"

"The blank walls?"

Hatshepsut chuckled. "No, not the walls." She looked up at the stars twinkling overhead. "The sky. The stars and the sun are always here, but always moving. I think Set would approve of the orderly chaos."

"And Sekhmet, too."

"She does like the sun."

"I know." His chest rumbled with laughter. "Do you remember the knife I gave you?"

"How could I forget?" She groaned and her cheeks flushed despite the cool air, recalling the hymn to the lion goddess painstakingly etched into its ivory handle. She really had been terrible to Senenmut then, but he had never given up on her. Sometimes she didn't think she deserved him, but then she remembered how alike they were.

"I still can't believe you gave it away. In front of me."

"You deserved it."

He chuckled. "You're probably right. But it took a damn long time to carve that handle."

"Perhaps you can make me another someday."

"Greedy little thing, aren't you?"

"Always." She nestled deeper into the crook of his arm. The gods had given her an incredible gift in Senenmut, and another one growing in her belly. She wondered if she dared trespass upon them further.

"There's something else I want, Senenmut."

He chuckled and she felt his lips on her temple. "And what might that be?"

She waited a moment, listened to the words growing ever louder in her mind. She'd never spoken them aloud before, but they had been her constant companions since the day of Tutmose's coronation.

"I want to be pharaoh."

The silence stretched so long that Hatshepsut wondered if she had shocked the words out of him. Finally, he rubbed his jaw. "I know you do."

She straightened, needing to see his face. "What?"

He shook his head. "You call me ambitious, but you're the most driven person I've ever met." She gave him a mock punch and he smiled, then grew sober. "Still, Hatshepsut, you must realize—"

"That I can only ever be regent." She clenched her fists and drew a ragged breath. "If I'd been born a boy—"

He chuckled. "I, for one, am quite happy that the gods made you otherwise."

She ignored his attempt at levity. "It's not fair that I can't rule simply because I'm a woman."

"I know, *nefersha*." He pulled her back to her place against his chest, the stars twinkling overhead. "This life is rarely fair, yet I know two things for certain."

"And those are?"

"First, that the gods favor you above all their other children. Be content with that, and perhaps they'll surprise you one day. And second, if you ever did sit upon the Isis Throne, I'd be your most ardent supporter."

"Really?" Senenmut loved her, but she hadn't anticipated that he'd even entertain the idea of her wearing the double crown.

"Of course." Laughter rumbled in his chest. "What man wouldn't want the pharaoh of Egypt in his bed?"

The expedition continued down the Nile toward Giza. At Asyût, reed flutes and castanets played as women danced along the banks to honor Mut and Taweret, the goddesses of motherhood and fertility. Girl-slaves lined the boats to shout at crowds of women on the shore, and both groups hitched up their sheaths to expose themselves, absorbing the fertility of the Black Land. The men politely pretended not to notice. Most of them, at least.

The trip continued in a more sedate manner after that, scheduled to end at the ancient pyramids before beginning the return trip to Waset. Senenmut had drawn the children a picture of the Sphinx with its pharaoh's head, and Tutmose and Neferure spent several days roaring like lions and pretending to be giant statues.

Most nights when Hatshepsut retired to her cabin, it was to discover folded scraps of papyrus that Senenmut had hidden in empty perfume pots or under her headrest. They contained tiny bits of poetry scrawled in the nearly illegible handwriting she so adored. Some brought tears of joy to her eyes, and still others made her laugh out loud.

> *I love you more than the everlasting earth,*
> *And worship at the temple of your body.*
> *The goddesses are bound together in you,*
> *Fearsome Sekhmet,*
> *The Great Mother Taweret,*
> *Cunning Isis,*
> *Even pliant Hathor.*

There was one he dared slip to her while they prayed at the Temple of Thoth—Senenmut's patron god—in the city of Khmun, home of the baboon-headed god of wisdom.

> *Atum ascended from the waters of chaos*
> *And bound together the elements of the world.*
> *So your love has transformed me*
> *Because we go together.*

And her favorite:

> *Your voice is sweet wine;*
> *I live to hear it.*
> *To see you with each look*
> *Is better than bread or beer.*
> *Get thee to my bed, woman,*
> *Lest I waste away!*

That one had been passed under the table after a night spent drinking pomegranate wine and feasting on fresh river catfish, surrounded by all the nobles from both barges. She and Senenmut had slipped away to her cabin and devoured each other in a furious bout of lovemaking that left her body aching for more. Aset had pursed her lips when Hatshepsut had returned to the banquet alone, then motioned for her to straighten her wig.

Hatshepsut treasured each precious letter, tied them all together with a dyed red string and hid them in the bottom of her jewelry box. Perhaps one day she and Senenmut would read them in their old age, and then chase each other to bed. She knew that they would be together as long as the gods willed it, until one of them flew to the West.

Re had started his battle with Apep by the time the boats reached the sacred necropolis of the pyramids, and Nut's belly was a soft haze of black. The timeworn monuments glowed in the light of the full moon, a testament to time. Khufu's Great Pyramid reigned over the plateau, the two smaller pyramids flanking their great king. The Sphinx sat at attention before the monuments, its limestone body aglow with white moonlight, while its painted face was shrouded in shadows.

The nobles and servants remained aboard their boats, silent witnesses as Nomti rowed Hatshepsut and Tutmose ashore. This sacred land of the dead was typically forbidden to the living, but not to the pharaoh and regent. They went ashore alone and meandered hand in hand through the Sphinx's red granite temple to pay their respects at Pharaoh Khafre's mortuary complex. The ancient building had fallen into disrepair, but Hatshepsut left a priceless bag of white frankincense pellets for the ancient pharaoh. She wondered what treasures lay beneath their feet, the tombs of royal mummies and *kas* of dynasties long since past. They skirted a cluster of smaller pyramids partially buried by ancient sand, the final resting places of Egypt's queens long since dead. These women had been the lucky ones, gifted by their husbands and sons with eternal tombs in recognition of their contribution to their dynasties, but their majesty had been scoured away by centuries of winds, leaving only heaps of mud brick, virtually forgotten.

Hatshepsut shuddered.

They stopped walking and she took Tutmose's hand. Khufu's

colossal pyramid was immense, a living manifestation of Re's light brought to earth. Tutmose touched the white limestone first, then her hand enveloped his. The rock pulsed with Re's warmth, despite the crisp night air. Nameless workers long since dead had hauled each massive block and toiled to fit each perfectly into place so the pharaoh could climb to the heavens and meet the gods. The records of his reign might be lost or his mummy destroyed, but the world would always remember Khufu because of this monument he had built. His name would live forever.

So would hers.

Tutmose craned his neck to see the pyramid's pinnacle, no easy feat. "Is it old?"

"Very old," Hatshepsut said. "This tomb was ancient many lifetimes ago and will remain here long after we've passed to the West. Remember this when you sit upon the Isis Throne. Everything we do is for the glory of Egypt."

They retraced their steps. Aset waited for them on board, but the rest of the deck was deserted. Snores drifted from belowdecks—they had been gone longer than Hatshepsut had realized.

She kissed the top of Tutmose's head and helped him stumble into his mother's arms, and stifled a yawn herself. Alone on deck, she watched the pyramids, spellbound, until a heavy cloud shrouded the moon; then she tore herself away and stepped over the girl-slave asleep outside her door. She had almost finished undressing when she felt something warm and wet between her legs.

A smear of crimson.

"No. Please, no." She grabbed her discarded sheath to staunch the blood, curled on her side on the narrow feather mattress. She knew from Enheduanna's miscarriages that terrible cramping urged a woman's womb to expel her unborn child. She waited an eternity for the pain, but none came, only the slow and steady flow of blood.

Her moon bloods.

Tears streamed down her cheeks at the stark realization. There had been no nausea, no tender breasts, no lethargy these past months. She'd never been pregnant, just missed her courses.

Only now that the hope of it was gone did she realize how much she'd wanted this baby, a child that had never existed. And then she knew without a doubt that this was a message from the gods, a warning not to reach too high. A son from her womb would imperil Tutmose's succession, just as Aset had predicted. Hatshepsut already had a precious daughter and the love of a wonderful man.

Still, she wanted more.

As she lay curled on her mattress, racked with silent sobs, something tiny and pale caught her eye on the wooden planks. A scrap of papyrus.

Another of Senenmut's poems. The handwriting was his, but this time it wasn't poetry he'd written. The words were bittersweet.

One day you'll build monuments to rival these.

CHAPTER 23

The second obelisk was ready to soar. Cushioned on the sand, its electrum-capped pinnacle was aimed at the horizon, but in moments the workmen would hoist it to forever pierce the sky. The men guzzled from dirty water skins, wiped sweat from their brows, and unclenched fists burned by the ropes. The first obelisk stood guard at Amun's entrance to Karnak, awaiting its mate.

"They're even taller than Grandfather's." Neferure shielded her painted eyes from the glare of the gilded monuments. The shafts of the obelisks were covered in gold foil and as blinding as the sun disk on today's cloudless morning.

Time marched loudly past as Hatshepsut gazed at her daughter, the only person aside from Tutmose left on this earth who shared her family's blood. Over the past years almost everyone from her father's generation had passed to the West—Sitre, Mutnofret, and finally even her own mother. Anubis had felled that aging branch of the family tree. There had been no more pregnancies either, due to her secret use of the Royal Physician's pessary. Her heart ached at the necessary deception, but she couldn't allow her desires to open the door to future civil war and bloodshed. Always she reminded herself of the sacrifices Egypt demanded of its rulers. Senenmut had only nodded when she'd told him of her mistake, and seemed to accept her hints that perhaps Neferure's difficult birth had made it impossible for her to bear other children. He never broached the subject of trying for another child and had since thrown himself into becoming Neferure's acting father. Perhaps things were better this way.

Now, only a hairsbreadth shorter than Hatshepsut, Neferure was about to celebrate her tenth naming day. A willowy wisp of a child, she possessed the translucent beauty of a pale moth and grew more quiet and reflective with each passing year. Sometimes she was too quiet.

"I dedicated the obelisks to my father," Hatshepsut said.

"And to Amun. I read the inscriptions," Neferure added shyly before confusion clouded her delicate features. "But Tutmose's name is on them, too. And he didn't have anything to do with them—he's too busy with the army."

"But he's the pharaoh," Hatshepsut said. "And one day, after all his military training, he'll be a great pharaoh, one worthy of your grandfather's name."

The workmen shouted as they hoisted the obelisk, pulling the heavy granite in unison while scrambling men pushed away the sand at its base. Hatshepsut squeezed Neferure's hand, barely able to breathe. The slightest crack would cause the magnificent monument to topple and obliterate in an instant what had taken seven months to create. These were the tallest obelisks ever raised in Egypt—as high as six men. To have one of them fall or crack now would be a horrible omen, not to mention dangerous.

The shouting continued. Somewhere in the melee of voices was the reassuring sound of Senenmut's deep timbre as he supervised. Over the years, Hatshepsut had gifted him with a multitude of titles until he outranked every other man in Egypt. Senenmut was her sun as she reigned over Egypt in all but name.

She felt a twinge at that thought, some emotion she refused to name. She had served Egypt faithfully these past years, had watched her kingdom prosper as Tutmose grew into a sturdy and intelligent boy. And yet, in a few more years she would hand over the kingdom and fade from public life. It would be painful to sit in the shadows and watch her stepson rule.

A loud cheer interrupted her thoughts as the obelisk sank triumphantly into its vertical position, its gold and silver top glowing.

The workmen parted to let Senenmut pass. His presence wrapped Hatshepsut in a warm embrace. "They're magnificent."

She resisted the urge to smooth the lines from his eyes as he squinted into the reflected sunshine of the two monuments. Senenmut was a wealthy and powerful man now, easily shouldering the mountain of titles and responsibilities she had bestowed upon him. There was still a small group of nobles—once Mensah's most ardent supporters—who resented the meteoric rise of a *rekhyt* to their ranks, but they knew better than to voice their dissent. By now the entire court, if not all of Egypt, realized the regent's relationship with the Steward of Amun, but the prosperity she had brought to their pockets made it inconsequential.

Standing in the shadows of her two greatest accomplishments to date, flanked by her daughter and the love of her life, Hatshepsut should have been deliriously happy.

But she wanted more.

Hatshepsut glanced up from her discussion with the Phoenician ambassador as Senenmut strode into the throne room, ignoring the herald that tripped after him, sputtering to get out all his titles. Senenmut looked as if he'd just come from the quarries—he probably had—but the court still cleared a path for him. Some even bowed in full *henus*. Thick leather armbands clasped both his wrists and heavy gold rings encircled most of his fingers. "A word with you, *Hemet*?" He looked about and spoke loudly enough for everyone to hear. "In private?"

Some courtiers had already headed for the door.

"We'll continue our discussion later." Hatshepsut smiled at the ambassador. The curls in his dark beard jiggled as he bowed and backed away from the dais. She'd never understand the Phoenicians and their preoccupation with facial hair. They truly were barbarians.

Before dismissing the slave and herald, she poured a faience glass of gazelle milk spiced with cinnamon and cardamom and offered a cup to Senenmut, but he ignored it. "You look as though Egypt's been invaded," she said.

"Worse. Your favorite cupbearer has returned to the capital and is on his way to seek an audience with you."

"No." She choked on the milk. "Not Mensah."

"In the flesh."

She wiped her mouth with the back of her hand. Mensah was a dung beetle, one that refused to die no matter how many times she stepped on it. The past years had seen a steady stream of scrolls from him in his outpost at Buhen, in which he borrowed verses from Egypt's ancient poets to laud her virtues and praise her beauty. He'd even built a temple to Horus in her name at the fort. The letters never failed to entertain Hatshepsut, but Senenmut rarely shared her humor.

He scowled. "When you sent him to Buhen, it wasn't far enough."

"I'd send him to Crete if I could, but I doubt their king would thank me for it." She smiled, but Senenmut only crossed his arms over his chest.

"This is serious, Hatshepsut."

"Mensah is nothing more than a pest."

"A pest that almost had me killed—"

"Because he was ordered to spy on us by Thutmosis."

"He lied to you."

"Because he loved me."

They'd spoken of this before, but that didn't make it any easier to say the words, to see the flicker of pain on Senenmut's face. Mensah's execution would have violated Ma'at, but that didn't mean her decision to let him live was any easier to stomach. "We were all young fools then," she said, "but he's harmless now."

Senenmut made some noise in the back of his throat, part laugh and part cough. "You're blind. The man wants the Isis Throne."

She resisted the urge to laugh, then recalled Mensah's proposition to do exactly that when she'd once visited him in chains. "Why do you say that?"

"Because my spies intercepted this." He pulled a rumpled scroll from his pocket and handed it to her.

A thin film of granite dust coated the outside of the papyrus, its seal already broken. Hatshepsut unrolled it, and gasped as she scanned the treason within.

"That filthy jackal," she muttered. The letter was addressed to a minor noble, asking for his support after Mensah had made Hatshepsut his wife and assumed the Isis Throne, as well as promising the petty courtier his share of titles and wealth in return for his assistance.

"Filthy and brazen," Senenmut said. "I don't know how many more of these he's sent out, but I suspect it's quite a few."

"Why would he think I'd ever accept his suit?" Hatshepsut stood, rapping the scroll angrily against her open palm. "I'm regent. I already have the throne."

"No. You only sit next to it. Egypt will soon clamor for Tutmose to wear the double crown, and if I'd been sent to rot in Buhen the past seven years like Mensah, then this would be my final effort to convince you to seize the Isis Throne."

"With him at my side."

"Naturally. The regent and a man from one of Egypt's most ancient families would have a good chance of winning a coup against a ten-year-old boy."

Senenmut was right. After seven years on the throne, if she chose to act against Tutmose, she would have more than a good chance of success.

"I'm no fool." Hatshepsut stood, starting to pace. "If I agreed to marry Mensah, he'd support a coup and be kind enough to lock me in the Hall of Women when it was over. I've already played that game."

"It may not matter if he has your support or not. He might force you, and with his family background, he could likely garner plenty of followers even if you did manage to refuse him." Senenmut waited for her to speak. "You *will* refuse him, won't you?"

She ceased pacing and stopped before one of the painted murals, a hunting scene of a crocodile with a brown duck pinned in its jaws. "Should I?" She glanced at Senenmut over her shoulder. His expression was murderous.

"Hatshepsut—"

She laughed, a low, throaty chuckle. "Of course I'll refuse him, you simpleton." Her hennaed fingernail traced the crocodile's jaw, picked at the duck's head until the paint flaked away. "I only wish I knew how he was going to react."

"He might slink off to Buhen to lick his wounds. Or, more likely, he'll go through with the coup anyway. He may try to kill Tutmose. Or you." He touched her arm and forced her to turn to look at him. "You can't send him back to Buhen after this treason."

"No. Whatever happens, this will be the end for one of us."

Senenmut blanched. "No, not us, not you. *Him.* Kill him now. Avoid the risk."

Mensah's plot might be a curse from the gods, or perhaps it was a gift in disguise. Perhaps even the best gift of all.

"I won't kill him now, not until he's revealed himself."

"That's the most ridiculous thing I've ever heard. You're willing to put your own life in danger—"

She touched a finger to his lips, leaving the faintest trace of plaster dust. "Mensah will set his own trap and then we'll snare him with it. There will be no escape for him this time."

Senenmut reached out to touch her, his hand barely brushing her cheek as he cupped the side of her face. "And if your plan fails?"

She shrugged, but her heart pounded against her ribs. "Then it won't matter anymore. I'll be dead."

She received Mensah alone in her private chambers, wanting him to speak plainly before she humiliated him for the last time. The fool actually dared to meet her eyes before he swept to the ground in a full *henu*. Her foot itched to kick the complacent smile off his face, but she managed to restrain herself.

Time had wrought changes on the former cupbearer. Mensah's skin was as weathered and tough as ox hide from years in the desert, but his braided black beard echoed the pharaoh's official false beard. His waist had thickened, but his chest was freshly oiled, his body as solid as that of a pharaoh carved onto some temple wall. There was a good chance his head would soon be decorating a pike on a similar wall.

When she spoke, her voice could have frozen the Nile. "You'd best have a good reason for leaving Buhen unattended."

"I do indeed." He rose and brushed imaginary sand from his shoulder. "Let's not play games, Hatshepsut. We both know why I'm here."

She bristled at the casual use of her name. "You want to rule Egypt. However, we already have a pharaoh."

"No, we have a boy who is too young to shear his youth lock, not a pharaoh. I've always said you and I belonged with each other, Hatshepsut, but now, together, we could do something great."

"And Tutmose?"

He shrugged. "I bear no ill will toward the boy. His death would be clean."

"To clear the way for our children." She stepped toward him, willing her face to take on an expression of Hathor's adoration when she really wanted to claw his eyes out.

"Naturally."

"I see you've given careful thought to your plan."

"I've had seven years to think about it. Your royal blood and my ancient family would usher Egypt into a golden age, supported by the nobles who've already promised me their loyalty." He stepped closer, daring to take one of the braids of her wig and wind it around his finger. "'Your hair snares my feeble heart, your breasts steal the breath from my lungs, and your eyes trap my *ka*.'"

She recognized the line of ancient poetry from one of his letters and jerked her head to pull the hair from his hand.

"I'd give you more than my *ka*," he said. "You know this is the right path, Hatshepsut. The only path."

"And if I have other ideas?"

"Like stepping aside when Tutmose comes of age? You'll never do that, not now that you've tasted power."

"That's where you're wrong." She shoved his hand away, ready to call for Nomti and the other guards outside the door, but Mensah grabbed her wrist and muffled her cry with his hand.

"Perhaps I misjudged you. Perhaps you're content to remain insignificant for the rest of your life, but I've been groomed from the day I was born to govern Egypt. Your brother realized that and made me his vizier."

"Just as I realized you weren't qualified for such a lofty position and rectified his egregious error."

Mensah bristled, anger simmering beneath the surface of his wicked smile. "You can't dispose of me so easily."

"Let go of me." She tried to twist out of his grasp, but his hand was as strong as any manacle.

He pulled her in to his chest, his breath hot on her ear. "There's something else I know about, a little secret you've kept that could destroy everything you've worked for these past seven years."

"I don't know what you're talking about."

"No? Allow me to refresh your memory, then." He pulled her to a cedar bench, pinning her on his lap so she could feel the hardness between his legs. "You may recall that you banished me to the Temple of Amun after your brother's death, that I served there first as *wa'eb* and then as Second Lector Priest."

She struggled against him, but it was no use. "I don't see the point of this."

Binding her wrists with one hand, he stroked the hollow of her neck with the other. "While serving the Great Cackler, I worked under the supervision of the High Priest, a man marked by the gods." He touched her right cheek. "Right here, a purple stain like a thumbprint."

She fell still and her body grew cold.

"That's right." He continued to caress her cheek with his rough thumb. "You bribed him the day the invisible god cast you off."

"You can't prove that."

"I don't have to prove it, Hatshepsut. All I have to do is mar your name and you'll be thrown into obscurity. That's your greatest fear, isn't it?"

"You can't bully me into marrying you."

"No? Amun rejected you, but you bribed the High Priest to hide that fact. You may not realize how thoroughly many of your nobles detest Senenmut and would rather see one of their own share the power of the Isis Throne. All of Egypt knows you consort with that foul *rekhyt* and shower him with undeserved titles, but do they know the Great God rejected you or that you bribed the High Priest to cover it up? How do you think your people would feel to realize Sekhmet's daughter has deceived them all this time?"

The metallic taste of defeat filled her mouth. A woman controlling the throne was an aberration, one the *rekhyt* would not tolerate long if they believed her to be corrupt. She swallowed hard, looked at him through her lashes. "You make a convincing case."

"Does that mean you accept?"

She smiled and leaned toward him as if to kiss him, but stopped short of his oiled lips, smelling the garlic on his breath. "It means you'd best get out of here before I scream for my guards. Get out of my palace."

His grip on her wrists tightened and his lip curled in the sneer of a feral dog. "Think carefully, Hatshepsut. I won't make this offer again."

"And I won't ask you to leave again."

He shoved her off his lap so hard that she fell to the ground, smashing her elbow into a table. He spat at her and stormed off.

She scrambled to her feet and rubbed her elbow, grimacing at the film of oil from Mensah's chest that covered her arms. The door slammed behind him, but reopened, and Nomti's huge frame filled the door.

"Is everything all right, *Hemet*?"

"No. Plans have changed." She had given strict orders that Mensah be allowed to go free, but his attempt at blackmail had changed all that. "Follow Mensah. I want what's left of his body to summon the crocodiles by morning."

Surprise flared in Nomti's eyes, followed by an eager flash of pleasure. He pressed his fist to his chest. "As you wish, *Hemet*."

He slammed the door and footsteps pounded down the hall. She sat on the same bench Mensah had vacated, the wood still warm from his body. Everything suddenly felt too tight—her crown, necklace, ribs, heart. Faience beads fell like a shimmering rainstorm onto the tiles as she yanked the woven collar from her neck, shed the matching bracelets, and tore the wig and crown from her head.

She hated Mensah for his threats, for destroying everything she'd worked so hard to achieve. But more than that, she hated him for what he would turn her into.

A murderer.

She didn't sleep that night, haunted by images of Mensah's sightless eyes staring up at her from the murky waters of the Nile, his rotting arms reaching up to drag her into the river with him. Her ears pricked at every rustle in the dark as she awaited word of Mensah's final moments, imagining his men coming for her, or, worse, an angry mob arriving to demand her removal. Finally, unable to control her impatience, she dressed herself and left her rooms, ignoring the silent guard who fell into step behind her.

Senenmut and Nomti found her in the Royal Treasury before Re had heaved himself over the horizon, counting burlap sacks filled with gold. Torches flickered to illuminate black hieroglyphs painstakingly printed on the bags, marking each with its place of origination. *Gold of the Delta. Gold of Nubia. Gold of the Mountains.* The stacks brushed the ceiling in some areas, enough gold to melt down and cover the pyramids if she chose. But would there be enough to buy the army's loyalty? The priesthood's?

She prayed it wouldn't come to that.

"Mensah is gone." Senenmut's voice echoed off the rafters of the treasury, frightening two speckled pigeons from their roost. A downy gray feather floated in lazy circles to the ground.

"Gone?"

"Disappeared," Senenmut said. "Without a trace."

"Sekhmet's breath!" She kicked one of the burlap sacks and was rewarded with a sharp pain that ratcheted through her big toe. She grabbed it and sat down on the bag, swallowing the rest of the curses on her tongue.

Senenmut exchanged a look with Nomti, then sat down next to her. "What happened with Mensah? What made you change your mind about him?"

She didn't care to spill her secrets of Amun rejecting her or of bribing the High Priest. Or the god's words in her head. Never that.

"Nothing important," she said.

He scoffed. "We need the truth, Hatshepsut. You rejected his plan, didn't you?"

"Yes. And told him to leave the palace."

"Well, he didn't follow your orders," Senenmut continued.

"What do you mean?"

Nomti scowled. "A girl-slave reported seeing Mensah sneak out of Aset's chambers and leave the palace this morning. It was one of the few places we didn't search last night."

The implication filled Hatshepsut's veins with lead. Mensah and Aset. It simply wasn't possible.

"Where is Aset now?"

"Gone." Nomti shifted from one foot to the other. "And Tutmose, too."

The stab of betrayal cut Hatshepsut deep. Aset was the closest thing she had to family, a sister made from the same clay. There had to be some mistake. Surely she wouldn't have joined with Mensah. Would she?

"If Mensah bribed the mother of the pharaoh to join his cause, he'll have a strong case to drum up support from the nobility." Senenmut rubbed his face, his eyes haggard. "Tutmose will be set aside, but he'll be safe, at least for now."

"But I'm still regent."

She didn't have to ask what that meant for Mensah's plan. The answer was clearer than the writing on the sacks of gold.

Senenmut touched her hair, his jaw clenched. "Mensah will come after you."

This was no longer a struggle for the throne, but a fight to the death like the famous battle between Set and Osiris.

Nomti's lips curled up like a hyena closing in on a kill. "You're not in danger, *Hemet*. My men will spear Mensah before he can come within a stone's throw of the Great Double Gate."

And she would continue as regent until Tutmose came of age, then retire to some sun-drenched estate, forgotten by the world. It was a fate worse than death.

"No. Let him into the palace."

"What?" Senenmut and Nomti both gaped at her with naked disbelief.

She shook her head slowly, her mind jumping several steps ahead to anticipate Mensah's next moves as if this were a simple game of *senet*. "Let him set into motion whatever plot he's hatched."

"Have you lost your mind? He'll try to kill you," Senenmut said.

"Exactly. We have to catch him in the act. There can't be any doubt of what he intends."

Realization lit his eyes. "You'll convict him of treason, expose him publicly?"

"Mensah won't wait long to reveal himself, and when he does we'll be there to crush him. Afterward, the people will see that the Isis Throne is vulnerable, that Egypt needs a true pharaoh."

She took a deep breath, daring the gods with her next words. "And that pharaoh will be me."

There was no bolt of lightning, none of Sekhmet's golden arrows to smite her for her heresy. Instead, she swore she could hear the goddess's laughter in her head.

Senenmut moved to protest, but she stopped him with a gentle shake of her head. "Don't you see? I've waited seven long years for this opportunity. Only now the winner of this match receives the double crown."

Senenmut motioned to Nomti and her guard stepped back, leaving her alone with Senenmut. "This isn't some game, Hatshepsut. This is your life."

"A life lived for the glory of Egypt, or a life lived in disgrace. There's no other option." She would be ruined if Amun's rejection and the bribery got out. She clasped Senenmut's hands, let them hang loosely between them. "Please. This is what I want."

He frowned. "We don't always get what we want."

She stood on tiptoes, brushed her lips against his. "I do."

"I can see I'm not going to win this argument." He turned away from her, his fingers still woven with hers and a look on his face as if she were already dead. "But I want you surrounded by *medjay* day and night."

He let her go and walked to a broad window looking over the palace gardens, his scarred back and strong shoulders already carrying this extra weight. Senenmut was a survivor; he would continue on in this life even if Mensah succeeded in sending her to the next. She wouldn't think on that now.

The trap was set. Now let Mensah—and anyone foolish enough to follow him—stumble into it.

Hatshepsut rolled over and reached across the bed for Senenmut, but her arm found only the softness of the goose-down mattress. Mouse's usual snores continued from the other side of the door, but tonight there was something else: a constant hum in the air. Outside, the wind tore through palm trees and cascaded over the garden walls, thick with sand that blotted out most of the light from the full moon, the stars tucked deep in Nut's black belly from the force of the *khamsin*. A furious howl of wind like a pack of starving wild dogs slammed the wooden shutters against the wall.

"Are you all right?" Nomti burst into the room, spear pointed, but relaxed when he saw her at the window, fumbling with the latch. Angry hot air and a spray of sand slapped her face, robbing her of the breath to answer. Together, they finally secured the window.

"I haven't seen a *khamsin* since I wore a youth lock," she said, rubbing the grit from her eyes and rinsing the sand from her mouth with a glass of warm wine. It was no use—the wine had sand in it, too. "I got yelled at by Sitre to come away from the window while my sister spent the entire night cowering under our bed."

Nomti didn't smile. "The gods must be angry tonight."

She didn't care to find out who had upset them. Instead she padded back to bed, pausing to brush grains of sand from her feet. She'd get an earful from Mouse in the morning about the mess.

"In peace, Nomti."

"In peace, *Hemet*."

He shut the door just as she saw something move out of the corner of her eye. She didn't react fast enough before she was slammed to the ground so hard the air flew from her lungs. Something soft and scratchy covered her face so there was no air, nothing but hot wool filling her nose and mouth. She bucked under the pressure, shoved at her assailant, tried to scratch, kick, punch—anything to free herself, but it wasn't enough. A heavy weight pressed on her lungs, and sunbursts exploded in her eyes. Her arms were pinned to her sides while something heavy pushed on her throat. The strength seeped from her muscles and lethargy overtook her limbs.

Her final thoughts were for Neferure. Senenmut. Tutmose.

Her chest grew light, her *ka* slipping free from her broken body to fly to the sky. Then the wool was yanked from her face. The air in her chambers was as sweet and cool as chilled honey wine on a summer afternoon. She coughed, choking as she curled into a ball, fingers clutching her battered throat.

"Hatshepsut!" Aset's face hovered above her, vague in the darkness and all the wrong colors. The oil lamp in her hand chased away the darkness. "Are you all right?"

Hatshepsut only nodded, unable to speak. Aset helped her to sit, a monumental task as Hatshepsut tried to drag air into her lungs again. It took a few moments to make out the scene before her. Nomti stood in the corner, hands on his knees with chest heaving and tattoos rippling like black waves. She followed his line of sight to the floor, but recoiled from what she saw there.

A man lay sprawled facedown on the floor, crimson blood seeping from his chest to creep like red fingers across the shadowy tiles. Hatshepsut had seen blood like that before when her father had slaughtered a bull at Karnak. She'd been riveted then as she was now, entranced as the stain spread across her floor. She couldn't see the man's face, but there was a stain on his cheek, one that might have been taken for blood at first glance. But it was darker, more like wine, and matched the larger stains on his arms.

"It appears the High Priest decided to pay you a visit," Nomti said, straightening and wiping the back of his curved blade on his kilt. It came away streaked with red. "Quite an honor."

Shocked, she looked to Aset. "How did you know to come?"

"Mensah came to me with a plot to get rid of you. I pretended to go along with his plan to find out the details." She shuddered and stepped away from the body with its still-expanding pool of blood. "I almost got here too late."

Not a traitor at all, but her savior. How could she have doubted Aset?

Hatshepsut winced as she touched her neck. "I'm grateful you got here at all, or I'd be on my way to Amenti right now."

Nomti inclined his head toward the window where the wind still howled, as loud as if the gods themselves were fighting. "The storm gave them the perfect opportunity."

"Was anyone else involved?" Hatshepsut asked.

"Only a few." Aset gave their names, several priests and a handful of inconsequential courtiers, including the one from the scroll that Senenmut's spies had intercepted. Nomti stepped out to bark orders to the other *medjay* to round up the traitors.

"Where's Tutmose?"

"I hid him at the Temple of Hathor. He's safe for now." Aset glanced around, her face falling. "Where's Senenmut?"

Hatshepsut shook her head. "Probably in his chambers. Why?"

Aset bit her lip. "Mensah wanted Senenmut brought down, too."

No. Not Senenmut.

Hatshepsut shoved past Nomti and flew down the torch-lit corridors, ignoring the shouts and pounding footsteps behind her. She shoved open the doors to Senenmut's apartments, terrified of what she might find.

A broken chair lay overturned near the open window, the carved cedar shutters thudding against the whitewashed walls. The wind was dying and the moon gleamed dully through the black clouds of Nut's belly. Sheets of pale papyrus rustled about the room. The one at her feet was dotted with a delicate spray of blood, as bright as pomegranate juice.

Senenmut stood beside his desk cradling his left arm, and blood dripped through his fingers to the floor. At his feet lay a man's crumpled body, still breathing.

Mensah.

"How bad is it?" She grabbed linen from the bed to staunch the flow from Senenmut's arm.

"It's nothing." He prodded Mensah with his foot, none too gently. "I managed to get him down, but he's still alive."

"I'll make him talk before he joins his friend," Nomti said. "They can greet Ammit together."

"His friend?" Senenmut asked.

"The High Priest of Amun," Hatshepsut said. "He tried to kill me."

"Son of a jackal!" Red-faced, Senenmut winced as Hatshepsut peeled his hand back from the gaping wound on his arm. She pushed from her mind the image of another injury long ago, her sister's *ka* seeping through her fingers. "Are you all right?" he asked.

"Fine. Aset warned Nomti in time."

Senenmut caressed Hatshepsut's cheek, and she turned into his hand, wishing they were alone so she could tell him how terrified she'd been. Not for herself, but him—she needed Senenmut here in this world, not lost forever in the Field of Reeds. But then he turned to Aset, and the moment was gone. "Thank you, Aset," he said. "I can never repay you for all you've done tonight."

She gave a tight nod and dropped her gaze to the floor. Senenmut turned to Nomti and gestured to Mensah on the ground. "Take your time with this one."

"I intend to." Nomti's lips twisted into a dangerous smile.

Senenmut swayed on his feet, his hand tight on Hatshepsut's arm and his face pale.

"You've lost too much blood. Sit down." Her hand was already sticky with all the blood that had seeped through the linen on his arm. "Aset, can you send for Gua?"

She nodded. "And then I'm going to check on Tutmose." She was almost out the door when Hatshepsut stopped her.

"Aset, thank you."

"Of course." Aset gave a strange smile, then slipped out the door.

Nomti and another *medjay* dragged Mensah from Senenmut's rooms in the time it took to summon the Royal Physician from his bed. Crimson flotsam spattered the tiles, leaving the engraved lotuses bedecked with drops of bloody dew. The physician sewed up Senenmut's wound and packed it with a honey poultice.

Hatshepsut kissed Senenmut as soon as Gua left. "I'm so sorry," she said. "I never planned for anyone else to get hurt."

Senenmut sat in a cushioned long chair and patted the space next to him, maneuvering her into his arms as best he could with the sling he now wore. The metallic smell of copper and honey filled her nose as she laid her head on his chest, relishing the feel of his arm around her.

"This wasn't your fault." Senenmut tilted her chin up and kissed her nose. "Although it might be a perfect excuse for you to spend less time in the throne room and more time in my chambers. I might need someone to help nurse me back to health."

She laughed, glad to hear the Senenmut she knew and loved, despite his ashen face. She nestled her head against his chest, simply enjoying listening to the steady beat of his heart. She hesitated on her next words, knowing that nothing would be the same once they left her lips.

"And now I'm going to be pharaoh."

Senenmut leaned back to look her in the eyes. "You still plan to go through with it?"

"I swore to do whatever was necessary to protect Egypt when I assumed the regency," she said. "Mensah's plot to seize the throne is a stark example of how vulnerable Egypt is without a single capable ruler wearing the double crown."

"And Tutmose is still far too young to rule."

She nodded. "It will be at least six more years before he can truly assume the throne." Hatshepsut waited for the gods to show their disapproval, for the storm outside to scream again, yet there was nothing. It was as if the gods held their breath to see what she might do next.

"A lot could happen in six years." Senenmut grimaced at his arm and stretched his legs before him. "After your victory in Nubia, the military will support anything you decide, and the *rekhyt* believe both you and the Two Lands are blessed by the gods."

The Nile's floods had gifted the Black Land with especially fertile soil since Thutmosis had died, filling Egypt's grain houses along with the Royal Treasury. Even the cattle and goats in the fields seemed fatter, the catfish in the markets bigger. Countless celebrations in Hatshepsut's honor had been held up and down the Nile over the past year as the *nomarchs* she'd met while on procession sang her praises to their people.

"And the position of High Priest of Amun recently became vacant," Senenmut said. "You'll have to appoint someone new, perhaps a distant relative who is inclined to support your wearing the double crown?"

Hatshepsut nodded slowly, awed and overwhelmed at the way events were falling together, as if the gods had blessed her decision and bent everything to her will. Perhaps her becoming pharaoh would actually fulfill the gods' wishes.

Still, there was one thing the gods had overlooked.

"Not everyone will be happy at my assuming the throne," she said. "One person in particular."

"Aset," Senenmut said.

Hatshepsut nodded. Aset had saved her life tonight, had taken Neferubity's place as her sister over the years, and now Hatshepsut would reward her with betrayal. "But I love ruling Egypt," she said, tears blurring her vision. "I can't give it up."

Senenmut gathered Hatshepsut into his arms. "Perhaps Aset will forgive you, even support you."

She snorted, swiped at her nose with the back of her hand. "You don't know Aset very well."

"It's not as if you're casting Tutmose aside, as Mensah planned to. You're only delaying his turn to wear the double crown."

She closed her eyes and nodded into his chest. "I'll ensure he has the best education and military training, everything he needs to succeed me after I pass to the West."

Senenmut's arms tightened around her. "Let's not talk about your dying while you're still covered in the blood of would-be assassins."

They held each other like that for some time, the events of the day and the enormity of their discussion settling like the silence of a tomb. Finally Hatshepsut tipped her head to look at him.

"Do you really think I can do it?"

"I know you can. And you'll see—Aset will come around eventually."

"I hope you're right."

He smiled. "I usually am."

They moved over to Senenmut's bed, his good arm wrapped around Hatshepsut, and almost everything right in the world. Senenmut settled into sleep, his chest rising and falling in perfect rhythm, but Hatshepsut stared at the ceiling, her thoughts whirling like the winds of the *khamsin*.

Aset might one day forgive her, but nothing would ever be the same when Hatshepsut took Tutmose's crown. There was a good chance her bond with Aset would become her first true sacrifice in Egypt's name.

She only wondered what other sacrifices the gods might demand of her.

CHAPTER 24

Bound by copper manacles on his neck and wrists, Mensah cowered on the flowered tiles before the empty Isis Throne, squinting through swollen eyes at Hatshepsut sitting in the glittering golden alcove. An angry purple bruise clamped his left eye shut and a dried crust of blood caked his forehead and chin. She wrinkled her nose at the stench of filth and feces. He must have soiled himself over the course of Nomti's torture. He was lucky to still have his hands and ears.

"Mensah, son of Imhotep." Hatshepsut looked down her nose into his bloodshot eye. "We find you and your fellow conspirators guilty of attempted regicide and murder. The penalty for such treason is death." The cross-legged scribe at her feet struggled to keep up with her words, his brush flicking frantically over the papyrus. The recordings would be kept for a short time and then burned so no trace of Mensah's name would remain to keep his *ka* alive. "You will be taken immediately to the Great Double Gate, where you shall be thrown onto a wooden spike." Mensah winced at the sentence, but she wasn't finished. "Once you are dead, your body shall be burned and the ashes flung into the Nile. You shall cease to exist in the afterlife, just as in this life. This is Ma'at's wish."

"Please, *Per A'a*," Mensah shrieked as two *medjay* hauled him away by his copper chains. "Not my *ka*. Let my body rest in my tomb, I beg of you."

He was a fool to think she would allow that. She already had plans to seize his tomb and reallocate it to another noble, perhaps Neshi or Ti. No one would meet Mensah or his fellow conspirators in the Field of Reeds. They wouldn't even make it to Ma'at's scales before their ashes fed the Nile's crocodiles.

Hatshepsut signed the bottom of the scribe's papyrus, listening to Mensah's wails fade down the corridor. In a few days' time, the hieroglyphs of her name would be wrapped with the sacred cartouche that only pharaohs were allowed. Ma'at's justice was sweet.

She traded the papyrus for the golden crook and flail, carried them with her as she strode to the lapis audience window above the Walls of the Prince to watch as Mensah's sentence was carried out. The occasional russet smear of Mensah's blood on the tiles marked the path for her to follow. A narrow set of stairs climbed to a small balcony with a view of the main gates—a window used only for formal appearances by the pharaoh to the populace, the same window where she'd once watched Enheduanna parade to the palace and her too-early death. A thick layer of sand left over from the *khamsin* covered the balcony. Carved ankh symbols formed a painted vine of life around the window, framing the hastily arranged execution ground waiting below.

A *medjay* shoved Mensah up a small wooden platform situated next to a cedar stake half the height of a man. The top of the pike was stained black, a remnant of other traitors' blood from generations past.

At the sound of the drums a crowd, consisting of a few curious *rekhyt* but mostly courtiers ordered to attend by royal decree, gathered. This was a public execution, witnessed by enough people to ensure that the traitor's death would soon be on the lips of every priest, farmer, and fisherman in Egypt. Everyone would know the price exacted from traitors, something to remember as Hatshepsut took the throne.

She caught Nomti's eye from where he was on the platform with

Mensah and nodded for him to secure the linen bag over Mensah's head. The former vizier bucked against his ropes like a bull about to be sacrificed, but he finally succumbed, although his shoulders still shook. There were only two possibilities open to Mensah as he left this life: a very quick death if the wood pierced his miserable heart, or a slow and agonizing demise if the spike missed its target. It was in his best interest to be still and allow the executioner to do his deed properly.

Hatshepsut held up her hands and the drums stopped. "Citizens of Egypt," she called out. "We banish this traitor's body and name from this world to ensure he shall never rise in Amenti. Let this be a warning to all those who might wish to incite chaos against Ma'at's perfect order."

The drums pounded a steady heartbeat as *medjay* guided Mensah to the edge of the platform. His bare toes hung off the edge. The crowd held its breath in complete silence, and then the *medjay* slammed their shoulders into Mensah's back. As stiff as a board, he fell forward with a spray of blood and a sickening squelch. The spike missed his heart, piercing his stomach and exiting out his back. He screamed—the high screech of a falcon—and scarlet blood trickled down the stake to stain the earth. A woman keened as Mensah writhed upon the shaft, his head still in the sack and arms and legs bound.

Re reached his pinnacle before all the life seeped from Mensah; perhaps Anubis was less than pleased at the prospect of claiming a traitor. Sweat gathered under Hatshepsut's arms, trickled like blood down her back. Still she stayed and watched.

Finally, he stopped moving and his chest stilled. Slaves poured oil on a nearby pile of imported cedar and pine, then tossed a burning light onto the logs. The bonfire roared to life as four *medjay* lifted Mensah's body from the pike. All his guts poured forth, entrails dangling from his stomach as his corpse was heaved onto the pyre. He wasn't the final obstacle in Hatshepsut's path to the throne, but she vowed that he would be the last blood sacrifice she would make.

She remained until the embers grew cold and the greasy smear of smoke cleared from the air. Slaves lit torches as dusk spread; then they gathered the ashes and doused the bloodied earth with buckets of water.

Hatshepsut hoped never to see another execution as long as she lived.

Hatshepsut's hair was still damp after her visit to the bath pavilion, her skin pink where Mouse had scoured her with natron until she thought she might bleed. Nomti fell into step behind her as she left her chamber, his hand on the hilt of his curved sword. Her skin prickled with fear at each stray sound and her neck was still tender, the black bruises from the night before hidden under a wide pectoral collar of lapis and a turquoise winged scarab.

Mensah lurked in the darkness every time she closed her eyes, impaled and slowly bleeding to death on the stake. Her body was clean, but her *ka* would carry the stain of his execution forever.

The greatest gifts in life came with the greatest costs.

She gathered her thoughts for what she was going to say when she reached the Hall of Women, the words she'd focused on during Mensah's drawn-out demise. Her feet slowed as she approached the massive gilded gate, wishing she could forestall what she was about to do.

A small price to pay. That's what she kept repeating to herself, yet this was another stain about to find its home on her *ka*.

She almost turned around, but the golden gate swung open. The one person she wished to avoid—yet desperately wanted to see—raised her hand in greeting.

Aset walked toward her and enveloped her in a warm hug. "I'd guess you can't wait for this day to be over."

Hatshepsut nodded. Her day of triumph didn't feel as victorious as she'd imagined. And she had a feeling it was about to get much worse.

Aset squeezed her shoulders. "You did the right thing, Hatshepsut. I know it doesn't make it any easier, but Mensah deserved to die."

"I know."

Aset rubbed her arm with one hand, then glanced at the ground. "How is Senenmut?"

Hatshepsut started. She hadn't expected Aset to show concern for the man she openly disliked. "He is well. Gua says his arm will heal so long as he rests."

"You might have to barricade him in his chambers, then." Aset smiled and Hatshepsut managed to return the gesture. "Speaking of rest," Aset said, "I seem to recall the Royal Physician saying the same thing about you."

"I'm fine." Hatshepsut took a deep breath. "I was coming to see you, actually."

"Me? Don't be silly. Go to bed."

"By the gods," Hatshepsut said, her voice low. This was so much harder than she had imagined. "Aset, there's something else, something important I have to tell you."

"Sekhmet's breath," Aset said. "You'd best get it out quick—you look like you're about to be ill."

"Egypt is vulnerable with Tutmose on the throne. Someone stronger than a ten-year-old boy needs to wear the double crown in order to avoid another rebellion like Mensah's."

"What?" Aset blinked, struggling to comprehend Hatshepsut's words. "But Tutmose is the pharaoh, the only heir to Thutmosis and your father. There's no one else who shares their blood—" She stopped and shook her head, the bells at the ends of her wig tinkling like a flurry of angry bees. "No—"

"Aset." Hatshepsut wanted to touch her, to stop her friend's trembling. "I'm going to be pharaoh. It's the only way."

Aset clenched her hands into fists at her sides and stepped toward Hatshepsut. Nomti moved closer, but Aset slowly raised her hands, palms open. "I must have misheard you," she said to Hatshepsut, the sharpness in her voice echoing down the corridor. "For a moment, it sounded like you were planning to steal my son's throne."

"Tutmose will still become pharaoh, but not until after my reign."

"So you'll keep the throne warm until my son is older and then step aside?"

"No. A pharaoh never abdicates."

Aset slapped her—hard—but Nomti pinned Aset's arms behind her back before she could do further harm. She struggled against him, and if the glint in her eyes was any indication, she wanted to do much more damage.

Hatshepsut touched the fire in her cheek, then dropped her hand and stepped close enough to feel Aset's breath. "Please," she said. "Try to understand—"

"I understand perfectly well." Aset spat at her feet. "I wish I'd let you die. You may as well be dead, at least to me."

Hatshepsut stepped back, struggling to keep her face a mask. "I'm sorry, Aset—I truly am. But this is the way it has to be."

"Only because it's the way you want it."

"This is for Egypt. I hope one day you'll understand." She turned and walked away, resisting the urge to look over her shoulder even as she heard Nomti fall into step behind her, and feeling as if she was leaving behind something precious and irretrievable with Aset.

"Ammit will eat your heart for this!" Aset screamed at her back. "I loved you like a sister, but you've betrayed Tutmose! And Egypt!" There was a splintering crash, and Hatshepsut turned to see shards of alabaster and pink lotus blossoms strewn about the floor, puddles of water on the tiles. "I hate you!"

Hatshepsut forced herself to continue walking, one foot in front of the other, all the way to her chambers. Nomti motioned for the guards outside to fall back and barred the entrance with his arm.

"Aset will be a dangerous foe after this," he said.

Hatshepsut's hand fluttered to her temples. She didn't care to discuss this now, but Nomti wouldn't be dismissed so easily. "It's my opinion that Aset should be removed from the palace," he said, "perhaps sent to your estates in Bubastis, at least until you can be sure she won't seek revenge against you. Your Keeper of the House there is loyal to you and won't shirk from the added duty of watching Aset for suspicious activity."

"Suspicious activity?" Hatshepsut closed her eyes and rubbed the bridge of her nose, not wanting to think on this new reality. Her friend and sister was now her enemy, all by her own hand. "Aset hates me, but I doubt she'll try to have me murdered in my bed."

Nomti clasped his hands behind his back. "Do you know exactly what transpired between her and Mensah before he almost had you killed?"

"He tried to persuade her to join him, but she refused." Hatshepsut's voice climbed until the waiting guards gave them a sharp glance. She drew a deep breath, ready to dismiss Nomti so this conversation could reach its end. "Then she fled to hide Tutmose."

"That was after Mensah spent the evening in her chambers. The possibility remains that she might have initially been tempted to join him."

Hatshepsut opened her mouth to reply, but the protest died before it could leave her lips. Nomti was right to be concerned, although she doubted Aset was capable of such duplicity, as she'd always worn her emotions plain on her face. But as much as Hatshepsut hated to admit it, Nomti was probably right about Aset being a threat to her safety. Still, she could scarcely stomach the thought of punishing Aset further. "I can't send away Tutmose's mother, not as I'm about to be crowned."

Nomti shrugged. "It might be said that the former concubine of Osiris Thutmosis requested time to recuperate from the recent coup away from the palace. Grant her some rich grazing land or dedicate a monument to her as Tutmose's revered mother as a public token of your appreciation. She'll forget soon enough."

Hatshepsut doubted very much that Aset would be so easily distracted. "That doesn't change the fact that I'd be banishing her. I can't send her so far away as Bubastis."

"It's not banishment if you plan to recall her in a few years, once she's had time to realize that Tutmose will still be pharaoh one day."

Nomti crossed his arms, his eyes narrowing like a desert cat's. "My only concern is for your safety. I stand firm by my warning: Aset cannot remain here, *Per A'a*."

Per A'a. Pharaoh.

She had thought the title would sound sweet, but the word seemed impossibly heavy now that it belonged to her. Had her father felt like this when he took the throne? Had Thutmosis?

Finally, she nodded. "Fine. Aset will be sent away, but not to Bubastis. She'll go to Dendera instead, so she's not as far away, and perhaps will even serve the Temple of Hathor. Regular reports will be sent to her regarding her son."

Nomti signaled to the guards to return to their places. "I'll make the arrangements immediately."

The doors to Hatshepsut's chamber shut silently behind her. The walls pushed in on her, the warm air threatening to suffocate her. Seams ripped as she yanked the neck of her sheath, clenched her teeth, and wanted to throw something as Aset had done. Instead, she climbed the ladder to the roof, gulping in deep breaths of the tempered night air.

"Is this what you wanted?" she yelled at the stars. "Another price I have to pay?"

But if the gods heard her, they didn't answer. It was possible that she had been wrong in assuming the double crown would fulfill their wishes.

Instead, perhaps the gods had finally abandoned her.

PART IV

pharaoh

1481 BC – 1458 BC

Her fragrance was like a divine breath,
Her scent reached as far as the land of Punt,
Her skin is made of gold,
It shines like the stars in the hall of festival . . .
She had no equal among the gods
Who were before since the world was.

—FROM THE OBELISK INSCRIPTIONS AT KARNAK

CHAPTER 25

YEAR ONE OF PHARAOH HATSHEPSUT

The coronation was not ostentatious. And unlike her brother's and Tutmose's ceremonies, held at the palace, Hatshepsut was crowned at Karnak, open for the world to see.

No woman had ever become Pharaoh in a time of peace, and only two others—Nitokerty and Sobkneferu—had ever worn the double crown. Both women were the last links in their dynastic chains—a trend Hatshepsut refused to follow. She would rule well, and prove that a woman could govern as well as a man. Then, should some catastrophe befall Tutmose after he assumed the throne, Neferure would be able to wear the double crown as undisputed leader of the Two Lands.

Perhaps it was her imagination, but Hatshepsut could feel the presence of each of the great nine gods as she entered Karnak's holy ground, all the gods and goddesses leaving their sacred shrines to flank her as she walked toward the golden pavilion where the High Priests of Horus and Set waited with the crowns of Lower and Upper Egypt. Interwoven papyrus reeds and lotus blossoms formed a fragrant carpet underfoot, and red and white standards fluttered in the breeze, further proclamations of the united Two Lands.

Tutmose stood under the pavilion, only ten years old and already as tall as she, while Senenmut and Neferure stood a step below him. A newly carved red granite statue of Amun that stood the height of two men gleamed brightly in the sunshine. Hatshepsut had herself inspected the god's body for cracks the night before and had laid the offerings of incense and myrrh at the feet of the hidden god with her own hands. She wasn't taking any chances today, having gone so far as to allow Nomti earlier this morning to personally escort Aset to the barge that was carrying her to Dendera. Only the gods knew when Hatshepsut would see her friend again, but she hoped the passage of time would bank her friend's anger and they would soon be reunited.

Senenmut winked in Hatshepsut's direction and she suppressed a smile and took her place in a massive golden litter. Led by the High Priest, it began its short journey from Amun's inner sanctuary. A solid gold statue of the Great Cackler in his double-plumed crown was balanced on the gilded sedan chair. Not even the sparrows dared chirp as Amun's sacred statue approached Karnak's outer courtyard. The supreme god rarely mingled with men, but Hatshepsut had persuaded the newly appointed High Priest to make an exception today. The golden statue had been anointed with precious myrrh oil so that the god of gods shone from his crown to his sandaled feet. Four boy-slaves bearing ostrich-wing fans cooled the god as supplicants laid offerings of flowers, incense, and jewelry at the edge of the path. Cornflower and lotus petals festooned the pebbled walkway to provide a scented carpet for the bearers' feet.

The High Priest of Amun held up his hands, and the litter stopped before the ancient altar. The new priest's upper jaw jutted out so that his lips could barely close, and his eyebrows joined together above the bridge of his nose. Hapuseneb was a distant relation through Hatshepsut's mother; Hatshepsut had taken to heart Senenmut's suggestion that their shared blood would guarantee that the priesthood wouldn't be tempted to rebel again.

The High Priest of Amun controlled the temples, and through the priesthood and the army, Hatshepsut would control Egypt.

At Hapuseneb's side, Set's priest held the white leather crown of Upper Egypt so that it hovered over Hatshepsut's head, and Horus' priest held Lower Egypt's copper-red crown. "The crown of Upper Egypt and the crown of Lower Egypt will unite at the word of the pharaoh," Hapuseneb said. "As you have kept your subjects and the Two Lands from evil, so may Amun, the king of the gods, be compassionate toward you."

Hatshepsut glittered in the sunshine as the High Priest of Set first placed the white crown upon her head and then the High Priest of Horus added the gleaming crown. The combined weight of the double crown was surprisingly light.

She grasped the crook and flail with cool hands and sank gracefully to her knees. The High Priest of Amun placed a piece of flatbread imprinted with an ankh, the symbol of everlasting life, upon her tongue. It was gritty, the dough having been sprinkled with sand blessed by all the High Priests before it was baked that morning. *"Ankh, udja, seneb,"* Hapuseneb proclaimed over her head. "May the great nine gods refresh your nose with life, prosperity, and health so your reign may shine like the star that does not end." Then he stepped back and beckoned her to stand.

The rehearsed words tumbled from her lips.

"It is with a humble heart that I, Hatshepsut, seek to lead the Two Lands as pharaoh. In the presence of Amun and my people, I ask for the Great Cackler's sacred blessing to rule Egypt. This shall be my privilege and burden until the day I pass to the West. O, Amun, will you accept me?"

All eyes were on Amun now, but the golden god remained silent. Then the litter tilted forward so that the statue bowed to her. It wasn't as clear a sign as the cracking statue in Karnak's temple years before, but one the High Priest had promised after a sizable donation of vineyards and oasis farmland.

"The King of the Gods blesses Hatshepsut," the High Priest exclaimed. "May the pharaoh's reign be long and prosperous. *Ankh, udja, seneb!*" Cheers loud enough to wake any gods who may have missed the ceremony erupted from the temple as the crowd repeated the prayer for Hatshepsut's life, health, and prosperity.

This moment would forever etch her name on Egypt's history. Twenty-six years old and dressed in a man's long kilt of cloth of gold, Hatshepsut wore all the pharaoh's trappings—the bull's tail to denote strength, false beard to associate her with Osiris, and the golden *uraeus* at her brow for protection. Instead of her usual titles—those that had identified her for the past seven years—the High Priest called out her new titulary, one that would forever mark her as pharaoh and join her with Amun.

"Horus powerful of *kas*, two ladies flourishing of years, Horus of gold divine of appearances, king of Upper and Lower Egypt, beloved of Amun-Ra, Maatkare Hatshepsut!"

The cloud of incense parted and she breathed in sweet air, felt the warm slick of sacred oil as the priest anointed her forehead in the name of the gods. Her name would now be engraved into the list of all the pharaohs who had ruled over Egypt, a living god in her own right.

She had earned it.

It was unbearably hot in the palace that night. Shomu had reared its head early and had them within its scorching grasp again, cracking the mud left from the Inundation and scalding the long leaves of the barley and emmer growing along the Nile. Hatshepsut and Senenmut climbed alone to her roof and escaped into the night air for some welcome relief. They lay together on a fresh reed mat, occasionally shifting to allow the breath of the gods to cool the dampness that clung to where their limbs touched.

"I want to build you something." The roughened skin of Senenmut's thumb traced her jaw in the subdued lamplight.

Hatshepsut's silvery laugh floated up to the half-moon above them. "You've already built so much for me." She kissed his hand. "I don't need anything else."

"None of that will compare with what I want to build. Today you achieved immortality. Your name will live forever," Senenmut murmured in her ear, his quiet voice a caress. "Now it's my turn."

Senenmut's statement brought back the echo of words Hatshepsut had heard long ago, words she hadn't thought of in years.

> Your name will live forever.
> You shall be the downfall of all those you love.
> Egypt will prosper, but those closest to you will find only
> anguish and ruin.

She trembled in the dark. Senenmut pulled her closer and kissed her hair. She had caused Aset anguish, but was still determined that her friend would forgive her. She'd never loved Mensah, only lusted after him; he had caused his own downfall. But what about Senenmut? The thought of a future without this man was inconceivable—he was as much a part of her now as her lungs or heart.

His next words ripped the air from her.

"Someday one of us will die like this—wrapped in the other's arms. But I want both our names to live for eternity."

She had to force herself to breathe, imagining Djeseret cackling at her terror, her panic growing now that the first part of the prophecy had come true.

Was she doomed to fulfill the rest?

"Don't say that," she said. "Neither of us is going to die anytime soon. I won't allow you to."

"And I always follow orders."

She felt Senenmut's smile as he kissed her neck. She refused to believe the witch's soothsaying or the words Amun had spoken in her head. Together, she and Senenmut would laugh over the ridiculous prophesy in their old age. Of course, that was only if she ever decided to tell him. Speaking the words aloud might give them too much power.

"What do you have in mind for this building project?" She nestled her head into the crook of his arm, willed her heart to stop its frantic pounding.

"I want to build your mortuary temple," Senenmut said softly, as if he was afraid she might reject the idea.

"A morose thought." Hatshepsut chuckled. "But practical. My father started building his as soon as he began his tomb."

"Then you'll let me build it?"

"Of course." She turned and rewarded Senenmut with a long kiss, her tongue teasing his. "You were saying?"

Senenmut groaned as she slipped back to his chest. "You drive me mad, woman."

"You wouldn't want it any other way."

He sighed, but she felt the happiness radiating from him like sunshine. "Your temple will be unlike anything Egypt has ever seen." He caressed the outside of her thigh. "I've been sketching it in my head."

"Let me see."

"Look." He reached off the mat to retrieve one of the charcoal nubs that was always tucked in the pocket of his kilt, then etched stark black lines on the mud-brick floor, giving birth to his vision. Tall columns hugged three sweeping terraces of an elegant temple, each level flowing into the next with flawless symmetry. The design was stately but fluid, resembling nothing of the geometric and static designs of traditional Egyptian architecture. Delicate trees stood in the temple forecourt, their branches stretching from the ground in fragile V's. Curious, Hatshepsut traced one of the trunks with her finger, smudging the charcoal.

"Myrrh trees," Senenmut whispered, his eyes ravenous for her response.

They were trees of the gods, more precious than gold.

"It's magnificent," she breathed. "Where will you build it?"

"I'll show you." Senenmut pulled her to her feet before she could object.

They sent slaves to wake Dagi and the rowers, dragging the bleary-eyed servants from their beds. The rest of Egypt slept, the pennants of the royal boat hanging drowsily, and all the birds and beasts tucked into trees and grasses for the night. The Nile gleamed like black glass in the moonlight as the boat traveled to the West Bank, retracing the path she and Senenmut had taken on that forbidden afternoon long ago. Things were so different now. It seemed as if she were looking back at someone else's life to remember that awful day.

She felt a twinge of guilt at Dagi's yawn as they leapt off the gang-plank, but Senenmut's elation was intoxicating. They ran hand in hand from the river's edge into the Western Valley while fingers of gray clouds reached across the black sky.

She was breathless when Senenmut finally stopped in the middle of a desolate amphitheater, hammered by the gods into the surrounding cliffs that towered above their heads, the sandy stage spread before them. To the left were the remains of an ancient temple, two lonely pillars and myriad carved blocks the only testament to whatever monument the blanket of sand had tucked in so long ago. Senenmut stood behind her and laid his arms atop her shoulders. His hands in front of her formed three sides of a square to frame the ground of the cliffs.

"Here," he murmured.

Hatshepsut closed her eyes and imagined the temple blueprint he'd drawn. She opened her eyes and saw it at the base of the cliffs—their rugged beauty melding perfectly into the porticoes and terraces of her temple.

"Yes." It was all she could say.

"Thank you, *nefersha*," Senenmut whispered into her hair. She turned in his arms and their lips met. She would ensure that part of the temple was dedicated to Hathor, a gift to the goddess of love for giving her this man.

On the way back, they walked instead of ran, fingers loosely inter-twined.

"We'll need to find myrrh trees," Hatshepsut said. She wanted Senenmut's vision to be complete, down to the last detail.

"I'll leave that part to you."

"I'll talk to Neshi and Ti—perhaps a trade expedition is in order."

They had caught sight of the boat floating on the glimmering surface of the Nile when Hatshepsut stopped.

"What is it?" Senenmut asked, his fingers still looped with hers.

"When you finish my temple, I want you to build something for yourself."

He chuckled. "Everything I build *is* for me. In case you hadn't noticed, I rather like seeing my name stamped on something that will last forever."

"No." Hatshepsut squeezed his hand. "I don't mean a temple dedicated to me or to the gods. I want you to build something for you. I don't care what it is, but it has to be perfectly selfish—something for you alone."

"Is that an order?" Senenmut's lips grazed her earlobe.

She shivered. "Yes." There had to be something he wanted, something she could give him.

"Then I'll think about it," Senenmut said. "I wouldn't want to disobey the pharaoh, now, would I?"

"No, you certainly wouldn't." She laughed and started back to the waiting boat, but his hand in hers anchored her to the path.

"There's something else I want, Hatshepsut."

The look on his face silenced her laugh. His eyes were soft, his expression more vulnerable than she'd ever seen it. There was only one thing more Senenmut could want, something she could never give him no matter how much she loved him.

For a moment, she feared what he would say, but his next words were more terrible than she'd expected.

"I want a child with you, Hatshepsut," he said, pulling her into his arms. He kissed her forehead. "I want to see your belly swell with my daughter. I want to watch you carry my son in your arms."

She struggled for words, but the only ones that came to mind seemed a pitiful joke. "And you call me greedy."

It was far too late for a child now that she had claimed the Isis Throne. A son borne of her body could supersede Tutmose's claim to the throne, would surely invite future civil war. It would be easier to give Senenmut her crown.

He touched her cheek, took her hand again. "When it comes to you, yes, I am greedy."

She stared at their hands entwined together, his dark from the sun and stained with charcoal, hers thin and delicate in comparison. "But we have Neferure."

"And I love Neferure." He kissed her hand. "But I want a child of our own, someone who will carry both our blood even after we've gone to the Field of Reeds."

She gave a watery smile. "The ultimate building project."

"In a manner of speaking, yes." He chuckled. "Although I think the building of this particular project would be far more enjoyable."

"I'm not sure I can still have children, not after Neferure—"

His expression hardened. "I know about the pessary, Hatshepsut, and about your visits to the Royal Physician. I won't pretend to understand why you've needed them all these years, but I feel I've been patient long enough."

She retrieved her hands and hugged her elbows. "We've already discussed this. Why now?"

"What do you mean, why now? I've wanted it for seven years. Longer, probably."

"Why didn't you mention it before? Why not after the first time—"

Her voice trickled away, the memory of her mistake a heavy weight on her *ka*. And then she realized why he'd never pushed to try for another child, why he'd fallen silent on the subject. "You believed I got rid of it, didn't you?"

His face contorted. "I did, for a while."

"You thought me such a monster?"

"I was hurt; I couldn't think straight. Having a child would have endangered Tutmose's future succession, made your bid for pharaoh a risk no one would have supported."

"That hasn't changed." That he could have thought her capable of destroying her own child made her want to scream at him, to rake her nails across his face.

The air around them seemed suddenly cold. "You're pharaoh now," he said. "You can do what you like."

She shook her head. "No, I can't *because* I'm pharaoh."

"You can't?" He gave her a sharp look, one meant to impale her. It worked. "Or you won't?"

She smoothed the lines that radiated from his tired eyes. "And what if I had your son? What would happen to Egypt then?"

"Who's to say you'd have a boy?" His tone was defensive, as if he already knew the impossibility of his dream.

"The gods would give me a boy." She'd worn her knees out praying for Neferure to be a boy, but to no avail. It was guaranteed the gods would send her a son if she prayed for a daughter. She sighed. "What would happen if the reigning pharaoh had a son while there was already a hawk in the nest? What would happen after I died?"

"You'd have to decide who would take the Isis Throne after you— our son or Tutmose."

"Exactly. And regardless of whom I named, both boys would have an equal claim to the throne. I won't plunge Egypt into civil war after I'm gone."

"So you sign some proclamation, choose one of them as your co-regent before you die."

"You know it's not that simple. There would be a power struggle no matter what I did. It's too late for us to have a child."

Silence shrouded them. A cloud passed over the moon and hid his expression. "I don't ask for much, Hatshepsut."

"I know." And it was true. All his titles, all his wealth, had been bestowed freely by her hand. She'd suspected that Senenmut might wish to share the double crown, to rule with her on the Isis Throne, but he was a much better man than she'd given him credit for. She didn't deserve him.

He sighed. "You won't give this to me, will you?"

His face was a dark blur as she drew in a ragged breath. "I can't. But I'll make it up to you, I swear it." She caught his hand to keep him from leaving. "Senenmut, I love you."

"I know," he said, striding away from her anyway and calling the final words over his shoulder. "But not enough."

It didn't take much to persuade Neshi and Ti to indulge Hatshepsut's desire for a trade expedition. Ti was overjoyed to have something to sink surplus treasury funds into—Hatshepsut had yet to splurge on anything other than her building projects—and Neshi was determined to lead the expedition himself. The only question that remained was where the voyage should go. Unfortunately, the project had lost much of its appeal for Hatshepsut after her argument with Senenmut, and she postponed several planning meetings with the twin brothers. Senenmut hadn't broached the subject of a child—she doubted he would again—and while she'd showered him with a clutch of fresh titles, even she knew that no title in the world would ever make up for his not being a father.

And then one day he was gone.

She waited for him on the docks for a trip into the valley to take measurements for her temple and recruit artists from the Place of Truth. Her impatience grew as Re climbed into Nut's belly, hampering their chances of making it there before the worst heat of the day. Finally, she sent a slave to fetch him, but the boy returned alone.

"*Neb* Senenmut is gone," he said.

"What do you mean, gone?"

The slave's hands trembled. "His slaves claim he left yesterday and that he packed for a trip of many days."

Many days. Yet he'd left without telling her. For a moment she wondered if there was a chance this was a permanent move, and felt loneliness crash upon her.

She left the slave cowering on the docks and hurried to inspect Senenmut's chambers, the sound of her sandals on the tiles echoing off the corridors' high walls. His largest chest was missing, as were many of his most precious belongings: the pectoral of golden bees she'd bestowed upon him a year ago for his service to Egypt, a cedar statue of Thoth, and even all his architectural plans for her temple. The rooms were filled with Re's light, yet they felt desolate.

He'd left her.

Surrounded by silent slaves, Hatshepsut had never felt so alone in her entire life. She retraced her steps to her own apartments, then sat at her desk, staring at a sheet of blank papyrus. She waited for the hieroglyphs to take form, for the right words to beg him to come back.

But there was nothing she could do or say to make this right. She would not order him to return or to stay with her; she loved him too much to demean him that way. It was only natural for a man to wish for a wife and children, the two things she could never give him. She had to remain loyal to Egypt.

Still, loyalty was a cold bedmate, and didn't fill her heart with happiness as Senenmut's laugh did.

The day slipped into another and yet another, until a week had passed. Her slaves learned to avoid her until only Mouse could stand to be in the same room with her, and then only because the poor dwarf had grown mostly deaf over the past years.

Darkness had fallen, and Mouse sat polishing a set of silver bangles as Hatshepsut curled at the window with a cat in her lap, staring out at the reflection of the Nile. On a still evening, it was possible to hear the murmur of the river's great god Hapy, one of Egypt's most ancient deities, as the bent old man adorned himself with papyrus reeds and spoke to the frogs. Hatshepsut had almost drifted to sleep when Mouse's voice woke her.

"I forgot to tell you," she said, so loud the cat startled and ran off. "*Neb* Senenmut returned to court tonight."

"What?" Hatshepsut straightened, wincing at the crick in her neck. "When?"

"While you were dining with Tutmose and Neferure." Mouse picked one of her back teeth, revealing a gaping hole where she'd recently had another pulled. "So, now you can stop moping about and let all your slaves get back to work."

Hatshepsut was already on her feet. She'd rehearsed this scene in her mind too many times to count over the past few days, usually at night, when she ached for Senenmut's reassuring warmth next to her. She'd beg him to come back if she had to, and had almost managed to persuade herself that perhaps it was the gods' will for her to have another child.

Almost. Yet in her heart she knew it would go against *ma'at* to invite possible chaos and civil war. Still, she'd do almost anything to have Senenmut back.

She ignored the guards outside his door and drew a steadying breath before stepping inside. It took a moment for her eyes to adjust to the dark; the shutters were closed against the moon and no oil lamps burned. Her heart lightened at the fresh scent of cinnamon she'd so missed, although there was another scent as well, something exotic. She stopped with a start as she approached the bed.

Senenmut lay on his back atop the rumpled sheets, his bare chest rising and falling in sleep. Curled on her side next to him was a young woman nestled under the sheets with her face toward the wall. The braids of her wig fanned over Senenmut's arm, as expertly woven as the most intricate fisherman's net. It was then that Hatshepsut recognized the source of the exotic scent in the room: the girl's costly narcissus perfume.

Hatshepsut's hands flew to her mouth, but the moan of pain escaped anyway. Senenmut didn't move, but the girl stirred.

Hatshepsut fled as fast as her feet would carry her, not stopping until she'd reached her chambers and slammed the door behind her, yelling at Mouse and the slaves readying her bed to leave. They'd barely scurried from the room before she fell to her knees in front of her shrine to the gods. Behind the tallest statues of Amun and Sekhmet was a small ivory figure, a smiling cow-faced goddess gifted to her by an albino hand so many years ago.

Hatshepsut grabbed the goddess, wincing as Amun clattered to the ground. She didn't realize how hard she squeezed Hathor's statue until something snapped in her hand. The ivory goddess lay in her palm, broken in two yet still laughing, always laughing. It was unfathomable that such a seemingly insignificant goddess, relegated to oversee only music, love, and dance, could topple all else. Such was the power, and curse, of love.

In denying Senenmut children, she'd also denied him immortality of the flesh and pushed him into another's waiting arms. Any number of women would be beside themselves to marry Senenmut and bear his children.

The one thing Hatshepsut had denied him had proved too much.

Head pounding after a night spent staring at the ceiling above her empty bed, Hatshepsut was unable to close her eyes against the image of Senenmut and his young woman that was now seared onto her mind. She'd alternated between the urge to storm back to his apartments and scream at him like a demon from the afterlife, and forcing herself not to curl up like a child and sob herself to sleep. She didn't know what she'd do or say to Senenmut when she saw him, but one thing was certain: She couldn't chance a scene that would fuel the gossips for years to come. Much as she hated it, she would have to go to him.

And so she dragged Mouse from her pallet long before Re had finished his battle with dark Apep, and ordered her dwarf to ready her for the day. She wore no crown or headdress, no pectoral of precious stones, not even any rings—only a sheath of the softest linen and two stark lines of kohl ringing her eyes. It wasn't as his pharaoh that she would speak to him, but as the woman who shared his heart.

She dismissed the guards posted outside his apartments and braced herself to step inside once again. These rooms would be empty after today, for much as she might wish to keep Senenmut near, she was not so magnanimous as to let him remain with his woman beneath her nose. Egypt's third district at the farthest reaches of the Delta was in a need of a *nomarch*; she would send him there and be done with this, go through life with only half a heart, and that half scarred beyond use.

She expected Senenmut to still be abed, but the door opened to reveal a multitude of burning oil lamps. Her heart tripped at the sight of him, bereft of his wig and golden armbands and seated behind a table covered with scrolls. His face was as hard as a statue as he looked at her, as if he'd been waiting for her. They started at each other for a moment: a man and a woman, both broken.

She glanced around for the young woman, but his chambers were empty.

"You look terrible," he said.

"I didn't sleep well last night."

He nodded, and a thick silence settled between them. Finally, Senenmut cleared his throat. "I expect we'll need to meet with Ti and Neshi today regarding the trade expedition—"

"I know about her." Hatshepsut clasped her hands around her elbows, as if cradling her heart to protect it from further damage. She needed to get the words out and leave here—leave *him*—before she lost her composure.

"Her?" Senenmut cocked his head, his brow furrowed. "What are you talking about?"

Her hand fluttered toward his bed, the mattress still bearing the imprint of two bodies. "The woman in your bed." The words stuck in her throat. "I understand, but I can't have you here, not with her—"

"You understand?" Senenmut spoke the words slowly and stared at her, thunderstruck. "What do you understand?"

"That what I can give you pales in comparison to the joys of a wife and child." Hatshepsut tilted her chin and dropped her arms. She would do this with grace and pick up the fragments of her heart later. "You have my permission to leave court, and I gladly gift you the governorship of the third *nome*. It is my most fervent hope that you are able to find happiness there."

For she would never be happy again, not without him.

Senenmut rose and came to stand before her, the vein under his jaw throbbing and his eyes sparking. "So I can leave with my *wife*—and that's the end of the matter?"

Her heart cried out at the word *wife*. There was no formal wedding ceremony for nonroyalty; a man and a woman moved into the same house, broke bread, and made their claims on each other's hearts. For all she was aware, Senenmut might have been married for a week by now. She managed a nod. "You may. Go well, Senenmut of Iuny."

He stared at her for a moment, then shook his head. "I didn't expect such generosity," he said.

"You are dismissed." She meant that he was dismissed from court, but the words seemed small and silly, as she was the one now left to retreat from his rooms. She turned to leave, but he grabbed her wrist and pulled her against his chest, a rumble of laughter growing in the back of his throat. She struggled against him, but his arms were as tight as any ropes. She would let him leave the palace, but she would not be laughed at.

"Let me go!"

"You are a stubborn little fool, *nefersha*," he said, grunting to keep her from breaking loose. "I presume you mean the girl in my bed last night?"

She winced at the painful truth, but struggled to keep her voice from wavering. "Why? Is there more than one that I should be aware of?"

"No, just that one. And this little show of yours would have been rather impressive, were it not for the fact that the girl you saw in my bed is *my sister*."

It took several moments for the words to penetrate her mind. She stopped struggling, feeling his breath on the top of her head. "Your sister?" It was a family duty for royal siblings to marry in order to model the gods and ensure the purity of the bloodline, but otherwise the practice was virtually forbidden to the rest of Egypt's people. "I'm sure you have an excellent excuse for keeping your sister in your bed. If she really is your sister, that is."

His arms tightened around her, and a glance at his face revealed an expression as if he'd like nothing so much as to strangle her. "I'll tell you the whole story, but only if you promise not to gouge my eyes out when I let you go."

She glared at him and he gave an exasperated sigh. "I suppose that's as close as I'll get to a promise," he said.

He released her, and she crossed her arms tightly in front of her chest. "Go on."

"I went home to Iuny to clear my mind."

"I don't see why you had to leave." Even to her own ears she sounded as if she were pouting.

He pursed his lips. "You have the gift of muddling many a man's thoughts. It's like having Sekhmet roaring in your ear day and night."

"And?"

"Nofret-Hor is my youngest sister," Senenmut said, taking his seat again. He looked far too relaxed for Hatshepsut's liking. "The baby of the family."

"She didn't look like a baby to me."

"Perhaps not, but she's still afraid of the dark, although she wouldn't thank me for telling you that. I fell asleep last night and she crawled into bed next to me after the lamp burned out." He smiled. "She's only two years older than Neferure. In fact, Neferure is the reason why she's here. Nofret-Hor asked to come to court, and I thought it good timing with the Beautiful Feast of the Valley coming up."

"I'm not sure I understand the connection."

Senenmut ran his hands over his bare scalp. "My little sister wished to meet my daughter, Hatshepsut. She wanted to meet Neferure."

My daughter.

"Oh." Hatshepsut's hands fell away, her eyes filling at the simple words.

Senenmut rose and gathered her into his arms, his chin resting where the double crown would have been. "It took me several days of moping around Iuny, watching my brothers with their children, before I realized that I already have what I wanted."

"But I thought—"

"I know what you thought. And as impossible as it may sound, you were wrong. Of course I'd be happy to fill several stables with our children, so it was hard for me to understand your decision. But I could never leave you, Hatshepsut. I may as well cut out my heart."

She pressed closer, listening to the heavy beat of that heart. "I'm glad to be wrong," she said, splaying her hand over his bare chest so she could feel its steady rhythm. "Just this once."

His familiar laughter rumbled above her and she smiled at the sound, another gift from the gods.

"I didn't make the decision lightly," she whispered. For a moment she allowed herself to imagine these apartments and the palace corridors ringing with the laughter of their children. Instead, there was only silence.

"I know," he said.

They stayed that way for a long while, until Senenmut pressed a kiss onto her forehead. "You'd best go change," he murmured.

"Change?" Hatshepsut looked down at her sheath. "Why?"

"Because I thought to present my sister to you this morning," he said, a smile creeping across his face. "I've told Nofret-Hor how beautiful the pharaoh is, but—" He shrugged.

"But what?" Hatshepsut stood with arms akimbo, lips pursed together.

Senenmut laughed and kissed the back of her hand. "But right now you look like an angry fishwife. One with nowhere near enough jewels to impress a girl of thirteen floods."

She kissed him then, a kiss full of apology and happiness. A kiss of promise.

Senenmut groaned, his lips still on hers. "Nofret-Hor just ran to the bathing pavilion. You'd best go before we give her an eyeful of more than just the pharaoh's jewels."

Hatshepsut laughed, her heart light as she danced from his arms. And she made a silent promise to the gods as she ran back for another kiss before darting out the door, lest she and Senenmut find themselves tangled in his bed.

Never again would she take this man for granted. Instead, she swore that their shared sacrifice for Egypt would bind them closer together.

Hatshepsut did meet Nofret-Hor later that afternoon, and gifted the awestruck girl with enough jewels to buy the entire village of Iuny.

"Am I supposed to wear all these at once?" Nofret-Hor whispered to Senenmut, her brown eyes bulging. She wasn't terribly pretty, but her eyes sparked with intelligence as they darted about, taking in everything around her. Hatshepsut was struck by the family resemblance between the girl, scarcely on the cusp of womanhood, and Senenmut, but also by the stark contrast between Nofret-Hor and Neferure. Senenmut's sister had been raised on the muddy banks of the Nile and had the energy of a water bug, while Neferure seemed as fragile as a lotus blossom.

Hatshepsut had hoped the girls would strike up an immediate friendship, but Neferure remained quiet and withdrawn, finally opening up on the morning of the Beautiful Feast of the Valley as they boarded the royal barge that would accompany Amun's cedar boat to the West Bank, the land of the dead and the setting sun. Today the golden statue of the Great Cackler had left its newly constructed shrine in the Red Chapel in Karnak and traveled in a stately procession so that the hidden god might be reborn and granted new energy after a tiresome year of ruling this world. Neferure's face lit with rapture as she described the ceremonies she dedicated to the god of gods each morning at Karnak, the singing of hymns and preparation of offerings to the sacred statue as Re rose and bathed the supreme god in his light. These new duties were training for the day she would receive the title of God's Wife, a royal title Hatshepsut currently held. Nofret-Hor had barely managed to stifle a yawn and fidgeted under the golden awning as Amun's ram-headed boat stopped at several places along the Nile's banks, allowing Egypt's people to place offerings of bread and flowers at the god's feet, but she squealed with glee when Dagi asked if she'd like to steer the royal barge. Neferure had paled when Dagi had offered her the steering rod, its end topped with the gilded head of Horus, and made an excuse about needing to sit in the shade to avoid the glare of the river.

Horus and his golden sons watched the scene with unblinking glass eyes from the tops of the standard shafts, the snapping of the red and white pennants mingling in the breeze along with the low tone of the rowers' song. Hatshepsut pretended to inspect the offerings of wine and natron pellets waiting for Amun but instead observed her daughter from the prow. There was no doubt that Neferure took after Thutmosis with her fair skin and hesitant nature, and Hatshepsut herself had favored Pharaoh Tutmose and not her mother. Was it common for the gods to cast daughters from the same clay as their fathers instead of their mothers?

Senenmut seemed to read her thoughts and gave her a hand a gentle squeeze. "We don't all follow the paths our parents plan for us. If we did, I'd be in a field in Iuny, sorting manure, and you'd only be regent. Neferure will chart her own course." His eyes grew soft. "She's growing into a thoughtful young woman."

"Perhaps. I wonder if your mother can spare her youngest daughter for a bit longer?" Hatshepsut asked Senenmut. It might benefit Neferure to spend time with another girl close to her own age, especially someone as vivacious and lively as Nofret-Hor. Hatshepsut smiled as Nofret-Hor motioned to one of the rowers to move over on his bench and took his place, her oar out of sync with the others. Senenmut's sister beckoned for Neferure, but she shook her head, her long white robe fluttering in the breeze. She looked ready to faint when Nofret-Hor jumped up and pulled her over anyway, but then she let out a peal of laughter as Nofret-Hor took up the rowers' song, belting out the words off-key and adding in her own bits urging them to row faster.

Senenmut smiled at the rare sound of Neferure's silvery laughter. "They do complement each other, but I promised to return Nofret-Hor after the festival. Our mother has grown frail and is almost deaf now," he said.

"Does she still deny receiving my message after Thut's death, asking you to return to court?" Hatshepsut kept her voice light, but it still stung that Hatnofer of Iuny despised her so much that she would keep up her ridiculous lie after all these years.

"She does," Senenmut answered. "So adamantly that I think in her old age she may have forgotten the truth." He sighed. "I've ordered builders to begin construction of her tomb. My brothers bring her food and their wives check in on her, but Nofret-Hor is the only one of us left at home to take care of her now."

Hatshepsut linked her arm through his and rested her head on his shoulder. "Then of course she'll return. After all, I owe Hatnofer of Iuny a considerable debt."

Senenmut smiled. "Yes, come to think of it, I suppose you do."

"And Nofret-Hor shall have whatever she needs to make your mother happy and comfortable. Is there anything in particular you'd suggest?"

"Nofret-Hor," Senenmut shouted to his sister over her exclamations about the expertise of Dagi's rowers. "If you could give any gift to our mother, what would it be?"

Nofret-Hor stuck her tongue between her lips, making quite a show of thinking before a slow smile spread across her face. "Jugglers," she said.

"Jugglers?" Hatshepsut gaped at her, dumbfounded. "Why jugglers?"

Nofret-Hor shrugged. "My mother hears little, but she still loves to laugh. There's nothing in this world funnier than a juggler."

Hatshepsut chuckled. "Then you shall have an entire boatload of jugglers to entertain Hatnofer of Iuny. Is there anything else she'd like?"

Nofret-Hor puffed out her cheeks, looking like a Nile perch. "And a big, fat ox to eat until the end of her days."

Hatshepsut laughed. "Consider it done. Your family shall dine on the fattest ox to be found in the City of Truth."

Nofret-Hor grinned, then remembered to bow before scrambling to her feet as Hatshepsut dismissed her. "It must be wonderful to be pharaoh," Hatshepsut heard her whisper to Neferure as she linked arms with her daughter. "Imagine being able to order all that with a flick of your hand!"

Hatshepsut smiled and bumped her hip against Senenmut's, earning her another grin as their barge dropped its mooring stake and Amun's barque floated into position behind them.

It was indeed good to be pharaoh.

Nofret-Hor's visit stretched from days into weeks, but she finally departed with an escort of Hatshepsut's own *medjay*, accompanied by a boatful of jugglers and one extremely well-fed ox. She stood on the stern of the royal barge, blowing kisses and calling out promises to exchange frequent letters with Neferure. Hatshepsut stood flanked by Senenmut and Neferure as they waved good-bye, and then she left father and daughter so they might spend the day together. One of Senenmut's official titles was Overseer of the Granaries of Amun, and he had asked Neferure to help him inspect the god's accounts, a task Neferure was eager to help with, as it benefited her chosen god.

In the meantime, Hatshepsut hummed with happiness at the thought of her great task of the day: meeting Ti and Neshi to search for a land of myrrh trees and spices, a task that no longer seemed onerous now that she and Senenmut were happily reconciled. Scribes sat cross-legged on the floor of the administration offices, silently copying ancient treatises and maxims from sages long since flown to the Field of Reeds. The walls were stacked with flaking papyrus scrolls, and dust motes hung heavy in the air, eliciting a sneeze from one of the scribes every so often.

They pored over maps and archaic histories in search of the right destination, until the grime of dust covered Hatshepsut's hands, itched her eyes, and filled her mouth. This was a trip that would stretch beyond Egypt's boundaries so that Ti and Neshi could bring back exquisite luxuries from foreign and mystical lands. Nubian gold or Phoenician cedars were commonplace, too easy to obtain. Her temple would be unprecedented; all its trappings had to be matchless.

They found precisely what they were looking for buried in musty old records from the reign of Amenemhat II. The pharaoh had ruled five hundred years prior, but tucked deep within the histories of his reign was a reference to the now-mythical land of Punt, a nation that Egypt had traded with since the days of the pyramid builders. Amenemhat's expedition to the obscure land was the last of its kind. No other trip had been undertaken since then and the maps that outlined the route had been lost to time.

"Give me a ship and I'll find it," Neshi said.

"We might as well throw gold into the Nile," Ti countered. "It's been too long since the last trip. There has to be something safer." It was interesting to watch the identical men argue—they so rarely disagreed.

"But there's a description of the route right here." Neshi smashed his finger into Amenemhat's account. A piece of the decrepit papyrus flaked off. "Sorry," he muttered.

Hatshepsut reread the vague account aloud, imagining the voyage in her mind's eye. "Down the length of the Nile, through the Delta's marshes, overland across the Sinai, and down the Red Sea. There you will find the Gods' Land, filled with myrrh and frankincense, ivory and ebony, giraffes and baboons. The land of Punt."

"Imagine all of that decorating your temple." Neshi was practically salivating. "There's something you could write about on one of your obelisks."

"Or on the temple itself," she said.

The idea was more than tantalizing—new luxuries unseen in Egypt for five hundred years, brought back to her mortuary temple, her single most important monument. It made her wish she could travel to Punt herself to witness it all firsthand.

"If you're willing to lead the expedition, I'll finance it," she said to Neshi. A grin broke across her face as he whooped with delight.

"I'll stay here, if you don't object," Ti said to Hatshepsut. Neshi sobered slightly, but Hatshepsut nodded. She couldn't recall a time when the two men had been separated. "Good," Ti said. "After all, someone has to stay behind to make sure you don't spend all your money on temples and expeditions."

It took many months to design and build the appropriate seaworthy vessels, but finally, as Senenmut broke ground on her temple, the entire court and most of Waset gathered to send off two hundred men and five ships from the docks. Hatshepsut wished she could join them, but as pharaoh her place was on the Isis Throne, not gallivanting off on some wild adventure. Such was the price of the double crown.

The outcome of such a massive and dangerous undertaking wouldn't be known for months, perhaps years. The voyage might be a wild success, or, should Neshi fail, it might be a dark shadow on her reign.

The red sails puffed like giant ruddy cheeks, and hundreds of sturdy cedar oars were raised in salute to Hatshepsut. The High Priest of Amun intoned a prayer, surrounded by a clutch of solemn *wa'eb* priests, as he overturned a vial of myrrh into the Nile to bless the waters. Neshi gave his a final bow from the front of his boat as acrobats and dancers took to the crowd on shore, vendors hawking overpriced melons and half-burned meats over the beat of the boats' drums. She prayed she would see them all again.

Hatshepsut stayed to watch as the last red sail melted into the brown horizon. The Great Cackler himself would protect the expedition, just as Sekhmet watched over her.

The gods loved her too much to forsake her now.

CHAPTER 26

YEAR FOUR OF PHARAOH HATSHEPSUT

The morning sky was aglow with buttery young sunshine, warming the granite in the forecourt of Hatshepsut's mortuary temple. The breath of the gods whipped puffs of white into a fluffy bird with the beak of an ibis and the feathers of an ostrich, then morphed it into a ship with billowing sails, a reminder of the ships that had set off from the City of Truth three years ago. Hatshepsut and the rest of Egypt had long ago given up hope of hearing from Neshi and his men. Surely they were lost, killed on the overland trek across the Sinai Peninsula or drowned in a storm while sailing the Red Sea.

This would be the greatest stain on her rule as pharaoh. What should have been one of the brightest accomplishments was instead an abysmal failure. And even that didn't plague her as did the thought of those two hundred men meeting unknown and possibly gruesome deaths while their *kas* were obliterated, with no bodies left behind to mummify and place in their tombs. It was as if the gods wished to remind her not to become complacent, to remember that disaster could strike at any time.

She had hoped that the discovery of Punt and the completion of her mortuary temple would be the crowning achievements of her reign, but now the temple would have to stand alone on that pinnacle. The sacred place was almost finished, christened Djeser-Djeseru, the "Holiest of Holies." It was all Senenmut had promised her, and more.

On this morning of dancing clouds, Hatshepsut traveled to the Western Valley to check the progression of the temple's final frescoes in the Hall of Birth. The northern portico of the mortuary temple was devoted to the story of Hatshepsut's divine birth to her mortal mother, Ahmose, and her hallowed father, Amun. The invisible god had been her father's patron, so it was scarcely stretching the truth to claim him as her divine father, yet another way to overcome the obstacle of a woman ruling. If the Great Cackler decreed it, so it would be.

Hatshepsut gazed at the chiseled outline of Osiris Tutmose, glad she had commissioned Aka to depict her father rather than a younger artist who had never met the pharaoh. The figure was stylized, but miniscule details identified him from the mass of other men depicted on the walls. He was there in the hook of his nose, the way the lips curved up slightly at the edges, and the receding chin. His figure loomed over everyone else's on the relief, even the gods'.

She wished he could see her now.

Another frieze depicted her as pharaoh. This time the figure bore no likeness to the subject. The cartouche above the image identified her throne name—Maatkare—but she wore the short kilt and false beard of a man, a mirror of her costume at all formal occasions. She despised it. Not only did the beard scratch and leave a rash on her chin for days afterward, but she hated the pretense. Her monuments were scattered about Egypt, but her advisers had deemed the deviation of a female pharaoh too outrageous for the illiterate *rekhyt* to stomach, so each image depicted her as a man. It was one thing for the commoners to accept the pharaoh as a living god, but quite another for them to swallow a woman as that god. She understood the logic, but that didn't mean she had to like it.

Footsteps crunched behind her, followed by the scent of cinnamon on the air and the low hum of Senenmut's voice.

"Do you like it?"

She nodded without turning around. "It's exquisite, more majestic than I could have dreamed."

This would be her tribute to Egypt, something to last for all time.

Her pyramid.

"Your father would be proud," Senenmut said. "He might even be a little put out to discover that thus far, his daughter's reign has been even more successful than his own."

Hatshepsut laughed at the truth. "You exaggerate."

"Humility doesn't sit well on you." He wrapped his arms around her waist. "Egypt has been at peace for over a decade, her enemies vanquished and her storehouses perpetually overflowing. Your people adore you. I adore you." His eyes swept over the columns and reliefs of the temple he had built for her. "And in case you hadn't noticed, Egypt is now littered with your monuments."

Her chuckle echoed off the columns and into the sunshine. "I suppose it is."

"Even your mother would be proud," he added.

"She'd be proud of this." Hatshepsut pointed to the carved depiction of Ahmose being led to the birthing chamber by her attendants. "You can't tell if she's pregnant or simply eaten too much at dinner."

Senenmut laughed, that throaty chortle that still had the power to make her feel a little warmer. "A final gift for your mother."

They stood that way for some time, swathed in each other's embrace. A timelessness imbued within the temple's stones made the rest of the chaotic world seem far away.

Hatshepsut was the first to speak, her voice so low it blended into the breeze. "I have a surprise for you."

"Really?" Senenmut arched a brow. "I have a surprise for you, too."

"The best minds think like me," Hatshepsut joked, and received a playful jab to her ribs in response. "Which one first?"

"After you." Senenmut released her with a mock bow.

She took him the long way through the temple, wandering through the chapels dedicated to Hathor and Anubis. Although Hatshepsut still favored Sekhmet and Amun, she had chosen to honor the cow goddess of love and the jackal god of death, having come to appreciate their positions as the creator and taker of life, greater even than that of the nine gods. One relief showed Hathor as a cow suckling the infant Hatshepsut, and another depicted Anubis introducing Hatshepsut to the world of gods in the next life. The rest of Hatshepsut's days would be written on the walls in between, but her story began with Hathor and would end with Anubis.

It was to Djeser-Djeseru's second terrace that Hatshepsut guided Senenmut, to a statue niche on the southern wall. Above the door were fifteen empty stone vessels, each dry now but soon to be filled with sacred oils and unguents. The alcove was empty as well, but would house a statue of Amun once the temple was finished. Senenmut stood back, unsure what he was looking for.

"Look carefully." She could hardly wait for him to find it, but the surprise was well hidden, just as she'd intended.

Senenmut perused the carvings, mumbling the hieroglyphs as he went. He finished scanning the wall and gave her a quizzical look.

"You're sure there's a surprise here?"

"Look closer."

He continued the search, lingering over an inconspicuous offering scene depicting a kneeling man holding two ankhs—the symbol of eternal life—to the supreme god. An image of Hatshepsut stood before the man, offering a green vial of perfume to Amun. Senenmut inhaled sharply as he read the hieroglyphs that identified the supplicant.

"Me? You put *me* in here?" He expression was blank with shock. "But this is a holy site."

In ordering the artist to include Senenmut, Hatshepsut had broken with a tradition countless millennia old. The portrayal of a person in a site as sacred as this one was not a mere picture, but a true substitute for the person represented. By placing Senenmut's image within the temple precincts, she allowed him to bask in the power and glory of Amun just as she would for all time. The sacrilege was no small favor.

She shrugged, trying her best to appear nonchalant. "For some reason I can't fathom the idea of eternity without you."

She'd barely lived through that once. There was still a pig heart buried in the garden to prove it. Yet Senenmut stared at the image of himself as if it were a cobra poised to strike.

She sighed. There was only one way to wake him from this stupor. "I'll have the workmen chisel it off tomorrow."

"No." Senenmut spoke quickly. "Don't do that. I'm just . . . in awe. To think that a *rekhyt*—"

"I don't care about that and you know it. All that matters is that you have a place with me in the next world."

Senenmut laughed. "You don't want to be bored when you get to the Field of Reeds."

It was Hatshepsut's turn to laugh. "Perhaps."

Senenmut clasped her hand in his and kissed it once. "Thank you."

"This isn't the only picture of you." She bit her lip and traced the white scars on her wrists, unfaded even after all the years since Neferubity's death.

His eyes narrowed. "How many secret Senenmuts have you hidden around here?"

"Well, they're all very small and out of the way, where no one will really notice." Hatshepsut stalled. She felt like a little girl admitting to stealing not one but dozens of honey rolls.

"How many?" Senenmut prodded.

"Sixty."

"Sixty!"

She had sworn to make it up to him when he asked for a child. Now she had returned him sixtyfold. "You're stuck with me for eternity, *sehedj ib.*"

One who gladdens the heart.

The name was fitting; Senenmut made her heart feel as if it had wings. She chuckled at the look of horror plastered on his face. "I asked the artists to scatter you all over the place."

"What in the name of Amun are you thinking?" He glowered at her now. "One picture might not be noticed, but sixty? *Sixty?*"

This she had expected.

"Just listen for a moment." She spoke calmly and gestured for him to sit at the base of one of the pillars with her. He did, but she had a feeling his fingers itched to wring her neck.

"What I did three years ago was an aberration tolerated only because my seven years as regent were idyllic. I can control what Egypt says about me during my lifetime, but not what will be said of me—of us—years down the road."

"I don't see how I play into this."

"When has a *rekhyt* ever risen so high?"

"I thought you didn't care about my birth."

"Answer the question."

"Never." It wasn't a bluff because it was the truth.

"What if history decides to erase us, to remove the female deviation and her consort from the record? What if our bodies are destroyed and my monuments torn down? Without some tangible evidence of our lives on earth, we could disappear from the Field of Reeds. I can't let that happen to either of us."

Senenmut pulled her closer. She shivered, trying to push the nightmare from her mind.

"I've planned the odds in our favor," she said. "Even if this temple falls to the ground, somewhere in the rubble the images of you and me will keep our *kas* alive."

"I think Egypt will laud you as one of their golden kings for all eternity." Senenmut entwined his fingers through hers. "But it's probably wise to be prepared."

"And we both know I'm extremely wise." She shot him a mischievous grin. "It's one of my better qualities."

His lips silenced her. "Thank you," Senenmut repeated. "This is the best gift I've ever received."

"You're welcome," Hatshepsut said. Then she poked his ribs. "I believe that's only half the surprises for the day."

A quick smile flashed across his face. "Follow me."

They passed the T-shaped pools in the lower courtyard and left the temple boundaries, but Hatshepsut envisioned the underground arc of her new tomb where it rested beneath their feet. She had abandoned the dangerous and unfinished cliff tomb and instead ordered a second tomb dug to physically link her with Djeser-Djeseru when she flew to the sky. They walked outside her temple's courtyard, stopping at an inconspicuous door dug into the rubble at the base of the lion-colored cliff.

"Wait here," Senenmut said. "And close your eyes."

She motioned to the limestone boulders strewn about them. "This isn't a surprise. It's the quarry for Djeser-Djeseru."

"Do what you're told for once, *nefersha*." Senenmut smiled. "Close your eyes and don't open them until I come back."

She pouted, then closed her eyes, enjoying the sun on her face before she heard Senenmut return, accompanied by the acrid smell of a burning torch. She felt its heat before he took her hand.

"Keep your eyes closed."

It was disconcerting as they started down a set of extraordinarily steep stairs. She stumbled once, but Senenmut steadied her. The temperature rose the farther in they went—a result of the heat and stale air trapped within—and beads of sweat dripped at her temples. She reached out several times to be sure the walls weren't closing in on them.

She lost track of the number of steps before the ground leveled out. Senenmut stopped, then dropped her hands.

"Open your eyes."

They were too deep in the earth for even the faintest reminder of the sun, but the torch cast a warm glow upon exquisitely painted walls.

Shadows danced to a silent melody, bringing the surreal figures of gods and goddesses to life. A false door was carved into one wall of the tomb, so painstakingly crafted that Hatshepsut was tempted to try to open it. She recognized the style—this door would serve its only purpose in allowing the *ka* of the deceased to enter and exit the room each night.

This was the closest she would come to the afterlife until she traveled to the Field of Reeds. The dark figures etched into the rock were fluid, lifelike. Seated above the unblinking eyes of Horus were three people enjoying a banquet—one woman and two men. The first man embraced the younger, and a woman held a lotus in full bloom to his nose.

Hatshepsut read the glyphs. "'Ramose and Hatnofer.' Your parents." She reached out to the middle figure, but her skin barely brushed the stone. "And you." She breathed deeply, inhaled the aroma of stale air and the burning oil of Senenmut's torch. "This is your tomb."

"My gift from you," Senenmut said. "I finally built something for myself, but I couldn't quite leave you out of it." He gestured to another scene, this one of a man in open adoration of the pharaoh before him. But this pharaoh was different from the ones cut into the stones of Djeser-Djeseru. The figure wore the double crown and bull's tail, but lacked the false beard and wore a sheath instead of a kilt. The curves under the clothing attested to the fact that this was no man, but a woman.

Her eyes stung. At least here in the darkness of Senenmut's tomb she could be depicted in truth. It was a precious gesture.

She read the inscription next to it aloud, focusing on each word to keep the tears from blurring her eyes.

"Live, Horus powerful of *kas*, two ladies flourishing of years, Horus of gold divine of appearances, king of Upper and Lower Egypt, Maatkare, beloved of Amun-Ra, living—"

The first was her titulary, all her titles repeated, but then linked to something else—*someone* else.

"—the sealbearer of the pharaoh of Upper and Lower Egypt, the steward of Amun, Senenmut, born from the bodies of Ramose and Hatnofer—"

She stopped, unable to read on for the stone lodged in her throat.

"You're not the only one breaking tradition," he whispered.

Senenmut had linked himself to her in a single line of text—proclaiming his relationship to her forever in stone. It was bold and brash, and she loved him all the more for it.

He shifted the torch from one hand to another so the hieroglyphs shuddered. "'A poor man's name is pronounced only on account of his lord.'"

She chuckled at the ancient proverb. "You are far from a poor man."

"Perhaps not, but I still didn't think you'd mind." He stood behind her now, the heat of the torch warming the flesh of her back. A single drop of sweat slipped down her spine. "There's one more thing," he added. "Look up."

The entire cosmos arched above her head, each haloed star and glowing planet flawlessly recreated in miniature. Senenmut had created the midnight sky, the universe of Nut's belly canvassing the tomb and enveloping it in eternal night.

She gasped. "It's beautiful."

"Your new tomb is so close that each night our *kas* can return here to sit under the stars. It only seemed fitting to take them into eternity with us." He pointed to the vault of constellations. "There's Sodpet and Osiris. And Set with the first planet." He continued talking, pointing out all the clusters of stars they both knew so well.

"I've never seen anything like this," she said. "It's amazing. *You're* amazing."

She had never seen Senenmut blush, but even in the shadows she could make out the blood rising to his face.

"I did it for you, *nefersha.*"

"It's supposed to be for you," she said. "This was your project, remember?"

"For us, then."

They stayed in the tomb until the torch threatened to sputter out, each lying on the floor with the crowns of their heads touching under the earthen stars and sky. When they finally stepped back into the land of the living, both had to blink away the searing pain of Re's light. They were halfway down the path that wound away from Djeser-Djeseru and toward the river when a runner from the palace intercepted them.

Hatshepsut's stomach turned sour to see the boy race toward them, running as if Ammit herself was chasing him. Perhaps Nubia had decided to revolt again or, Amun forbid, something had happened to Tutmose or Neferure. It wasn't until the slave got closer that Hatshepsut could see his face ablaze with excitement.

She didn't allow him a moment to bow. "What is it?"

"They're back!" The messenger gasped for breath, hands on his knees and chest heaving. "The ships from Punt have been spotted upriver—they're only two days away!"

Hatshepsut was struck speechless. It had been so long since the ships had left that she'd given up hope of ever seeing Neshi and the rest of the expedition again. There had to be a mistake. "Are you sure?"

The youth nodded, his head ready to fly from his neck. "Four ships, flying the royal pennants—the same ones that left three years ago."

"Four ships." Hatshepsut thought out loud. "One was lost."

"The runners claim they're carrying all sorts of wonders. The ships are so heavy they can hardly make it up the Nile!"

Senenmut grinned. "So the trip was a success after all."

If the expedition had been a success, her temple would be outfitted with grandeur to impress even Amun. New trade routes would be established with the Gods' Land, and Egypt would gain prestige and stature. Hatshepsut recited a silent prayer to Amun to thank him for such a blessing.

"Are you coming?" Hatshepsut, already running back down the path, hollered at Senenmut over her shoulder.

"What's the hurry?" His voice grew closer as he chased after her. "They won't be here for at least two days."

She twirled to face him, grinning like a jackal and flinging her arms open to the sky. "Because this will be a homecoming like none Egypt has ever seen before!"

The drums beat in time to herald Neshi's approach before he entered Amun's gates at Karnak. Shielded from Re's glare by the shadows of her twin obelisks, Hatshepsut stood on a makeshift dais, the smell of new wood and fresh whitewash still lingering in the breeze and the *atef* crown with its white dome, red ostrich feathers, and gold disk light on her head. Too excited to sit, she ignored the gilded traveling throne and its footstool with engravings of Egypt's nine enemies behind her. To her left, Tutmose stood on tiptoes to see what wonders Neshi had retrieved from the land of Punt. Senenmut, Neferure, and the rest of Hatshepsut's counsel clustered at the foot of the dais, each straining to catch the first glimpse of the coming treasures. The temple forecourt overflowed with nobles and *rekhyt* alike, so that even the causeway outside was jammed with eager onlookers.

It wasn't long before Neshi entered, his skin baked almost black and his frame much thinner than when he had left. Weather-beaten men flanked him, each carrying a large basket of woven papyrus. The men placed their baskets far in front of them, then stepped back to kneel and dropped their foreheads to the flagstones.

"Greetings, *Per A'a*." Neshi grinned as he knelt before her. "Your weary explorers have returned with ships full of riches beyond your imagination, all for the glory of Egypt."

"We are happy to bear witness to your safe return." Hatshepsut spoke formally, but couldn't keep the excitement from her voice. "We feared the entire expedition had been lost."

Neshi's grin faltered. It took a long moment for him to gather his words. "We hit a storm wind after coming out of the Red Sea. One boat was lost, but we saved as many men as we could. Some didn't make it." Hatshepsut could only guess at the horrors he had witnessed as men drowned around him. "Their names are preserved and they died with honor. Osiris feasts with them in the Field of Reeds," he said, finding his feet and his smile again. "We reached the Gods' Land as the egrets were nesting and were greeted by Chief Parihou and Queen Ati. She is so massive it takes six men to carry her about the town in her litter, but her husband is as thin as sedge grass and wears golden bracelets on his ankles as if he were a woman!"

There was a rumble of excitement from the forecourt.

"Punt is a strange land, *Per A'a*, both wild and civilized. The people's skin is darker than even the Nubians', but they are much more sophisticated than our rebel neighbors. The houses in Punt are built on stilts higher than giraffes and they have to climb into them every night using ladders."

Neshi pantomimed climbing, causing a burst of laughter, and then paused for dramatic effect. "But the splendors!" He threw his hands into the air. "I wish we could have brought back all of Punt to show you, but we managed only a sample of the wonders from that strange land."

He motioned to the men flanking him, and one by one each swept the lid off his basket with a flourish. Neshi called out the contents as scribes hastily recorded each item.

"Ebony!"

"Cinnamon!"

"Coriander!"

"Marjoram!"

"Gold ingots!"

Neshi grinned again, his face cleft by excitement. "And there's more!"

A single boom of the drums swept in the beginning of a long procession of temple priests, each heavily laden with items now dedicated to the Great Cackler himself. Hatshepsut's eyes welled as she watched. A mountain of black panther skins weighed down one of the marching

priests, followed by a river of elephant tusks, and more hills of mul-
tihued spices than she could count. There were boxes of creamy frankincense pellets—the opaque tears gathered from the trunks of the
sacred trees—and two priests struggled to contain a bevy of collared
baboons. The furred monkeys of Thoth squawked at one another, more
interested in playing with the contents of each basket than in looking
like official prizes.

"We brought back giraffes, too, but they're still on the ships. We
had to untangle their necks before they could be added to the royal
menagerie." Neshi joked loud enough so that everyone in the whole
temple could hear, inciting still more laughter from the amazed onlookers.

If that wasn't enough, Hatshepsut nearly wept as she saw the final
acquisitions being paraded beneath Amun's gate.

Her trees.

The breath of the gods carried the gentle aroma of myrrh as a dozen
precious trees were marched before her, their delicate white trunks
topped with a dusting of pale green leaves. Each would be planted in
the Garden of Amun at Djeser-Djeseru to cloak the entire complex
with their scent and allow the hidden god to enjoy their fragrance.
Senenmut's vision of her temple was complete.

Gone was the smudge on her reign, the dark spot that would have
marred her rule as pharaoh.

Everything was perfect.

CHAPTER 27

The clang of bronze scimitars accompanied the grunts of the two men sparring on the packed earth of the training ring, their ox-hide vests denoting their elite ranks within of the Division of Amun. Seasoned soldiers with leathered skin and scarred chests surrounded the hawk in the nest and his sparring partner, but the typical jeers and teasing were tempered today in deference to the three women seated on the raised wooden platform at the edge of the ring. It wasn't often that royalty descended to join their ranks. Neferure sat to Hatshepsut's right, picking at a stray thread on her otherwise pristine sheath, and Aset perched on the left, beaming down at her son.

Nomti wasn't pleased with Aset's recent return to the palace, but Hatshepsut felt sure that the past years had been more than enough time to dull the edge of Aset's hatred. She'd broached the subject of allowing Tutmose's mother back to court several times, especially as she received an increasing number of letters from Aset begging to be allowed to return to her son, but each time Nomti and her other advisers had managed to persuade Hatshepsut against the decision. In the end, it was Tutmose and Neferure who had convinced her.

Tutmose had mentioned his wish for Aset's return during his most recent naming ceremony at the end of Peret, when the seeds that would bring forth the next season of wheat and barley were already sprouting. He had seen seventeen floods and been apprenticed to the army for several years now. The royal family had sat on a rooftop terrace over-looking the Nile, the river shimmering like a long brown snake cutting through green grass. Slaves had hovered behind them, ready to move Tutmose's many gifts to his chambers as soon as Re's disk grew too hot and they all retreated inside. "It's been a long time since I've seen my mother," he'd said, his gaze fixed on the leather helmet Senenmut had given him. "I sometimes wonder if she'd recognize me now."

"I miss Aunt Aset, too," Neferure had said. "Her letters from Dendera sound so lonely."

Cold guilt settled around Hatshepsut's heart. She still hated what she'd done to Aset, knowing it was an affront to *ma'at*, the same sacred principle of truth and justice she'd always sworn to uphold. Her gaze caught Senenmut's, and he gave an almost imperceptible nod.

"Then she shall return," Hatshepsut said, folding her hands in her lap.

Tutmose's head jerked up. "Truly?"

Hatshepsut felt another sharp stab of guilt. She'd told Tutmose that his mother had retired from the City of Truth so he might pursue his schooling and military training unencumbered. He'd seemed to accept the story, yet now Hatshepsut wondered if perhaps he had suspected the truth but was too perceptive to question her motives, at least not aloud.

And so Aset had returned, escorted by two royal ships with mast-heads carved like giant lotus blossoms. Hatshepsut had toyed with the idea of not greeting Aset upon her arrival, but she refused to take the coward's route. If she could face the chiefs of Nubia and order the ex-ecution of criminals, then surely she could confront a lone woman who bore her a grudge. She commanded a modest celebration befitting the return of the mother of Egypt's future pharaoh and ordered her ad-visers to attend.

The first boat slipped into its place against the dock, and Aset waited on the prow, staring at Hatshepsut with an expression so regal that it reminded her of her own mother many years ago. Finally, the ropes were secured and Aset stepped onto the fresh flower petals laid out for her arrival. As if on cue, the courtiers—including Senenmut—bowed their heads, leaving only Hatshepsut, Tutmose, and Neferure to witness Aset's slow progress up the dock. Tutmose stepped forward and clasped his mother's hands, kissing each of her cheeks before accompanying her to Hatshepsut. Neferure dabbed at the corners of her eyes, her face aglow with happiness at the return of her second mother.

"Welcome home, Aset," Hatshepsut said in a low voice, her heart fluttering like a falcon's wings.

"I hardly know what to say." Aset glanced about at the nobility, their heads still bowed. Her eyebrows had been plucked clean away and replaced with thin slashes of kohl, giving her an unnaturally severe expression. "I didn't expect such ceremony to herald the end of my banishment."

Hatshepsut fingered the golden snake bangles at her wrist. "Such a homecoming is worthy of a little celebration."

Aset gave her a strange look, but Tutmose seized that moment to take his mother's arm and lead her into the palace, Neferure trailing after them. Hatshepsut watched them go, wondering how she had escaped so easily. She assumed Tutmose and Neferure would keep Aset to themselves for the rest of the day, so her heart thudded when Aset was announced into the royal menagerie later that night.

Hatshepsut tossed the last bruised turnip from her basket onto the ground before one of the giraffes from Punt, smiling as the beast bent its graceful neck and nibbled the vegetable, then blinked at her. "I know," she chuckled. "I wouldn't eat it either."

She liked to come here to visit the animals on occasion, laughing as the baboons groomed one another and watching the giraffes strip the leaves from the trees that were constantly replaced in their stone enclosures. The giraffe wandered off, leaving the half-eaten turnip as Nomti announced Aset, looking none too happy with the unexpected visitor.

A guard trailed Aset, a lean *medjay* whom Nomti had chosen to keep an eye on Tutmose's mother. Aset was dressed in a form-fitting sheath far too tight and translucent to hide any weapons; her nipples had been rouged under the fine linen and all her body hair had been plucked away. The second *medjay* followed her with his eyes, his gaze lingering on the curves of her backside. Both guards fell back at Hatshepsut's signal, although Nomti didn't look pleased at the silent order. Aset's features twisted into an expression of pure malice as she passed Hatshepsut's guard, but then she turned her attention to Hatshepsut and swept into a deep *henu*. "I've come to make peace with you, Hatshepsut," she said as she straightened.

Hatshepsut was caught momentarily off guard, then recovered and motioned Aset to a bench. "That's hardly the reaction I expected from you," she said, smoothing the pleats of her skirt and trying to collect her thoughts.

"I've carried this grudge against you for years now. I don't wish to face Anubis' scales and find my heart so heavy with bitterness that I'm unable to enter the Field of Reeds."

Hatshepsut didn't speak for a moment, startled again at the stunning ease of Aset's return. She'd hoped to have a conversation like this with her, but as time had worn on, it had seemed more likely that frogs would fall from the sky. A glance at Nut's clear belly told her that wasn't going to happen, at least not tonight.

"I've missed you," Hatshepsut said, finding a truth in the words that she'd held at bay these past years. "I don't deserve such kindness."

"I don't agree with what you did." Aset dropped her hand and picked her nails. Her thumb had started to bleed. "But I understand why you did it."

"Can you forgive me?"

Aset sucked the tip of her finger, then clasped her hands before her. "Does it matter?"

"It does matter. To me."

"Then yes. I forgive you."

Hatshepsut searched Aset's face for any trace of malice, but her features were scrubbed clean. She seemed to have aged at least twenty years since the coronation.

"I never meant to hurt you."

"I know that now, but I couldn't help being angry. For Tutmose."

"He'll be pharaoh after me, I swear on Sekhmet's sun disk."

"Good." Aset studied her. "He seems to be doing well in his apprenticeship to the military. I hope one day to see him follow in his grandfather's footsteps."

"He's a smart boy and a quick learner."

"Good," Aset said stiffly. "Thank you for taking care of him."

There was still a wall between them, but it wasn't so tall that it couldn't be chipped away in time. It was more than Hatshepsut had hoped for.

She stopped Aset as she stood to leave. "I've missed you, Aset."

Aset smiled, yet traces of sadness clung to her dark eyes. "I've missed you, too."

Aset walked from the garden, and the lean *medjay* fell into step behind her. Hatshepsut wanted to trust Aset again. She just didn't know if she should.

Several weeks had passed since that night, and although Aset had offered her friendship, Hatshepsut had grown accustomed to the sight of Aset's retreating back each time she entered a room, followed by the shadow of her guard. Finally, Hatshepsut decided their single shared interest was the only route to earning back Aset's friendship, so she invited Aset and Neferure to watch Tutmose's skirmish at the military training ground. Egypt's hawk in the nest filled out his armor and was taller than most of the other soldiers; Tutmose slept in the barracks and could swear and spit with the best of the men, much to his mother's chagrin. Of course, few soldiers were as well-read or could speak as many languages as the hawk in the nest, but the men seemed willing to overlook these shortcomings in their future pharaoh.

The other soldier—a young man with dirty feet and overly large teeth—danced around the ring, looking for a hole in Tutmose's defense.

"Want me to let you win?" The wind carried Sennedjem's words to Hatshepsut. "It might help you impress your princess."

Hatshepsut snuck a glance at Neferure through her lashes. The poor girl winced as if the men were strangling kittens instead of talking about her.

Tutmose charged the other soldier, slammed his shoulder into his friend's flank to throw him off balance, then smashed the butt of his scimitar into Sennedjem's shield. The force of the blow knocked Sennedjem back. He fell, his head and shoulders landing outside the ring drawn in the dirt.

"Match!" The trainer's hand cut through the air. "The round goes to Tutmose!"

Tutmose grinned and offered his hand to his friend. It didn't matter now who was watching—the soldiers cheered and many collected bets from those who had wagered against the hawk in the nest.

"Caught me off guard there." Sennedjem laughed and brushed the dirt from his kilt. The two clapped each other on the back, releasing puffs of red dust before Sennedjem waved at the stands.

Tutmose bowed in their direction, but his eyes lingered on Neferure. Her hair was loose today, a shining sheet of mahogany held back by a thin gold diadem to emphasize her cheekbones. Without asking permission, Hatshepsut's daughter had grown into a woman, just as Tutmose had become a man.

Perhaps too much of a man for one still so young. Senenmut's spies had recently reported Tutmose's nightly visits to Satiah, a girl-slave in the kitchens with breasts as big as water jugs that swayed enticingly when she kneaded bread. For now, Hatshepsut was willing to ignore the indiscretion, allowing a reminder regarding Tutmose's duties to Neferure to suffice as his only consequence. Once he married Neferure he could have as many *rekhyt* as he wanted in his bed, but until then he needed to restrict his interests to his books and military training, despite the allure of certain kitchen slaves.

And yet Hatshepsut wondered how Neferure would react if she heard of Tutmose's interest in Satiah. Neferure reminded her of a spring butterfly, graceful and rare, but so fine that the slightest touch would irrevocably damage its wings. She fluttered about at all the palace functions Hatshepsut required her to attend, and would bolt at the first opportunity with some excuse about her temple duties.

Hatshepsut had bestowed the title of God's Wife upon Neferure, and with that came heavy responsibilities. Her daughter was usually up before Re rose to dress and anoint Amun's gold statue at Karnak. She spent most of her afternoons singing and chanting prayers to the god, and saw to the distribution of temple offerings. The musk of incense had become Neferure's permanent perfume, the holy scent made from countless sacred ingredients clinging to her pale skin.

And now, just as it seemed Neferure might crawl under her seat, Tutmose freed her from his eyes to spare a smile for his mother, then gave a deep bow of acknowledgment to Hatshepsut. She often wondered what he thought of her now that he was older, whether he truly realized what she had done in claiming the throne as her own. The idea that he would receive the finest military training and gain a calm and stable Egypt after she passed to the West was usually more than enough to soothe the occasional qualms of her *ka*.

She smiled as he picked up his belt and walked to the observation stand, the men behind him already dispersing in search of their mats or a cup of beer.

"Well done." Aset glowed at her son. "That was quite a maneuver you pulled out there."

Tutmose buckled his belt and glanced warily over his shoulder as if to check whether anyone had heard his mother's praise, but they were all out of earshot. "Luck. Tomorrow Sennedjem will probably throw me."

"I see you've moved on to the scimitar." Hatshepsut eyed the bronze weapon hanging at his hip. "Do you like it?"

"Senenmut showed me the trick to holding it." He tossed the blade lightly and caught it by its hilt. "The Syrians knew what they were doing when they came up with this. It's like an extension of your arm."

"It's time to eat." Aset clapped and stepped down from the stands, holding out her hand for Tutmose. She ignored the sheen of sweat and dust on his skin and linked her arm through his. "As your mother, I claim you for lunch. I thought I'd see you more now that I've returned to the palace, but it seems like ages since we've talked. Perhaps we can discuss Pharaoh Kamose's military victory against the Hyksos over oxtail soup."

"It's Pharaoh Ahmose," Tutmose muttered. "Kamose died before the Hyksos were defeated, as did his father."

"Such similar names," Aset said. "Does it really matter?"

Hatshepsut winced, hoping Tutmose would bite his tongue. It mattered very much, for Pharaoh Ahmose had expelled the terrible foreigners from Egypt and founded their family's dynasty. Aset had always detested history—she'd once claimed Hatshepsut's scrolls on the reigns of Khufu and Khafre would be best suited for lining cages in the palace aviary—but at least she was making an effort for her son.

Tutmose's gaze trailed after the men and for a moment he looked as if he'd rather clean chamber pots than spend the afternoon with his mother. But then his face cleared and he patted her hand. After all, duty was duty.

"I can think of nothing better I'd like to do." He sheathed the scimitar and bowed to Hatshepsut and Neferure, but turned around as an afterthought. "Neferure." Did she cringe as he spoke her name, or was it the sun making her squint? "You look lovely today, your eyes especially."

A rosy blush overtook Neferure's cheeks. And it was true. The sun made her eyes shine so that she looked even more ethereal than usual, her skin as translucent as a lotus petal. Tutmose bowed to his future wife and continued down the path with his mother, Aset's guard following a few steps behind them.

Hatshepsut and Neferure watched them go, then ambled back up the path to the palace, taking the long way around the lake. Neferure plucked a lily from the waters, absentmindedly picking the petals and dropping them as they walked. The yellow petals fluttered to the ground, scattered by the princess's footsteps. She bit her lip, showing slightly crooked teeth, seemingly lost in thought.

"How is Nofret-Hor these days?" Hatshepsut asked.

"Fine," Neferure mumbled. "She's to be married soon."

"I'm sure she's excited." Hatshepsut knew from Senenmut that Nofret-Hor had chosen her own husband, a scribe from the Temple of Thoth. Hatshepsut planned to send them a lavish wedding gift, perhaps even present them with a plot of land and vineyards in Iuny.

Neferure only shrugged and sighed, dropping more flower petals to the path.

Hatshepsut wished she could catch a glimpse of the inner workings of Neferure's mind. It was easier to discern the secret motives of glossy courtiers than it was to pull one solid answer out of her silent daughter.

"I can't stand it anymore." Hatshepsut motioned for the guards to fall back. "What are you thinking?"

"Nothing." Neferure flushed again, her cheeks crimson fire now compared to the gentle pink that had warmed her face earlier. Those same eyes now darted to her mother's face and down to the mangled lily.

Hatshepsut took her daughter's fingers and squeezed them. "Neferure, anyone can see you're upset. Was it Tutmose? I'm sure he didn't mean for his comment to embarrass you."

"No, I know, it's not—" Neferure stumbled over the words. "It's not Tutmose." Her lower lip trembled. "It is, but it's not."

Hatshepsut pulled Neferure into her arms and held her tight. Her daughter's heart fluttered like a sunbird. "Whatever's bothering you can't be that terrible. And you can tell me anything, you know that."

"I know." Tears clung to the corners of Neferure's eyes, but she allowed Hatshepsut to lead her to a granite bench at the edge of the lake. They sat in silence for some time as a pair of swans built a nest in a clump of reeds. Past the lake, the heads of two giraffes stood tall above the menagerie buildings. The baboons and monkeys squawked from behind the wall.

Finally, Neferure spoke, twirling the same loose thread on her sheath between her thumb and forefinger. "Did you ever doubt the path the gods had chosen for you?"

So that's what this was about.

"Every day until the double crown was placed upon my head," Hatshepsut replied. It felt strange to say the words, but they were true. "I've been terrified of failing since the day my sister died and I realized I'd have to become Great Royal Wife."

"But you didn't fail." Neferure's eyes welled with tears and she tugged at the thread, opening a hole in the linen. It broke Hatshepsut's heart to see her so miserable.

"You won't fail either." Hatshepsut slid closer. "You're doing beautifully at the temple. The priests inform me of your progress every time I see them."

"What if that's all I want?"

There was a long silence. Reeds snapped as the swans worked to build a home for their cygnets.

"Neferure, the gods have given you a gift, an opportunity to serve them in more ways than one. Your work at the temple is infinitely important." Hatshepsut knelt on the ground so Neferure had to look at her, clasped her hands to keep her from picking at the thread. If she kept at it, she wouldn't have much of a sheath left to ruin. "But serving Egypt as Tutmose's Great Royal Wife and partner on the throne is even more important."

Tears spilled onto Neferure's cheeks. She was young. It was natural for her to be frightened of the future.

Hatshepsut hugged Neferure, feeling the delicate wings of her shoulder blades. "You'll make a wonderful Great Royal Wife. And Tutmose is a smart young man—"

She stopped, realization dawning as her arms dropped back to her lap. "It's Tutmose you're worried about, isn't it? You don't want to marry him."

Neferure stiffened. "No, it's not that. Tutmose always tries so hard to please me. Too hard, perhaps." She stared past Hatshepsut to the swans, fingers unfolding in her lap like lotus blossoms. "I don't think I'll ever make him happy."

Hatshepsut laughed in relief. "My precious girl, you couldn't be more wrong. I can't think of a better pair to share the throne."

"Better than you and Father, I suppose."

Hatshepsut sobered. She had never belittled Thut to his daughter, but it was no secret that theirs had not been a love match. "I suppose so."

"And you won't allow someone else to become Tutmose's Great Royal Wife?"

"You know I can't do that. Your fully royal blood completes his claim to the throne. And if something were to happen to him as it did your father, you would need to rule Egypt in his place."

Neferure's face turned whiter than the swans' feathers. She shook her head. "That can't happen. I wouldn't be able to—"

"You could," Hatshepsut chided her gently. "I had to."

Neferure's face crumpled, her hands fluttering in her lap. "I'm not you, Mother. I don't have your gifts. I want to stay at the temple, become a chantress or perhaps a priestess."

"That's not an option, Neferure." Hatshepsut stood and shook her head. "You are destined for greatness, not obscurity."

"What if I don't want greatness?"

"Then you'll need to content yourself with doing your duty."

Neferure wished for the impossible. This was the way things had to be, the only possibility.

"You'll grow into the idea with time." Hatshepsut offered her hand to Neferure and was shocked by the chill of her fingers. "You won't marry Tutmose until you're ready."

"You promise?"

"I give you my word." She kissed Neferure's forehead, inhaled the scent of sunshine on her skin. "And I promise one day you will be ready."

She would have to be.

CHAPTER 28

YEAR EIGHT OF PHARAOH HATSHEPSUT

Alone in the Pharaoh's private garden, Hatshepsut and Senenmut were silently absorbed in their scrolls as two peacocks—recent gifts from the Phoenician ambassador—meandered through the garden, idly picking at flower petals and insects. The birds were terribly loud and gaudy, but Hatshepsut rather liked the unique addition to the royal menagerie. If their screeching became unbearable, she'd order the cooks to come up with a sauce that would complement roast peacock.

She closed her eyes to the morning sunshine, letting the well-worn papyrus of *The Tale of the Shipwrecked Sailor* drop to the grass. She'd read the story countless times as a child, but now the adventure reminded her of Neshi's trip to Punt. Of course, that expedition had lacked the talking golden serpent.

Eyes still closed, she allowed Re's warmth to lull her toward sleep, until the angry slap of sandals on the garden tiles pulled her back to reality. Nomti had intercepted an unfamiliar messenger at the garden entrance, and now he gestured toward her and Senenmut.

"That doesn't look good," Senenmut said, shielding his eyes to peer in Nomti's direction.

Nomti dismissed the messenger and walked slowly toward them, arms tight at his sides. Whatever tidings the messenger bore weren't pleasant.

He stopped several paces away, his face unreadable beneath the tattoos.

"What is it?" Hatshepsut asked.

"The messenger was from Aswan," Nomti said.

"What happened to the obelisks?" Senenmut set down his papyrus.

Hatshepsut had ordered two more colossal obelisks hewn from Aswan's quarries to accompany the pair already raised at Karnak. These newer obelisks were scheduled for completion in two months, to commemorate the anniversary of her ascension to the Isis Throne. And they were massive, a third larger than the previous ones.

She'd never been one to dream small.

Nomti clasped his hands behind his back. "The workers followed common procedures for removing the granite from the quarry, placing wood in the vertical cuts and wetting it to allow it to expand."

"And?"

"The first obelisk released unanticipated stress while still attached to the bedrock."

"Unanticipated stress?" Hatshepsut asked.

"It cracked," Senenmut interpreted, his voice strangled.

"Yes," Nomti said. "It's unsalvageable."

"Son of Set!" Senenmut crumpled the papyrus in his fist. "We scoured the quarries for that granite for weeks. The stone was perfect!"

Hatshepsut couldn't stop a shiver from climbing up her spine, as if a cloud had suddenly crossed over the sun. Perhaps this was an admonishment from some offended god?

She pushed away the ridiculous worry. She had done nothing to anger any of the gods. This was simply nature, an undiscovered aberration in the stone that was only now making itself known.

"We'll simply have to survey Aswan for another suitable site," Hatshepsut said. "There's nothing wrong with the second obelisk?"

"Nothing the messenger reported," Nomti said.

"I'll send new orders to Amenhetep immediately." Senenmut was already on his feet. "If he doubles the pace of construction on the new one, the two obelisks can sail at the same time." He glowered, as if somehow the rock had cracked to spite him. He disliked the taste of failure as much as Hatshepsut did.

She nodded her dismissal to Nomti. "We knew this might happen," she said to Senenmut once they were alone.

"It shouldn't have happened. I handpicked that slab."

"What's done is done. The work will start over and, as you've said, the obelisks can still sail together as planned. There's nothing else we can do."

Senenmut stared at the battered papyrus in his hand, attempted to smooth it out. "You're right," he said. "It doesn't matter, as long as it's ready for the *sed* festival."

"It will be." She kissed his cheek. "And the festival is going to be perfect."

The obelisks were barely ready in time for the first day of Peret, the planting season and the start of the five-day *sed* festival. As the celebration was one of rebirth and rejuvenation, it seemed only fitting that the season match the mood. The rest of the celebration—raising the obelisks, reenacting Hatshepsut's coronation, and assorted physical competitions—would prove that at thirty-four years old, the female pharaoh still possessed the vitality and physical ability to rule Egypt.

Hatshepsut marveled at the behemoth sycamore barge that was transporting the two massive lengths of stone upriver toward the docks. Just as had occurred eight years ago, the entire town lined the riverbank to witness the approach of the gold-capped monuments. In years to come, the *rekhyt* would regale their children and then their grandchildren with the story of the incredible feat accomplished before their very eyes. For her part, Hatshepsut would ensure that this monumental undertaking was recorded in stone at both Karnak and Djeser-Djeseru.

Future generations would sing her praises long after she was gone.

This time, she wasn't taking any chances of angering the fickle gods and earning further wrath directed at the obelisks. On her orders, and only after the stretch of river had been cleared of crocodiles, a herd of white cattle had been driven across the Nile for good luck before Re had risen. Three small boats packed with priests now plied the waters to bless the obelisks, the river, and even the oarsmen of the twenty-seven boats pulling the barge. The *sed* celebration would start according to plan.

Priests led a sleek black sacrificial bull from the crowd as oarsmen threw ropes to the barge, like oversized spiders spinning a web. The bull's muscles rippled as if made of quicksilver and its nostrils flared at the priests' attempts to calm it. Catching the scent of death on the breeze, the beast lost its temper, braying and snorting, its yellow eyes flaring. The priests scurried to contain the animal, but one took a horn in the ribs and was carried into the crowd to die. The crack of a whip finally persuaded the animal to step foot on the gangplank. The crowd held quiet as the High Priest of Amun intoned a prayer to the Great Cackler to ask his blessing for the occasion. The blinding flash of Re's light on the priest's dagger was no doubt the last thing the bull saw before blood surged from its neck. It knelt, then collapsed to the ground as the death spasms twitched their way along its dying body.

The High Priest crouched over the pool of warm blood to consult the frothy redness before looking into the pattern of clouds overhead. He gave a succinct nod, then turned to face Hatshepsut. "Amun is pleased with the sacrifice!"

The crowd roared in delight, and two drums beat out a single deafening heartbeat. Then it was Hatshepsut's turn to speak.

"We commissioned these obelisks to commemorate our fifteenth year as ruler of the Two Lands and to dedicate the precious monuments to Amun, our sacred father. May the Great Cackler accept these gifts and continue to shower Egypt with his blessings!" She marveled at the crowd as it thundered its approval. She had broken the rules once again. Pharaohs planned the sacred *sed* celebration only after they had ruled for thirty years, but she had included her years as Tutmose's regent to reach only half that. Why wait when there was no guarantee she'd ever see thirty years on the Horus Thorne?

An imperceptible nod to Tutmose gave the signal for him to follow her across the gangplank and onto the barge. Together they uncorked the sacred vials of myrrh and overturned them, dousing the giant stone needles with one final offering to Amun.

She turned back to address her subjects. "Tomorrow you will bear witness as these obelisks are raised within the walls of Karnak." Happiness radiated from her voice. "But tonight each of you shall enjoy ox flesh, bread, and beer from the palace!"

Her announcement was met with another mighty cheer. This would be the one and only time most of the *rekhyt* tasted meat, a welcome change from their usual diet of dried fish, onions, and bread. The beer was a welcome gift, too, far superior to the thick barley sludge they usually drank.

"A deft political maneuver, *Per A'a*," Tutmose commented as they stepped back on shore.

"You think so?"

"You have a gift, an ability to draw people to you, like bees to a lotus blossom." Tutmose looked askance at Hatshepsut, as if choosing his words carefully. "I didn't understand why you planned a *sed* festival after so short a time on the throne."

She waited for him to continue, but Tutmose remained silent, his smooth features a perfect mask.

"Some rules are worth following," she said, "but others exist simply because that's the way things have always been done." She gestured to the throng of Waset's jubilant denizens. "Look how happy they are."

Tutmose seemed impressed. "There's no doubt the people love you. And you've just sacrificed enough to Amun to keep him content for the next fifteen years."

"At least." Hatshepsut gave a wide smile. "Remember that when you're pharaoh. Keep the people and the gods happy, and everyone prospers."

Hatshepsut woke the next morning to priests singing hymns to herald Re's glorious victory over black Apep. The fuzzy rectangles of light streaming from her windows were softer than usual, and dust motes danced languidly in the air. The sun god hid his face behind a thick bank of clouds—a perfect day for the *sed* festival chariot race.

Hatshepsut leapt from her bed, startling the sleek black cat curled at her feet. Today there would be a reenactment of her coronation and the chariot race—one she hoped to win. Her mattress was still dented with the imprint of Senenmut's body; he had already left to oversee the raising of the second pair of obelisks. She wanted to be there, but knew anxiety would leave her without any hair or fingernails if she went to watch.

Mouse waited with a breathtaking linen kilt shimmering with thousands of silver beads and a pectoral and corselet strung with bands of gold and lapis, layered to represent the feathering of birds. Gold was revered as the skin of the gods, but silver was even more precious, symbolic of the bones of the sacred deities. Today Hatshepsut would be drenched with both precious metals to remind everyone of her link to the gods.

After she was scrubbed, plucked, and oiled from head to toe, a barrage of slaves ushered her to her dressing table. The heavy pectoral and matching earrings Mouse draped from her neck and ears had been a gift from Senenmut for her naming day several years back. The electrum moon hovered over lapis lazuli stars, that startling blue-and-gold-flecked gem reserved for royalty, and matched a ring of Senenmut's that she had taken to wearing on her thumb. Mouse drew thick lines of kohl to her temples and brushed gold dust over her eyelids, then dabbed delicate drops of jasmine perfume behind her ears. The bull's tail went round her waist and the pharaoh's braided false beard was strapped to her chin. The dwarf finished the ensemble with a new Nubian wig—one that smelled of beeswax and scratched worse than sand—and the striped blue-and-gold *nemes* headdress, the *uraeus* bearing its fangs and poised to strike.

Hatshepsut was ready.

Nomti waited to drive her by chariot in stately procession to Karnak for the ceremony. Despite the early hour, most of the City of Truth had roused itself to catch another fleeting glimpse of its pharaoh. The streets had been swept clean of signs of last night's debauchery in preparation for the most royal of eyes.

Hatshepsut's heart swelled under the weight of the moon pectoral, and she twisted Senenmut's silver star ring on her thumb as the chariot drew closer to the avenue before the Gate of Amun. Four stately obelisks now stood at attention, the two originals wrapped entirely in gold, now joined by two massive granite sisters capped with electrum, all reflecting Re's light to flood the Two Lands. Despite the overcast skies, the monuments rippled with light so pure that only the nine gods could have sent it. After all of Hatshepsut's heartache and worry, the obelisks were home safe.

The gods smiled upon them after all.

The coronation reenactment went smoothly. As the High Priest of Amun removed the *nemes* headdress to replace it with the red and white double crown, Hatshepsut saw most of the same players gathered once again—including Neshi, Ti, and Ineni—all with more wrinkles around their eyes and a little extra weight to pad their waists. Tutmose and Neferure stood below the dais, their shoulders not quite touching.

And then it was over.

The scent of the myrrh used to anoint Hatshepsut's forehead swirled on the breeze as she stepped outside. Gooseflesh crept up her arms at the uncustomary chill brought about by the clouds overhead.

Senenmut and Nomti stood on either side of her electrum chariot, arms crossed before their chests. Her black stallion pranced and snorted, the golden bells on his leather girths tinkling. She stopped, feet braced as if expecting a battle. "It's a good thing your expressions can't injure, or I'd be seriously maimed right now," she said.

Nomti stepped into the basket to secure the reins. "Are you still set on doing this?"

"Doing what?" She knew full well what Nomti meant.

Nomti looked down on her like an errant child. "Driving yourself."

"I've driven my own chariot since I was old enough to see over the basket," Hatshepsut said. "Earlier, actually, since my father had a step built for me."

"We're well aware of that," Senenmut said. "We're also aware that you prefer to drive your chariot like a cheetah on the hunt."

"Well, that only makes sense." She grinned. "After all, it *is* a race."

"I didn't save you from Mensah all those years ago only to watch you get trampled by a horse," Nomti said. "I'll drive you."

"You most certainly will not." Hatshepsut slapped his hands off the reins. "You two are worse than a couple of old women. These games are in my honor. I can't be driven around the arena."

"There are other games over the next few days you're supposed to participate in as well." Senenmut rubbed the stallion's forehead. "You can't compete if your neck is broken."

"You don't have to worry about me breaking anything." She waved Nomti out of her chariot. "Except my opponents."

Nomti looked like he wanted to use the whip on her. "I scoured your chariot myself—it's oiled and as safe as can be."

Hatshepsut rolled her eyes. "Nothing is going to happen to me."

"Promise you'll be careful," Senenmut said.

"I promise to be careful," she gave him a wicked grin, "to win."

"Hatshepsut!"

She turned to see Aset running toward them, waving her arms. She stopped before the chariot, bracing her hands on her knees and struggling to draw deep breaths. "Tutmose informed me that you plan to drive yourself today."

"You're too late." Hatshepsut gestured to Nomti and Senenmut. "They already tried to stop me."

Aset straightened. "You didn't listen to them, did you?"

"Never."

"Good." Aset grinned and slapped the horse's rump. "Don't kill yourself. But don't let those boys beat you either!"

At least someone understood her.

The stallion leapt forward at the crack of her whip, trotting toward the makeshift arena that had been constructed for the *sed* festival outside the city. Anemone petals littered the path; the fragrant confetti blew in the breeze as the crowd cheered. It didn't take long to reach the track seething with its mass of spectators. Hatshepsut counted eight other chariots waiting to start as she pulled into line, and Ti was the only other person remotely close to her age. He smiled and bowed before fiddling with his horse's girths. Tutmose joined them, navigating his chariot between her and Sennedjem, rounding out the number to an even ten.

"Are you sure you want to race today?" Tutmose asked her, his usual somber expression out of place today amongst the cheering and bets being placed. There would be plenty of prizes for the winner—a necklace of golden bees, a tract of fertile land in the Delta, and a clutch of fresh slaves from Nubia—but Hatshepsut wished only to prove that she still possessed the vitality to win a race like this one, symbolic as it was of her ability to rule.

"Of course I want to race. Don't you?"

"I suppose."

"Is everything all right?" Hatshepsut had to holler over the growing din as she checked her reins.

"Yes." Tutmose pursed his lips together, then sighed. "Actually, no. But I didn't want to mention it until after the *sed* festival."

Clouds passed over his face, and he avoided her eyes. Whatever it was, Tutmose wasn't happy about it.

Neshi was scheduled to start the race, but he was engrossed in conversation with one of the scribes who would record the order of the finishers. "We have a moment," she said. "You can tell me now."

Tutmose stared at his horse's rump. "Satiah is pregnant."

"Satiah?"

"One of the kitchen slaves. Her mother is Ipu, one of Neferure's old *menats*."

Hatshepsut recalled the name then and the girl-slave with heavy breasts that bounced as she kneaded bread. Her fingers tightened on the reins. "And I presume the child is yours?"

Tutmose nodded.

"You're sure?"

His eyes finally met hers. "Quite sure. The child is due in a few months. I haven't told anyone else, just my mother."

Too late for any herbs to take care of the pregnancy. Hatshepsut forced herself to relax her grip on the reins, yet her nails had already cut angry purple grooves into her palms. Tutmose was young, and as was often the case with the young, stupid. Thank the gods she sat on the Isis Throne, and not a youth still driven by what he carried between his legs. "You must marry Neferure immediately. A kitchen slave can be a concubine, but only Neferure can be your Great Royal Wife. This child is a threat to the succession."

"I know. I'm sorry I've disappointed you."

How could he have been so utterly careless?

She wanted to rail at Tutmose, but his hangdog expression told her he'd already done an ample job of tormenting himself. Now it was left to her to clean up his mess. Still, she recalled a time when she was young and brash and had done more than her share of stupid things. Tutmose would learn from his mistakes as she had, and become a better man for it.

The race seemed suddenly inconsequential, but Neshi stepped onto the track, passing from hand to hand a rock the size of his fist and painted with red ochre. Representative of the hearts laid upon Anubis' scale, the red stone would be flung in the air by Neshi to signal the start of the race. When it hit the ground the drivers would attempt to drive their chariots around the track four times, and try not to usher themselves, or any of the other drivers, to meet the jackal god prematurely.

"Let the race begin!" Neshi's arms tensed and the stone flew into the air in a blur of red, only to be trampled underfoot moments later. Hatshepsut's stallion bolted forward in a cloud of dust. Only Ti, Tutmose, and Sennedjem ran ahead of the pharaoh's electrum chariot. She leaned as far forward as she could, shouting wildly and flicking the reins.

She felt like Horus hurtling to earth in pursuit of her prey with the wind slicing her skin. Despite Tutmose's news, the race was exhilarating, the wheels grinding under her, the sheen of her horse's flanks flashing.

She plied the whip and urged her horse to pass Sennedjem as she completed her first lap. The second lap continued at the same fierce pace, with Ti and Tutmose neck and neck and Hatshepsut a chariot's breadth behind them. She could hear Sennedjem behind her, cursing at his horse, and she laughed at the sound.

By the third lap, her stallion discovered some untapped well of energy and sprang forward to overtake Ti on a straight stretch. Surely the crowd was yelling, but she could hear only the panting of her horse, her own ragged breathing, and the tinkle of golden bells.

Tutmose was the last left to beat, pushing his mare as if a demon chased them. Hatshepsut's single chance at overcoming him would come on the final lap. She jerked the reins to force her horse to the left, and planned to push to Tutmose's side and overtake him on the next curve. There was no way she was going to let Tutmose beat her, not after the disaster he'd just created.

The stallion was creeping forward on the curve, his nose past Tutmose's flank, when the world came apart. There was a crack and the stallion bolted ahead as the chariot shaft fell to the sand. The chariot shuddered beneath Hatshepsut and tipped forward, upended like a child's toy. She careened into the air, carried as if by the gods' arms, watching the sand of the track pass slowly under her. Something hard stopped her flight and yanked the breath from her lungs.

A sound like the snap of a twig.

A blinding flash of pain in her arm.

Then a horse whinnied in the distance and the perfect stillness of unconsciousness overtook her.

CHAPTER 29

She was being crushed, pulverized by the teeth of Ammit's fury. Or tormented by demons, her arm twisted and pinned to a wooden stake while she was forced to float in the darkness of her own blood.

She tried to move, but every limb cried out in agony and each labored breath threatened to smother her. There was a terrible moan of some creature in misery.

The sound was coming from the back of her throat.

"The pharaoh is waking up." A solid voice waded through the haze of pain.

"Thank Amun." Senenmut's voice traveled to her from far away. "Hatshepsut, can you hear me?"

Someone squeezed her hand. She returned the squeeze, or at least she thought she did. Her mouth refused to move.

"You've been badly hurt." A cauldron of relief and anguish boiled in Senenmut's voice. "Your arm is broken, but Gua set it while you were unconscious. He believes that's the worst of your injuries. Your chariot overturned and you went flying. We thought we might lose you." He cleared his throat, his voice thick. "You hit your head, probably when you slammed into Ti's chariot. Tutmose got to you first—he had to pull the chariot off you."

Her mind sifted through all she had been told, but it was like wading through quicksand.

"I'm sorry." She managed to open her eyes a crack as she mouthed the words. How could she have been so reckless?

"Don't worry." Senenmut kissed her forehead, his eyes watery with relief. "Now that I know you're not going to die, I plan to burn your chariot."

But something didn't make sense. There was the shudder of her chariot, the horse bolting away with the yoke still attached.

"How?" She was glad the word was only one syllable.

Senenmut pursed his lips together, his gaze flickering toward someone she couldn't see. "The girth had been cut."

Gua cleared his throat somewhere in the background. "I think the pharaoh would benefit from some rest now." And before she could protest, a sweet syrup was poured down her throat.

"Physician's orders." Senenmut tucked the linen sheets tighter around her. "I'll be right here if you need anything. Just rest."

She couldn't fight the potent herbs pulling her toward sleep. One final thought followed her into the bleak nightmares of Ammit's fearsome snarl.

Someone had tried to kill her.

A thick haze still clouded her mind when she woke, but she could make out Senenmut sitting next to her bed, chin drooping to his chest in the flickering torchlight. The dark stubble on his cheeks told her she had slept for more than a few hours. She watched him for some time before deciding that he was real and not part of her constant nightmares, which were filled with rearing horses, flashing knives, and demon mouths packed with sharp teeth. She couldn't afford the luxury of that medicine again if all her dreams consisted of such tortures that not even the gods could concoct.

"Who did it?"

Her voice sounded rusty, but Senenmut's head jerked up and he took her hand. He felt warm, alive. "You're awake."

She swallowed, her throat getting used to the motion again. "You said one of my girths had been cut. Who did it?"

He rubbed his cheeks, dropped both hands into his lap. His shoulders sagged. "Nomti."

She drew in a sharp hiss of air. "Are you sure?"

"The leather had been sliced under the harness, and Nomti was the last one to check your chariot. You heard the words from his mouth as well as I."

"I can't believe Nomti would try to kill me." She shook her head, closed her eyes to block out the truth. "That's too blatant."

Senenmut shrugged. "That wouldn't have mattered if—"

"If I'd died." She rubbed her temples, a drum starting to pound behind her eyes. "Where is he now?"

"In the same cell that once housed Mensah. He claims he's innocent, but I thought you'd want him questioned."

She shuddered. Life came in cycles, ever changing yet always the same. Here she was, repeating the same scene of treason, near death, and torture.

"Question him," she said. "But don't kill him."

At least not yet.

The purple bruises on her face and body faded to a murky yellow and then disappeared as her flesh healed, but her mind remained battered, and Gua insisted she continue to wear the stiff wooden splint so that her arm would heal properly. Nomti refused to admit to his treason, regardless of the creative methods being used to extract his confession, and the accident and Tutmose's news of Satiah's pregnancy made Hatshepsut painfully aware of the vulnerability of the Isis Throne.

There was only one way to remedy the problem, yet she'd have sold her *ka* to Anubis to avoid it.

She stared at the frescoes dedicated to Thoth on Senenmut's walls, wishing the god of wisdom might provide a better solution than the only one she could work out, waiting what seemed an eternity for Senenmut's response. The gods had been cruel these past weeks. From his youngest brother, Senenmut had received word of Nofret-Hor's unexpected death shortly after the *sed* festival; his sister had flown to the sky after struggling for two days on the birthing blocks to give life to her first child. Instead Anubis had claimed both mother and child. Senenmut had traveled to Iuny for the funeral and returned only today, still smelling of camphor and juniper oil, the scents of embalming and death. Now Hatshepsut had informed him of Tutmose's talent for impregnating kitchen slaves, a mistake that could lead to future chaos, possibly even civil war.

"Neferure doesn't want to marry Tutmose," Senenmut said. Their shared platter of roast pigeon sat between them, virtually untouched. "She's not going to be happy about being forced before she's ready."

"She has to marry him, and now." Hatshepsut squished a clove of roasted garlic with the thumb of her good hand. "What if Satiah bears a son?"

"A boy could be disastrous—the firstborn son would belong to a servant instead of the Great Royal Wife." Senenmut rubbed the bridge of his crooked nose. "But it might not be."

"Don't lie. It could be chaos even if Satiah has a girl. I've thrown open the doors on who can be pharaoh. The best thing for Egypt would be for Satiah to lose the child." The words were harsh but true.

"What about your promise to Neferure?"

"I wish I'd never made it." She exhaled and laid her forehead on her hands. The grainy surface of the table filled her eyes even as her temples throbbed. She'd rather face an army of spear-wielding Nubians than force Neferure into a marriage she didn't want. Unfortunately, there wasn't an angry army of Nubians handy for her to gamble on. "I don't want to force her, but I have to."

"Don't force her. Persuade her. Neferure isn't like you."

"I know that," she snapped. She stood and walked to an ebony table carved with gazelle's feet. Atop it sat a gray granite block carved to show Senenmut holding Neferure as a child with a youth lock, his robe wrapped around her for protection and gleaming dully in the lamplight. Neferure remembered so little of Thutmosis; Senenmut was the only father she had ever known.

"Your differences are not a bad thing for either of you." Senenmut wrapped his arms around Hatshepsut, just as his granite likeness did for Neferure. "Your *ka* is like a giant cedar, shouldering all of Egypt, but Neferure's is—"

"Like a fragile lotus."

Senenmut nodded, reaching out to touch Neferure's stone cheek. "Be gentle with her."

"I love Neferure," Hatshepsut said, "but she's seen eighteen naming days. Even I was married before then."

"And think of how miserable you were."

She closed her eyes and thought of Neferure. The only time her daughter's smiles and laughter rang true was at Amun's temple when she performed her duties as God's Wife. Just before the *sed* festival, Hatshepsut had watched her at a ceremony celebrating the anniversary of the victory at Nubia and was awed at Neferure's calm and the confidence with which she moved while in the god's presence, so different from her behavior in the palace. She still panicked over formal events and darted about like a startled chickadee when Tutmose was around.

Senenmut stood and rubbed her shoulders. "Would you like me to talk to Neferure instead?"

She leaned into him, shook her head. "I need to do this."

"If anyone can persuade her, it's you." He kissed the top of her head. "I'll see you tonight."

She made her way to Neferure's chambers, scowling to herself as a nameless *medjay* followed behind, his footsteps echoing loudly down the corridor. She found that she missed the reassurance of Nomti's quiet presence and his ability to meld into shadows, traits that none of her new string of guards seemed to possess.

It took longer than usual for her to finally reach Neferure's apartments, both because Hatshepsut got exhausted far too easily now and because she dreaded what she was about to do.

"Mother! I wasn't expecting you." Neferure ushered her to a chair before the door opened all the way. Her eyes were slightly bloodshot and dark shadows like thumbprints stained the delicate skin underneath. She'd taken the news of Nofret-Hor's death especially hard. "Shouldn't you be resting?"

Hatshepsut looked at the ceiling and prayed for some intervention from the gods. Perhaps a sudden earthquake or a plague of locusts. Anything.

Of course, there was only silence and Neferure's wide eyes, her lips parted to show slightly crooked teeth. Her beautiful daughter.

Hatshepsut had no choice except to plunge forward. This was for Egypt.

"We need to talk." She drew a deep breath. "About Tutmose."

Neferure frowned. "I heard about Satiah."

Hatshepsut cursed under her breath. Word traveled fast.

"A youthful blunder." She took her daughter's hands. "But you and Tutmose must be married before the child is born."

"I can't do that." Neferure's gaze flitted about the room like a panicked gazelle recognizing its imminent slaughter. She retrieved a small ivory statue of Amun from its golden shrine—the same carving that had once graced Hatshepsut's own shrine of gods before she gifted it to Neferure along with the title of God's Wife—and clutched it as if willing the Great Cackler to give her strength.

"Neferure, you have to do this," Hatshepsut said. "I won't live forever—the chariot accident made me realize that. When I'm gone you must share the throne with Tutmose and give him sons."

"I'd rather die than take the throne." Neferure's face crumpled and she pressed the statue into Hatshepsut's palm, then grasped Hatshepsut's other hand in a vise grip worthy of a woman giving birth. "I'm the God's Wife. To give myself to a man—even Tutmose—would destroy that."

Hatshepsut gave an exasperated sigh. "Neferure, all the royal women who have held that title have also been Great Royal Wives. We serve the gods, but we also serve Egypt."

"But if I marry Tutmose I might end up like Nofret-Hor, dead on the birthing blocks with a babe locked inside me. I don't want that life or that death. All I want is to serve Amun."

"That's not possible."

"Why not?"

"You are the daughter of not one, but two pharaohs. You have responsibilities!"

"But I'm not good at them." Tears filled Neferure's eyes and her chin trembled.

Hatshepsut forced a breath into her lungs and pulled her daughter to her, setting aside the ivory god. Now she knew how her own father had felt so many years ago. It seemed a cruel trick of the gods that youth and wisdom were never joined together.

"You have the blood of kings in your veins." She stroked Neferure's hair. "You can do this."

"I'll fail—disgrace you, Tutmose, Senenmut, Father, Grandfather." Neferure's voice was so quiet Hatshepsut could barely hear her. "Everyone."

"You'll do no such thing." She tapped Neferure's chin to look in her eyes. "That's not possible."

"I've tried so hard to make you happy. But it's not enough, is it?"

"Of course you've made me happy. That's not what this is about."

Neferure looked at the ground. "I'm not like you, Mother."

"You don't have to be like me." Hatshepsut smoothed the hair of Neferure's wig, letting her palm linger on her daughter's damp cheek. "The gods sculpt us all differently. You're *you*—princess of Egypt and Tutmose's Great Royal Wife."

Time slipped past. She could feel Neferure giving up thread by thread, unraveling the tapestry of everything she had planned for her future.

"You promised you would never force me to marry Tutmose—that I would get to choose when I was ready." Neferure's lower lip trembled when she spoke. "But I'm not ready."

"I can't keep that promise any longer."

"Please, can't Tutmose marry someone else?" Neferure's voice was no more than a whisper. "Anyone but me?"

"You know that's not possible, *sherit*. Your fully royal blood is Tutmose's only living link to the double crown. I'd sacrifice my heart to Ammit if it would clear another way to the throne, but there's no other choice. I can't risk it."

"Egypt is too important." A tremor quavered in Neferure's voice.

"You are important," Hatshepsut reassured her. "Never doubt that, Neferure. I treasure you above all else in this world. You've made me happier and prouder than you can ever know."

"I love you," Neferure whispered, finality weighing down her words.

"I love you, too," Hatshepsut answered. "Forever and always."

The following evening the pharaoh's private garden was awash with hundreds of tiny lamps that illuminated the air even as darkness strode across the sky. Mouse had arranged the lights on every surface that would hold them, and now the miniature flames danced merrily in the night. Five ebony dining couches had been arranged amongst the trees and flowers in the garden's grassy center. The background chatter of crickets and splashing fountains imbued the air with perfect tranquility. It had rained long and hard earlier in the day—a rare gift from the gods that had scrubbed the air clean—but now the storm had broken, so the full moon and only a few wispy remnants of clouds were reflected in the fountains. Humming to herself, Hatshepsut smelled the aromas of all of Tutmose's and Neferure's favorite foods from the kitchens—chilled cucumber soup, roast goose with almond dressing, and plenty of honeyed desserts—as they mingled with the wet-earth scent of her garden.

Tonight the royal family would celebrate the future of their dynasty.

Senenmut arrived first. The sight of him still made Hatshepsut's breath catch in her throat even after all their years together. Despite the importance of tonight's dinner, he had skipped the formal wig and wore his customary long kilt. He gave her a quick kiss, but her lips lingered longer than usual. The faintest taste of wine clung to his lips, wedded with the cinnamon scent she so loved. She felt his smile before their lips parted.

"You can't have missed me *that* much since this morning," he said.

"I'm just reminded of how blessed I am."

His eyes crinkled. "I'll remember that kiss for later."

"How was the hunting trip with Tutmose?"

"Terrible." Senenmut attempted a stern expression, but she could see the laughter in his eyes.

"After all these years at court, I'd have thought you might have learned to tell a better lie." She strummed the fingers of her good hand against the wooden splint that had kept her from joining them this morning. "You can tell me what you took down, as long as it wasn't an elephant or a water cow."

"Nothing so exciting—just too many geese to count and a couple swans. Tutmose has quite the arm with his throwing stick."

"Aset didn't join you?" Hatshepsut had hinted that they should invite her, hoping to provide a common interest for Aset and her son. Tutmose seemed to go out of his way to avoid his mother since her return, as if he couldn't reconcile the rough-mannered woman who constantly hovered about him with the remembrance of the mother of his youth.

"We invited her, but she wasn't interested," Senenmut said, more relaxed than she'd seen him in a long time. "I'm proud of Tutmose. He's grown into a fine young man."

Hatshepsut smiled. It was true, and, overlooking the incident with Satiah, Tutmose was all Hatshepsut could have hoped for in her heir. That fact alone made it easier for her to insist upon his marriage to Neferure, knowing that in time her daughter would come to realize her good fortune in having Tutmose as her husband.

Aset and Tutmose appeared next, entering the garden under one of the arched canopies of creeping foliage and followed by Tutmose's sleek black hunting dog. The animal was beautiful, despite his striking resemblance to the jackal god of death.

"What a lovely night." Aset gave a warm smile. "Especially for such an important celebration."

"Thank you for all this." Tutmose gestured to the transformed garden, looking uncomfortable in his formal kilt and wig. He glanced about as if searching for something. Or someone. "Is Neferure on her way?"

"I'm sure she'll be along in a moment," Aset assured him, picking at her fingernails, then clasping her hands behind her back when she realized Hatshepsut was watching. Aset's fingers were stained black, but also cracked as if with dried blood. What in Amun's name had she been doing?

Aset gave a bright grin, showing off her dimples. "Neferure probably wants to look perfect for you tonight."

Tutmose didn't seem to swallow his mother's explanation, but took a seat anyway, his lean dog curling at his feet. Hatshepsut hoped he hadn't deduced Neferure's reaction to being told she had to marry him.

Slaves marched in carrying blue faience glasses of wine and golden trays of imported Minoan olives, pomegranate-melon salad, and bread with cloves of garlic baked inside. Hatshepsut waved away a basket of mandrake berries with their intoxicating flesh. They didn't need help celebrating tonight.

"Are you enjoying your training in the Division of Horus?" Senenmut asked Tutmose between bites of salad. To Hatshepsut's delight, the two had been spending more time together lately as Tutmose grew into his role as soldier. At first Hatshepsut had thought Tutmose only endured Senenmut's tales of the campaigns to Canaan and Nubia, but she had watched more than once as Tutmose had listened with rapt attention, asking questions about battle strategies and fighting techniques.

Tutmose's face lit with pleasure as he looked down at the symbol of Horus on his pectoral, the falcon god's wings spread wide. He tossed his dog a few scraps of bread. "It's hard work, but I love it. I can't wait for the opportunity to campaign."

Hatshepsut smiled. Since the skirmish in Nubia, she'd made it a point to keep the military close to home. There had been no further rebellions, but she saw no reason to expand Egypt's borders at the expense of her soldiers' lives. If Tutmose so wished, he could make that a focal point of his own reign.

She turned to Aset and nodded at her hands. "It looks like you've been busy."

Aset's fingers curled into balls, as if she was trying to hide the stains and cuts. "I've been practicing my hieroglyphs."

"It appears they're winning the fight."

Aset stretched her fingers out, picked at the nails. "The stains are from the ink, but the cuts are from trimming papyrus reeds. I've taken up weaving. I make a fairly decent lotus-blossom basket."

To Hatshepsut basket weaving sounded like as much fun as gouging her eyes with a dull needle, but she kept her tongue. She was happy Aset had a new interest all her own, especially now that Tutmose and Neferure were to marry.

Aset left her couch to sit next to Hatshepsut, her golden plate balanced on her lap. She peeled the flesh from an olive with her teeth and dropped the pit to the ground. Tutmose's dog glanced up at the possibility of a treat, then rested his head back on his paws. "What have you decided to do with Nomti?"

Hatshepsut set her plate between them, her appetite fleeing. "He claims he's innocent," she said. "I'm not sure what to do with him."

Aset glanced to Tutmose and Senenmut, but they were still absorbed in conversation. Her voice dropped to a conspiratorial whisper. "Have you ever wondered about the night of the *khamsin*?"

"What do you mean?"

The only time Hatshepsut thought about that night was when she woke up from a nightmare of a pillow pressed over her face and a pair of strong hands pressed around her neck.

"Do you think Nomti might have been involved?"

"What?"

Senenmut glanced up at the sharpness in her voice, but Aset shifted on the couch next to her. "What if Nomti knew Mensah was going to use the *khamsin* to sneak into your rooms? What if he allowed it to happen?"

Hatshepsut shuddered. The idea was plausible, but she didn't care to know if Nomti had betrayed her more than once. She sipped her wine, hoping its warmth would chase off the sudden chill in her bones. "Nomti's involvement could never be proven. And that was years ago. I can't imagine that the two episodes would be linked."

"No," Aset said, "but still, it's something to think about."

Aset moved back to her couch and an awkward silence settled around them. Hatshepsut easily drew Tutmose into a discussion of the historical conquest of the Nine Bows, Egypt's enemies over the ages and one of their favorite topics to debate. Aset tried several times to join in the conversation, but she knew little about the subject and had to be corrected on inaccuracies about the Hyksos and the Mitanni. Tutmose's exasperation with his mother grew the more she tried to please him, until finally Aset ceased talking altogether and Hatshepsut had to ask her about the intricacies of basket weaving. They continued talking until their plates were empty and the slaves were ready to bring out the cucumber soup and roast goose. Still Neferure hadn't arrived.

Tutmose stood and brushed imaginary crumbs from his kilt. The dog sat up, tensed as if ready to run after his master. "I'm going to see if I can track down Neferure."

Aset shook her head and took a hurried sip of wine before standing. "I'll find her—she's probably in her room, fretting over which sheath to wear."

"No, Mother, I'll go," Tutmose said.

"I'm sure he can find her," Hatshepsut said. Perhaps a moment alone with Neferure would allow Tutmose to smooth things over.

Aset looked unsure, but she relented and sank back down on her couch. "Hurry back."

Aset waited for Tutmose's silhouette to disappear into the lamplight of the corridor before she spoke. "Is Neferure really ready to marry Tutmose?"

"I told her she had to be." Hatshepsut pursed her lips. "Your son's indiscretion left me no choice."

Aset frowned. "I'm not pleased about the situation with Satiah myself. Tutmose should have known better."

At least they agreed on that.

The conversation slowed. Senenmut attempted to draw Aset into a discussion of the upcoming wedding, suggesting which food to serve and what jewelry to commission for Neferure, but clearly neither was his area of expertise. Finally, they all settled into an uncomfortable silence.

And then they heard it. A feral howl splintered the night air and shattered the peace of the garden. At first Hatshepsut thought it might be Tutmose's dog, but she realized the sound was human, not animal.

"Tutmose," Aset said.

"Neferure." Fear flooded Hatshepsut's body.

Senenmut made it into the corridor first, Hatshepsut and Aset close behind him. They tore past Hatshepsut's chambers and the palace offices, but he came to a stop just inside the gilded gate to the Hall of Women.

"No, Hatshepsut." He grabbed her arm, his face stricken, but she pushed him off and continued into the courtyard, drawn to where Tutmose stood with his dog at the edge of a deep pool ringed with lotus-blossom tiles, the same one she had stepped into so many years ago after the banquet announcing her own betrothal to Thutmosis. The granite statue of Amun stood at the edge, the god's face sneering at her beneath his plumed crown.

Floating below the surface of the pool was Neferure.

Her sheath billowed around her like gossamer wings. The full moon swam in the pool's reflection, surrounding her in its cool embrace and illuminating the drowned fabric with an ethereal glow. But nothing could light Neferure's serene face. The life had leached from her so that her skin was tinged an insubstantial white. She was a glorious butterfly, one whose tenuous hold on this world had slipped away.

Hatshepsut moaned and fell to her knees, biting her fist and closing her eyes to the image that would remain imprinted forever on her *ka*. Her lungs collapsed, her heart eviscerated from her heaving chest as she sank even deeper onto the floor, smothered in a veil of grief. She wanted to tuck its edges around her and dive into the black abyss to join her daughter.

She was only distantly aware of Aset's keening behind her, of Senenmut's shaky arms as they enveloped her to pull her from the ground. In the midst of her grief, the words of the past returned, garroting what remained of her heart.

Your name will live forever.

You will be the downfall of those you love.

Egypt will prosper, but those closest to you shall find only anguish and ruin.

She had done this. She had broken her promise by forcing Neferure to consent to a future she couldn't fathom and had caused her daughter to flee this life as surely as if she'd held her under the water herself. Hatshepsut howled in pain and tore at her hair, her clothes, her skin.

It was from Hatshepsut's sense of duty that Neferure had been borne, and it was also what had killed her.

Hatshepsut shoved Senenmut away, unable to bear his touch or the tears welling in his eyes. Stumbling to her feet, she collapsed again, almost falling into Tutmose as he comforted Aset. Her eyes locked with Aset's.

"You did this!" Aset screamed. Black rivers ran from her kohl-lined eyes; saliva and snot dripped from her face. "You killed her!"

She lunged at Hatshepsut, but Tutmose and Senenmut held her back. It took two *medjay* to pull her from the garden as she spat and clawed at them. Hatshepsut almost wished they'd let Aset go. She was right.

She had killed her daughter.

"Help me move her," she whispered to Tutmose and Senenmut, the words pulled from her throat by their roots.

Misery warped Tutmose's handsome face. She couldn't bring herself to look at Senenmut—he, too, had lost the only daughter he would ever have.

"Tutmose and I will get her," Senenmut said as they approached the pool, his voice strangled.

"No." Hatshepsut shook her head violently. "She's my daughter."

Looking down on the exquisite creature held in the water's embrace, Hatshepsut's vision blurred as her tears overflowed. She slipped and smothered the sob that threatened to escape her throat. She waded to Neferure and pulled the limp body into her arms—the warmth already fleeing with her *ka*. A wail broke from the back of her throat as she smoothed her daughter's dripping hair and wiped the rivulets of water that ran down her face. She would never again hold her daughter in her arms, comfort her, tell her how much she loved her.

It took little strength to lift Neferure from the pool and into Senenmut's waiting arms. Even with her sodden hair and clothes, she still weighed scarcely more than a fledgling. Reverently, Senenmut laid her out on the tiles, his tears anointing her forehead.

A crowd of horrified slaves had gathered. Many of them scratched their skin and ripped their clothes in a display worthy of professional mourners. Tutmose's dog howled into the night once and then fell silent, as if announcing the departure of the god he so resembled.

Only then did Hatshepsut notice the bulge under Neferure's water-logged linen sash, tucked right at her heart. Hatshepsut knew what it was before she retrieved it: the ivory votive statue of Amun. Unable to serve her god in this life, Neferure had taken him with her to her death. Hatshepsut flung away the god, wincing as the statue clattered across the tiles.

"Bring her to my chambers," Hatshepsut said.

She had to get away from the slaves, away from their howls and Tutmose's pain. She barely waited to see Senenmut scoop the lifeless princess from the ground before blindly retracing the path to her own chambers.

Senenmut closed the door behind them and laid Neferure on the bed. The water from her hair and clothes bled onto the linen sheets.

"I need to be alone with her." Hatshepsut choked on the words.

"Hatshepsut, this isn't your fault."

"Get out!" She picked up an alabaster vase and hurled it at him. It hit the wall and shattered into hundreds of sharp white pieces, each the same pale hue as Neferure's skin.

Sobbing, she crawled into bed and clutched Neferure to her as Senenmut closed the door. The warmth of her skin had fled entirely, leaving it cold and clammy.

She was gone.

"I'm sorry, Neferure. I'm so, so sorry." Weeping, she kissed Neferure's cheek and breathed in the wet scent of her daughter's hair, the waterlogged trace of sunshine.

She wanted to die, to join her daughter in the next world.

But that was an honor she would never deserve.

CHAPTER 30

She dreaded night.

Somehow Hatshepsut had managed to rise from bed in the days following Neferure's death and accomplish the bare necessities to keep her kingdom running, yet she wished for the power to stop Re from setting and the moon from rising. It was in the black of night, despite the spells carved into her ivory headrest and the protective amulets tied about her wrists and neck, that the nightmares descended.

Senenmut had woken her last night and stroked her hair until she calmed, but the same nightmare tormented her each time she closed her eyes: Neferure flailing in the moonlit pool while Amun's broken statue from the temple of Karnak chained her below the water. Some invisible force held Hatshepsut back at the water's edge, and the god's lips morphed into a malicious grin, his glee demonic in the face of her suffering. Her eyes would snap open to her dark chambers, her heart pounding and her scream lingering in her throat.

She often wished that Nomti had managed to kill her, that she might be waiting now in the Field of Reeds to greet Neferure after her daughter's long, happy life.

Only one dream over the past few days had been unique. She and

Neferure lay in a hammock, arms linked together and a canopy of green above them. Neferure's contented breath fluttered on Hatshepsut's cheek as her daughter slept. Black-and-yellow butterflies danced from flower to flower to sip sweet nectar while puffy white clouds lingered high in Nut's belly.

Then Hatshepsut woke up.

And her arms were empty.

She thought she had discovered the bottom of her well of tears, but that dream found a hidden spring not yet tapped. Her mattress was drenched by the time she managed to dam the tears again.

Hatshepsut found no solace in knowing that Neferure would be in the Field of Reeds after the seventy days spent preparing her body had ended, that her daughter's heart would easily pass the test of Ma'at's scales. Neferure would be happy in the afterlife as she never had been in the mortal world, but Hatshepsut didn't care. Her daughter belonged in *this* world, not in the afterlife with Anubis.

She was a monster, a mother who had killed her own child.

Her head shorn in mourning and the skin of her chest scratched to bloody ribbons, Hatshepsut knelt before a shrine of Amun and mouthed the words of what was becoming her regular prayer. She begged for forgiveness, but most of all she hoped that the curse she bore had now been fulfilled. She had sacrificed Neferure on Egypt's altar.

She could only pray that the gods wouldn't demand further penance.

Nut's belly glowed pale pink with the approaching dusk. For once she was glad for the required seclusion during the seventy days of mourning, thankful to forgo the formal banquets and never-ending meetings with ambassadors and courtiers. Even so, she had asked Tutmose and Senenmut to dine in her chambers tonight. Traces of grief were etched deeper in the granite carved lines around Senenmut's eyes and in the slump of Tutmose's shoulders. But, then, she must look worse.

She would right something tonight, something she should have done a long time ago.

The three traded tired niceties as barefoot slaves padded out bearing tureens and platters of oxtail soup, roast quail stuffed in roast duck, white cheese dusted with cumin, and slices of melon drizzled with honey. The smells and silence were so thick, they threatened to suffocate the room.

"Tutmose." Hatshepsut folded, then refolded her linen napkin. Would nothing ever sit right again? "I've been remiss in my duties by not promoting you to Supreme Commander of Egypt's armies, an error I'd like to correct now." She waved a hand, and Mouse appeared with a golden platter bearing Egypt's blue war crown, the same helmet that Hatshepsut had worn in the campaign against Nubia almost fifteen years ago. It was a true work of art—blue leather with hammered gold disks and the *uraeus* poised to strike. "Wear it with pride."

"Really?" Tutmose blinked, waved away the slave serving his portion of stuffed duck. His face lit like a boy's, yet there was no doubt that Tutmose was now a man, his skin toughened from all the time he'd spent under Re's glare and his muscles hardened from years of training. The hawk in the nest was not born from her body, yet Hatshepsut understood him better than perhaps anyone else who had shared her blood. "You'd promote me?"

The accusation hung heavy in the air, or perhaps she only imagined it. She should have done this before, but even now she sought to placate the gods. This title might begin to atone for her mistakes while giving Tutmose a chance to make up for his carelessness with Satiah. Yet she was too weary to explain all that now.

"Your performance in the Division of Horus is exemplary," she said. "It always has been."

Tutmose cleared his throat and reached out to touch the blue crown with reverent hands, like a boy touching a woman for the first time. It was quite likely that this man who sat before her would relish wearing the war helmet more than he'd ever enjoy the double crown. "I'm honored," he said. "With your permission I plan to strengthen our forces near Megiddo—I don't trust the king of Kadesh."

"You don't need my permission." She managed a smile. "You're in charge of the military now."

"You've deserved this promotion for some time," Senenmut said. "We're both extremely proud of you."

The two talked about Tutmose's plans for Megiddo, but Hatshepsut let her mind wander, eating whatever the slaves placed before her without tasting any of it. She was painfully full by the time the men finished their discussion, only a pile of quail and duck bones left. Food and misery made excellent companions.

Mouse shuffled in with a golden platter of sweet-smelling desserts, squinting as she neared the table. Mostly deaf, Mouse still insisted on serving her mistress regardless of Hatshepsut's multiple offers of retirement, claiming she'd rather die while polishing the leather of the double crown than while reclining in luxury in a vineyard. Despite her stomach's protests, Hatshepsut took a honey cake dotted with dried apricots, but it was as dry as sand. Senenmut claimed a papyrus basket of candied almonds, one with a pattern of pink and yellow lotus flowers. He held it out to Tutmose and Hatshepsut. "Care for one?"

Tutmose stood. "No, thank you. I told my mother I'd be at the barracks all night before I received your summons. I saw her last night, but she was too unsettled for me to stay long. . . ." His voice trailed off and he cleared his throat. "I think I'll check on her before she retires for the night." He picked up the blue-and-gold helmet, stared at it a long moment. "Thank you," he said to Hatshepsut. "For everything."

Senenmut popped a nut into his mouth as Mouse showed Tutmose out. "A little too much cinnamon, but not bad."

Again he offered the basket to Hatshepsut, but she waved it away. The confection reminded her of when Neferure was a child. She would stuff as many of the special treats into her mouth as she could until her cheeks puffed up and she looked like a little brown squirrel. Hatshepsut packed the memory away before the tears began again.

It was her fault that only memories remained of Neferure.

Senenmut ate a few more nuts before he drained the last of his spiced wine. "It's late," he said. "We should both get some rest."

"Will you stay tonight?"

She needed him, ached to feel his arms around her, grounding her to this world.

"Of course."

She took the hand he offered and tipped her chin for a kiss that tasted of cinnamon and wine. Suddenly she needed more than his arms around her, needed him to fill the emptiness that threatened to overwhelm her *ka*. He seemed to sense her urgency and shrugged out of his kilt, untied the shoulder strings of her sheath. He seemed warmer than usual, so alive compared to the shades of death that lurked in every shadow.

Their lovemaking was slow, their bodies fitting perfectly together with a knowledge only a lifetime of love could bring. Hatshepsut drifted afterward, her mind floating in the gray area between wakefulness and sleep, unwilling to let the nightmares intrude on this small bit of contentment. Then there was a sudden crash, and Senenmut staggered from bed.

"What's wrong?" Hatshepsut sat up as he stumbled and sprawled to the floor. She tried to help him stand, but he was like a sack of grain and only collapsed to the tiles again.

"I need wine." His words slurred together.

"I'll get it." She slipped into a linen robe and found a jug of wine left on the table, tilted his head so he could drink. He gulped from the jug like a drowning man, the dark liquid dribbling from the corners of his mouth.

She fumbled to strike the wick of an oil lamp and almost dropped the dim flame at the sight before her. Senenmut's eyes were fully dilated, the irises eclipsed by the total black of his pupils. Angry red blotches stained his skin, discoloring even the white scars on his back.

"Blow that out!" Senenmut shielded his eyes from the feeble light.

"You need a physician." She flung her door open to shout at the *medjay* in the corridor. "Something's wrong with Senenmut. Get Gua. Now!"

Whatever demon had taken hold of Senenmut progressed to a new, terrifying stage. The love of her life convulsed on the floor, went still for a moment, and then began shaking with a force that only the gods possessed. His mouth opened and closed, but no sound came out. Finally, he shoved out a mangled whisper. "I'll wait for you in Amenti."

"Don't say that," she sobbed. "Gua is on his way. Everything will be fine."

But she could see that nothing was going to be fine. Senenmut clutched the last strings that bound him to this life.

"Granite's all wrong." His words came in harsh gusts. "Stars in the heavens." Terrified and not knowing what else to do, she felt his forehead and was horrified at the fire on his brow.

She clasped one of his hands between hers as he flailed about. His eyes sought hers, raw agony shining in the midnight depths of his pupils. The stars twinkled through the long windows. "Please, Sekhmet," she prayed, desperate for any reassurance from the gods. "Don't take him from me." She squeezed Senenmut's hand and whispered in his ear, tasting the salt of her tears. "I can't live without you."

He moaned and his head banged against the hard tiles of the floor, but his eyes were glassy now, unseeing. She cradled his head in her lap and wrapped her arms around him in a vain attempt to stifle his convulsions.

"I love you," she said. Tears coursed down her face, splashing onto his bare chest. Still she clung to him, more frantic and helpless than she'd ever felt in her entire life.

She prayed as she'd never prayed before, invoking every being in Egypt's vast pantheon. She promised the fickle gods whatever they wanted, bargained away her kingdom if they would spare Senenmut's life.

The *medjay* ushered Gua into the pharaoh's chambers, his wig askew and a cedar medical box inscribed with spells in hand. The physician's face flickered with alarm, but he knelt to take Senenmut's pulse, eyes bulging as he counted the frenetic beats. He retrieved the Eye of Horus—the strongest amulet in his collection—from his box and placed it on Senenmut's chest.

"What did he eat tonight?" he asked.

"Everything I had—wine, sweetbread, oxtail soup, roast quail, olives—" She swallowed hard as the awful realization blossomed in her mind. "He ate everything I ate, except the almonds. I was going to have some later—"

"Where are they?"

She pointed to the basket on the table, unwilling to relinquish Senenmut for even a moment. The convulsions weakened and his body began to stiffen. Anubis had almost won.

"Please don't leave me, *sehedj ib.*" Tears streamed down her face unchecked. "You can't leave me."

Senenmut's last moments on earth were horrific, a war between his unwilling *ka* and the jackal god of death. The convulsions continued until the *medjay* had to help Hatshepsut and Gua restrain him. In the end, his body simply fell still, limbs frozen and eyes open wide to greet the god of death.

He died clasped in Hatshepsut's arms, just as he had foretold so long ago.

CHAPTER 31

T he copper blade was coldly reassuring against her wrist, an old friend long forgotten and suddenly returned. She had contemplated taking her life once before, but the heady promise of a life yet to live had tempted her away.

Neferure was dead. Senenmut was dead.

Now the Field of Reeds promised everything.

The dagger bit into her flesh and a trickle of fresh blood dripped down her hand to consume the silver-star ring—Senenmut's ring—on her thumb. Even his body was gone, removed by the Royal Physician before the priests of Anubis could be summoned, although the scent of cinnamon still lingered in the air. Gua had taken the basket of almonds as well. He planned to feed them to his cats to confirm his suspicion of poison. Hatshepsut didn't care. She didn't plan to stay one more day in this world without him, without Neferure.

She would see them soon.

"The pharaoh is not receiving visitors." Mouse's voice came from the other side of the door, her voice muffled by the thick ebony. She'd taken up the post next to the *medjay* after Hatshepsut had thrown her out, but the dwarf peered inside often enough to make it clear that she didn't trust Hatshepsut not to hurt herself.

But slicing open her wrists wouldn't take long. Once the blood flowed, it would be too late.

"I don't care if the pharaoh doesn't want to see me." The door slammed open, and Hatshepsut's knife clattered to the floor.

Tutmose barged into her dark bedchamber, but stopped short at the dim light. He rushed to her when he finally saw her on the ground. "Are you all right? Did you eat any of the almonds?"

She didn't answer. He needed to go, to leave her with her knife.

"Where's Senenmut?" Tutmose glanced about her rooms. When she didn't answer, he finally seemed to absorb the details before him: the knife in her hand, the cuts on her wrist. "Where is he?"

"Dead." She choked on the word, clutching the hilt of the dagger. The sweet promise of the blade was the only thing grounding her *ka* to this life.

"Son of a jackal!"

She flinched as Tutmose slammed his fist into the wall. Then she realized what he'd said. The veil of grief was ripped away, replaced by Sekhmet's seething fury.

She lunged at him, the tip of the dagger touching the bare skin over his heart before he had time to react. A drop of blood pearled there, then trickled down his chest. "How did you know about the almonds?"

Surprise flickered over his face, but he didn't move. His next inhale drove the blade a hairsbreadth deeper into his flesh, and another drop of crimson followed the first. Even in the dark she could make out his clenched jaw, the hard line of his mouth. "I was so excited about the promotion, I went straight to my mother's chambers," he said. "She was frantic when she realized I'd just come from dinner with you, asking all sorts of questions about what I'd eaten. Do you know what she said when I told her about my new position? 'Hatshepsut may have promoted you to Supreme Commander of the army, but I've just promoted you to pharaoh.'" He drew a ragged breath. "My mother sent the basket of almonds."

And then Hatshepsut remembered Aset's words at the banquet.

I've taken up weaving. I make a fairly decent lotus-blossom basket.

A pink and yellow papyrus basket, woven with a lotus blossom design.

She would kill her.

She was halfway across her chambers, the knife clutched in her fist, when Tutmose's strangled voice stopped her. "My mother deserves to die a traitor's death, but I'm at fault as well. She came to me last night, ranting like a madwoman that you needed to be removed from the throne. I thought her raving was simply a mother's grief and sent her away. I could have stopped this, but I never thought she'd do anything. I suppose I knew her even less than I thought."

"Your mother did this, not you."

Blood dripped from Hatshepsut's wrist as she followed the maze of corridors to the Hall of Women, but she couldn't think of that now. Later.

Aset's chambers were dark, conveying the sense of rooms quickly abandoned. Statues of Hathor filled each corner, and vases crammed with dying flowers spilled onto the floor. The musty scent of wilting lotus blossoms choked the air, but otherwise the chamber was empty.

Hatshepsut startled as Tutmose stopped behind her; she hadn't realized he'd followed her.

Hatshepsut glanced about. "If she fled—"

She'd hunt her down. She'd have her revenge, no matter how long it took.

"The garden," Tutmose said.

They found Aset sitting in moonlight on the lip of a fountain, a white cat weaving between her ankles as she stroked the black granite statue in her lap. Hatshepsut recognized the figure as Thutmosis, dressed in the double crown, with his shoulders squared against the world. The statue's mate stood on the fountain, a smaller version of Aset, both gifts from

Thutmosis after his fight with Hatshepsut. Aset leaned over the statue of Thut, pressed a kiss to his lips, and smiled.

Her eyes flicked up at Hatshepsut's approach and her face drained of color. She returned the statue to her lap, her hands hovering over his body before she clasped them together. "I didn't expect to see you here," she said to Hatshepsut. "At least not alive."

Something within the woman had died; a festering infection had spread and overcome every bit of good in Aset's *ka*. But, then, something had died in Hatshepsut's *ka* as well.

Tutmose stood at Hatshepsut's side, his hands clenching and unclenching. She had never seen him so angry. "What made you think you could poison the pharaoh?" he demanded.

"Imposter pharaoh." Aset's eyes hardened as she spat out the words. "I only wish I'd succeeded." Then she smiled and lifted Thut's statue from her lap, standing it so close to her own statue that their shoulders touched. "What about Senenmut? I notice he's absent from your little entourage."

Hatshepsut swayed on her feet, clenched the knife in her hand.

Tutmose answered for her. "Senenmut is dead."

"So I've finally finished the job Thutmosis should have done long ago," Aset said.

Hatshepsut could scarcely form the words through her anger. "Yet long ago, you saved Senenmut from execution."

"You still believe that?" Aset exhaled through her teeth, the sound of a cobra's hiss. "I told you that only after Thutmosis died to make you love me more. Thutmosis was weak. He couldn't bring himself to kill his friend, so he sent him to Aswan instead. I wish he'd finished him off instead and spared me the trouble of hating him all these years."

The realization dawned in Hatshepsut. "You never delivered my message to Senenmut's mother, did you?"

"Of course not. The last thing I wanted was his return to court."

Tutmose sent the cat screeching as he yanked his mother to her feet. "Senenmut was the only father I've ever known. How could you do this?"

Aset blinked at him, some of her euphoria falling away. "I did it for you, Tutmose, to reclaim your throne. Everything I've ever done has been for you, to remove those who stood in your way. Who do you think poisoned that Akkadian whore all those years ago and made sure all her babes died in the womb? Who fed your father herbs to ensure he would sire no more sons, even as he gathered more and more women into the Hall of Women?"

All these years and no one had ever suspected the truth of Enheduanna's death or Thut's impotence. Hatshepsut's mother had been right: Aset had probably poisoned Hathor's dancer, too, so she could dance at Thut's Festival of Intoxication and meet the pharaoh.

"My only regret," Aset continued, "is that I didn't do a better job at the *sed* festival. If I'd cut that girth properly, Neferure would still be alive and Tutmose would be pharaoh."

Hatshepsut's fingers curled around Aset's neck, and she ignored the lancing pain at her wrists. Rage slithered through her brain, hissed in her ear. "How could you do this?"

Aset's mouth twisted into a smile. "How can you ask me that, you who stole my son's crown and banished me from the palace so that when I returned I hardly knew him? I loved you, but you betrayed me. You caused all this chaos, Hatshepsut, not me."

Hatshepsut shoved her away, wiping away the film of evil on her hands. Demons stalked the shadows of the garden, baring their teeth at her. "You would have been loyal to me if you'd truly loved me, but instead you've only been loyal to yourself all this time."

"No," Aset said. "Not to myself. To my son."

"Why now?" Hatshepsut asked. "Why not kill me when I first took the throne?"

Yet she knew the answer before she even finished the question.

"I'd have been happy to kill you then," Aset said. "But I couldn't get close enough, not after you sent me to rot in Dendera. And that beast of a *medjay* never left your side once I returned."

Nomti had been right to insist on Aset's banishment, but his imprisonment after the chariot accident had opened the way for the full onslaught of Aset's destruction.

"But you were under guard during the *sed* festival—"

Aset snorted. "That slobbering fool was all too happy to look the other way after I'd had him in my bed. You thought you were invincible, protected by the gods, but it turns out you're mortal like the rest of us, one with as much blood on her hands as I have."

Hatshepsut stepped forward. "You're nothing more than a demon sent from the pits of the netherworld. The gods should have destroyed you the day you were born."

Aset glared. "The gods have never watched over me. I've always had to take care of myself." She stumbled toward Tutmose and fell to his feet, clasping his hand. "Everything I've ever done has been for you, Tutmose. Surely you see that."

"You may have carried me in your womb, but we were never made from the same clay." Tutmose shook her away. His fists clenched at his sides; he looked ready to tear her apart at any moment. "I told you I didn't want this, and Neferure would have hated you for it. You're not my mother, only a traitor possessed by the darkness of Apep."

Aset's eyes filled with tears and she pressed her fingers to her lips, too late to stifle a moan. Her eyes flicked to Hatshepsut and the knife, and she straightened her shoulders, her eyes rolling madly. "A traitor's death on a pike outside the palace won't do?"

"No one is to know that the hawk in the nest's mother is a traitor and a murderer," Hatshepsut said. "But you will die and your body will be burned. Ma'at demands it. *I* demand it."

"Of course you do." Aset tilted her chin up in defiance, but shivered as Hatshepsut stepped forward with the knife. "I'll be just one more body on your path to immortality."

Ma'at's justice should have stricken Aset long ago, should have kept Neferure and Senenmut safe. The gods had failed Hatshepsut.

Tutmose held his mother as Hatshepsut pressed the dagger to her throat and released a thin stream of red. She felt a moment's remorse at spilling more blood, but the remembrance of Senenmut's empty eyes steadied her hand. Aset flinched but squared her shoulders, her eyes hard. "Ammit will eat your heart for this."

"Then she'll feast well tonight."

Hatshepsut slashed the dagger deep across the pale skin of Aset's throat. The spurt of scarlet blood showered both their sheaths with brilliant red petals. Wide-eyed, Aset opened her mouth to gasp, but only gurgled as a crimson froth broke over her lips and slipped down her chin.

She fell forward into Hatshepsut's arms, and the knife clattered to the floor. Each beat of her pulse bathed Hatshepsut in warm blood and filled her nose with its coppery taste. She rolled Aset on the ground as the blood blossomed in a dark stain across the earth, waited until her body stilled and the final bit of blood spurted from her neck.

She was gone.

Jaw clenched, Tutmose folded one arm over her chest, the death pose of a royal wife. The hawk in the nest was pale as he closed his mother's unseeing eyes, even as his own squeezed shut.

Little brown sparrows chirped as they flitted amongst the juniper bushes and Re pulled himself over the horizon. Slave gossip drifted from the garden. Life continued its ceaseless march, but Hatshepsut wanted no part of it.

She was a murderer many times over. The voices of the dead beckoned her.

"May the soles of her feet be firm." Tutmose choked on the words, his mouth set in a grim line as he picked up his mother's black granite statue.

Hatshepsut stared at the knife on the ground, at the spreading pool of blood.

It had taken less than a week to fulfill Djeseret's prophecy.

Tutmose followed Hatshepsut's gaze to the knife and then to her mangled wrists. The blood there was thick, a mottled shade of rust compared to the fresh slick of red on the copper blade.

"A pharaoh's sacrifices never end." He spoke slowly. "This is a lesson I'm just beginning to learn."

Hatshepsut silently picked up the knife. She would finish what she'd started.

He crouched in front of her, his voice no more than a whisper. "There have been enough deaths to sate Anubis for years to come. Egypt needs you."

"No." Hatshepsut shook her head violently. "It's my turn to face Ma'at's scales, to answer for what I've done."

"In due time," Tutmose said. "You still have a kingdom to rule."

"Egypt is yours."

He shook his head. "Nothing in this life is that easy." He held his hand out for the knife, but Hatshepsut didn't move.

He dropped his hand. "It would be simple to let you slit your wrists and take the throne as you greeted Senenmut and Neferure in the Field of Reeds," Tutmose said. "But that's not what's best for Egypt."

She knew what he was going to say. And she didn't want to hear it.

"I need to take command of the armies," Tutmose said, "both in the City of Truth and abroad." His face was set in grim lines. "Egypt would best be served if you continued as pharaoh, no matter how you may wish otherwise. Ma'at demands it."

There was a long silence while Hatshepsut twisted Senenmut's ring on her thumb. The weight of empty years stretched before her.

"Facing Ammit would be easier," she said.

Tutmose nodded. "I know."

This time she allowed Tutmose to take the knife from her when he reached out his hand.

Remaining in this life would be the hardest thing she'd ever done, another sacrifice in Egypt's name.

A fate worse than death, and it was all she deserved.

CHAPTER 32

Aset's rooms were almost empty.

The cool days of Peret had boiled into the full heat of the harvest season and cooled again as Isis cried and the Nile flooded before Hatshepsut had found the will to order Aset's apartments cleared. Now only a couple of stray cats and a handful of rough cedar boxes remained after slaves had swept the dust and dried flowers from the chambers and packed up the majority of the former concubine's belongings.

Hatshepsut took up the task of sorting Aset's jewelry, pausing over each piece to remember the occasions when she had worn the baubles. She untangled a lapis-and-gold vulture pendant worn to one of Neferure's naming-day celebrations and set aside Aset's favorite collar strung with carnelian and turquoise beads from the expedition up the Nile, and the turquoise earrings Hatshepsut had given her when Tutmose was born. Perhaps Satiah would want them.

"I came to see if I could help."

Tutmose stood in the doorway, for once not dressed in full military regalia, but instead wearing a plain white kilt and a gold pectoral depicting Horus with his wings spread wide over his heart. He would depart for the northern frontiers the following morning.

Nomti poked his head inside. "Do you mind, *Per A'a?*"

"Not at all." She smiled as Nomti took up his post. He'd been quickly reinstated as *medjay*, amidst apologies that she'd ever suspected him guilty of treason.

He'd only given that fearsome smile, which was now even more frightful with several new scars to accompany his black tattoos. "You'd have known if I'd been guilty," he'd said.

"Because you wouldn't have failed."

"Precisely." Then he'd dared to draw her into his arms and let her sob out her pain and anger. There had been no mention of the past then, only his steady presence. And now Tutmose waited to help her pack away so many more memories of the past.

"This is all that's left." She motioned to the boxes on the floor.

Tutmose opened one of the smaller ones and lifted out an alabaster carving of Taweret. The hippo goddess's swollen white belly filled his palm. "Do you mind if I take this? Satiah might appreciate it when the next baby comes. Perhaps this one will be a boy."

Satiah's child, which Hatshepsut had so feared, had been born perfectly formed, a baby girl with her mother's eyes and Tutmose's somber expressions. With Neferure's death Tutmose was now free to marry as he saw fit and, after a suitable period of mourning, he had taken Satiah as his first wife. The sight of Tutmose doting on his young wife and daughter— and dote he most certainly did—would make any woman's heart light.

"I'm sure Taweret will bless you and Satiah with many more children. At least I hope so."

And Hatshepsut meant it, even if she sometimes had to leave the room when watching Satiah nurse her daughter, wishing it could be Neferure sitting there with such a perfect expression of love on her face. Hatshepsut would never forgive herself for all she'd done in this life, and she had yet to find it in her heart to forgive Aset, but time and her trials had tempered her, for better and for worse.

Tutmose stacked some of the boxes. "I can take care of all this if you'd rather."

"I don't mind." All the same, she was touched by the offer. Egypt would be in capable hands when she passed to the West. Tutmose's honor and loyalty would serve her kingdom well. "I'm trying to remember your mother the way she was when we were young. It seems so long ago."

Silence enfolded them as they sorted through the crate. The box was filled with gold ointment jars, a collection of amulets including one of a giant phallus and another of a scarab, and a broken statue of Hathor. At the very bottom Hatshepsut found the dagger. Intertwined papyrus and lotus blossoms climbed their way up the knife's ivory hilt and a hammered sheath of decorated bronze covered the blade. Her breath caught in her throat as she turned it in her hands. Re's light hit the metal, glinting off images of a lioness attacking an ibex and a cow. Flawless hieroglyphs marched down the middle.

> *The one who is powerful, Sekhmet, lady of slaughter and wearer of the solar disk*

She struggled to draw a breath, remembering an identical inscription from long ago. Grief and time must have marred her memory, transformed it into this impossible trick.

Alone now at the bottom of the cedar box, a tiny scroll of papyrus lay tied with a bit of frayed rope. Dreading what she might find, she unrolled the paper carefully, ignoring the flakes of papyrus that floated to her lap. Formal hieroglyphs stood in perfect columns, the elegant and precise handwriting that could only belong to a well-trained scribe.

> *In the name of Ma'at, goddess of truth and justice, I bequeath this dagger to my daughter, Aset, upon my death, and entrust the Temple of Hathor to keep her safe until she and I meet again in the Field of Reeds.*
>
> *Blessed be Hathor, goddess of love, to whom I dedicated my life as chantress.*

And then, in stilted hieroglyphs, like the hand of a child with its first brush, was a single name.

Merenaset

Hatshepsut stared at the note for a long moment, dumbstruck at the secret the gods had hidden from her for so long. Then she laughed, little chortles at first, but soon great peals of laughter echoed off the ceiling. The wild sound ricocheted off the whitewashed rafters and scattered the cats who had been sunning themselves on the window ledge. She covered her mouth as tears poured from her eyes.

Alarmed, Tutmose set down the *senet* board he'd been wrapping. "What is it? What's so funny?"

It took a long time for her to gain control of herself. Hiccupping with unspent laughter and wild sobs, she gave Tutmose the dagger and wiped her eyes with the back of her hand.

He stared quizzically at the knife, turned it over in his hands. "I don't understand."

She shook her head, her wig wild and the kohl around her eyes smeared where tears still ran.

"Senenmut made this for me," she said. "And I gave it to your grandmother."

"My grandmother?" Tutmose looked at her as if she'd lost her mind. Perhaps she had. "But you didn't know my grandmother."

"A merchant dragged her to the Court of Reeds because she'd stolen bracelets from his stall. Your father wanted to cut off her ears, but I gave her a position as chantress in Hathor's temple so she could support her daughter. I gave her this knife, too." She sighed, wiped her cheeks, and let her hands float to her sides in a gesture of surrender. "Her name was Merenaset."

Understanding dawned across Tutmose's face. "And she gave it to her daughter. My mother."

She had saved Aset, only to kill her.

Tutmose seemed to read her thoughts and clasped her cold hands within his warm ones. "If it hadn't been for you, my mother never would have come to the palace to dance for my father," he said. "I would never have been born."

And Neferure and Senenmut wouldn't have died.

Silent tears streamed down her cheeks. She recalled Senenmut's words from the temple of Set long ago. There was always order amongst the chaos, even when it wasn't possible for her to see it.

"Things are as they were meant to be," Tutmose said. "Everything is as the gods will it."

epilogue

Tutmose leaned on his ivory walking stick—the same one his father had used after an accident with an elephant in Canaan—while standing under the shade of a myrrh tree, its fragrance wafting faintly on the breath of the gods. Time, rather than a glorious battle with some wild beast, had eaten away at an old combat wound so that he needed the cane. Now he stood in the Western Valley, a wizened old man about to commit the greatest crime of his life.

Hatshepsut's temple at Djeser-Djeseru shone like a mirage amongst the ruddy cliffs, the entire complex guarded by a walkway of solemn granite sphinxes and rows of statues all wearing his stepmother's face, a woman he hadn't seen in almost three decades. Each wore the remembrance of a smile, something Tutmose could scarcely recall the pharaoh wearing in this life. In her later years, Hatshepsut had grown fat and more ill-tempered than a mule as her health had deteriorated. She'd found solace in food and in memories, and Egypt had prospered under her guidance as it always had. Tutmose had maintained her mortuary temple after she had passed to the West, even as he had ordered his own, grander temple to honor Amun while expanding the kingdom left to him. Under his hand, the borders of the Two Lands had stretched to the ends of the sky, reaching from the Levant in the north far past Dongola in the south, making his Egypt the largest in history.

And yet he knew he owed all his successes to Hatshepsut, to the woman who had usurped his throne and passed to him a stable and peaceful country, despite all it had cost her.

Tutmose's heart was heavy, weighed down with the dishonor of the decision he was now forced to make. He hoped Ma'at would forgive him for what he was about to do.

He prayed Hatshepsut would forgive him.

"Tear them down."

Tutmose's voice was quiet as he spoke to Amenhotep. His youngest child and only surviving son, Amenhotep had seen seventeen years and was soon to take his place on the Isis Throne in what Tutmose hoped would be a peaceful co-regency. The transition from his reign to his son's must be smooth, so no scheming courtier could rally behind one of his many older daughters, including Weretkhetes, the daughter Satiah had borne after Neferure's death. Weretkhetes was no Hatshepsut; she was too self-centered to wear a crown that required such sacrifice. Tutmose's spies had intercepted whispers of those who supported Weretkhetes, courtiers who wished to seize the throne from young Amenhotep. Before Hatshepsut, the scenario would have been implausible, but one of Egypt's most successful and peace-loving pharaohs had opened the door for future strife and bloodshed based on the new precedent that allowed a woman to rule.

The next pharaoh had to be Amenhotep. Anything less could plunge Egypt into civil war.

"Every image depicting Hatshepsut as pharaoh must be destroyed," Tutmose said.

"Of course, Father." Amenhotep's voice cracked as he bowed and carried the order to a large pit clustered with workers. Dressed only in loincloths in the heat, the men would work through the day and still not finish pulling down Hatshepsut's statues.

Amenhotep gave the orders to the foremen, too quietly for Tutmose to hear, but the overseers glanced at the strange sight of the pharaoh standing alone under a myrrh tree. Tutmose had preferred to spend his time planning military campaigns and had rarely overseen a building project, but this was a duty he could not shirk, no matter how much he wished to.

His son returned to his side as the workers clustered around one of Hatshepsut's sphinxes. One man raised his hammer, then let it fall with a resounding crash. The men cheered and the sound of the blows echoed through the valley. Tutmose cringed.

"Are you sure you want to stay, Father?" Amenhotep asked. "These overseers worked at Karnak. I told them this was the same job, only that here there are no images of Hatshepsut as Great Royal Wife to save."

"I'll stay," Tutmose said. "For a while."

The workmen crawled over the statues like ants, decimating Hatshepsut's smiling images. Hammers and adzes flew in a frenzy, the overseers urging the men along.

"You are big, fat water buffalo," yelled a foreman. "You are dung!"

The men rolled their eyes, laughed, and made obscene gestures at the overseer's back, as if they were on some sort of holiday.

It was too much to watch.

"I'm going into the temple." Tutmose started down the avenue of sphinxes, his eyes trained on the temple's entrance, as Amenhotep fell into step behind him. They passed a scrawny worker struggling to hammer away the head of one of Hatshepsut's sphinxes. Finally, he hit his target with a crack like lightning, and her smiling face sheared away from the *nemes* headdress and fell to the sand with a dull thump.

Tutmose forced himself to walk up the causeway to the top terrace as similar sounds of destruction continued behind him. Here in the temple's innermost sanctum, painted scenes of Hatshepsut before Amun filled the temple walls. In one corner was a nondescript mural of her in open adoration of the hidden god; she was dressed in male attire with a green perfume bottle in her hand. Behind her stood a smaller man with his head also bent in worship.

Senenmut.

"I want that." Tutmose pointed at the image with his walking stick. "And I want it left intact."

Amenhotep's brow furrowed and he opened his mouth to speak, but seemed to think better of it and fetched a worker with sweat pouring down his temples. Between wiping his palms on his kilt and mopping his brow with his hem, the man used his adze to chip away the portrait, and after what seemed an eternity, he presented it to the pharaoh.

"May I ask why you wanted that?" Amenhotep asked as the workman backed out of the temple, almost tripping in his haste.

"Hatshepsut's public monuments—the obelisks and her temples— must be cleansed to purge Egypt of its memory of her reign as pharaoh and protect your claim to the throne." Tutmose stroked the image of Hatshepsut's double crown with his thumb, brushed the plaster dust from Senenmut's wig. "But I won't jeopardize Hatshepsut's *ka*. Her name must live on, so some of her images must remain."

"And Senenmut?"

"I want all my family to greet me in the Field of Reeds one day."

Amenhotep offered his father his arm. "Where will you put them?"

Tutmose took his son's arm, feeling suddenly tired. He smiled. "In my garden, next to the black granite statues of my mother and father."

Amenhotep chuckled; he knew the family saga and how little the four would enjoy spending eternity together. "I'm sure all of them will have choice words for you when you arrive in the Field of Reeds one day."

Tutmose grinned. "I know they will."

The two walked out into Re's brutal heat. The workers had assembled a line of wooden carts containing fragments of Hatshepsut's statues. Several ochre-painted heads and crowns lay on top of the closest cart, and Tutmose stopped to watch as the first load was dumped into the pit's open mouth. The statues fell with a crash and an explosion of dust, an inappropriate ceremony for their eternal burial.

He hoped Hatshepsut's own sacrifices in Egypt's name would make her more forgiving toward him when he finally greeted her in the Field of Reeds. The woman did have a nasty temper.

Tutmose clutched the painted temple fragment with one hand and his walking stick in the other. "Come, Amenhotep. It's time to go home."

AUTHOR'S NOTE

Hatshepsut was one of the greatest rulers during the Golden Age of Egypt's New Kingdom, but her memory was almost lost to history during a concerted campaign to erase every image and reference to her as pharaoh. The real story of Hatshepsut's life was one of the great mysteries in Egyptology for many years, as historians struggled to reconcile why various monuments around Luxor included her name and the title Great Royal Wife, yet other obscure monuments (such as the pinnacles of toppled obelisks) bore this woman's name with references to a male pharaoh. Added to the mystery were the many likenesses and cartouches in temples like Karnak and Deir el-Bahri of an unknown pharaoh that had been removed in antiquity. Finally, Egyptologists realized they had found a case of a woman successfully ruling Egypt as pharaoh, but, for some reason, someone shortly after her rule had tried to erase her memory. Now the only question they had to answer was why.

The most common response was that Hatshepsut's stepson (and nephew) Tutmose III, had sought revenge against her for usurping his throne and therefore tried to erase her reign from Egypt's king lists. However, later archaeological digs uncovered evidence that the destruction of her monuments took place at the very end of Tutmose's reign, hardly the act of a young man bent on revenge. Instead, it is most likely that Hatshepsut's rule as a female pharaoh was seen as an aberration not to be repeated, and one that needed to be erased from the historical record. Shortly thereafter came a new discovery: Hatshepsut's mummy. A thorough investigation of the body revealed that Hatshepsut died of natural causes (she was not murdered by Tutmose III, as had been speculated) when she was close to fifty. She was balding, extremely obese, and suffered from a variety of ailments, including a cancerous tumor in her pelvis, osteoporosis, and arthritis.

Although most of the characters and major events in the story did take place, this is a work of fiction, and, thus, I took a few liberties within the frameworks of what is documented in the historical record. I am deeply indebted to Joyce Tyldesley's excellent biography *Hatchepsut: The Female Pharaoh* and Janet Buttles' *The Queens of Egypt*. One of my first tasks was to make sense of the many tongue-twisting and similar names of the gods, goddesses, and courtiers during Hatshepsut's time. Hatshepsut's father, brother, and stepson were all known as Thutmose; I tweaked the spellings for the sake of clarity and ease of reading. I did the same for Aset and the goddess Isis, as both were known as Aset during Egyptian times, but the Greeks then changed the name to Isis.

Mensah was not a real courtier in Hatshepsut's court, and while we don't know what made Hatshepsut seize the throne seven years after becoming regent, it is possible that there was some sort of internal coup. The names of the worst criminals in ancient Egypt were obliterated, so if someone like Mensah did exist, his story is now lost to history.

Speculation is rife regarding Hatshepsut's relationship with Senenmut, but there is evidence pointing to their possible romantic involvement. While we will never know the truth with any certainty, the romantic in me has always believed they were lovers. Senenmut appears in many out-of-the-way places in the temple of Deir el-Bahri, he received more titles than any commoner in Egypt's history, and there is also a tomb graffito that is commonly assumed to depict Hatshepsut and Senenmut in a rather compromising position. The causes of Neferure's and Senenmut's deaths are also unrecorded, but both likely predeceased Hatshepsut by many years. Thus, the pieces of Hatshepsut's life always seemed to be a tragedy to me; after ushering Egypt into its golden age, she witnessed the death of her only daughter and then her lover, only to die later and have her memory almost wiped from Egypt's history.

Many people leave their imprint on a book, and this novel has been touched by a small village. I owe my early readers a debt of gratitude for their invaluable feedback: Julie Barry (who deserves a medal of bravery) for being my very first reader; Cindy Davis, Kristi Senden, and Merle Askeland for all their feedback over enchiladas; Shannon O'Donnell, Lessa Host, Amalia Dillin, and Joshua McCune for not suggesting I use early versions of the story to line birdcages; Janet Reid for giving me a well-deserved smack upside the head; Gary Corby for his patience and query regarding why there was no evil priest in the story; and Renee Yancy and Jade Timms for helping me whip the story into shape.

To my wonderful agent, Marlene Stringer, for her excitement over my fascination with obscure women from ancient history; and to my superhuman editor, Ellen Edwards, for making this story better than I ever could have written it alone.

And to my friends and family: Megan Williams, Claire Torbensen, and Eugenia Merrifield for their constant cheerleading over lunch; Dad, Daine, and Hollie for their never-ending well of enthusiasm; and especially Stephen and Isabella for putting up with this five-year roller-coaster ride. I promise not to drag you through the Valley of the Kings during midday in August again anytime soon.

Finally, to my mother, Kristin Louise Crowley, who read countless stories to me when I was a little girl, but never had a chance to read any of my books. This one is for you.

Photo by Katherine Schmeling Photography

Stephanie Thornton is a writer and history teacher who has been obsessed with infamous women from ancient history since she was twelve. She lives with her husband and daughter in Alaska, where she is at work on her next novel.

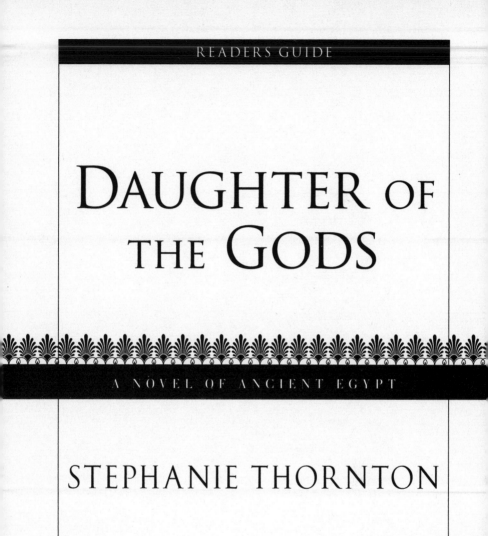

DAUGHTER OF THE GODS

A NOVEL OF ANCIENT EGYPT

STEPHANIE THORNTON

A CONVERSATION WITH STEPHANIE THORNTON

Q. This is the second novel you've written about the "forgotten women of history." Why did you choose Hatshepsut? What do you think makes her extraordinary?

A. The historian Laurel Thatcher Ulrich once wrote, "Well-behaved women seldom make history," and, from my perspective, that's totally true. Hatshepsut broke the mold of established history, arguably becoming the world's first successful female ruler. Before her, women had worn Egypt's crown, but their reigns were short-lived and always necessitated by the lack of a suitable male pharaoh. Hatshepsut ruled as regent for seven years, usurped the throne from her stepson for unknown reasons, and then went on to reign over Egypt's Golden Age. She left impressive monuments scattered throughout her country, organized one of Egypt's greatest trade expeditions, and may have had a rather steamy affair with a commoner. Nothing about her was expected or mundane, and no queen of Egypt—and few male pharaohs—successfully wielded as much power as she did. In fact, the list of women who managed to do so even in the millennia after her death is a short one.

Q. Reading Hatshepsut's story, I'm struck by the continuity of ancient Egyptian civilization, which lasted for three thousand years and was already ancient when Hatshepsut took the throne. Is there any other comparable civilization, in length and sophistication, in human history? What made ancient Egypt so stable?

A. The Chinese actually win the award for the longest-running continuous civilization because they were never fully conquered, and much of their culture and traditions can still be traced back to ancient times. Chinese civilization has lasted more than five thousand years, while Egypt was conquered by ancient Rome more than two thousand years ago.

That said, ancient Egypt was the most stable of all the ancient civilizations because of one geological gift: the Nile. While the Tigris, Euphrates, and Indus rivers were all unpredictable, the Nile flooded fairly reliably every year. The Egyptians even invented Nilometers—a series of steps marked with measurements—in order to predict how much the river would flood and to determine the time of harvest. The Egyptian government had two major collapses in its history before finally falling to Rome, but the Nile continued to feed the people, allowing their civilization to continue.

Q. Are any particular Egyptologists associated with the gradual acceptance that Hatshepsut was a female pharaoh? Were there noteworthy and exciting archeological discoveries made along the way?

A. Some early Egyptologists slandered Hatshepsut's reign as unnatural, especially considering her constant depictions as a man, but historian Édouard Naville (1844–1926) was a staunch supporter of the female pharaoh. At the turn of the twentieth century he wrote that it was because Hatshepsut had passed such a stable nation on to Tutmose III that he was able to expand the empire, becoming a sort of Napoleon of ancient Egypt. Naville also posited the theory that Hatshepsut's monuments weren't destroyed by Tutmose III until the end of his reign, rendering unlikely all the hypotheses that Hatshepsut's stepson had sought revenge and possibly even had killed his stepmother.

Probably the most exciting archaeological discovery in Hatshepsut's saga was the recovery of her mummy in 2007. Howard Carter (1874–1939), the famed Egyptologist who discovered King Tut's tomb, had excavated KV60 in 1903, but because the undecorated tomb held only two female mummies, he left them there (one on the ground), and resealed the tomb. More recently, Dr. Zahi Hawass decided to search for Egypt's female pharaoh and, among others, turned to the possible candidates in KV60. Very few objects from Hatshepsut's tomb exist to this day, but a sealed wooden box bearing her cartouche was x-rayed and found to contain a molar. After scanning all the possible mummy candidates, experts found that the mummy of the obese woman on the ground was missing the exact same molar. The tooth and the hole left behind were a perfect match, thus making way for the very rare, and very exciting, identification of a 3,500-year-old royal mummy.

Q. The novel gives us a good idea of what life was like for highborn women. What was it like for women who were commoners?

A. Compared to other ancient civilizations, women in Egypt had a substantial number of rights, many of which weren't granted to Western women until more modern history. By law, ancient Egyptian women were seen as equal to men, and could take part in court cases as jury members or as plaintiffs, own land, and initiate divorces. Upper-class women tended to remain home to manage their households, but most Egyptians during this time were farmers, and, as such, a wife worked in the fields alongside her husband. However, women could also own their own businesses as merchants, midwives, mourners, or doctors, and the temples often employed them as acrobats, singers, and priestesses.

Q. Senenmut's rise from humble beginnings to the nobility is almost as impressive as Hatshepsut's becoming pharaoh. What do we know from the historical record about the real Senenmut?

A. Senenmut's early life remains a bit murky, but we do know that he was born to a large family in Iuny and quickly worked his way up the ranks as an efficient bureaucrat. The key to Senenmut's rise is that he was educated. Few people in ancient Egypt could read and write, and therefore they were unable to advance themselves as he did.

While Senenmut almost certainly served under Hatshepsut's father and/or brother, it is during her time as regent and pharaoh that his meteoric rise occurred. Hatshepsut heaped titles upon him, ranging in importance from Steward of the God's Wife to Overseer of Amun's Gardens, and, my favorite, the Superintendent of the Royal Bedroom. Senenmut gained enough titles and riches to rebury his parents in grand style and to build himself not one, but two tombs, including one with an impressive astronomical ceiling. As the Overseer of the Works at Djeser-Djeseru, he was also allowed the high honor of building a tomb within the sacred confines of the temple grounds and linking his name to Hatshepsut's. There is no mention of a wife or children in either of his tombs, leading historians to believe he never married. Approximately twenty-five statues of Senenmut exist today, but, unfortunately, his sarcophagus was destroyed in antiquity, and his mummy has never been found.

Q. The idea of siblings marrying each other as Hatshepsut and Thut do, is, of course, very strange to us. It goes against some of our strongest cultural taboos. Can you explain the Egyptians' thinking about incest? When did this practice begin to fall out of favor?

A. Contrary to popular belief, ordinary Egyptians didn't engage in incest on a regular basis. (This can be a bit confusing, as their love poetry uses the terms *brother* and *sister* when addressing their lovers.) However, in order to secure the ruling dynasty and keep the crown in the family, incest was a common practice among royalty. Brothers typically married their sisters, and, as squeamish as it makes us, fathers even occasionally married daughters. When the royal family ran out of men, as happened after King Tut's death, the new male pharaoh often married into the royal family. The practice of royal incest continued well past Hatshepsut's dynasty, as Cleopatra VII married two of her prepubescent brothers before getting tangled up with Caesar and Marc Antony.

Q. The years during which Hatshepsut reigned were particularly peaceful and prosperous. How do they compare to the reigns of other rulers during that time? Would it be misleading to suggest that as a woman, she was less interested in expanding her kingdom through war and acquisition and more interested in building a healthy, vibrant civilization at home?

A. Hatshepsut and her family dominate any list of famous rulers of the fifteenth century BC. Ancient Greece was barely getting started, and Mesopotamia was already waning. Egypt's Eighteenth Dynasty is considered the start of the civilization's Golden Age, leading to the Nineteenth Dynasty of Amenhotep III, King Tutankhamen (who didn't do much while alive, but had a really great tomb), Seti I, and Ramesses II.

Hatshepsut's reign is bookended by both her father's and step-son's extensive military campaigns and, therefore, she's often por-trayed as a peace-loving queen intent on developing trade routes and initiating building campaigns. However, her treasurer, Ti, and other court officials recorded on their tombs that she was seen in a cam-paign in Nubia collecting hands from the enemy dead for the of-ficial casualty count. Granted, this may have been propaganda, but it's interesting to realize that, like Queen Elizabeth I of England, Hatshepsut may have been willing to wage war for the good of her country.

Q. Hatshepsut sends an expedition to the ancient land of Punt. Do we know where that would be in modern-day terms?

A. The location of the land of Punt, or "Land of the Gods," is still debated by historians, but most Egyptologists agree that it was roughly where Somalia lies today. Expeditions from Egypt were sent to the famed land of gold and frankincense as far back as almost 2,500 BC, but Hatshepsut's trip is the most famous, mostly because she recorded it in great detail on her temple walls at Djeser-Djeseru. The roots and trunks of the myrrh trees that she planted in the fore-court of her mortuary temple remain to this day.

Q. What would you like readers to most take away from the novel?

A. My goal in writing this book was to breathe life into Hatshepsut's story. Her name isn't as famous as Cleopatra's or even Nefertiti's, but, to me, she did so much more for Egypt and for history than either of those women. I hope people enjoy reading about this passionate and determined woman, and learning about her many accomplishments.

Q. In your research, have you come across exceptional women whom you have decided not to write about, but whom readers might want to investigate on their own?

A. I've been struck numerous times by the parallels between Hatshepsut and Queen Elizabeth I of England. Both women were seen as unlikely candidates for their country's thrones, both conducted military campaigns to secure their borders, and both ushered in golden ages for their nations. In addition, I've always been intrigued by Elizabeth's possible relationship with Sir Robert Dudley, a similar situation to that of Hatshepsut and Senenmut. I can't resist a good romance!

Q. What famous woman are you writing about next?

A. I'm currently writing about the very complicated and almost entirely unknown wife and daughters of Genghis Khan. These women were able administrators who fought tirelessly for their kingdoms while Genghis' sons spent their time waging war and getting drunk (only one of his sons wasn't a confirmed alcoholic), but because they were women, they were subsequently cut from much of Mongolian history. It's time the world saw how ruthless and talented those amazing women were, almost more so than the great Khan himself.

QUESTIONS FOR DISCUSSION

1. What did you most enjoy about *Daughter of the Gods*? What do you think you will remember about it six months from now?

2. Hatshepsut begins as a tomboy, lively and unrestrained. Discuss how her sister's death changes her. Do you think that a tragedy suffered during one's formative years tends to have an outsized affect on us?

3. What most surprised you about the author's depiction of ancient Egypt?

4. Discuss the various mothers in the book—Ahmose, Mutnofret, Hatshepsut, and Aset—and their child-raising methods and choices regarding their children's future. Consider in particular Hatshepsut's response to Neferure's desire not to marry Tutmose, and Aset's response to Tutmose's choice of Satiah. If you were these women, how would you have acted in their situations?

5. Did you find the relationship between Hatshepsut and Senenmut satisfying? Discuss the possible consequences if Hatshepsut had ever become pregnant with Senenmut's child.

6. Talk about the many animals in the novel, both the living animals and the animals used as symbols of different gods/goddesses and powers. What animals have played a part in your own life?

7. Why does Hatshepsut declare herself pharaoh? Do you applaud her or condemn her for it, especially in light of what happens to both the kingdom and to her loved ones afterward?

8. Once Hatshepsut usurps full power, she banishes Aset to a distant province. Was that a wise move? How might she have handled the situation differently? Did you feel sympathy for Aset?

9. Do you agree with this statement: Often women in power have few or no children. Discuss why this might be, pulling examples from history and current times.

10. The ancient Egyptians were extremely religious and also believed in the use of magic on a daily basis. How much of Hatshepsut's religious expression seems to be based on pure superstition and how much on actual religious belief?

11. Egypt enjoyed thousands of years of relative stability and changelessness. Would you like to have lived then? Compared to our time, which is so full of change, what might be some pros and cons of living during a time when life continued very much the same, generation after generation?

12. How does this novel compare to other novels or movies about ancient Egypt that you may have read or seen? Does it explode any misconceptions you might have had?

13. Can you think of some ideas and traditions that started with the Egyptians that we embrace even today, so many thousands of years later?

In the twelfth century, Genghis Khan built an empire
in central Asia greater than the world had ever known.
But it was the women in his life—his wives and daughters—
who ensured that his achievement would live on
long after his death. . . .

Read on for an excerpt from
Stephanie Thornton's exciting new novel
in which four women tell this story.

THE TIGER QUEENS

A NOVEL OF GENGHIS KHAN'S WOMEN

Available in paperback and e-book
in November 2014

PROLOGUE

Our names have long been lost to time, scattered like ashes in wind. No one remembers our ability to read the secrets of the oracle bones or the wars fought in our name. The words we wrote have faded from their parchments; the sacrifices we made are no longer retold in the glittering courts of those we conquered. The deeds of our husbands, our brothers, and our sons have eclipsed our own as surely as when the moon ate the sun during the first battle of Nishapur.

Yet without us, there would have been no empire for our men to claim, no clan of the Thirteen Hordes left to lead, and no tales of victory to sing to the Eternal Blue Sky.

It was our destiny to love these men, to suffer their burdens and shoulder their sorrows, to bring them into this world, red-faced and squalling, and tuck their bones into the earth when they abandoned us for the sacred mountains, leaving us behind to fight their wars and protect their Spirit Banners.

We gathered our strength from the water of the northern lakes, the fire of the south's Great Dry Sea, the brown earth of the western mountains, and the wild air of the eastern steppes. Born of the four directions, we cleaved together like the seasons for our very survival.

In a world lit by fire and ruled by the sword, we depended upon one another for the very breath we drew.

Even as the steppes ran with blood and storm clouds roiled overhead, we loved our husbands, our brothers, and our sons. And we loved one another, the fierce love of mothers and sisters and daughters, born from our shared laughter and tears as our souls were woven together, stronger than the thickest felts.

And yet nothing lasts forever. One by one, our souls were gathered into the Eternal Blue Sky, our tents dismantled and our herds scattered across the steppes. That is a tale yet to come.

It matters not how we died. Only one thing matters: that we lived.

CHAPTER 1

CE 1171

YEAR OF THE IRON HARE

He came in the autumn of my tenth year, when the crisp air entices horses to race and the white cranes fly toward the southern hills.

A single man led a line of horses between the two great mountains that straddled our camp. Startled, I set down my milking pail and wiped my hands on my scratchy felt *deel*—the long caftan worn by men, women, and children alike—as my father joined me, grunting and shielding his eyes from the last rays of golden sunlight. Visitors and merchants often found their way to the door at the western wall of our domed *ger*, silently filling their bellies with salted sheep fat until our fermented mare's milk loosened their tongues. I loved to hear their tales of distant steppes and the mountain forests, of clans with foreign names and fearsome khans. My father was the leader of our Unigirad clan, but life outside our camp seemed terribly exotic to a girl who had never traveled past the river border of our summer grazing lands.

I finished milking the goats and watched the shadows grow, eager for the trader's stories, which would carry me to sleep that night.

"Borte Ujin." My mother, the famed seer Chotan, called from the skin door of our *ger*, her gray hair tied back and a chipped wooden

435

cooking spoon in her hand. I hated that spoon—my backside had met it more times than I could count on my fingers and toes.

I was a twilight child, planted in my mother's belly like an errant seed long after her monthly bloods had ceased. After being childless for so long, my parents welcomed even a mere girl child, someone to help my mother churn butter and corral the herds with my father. And so I grew up their only daughter, indulged by my elderly father while my mother harangued me to sit straighter and pay more attention to the calls of geese and the other messages from all the spirits.

My mother was by far the shortest woman in our village, but the look she gave me now would have scattered a pack of starving wolves. "Pull your head from the clouds, Borte," she said. "The marmot won't roast itself."

I lugged the skin bucket of milk inside, ducking into the heavy scents of hide, earth, and burning dung. The thick haze of smoke made my throat and eyes burn. The felt ceiling was stained black from years of soot and the smoke hole was open to the Eternal Blue Sky, the traditional rope that represented the umbilical cord of the universe dangling from the cloud-filled circle. A dead marmot lay by the fire, the size of a small dog with prickly fur like tiny porcupine quills. Our meat usually came from one of the Five Snouts—horses, goats, sheep, camels, and cattle—but my father's eyes sparkled when he could indulge my mother's taste for wild marmot. The oily meat was a pleasant change.

"There's a visitor on the path." I hacked off the marmot's head with a dull blade and yanked out the purple entrails. My father's mottled dog pushed at my hip with her muzzle, but I swatted her away, daring to toss her the gizzards only when my mother wasn't looking.

Mother sighed and rubbed her temples, squinting as if staring through the felt walls at something far away. "I knew about the visitor before he stepped over the horizon," she said, the beads that dangled from her sleeves chattering with her every movement. Each was a reminder of a successful prophecy breathed to life by her lips, bits of bone and clay gathered from the spine of the Earth Mother to adorn her blue seer's robes.

I glanced at the fire. Two singed sheep scapulae lay on the hearth, cracked with visions of the future. My mother's father had been a holy man amongst our people, but he had passed to the sacred mountains the night I fell from her womb. There were whispers that my grandfather's untethered powers might have found a new home in my soul and his Spirit Banner still fluttered in the breeze outside our *ger*, strands of black hair from his favorite stallion tied to his old spear, so that his soul might continue to guide us.

My mother stuffed the marmot's empty stomach cavity with steaming rocks. "These strangers will bring great fortune, and great tragedy." She spoke as if commenting about the quality of our mares' dung, then pushed a strand of graying hair back from her face and glanced at my palms, slick with blood. "You'd best not greet your fate with foul hands."

My skin prickled with dread. My mother was an *udgan*, a rare female shaman, and had cast my bones only once and then forbade me from speaking of the dark omens to anyone, including my father. Lighter prophecies than mine had driven other parents to fill their children's pockets with stones and drown them. And so I had swallowed the words, and promised never to speak of them.

The Eternal Blue Sky was bruised black when I stepped outside, and the scent of roasting horsemeat from a nearby *ger* made my stomach rumble. The water in the horses' trough clung to the warmth of the day and I scrubbed until the flesh of my hands was raw. As on any other night, voices floated from the other far-flung tents. My cheeks grew warm at the grunts of lovemaking from the newly stitched *ger* of a couple freshly wed, the young man and woman that my mother claimed mounted each other like rabbits. The moans were muffled by a new mother crooning to her fussy infant and an old woman berating her grandsons for tracking mud into her tent.

And my father's voice.

I started toward him but retreated into the shadows as a wiry stranger stepped into view. About the same age as my father, the man wore two black braids threaded with gray hanging down his back, topped with a wide-ruffed hat of rabbit fur. Five dun-colored horses, laden with packs and their dark manes cropped close, grazed in the paddock. I strained to hear the conversation, but my father only complimented the man on the quality of his animals. The stranger patted the flank of a pretty mare, releasing a puff of dancing dust into the air. Early moonlight gleamed on the curved sword at his hip, an unusual sight amongst my peace-loving clan, but then the light hit his face. I stumbled back, nearly landing on my backside.

His right eye glittered like a black star, but the left socket was empty, a dark slit nestled between folds of wrinkled skin at the exact center of a long white scar, likely an old battle wound.

"And I thought they called you Dei the Wise." The man grinned at my father, revealing two lines of crooked brown teeth. "You didn't think I'd come without something to trade this time, did you, Dei?"

This time. So my father knew this traveler.

I thought to stay and listen, but the stranger shifted on his feet and his gaze fell on me. I expected a one-eyed scowl, but instead the man's bushy eyebrows lifted in surprise.

I shrunk farther into the shadows, pulling the darkness around my shoulders. My mother would have my skin if she knew I'd been eavesdropping. Learning more about this stranger would have to wait until he'd filled his belly with our marmot.

I scuttled back to our *ger*, feeding the fire with dried mare dung until the flames crackled and my cheeks flushed with heat. My mother bustled about, mumbling to herself as she set out five mismatched wooden cups.

"There's only one visitor, Mother."

She ignored me and poured fresh goat milk into two cups, then filled the other three with *airag*. I knew better than to argue about what I'd seen with my own eyes.

My mother pulled the rocks from the marmot's belly as the wooden door opened, ushering in a gust of cool air along with my father and his guest. Behind the man skulked a scrawny boy scarcely my height, dressed in the same ragged squirrel pelts as his father and fingering the necklace at his throat, a menacing wolf tooth hung from a leather thong. His black hair was cropped close to his head and his eyes gleamed the same gray as a wolf pelt. My father's dog gave a happy bark and jumped up, paws on the boy's shoulders as if embracing a lost friend. The boy's hand went to the hilt of his sword, a smaller version of his father's, and for a moment I thought he might stab the dumb beast. I dragged her away by the scruff of her neck and forced her to sit at my feet, prompting a raised eyebrow from the boy.

I turned my nose up at him and looked to the one-eyed visitor as he bowed to my mother. At least the father had manners.

"Chotan," he said to my mother, straightening, "I bear warm words from Hoelun, my first wife and mother of my eldest son."

My mother grasped the wooden cooking spoon so hard I thought it might crack. It took me a moment to recall the story of my mother's childhood friend Hoelun, married to a handsome Merkid warrior who loved her, and kidnapped by a destitute Borijin hunter while en route to her new husband's homeland.

A one-eyed man.

This man wearing a sword curved like a smile was no exotic trader, but instead a kidnapper of women.

The fire suddenly burned too hot, yet a cold sweat broke out on the back of my neck. I stepped toward my mother, well away from the men's side of the tent. "And this must be your daughter," he said, opening his arms toward me. "Her face is filled with the first light of dawn, yet her eyes are full of fire like the sun."

It wasn't my eyes that filled with fire then, but my cheeks.

"Borte's soul is full of fire," my mother snapped. "As was Hoelun's."

"Still is," the stranger said with a laugh. "Fiery women make the best wives." He elbowed the black-haired boy, still standing sullenly at the edge of the *ger*. "They're certainly the best in bed."

At least I wasn't the only one with burning cheeks. The boy looked as if he wished the Earth Mother would open her maw and swallow him.

My father cleared his throat and handed the largest cup of *airag* to his guest. "You must be thirsty after so long a journey, Yesugei. Rest a while and then you can tell us why you've come."

The men stuffed their bellies with so much marmot that my stomach still rumbled when I lay on my pile of furs later, listening to Yesugei's wild tales. His son hadn't yet spoken, only sat on the west side of the tent as though forgotten by his father and crammed his mouth with marmot as if he might never eat again. His gray eyes darted about, no doubt taking in everything. I burned to know why this one-eyed man dared return to the village of the woman he'd kidnapped, but the heat of the fire pulled me into sleep. The furious whispers of my mother and father entered my dreams, but the rosy fingers of day were pushing their way through the cracks of the *ger* when I next opened my eyes.

I wished I hadn't woken when I heard what the men were discussing.

"Temujin would make Borte a good husband," Yesugei said.

Temujin. So that was the boy's name. It meant to rush headlong, like a horse racing where it wished, no matter what its rider wanted. He sat cross-legged by the door, sharpening a stick with a wicked-looking knife as his foot twitched. I had a feeling he was ready to bolt at any moment, to saddle a horse and tear across the steppes.

I might beat him to it.

"They're too young." My mother's voice bit like a wasp. I peered through slitted eyes to see my father lay a gentle hand on her arm, the platter of dried horsemeat to break our fasts untouched between them. "I'll not give the only treasure of my womb to a Tayichigud raider," she muttered.

I wondered then whether she wished she had told my father our secret instead of keeping it hidden all these years. Now it was too late.

"Since the days of the blue-gray wolf and the fallow deer, the beauty of our daughters has sheltered us from battles and wars. Our daughters are our shields." My father's words were an oft-repeated maxim amongst our Unigirad clan, yet Yesugei's people were well-known as the lowest and meanest of the steppe's families, as sharp-clawed and sneaky as battle-scarred weasels. No single man ruled the grasslands, meaning that belligerent Merkid, wealthy Tatars, fierce Naiman, and even the Christian Kereyids all fought continuous wars for supremacy.

"Borte," my father said in a stern voice, but I kept my eyes closed. "Stop pretending to sleep and come here."

I sat up and my mother handed me a cup of goat milk to wash away the bitter taste of sleep from my mouth, but I found it hard to swallow.

"I'd keep my little goat with us as long as possible, forever if I could." My father twirled a strip of dried meat between his gnarled fingers, then sighed. "But as much as I might wish it, it is not my daughter's fate to grow old by the door of the tent she was born in."

"My husband," my mother said, "it is not wise—"

My father didn't allow her to finish, only raised his hand for silence.

"I don't wish to be married," I said, praying the Earth Mother would send up roots from the ground to bind me forever to this *ger*. I had no desire to be saddled to the half-wild son of a barbarian raider. Surely my father would not match me to a boy so far below us and thereby banish me to the farthest and most barren expanse of the steppes.

"One day I'll give you my daughter to keep the peace between our clans," my father said over my head to Yesugei, his hand on my shoulder. I had no doubt that Yesugei might steal what he wanted, as he'd done before with Hoelun, thereby disgracing me forever. I waited for my father to nudge me forward, yet he didn't move. "But that day is not yet born."

I stared up at him, only then noticing the fast ticking of blood in the vein in his neck. "Instead," he said, "I invite you to leave Temujin with us for a while, to hunt and herd for me so we can get to know our new son."

Yesugei gave a bark of laughter and clapped the boy on his back, grinning as if he'd just returned victorious from a raid on a neighboring village. "Do you hear that, boy?" he asked. "I just gained you a wife!"

In that moment I wondered whether all girls' hearts curled up in their chests and their knees threatened to give way upon hearing the news of their betrothals.

Many cups of *airag* later, Yesugei swung up unsteadily onto his horse's bare back, then dropped the rabbit fur hat onto Temujin's head. "I leave my son to you," he said to my father, then straightened and glanced at his boy. Temujin bore traces of his father in his bushy brows and the wry twist of his lips, but they differed in the set of their jaws and the slant of their eyes. I wondered whether he favored his mother instead, or some ancestor long since passed to the mountains. Yesugei circled his son on horseback, then bowed to my father. "I fear you're not so clever as they say, Dei the Wise, for I have gotten the better end of this deal." He turned his horse to leave, then called over his shoulder, "And you should know this whelp of mine is frightened by dogs."

Then Yesugei trotted away with his string of horses, heading back to his people, leaving behind a single dun-colored filly as a gift to my father, and a black-haired boy with a scowl like a storm.

My future husband.